I0649785

FREDDIE OMM

HONOR

Published by **Mad Bear Books**

ISBN №º 978-3-943829-02-0 (hardback)
ISBN Nº 978-3-943829-03-7 (paperback)

First published in the USA, 2012
Second edition, 2013

Cover design: Bradley Wind
Cover photography: Hilary Tullberg-Dotson
Author photo: de FOTOGRAF Viersen

Thanks to Sandie for stellar support

MAD BEAR BOOKS

For my father

"He who does not get angry (for his honor) is the one whose heart is upside down."

Ali ibn Abi Talib

"The wrath of brothers is fierce and devilish."

Arab proverb

"… if anyone slays a human being—unless it be in punishment for murder or for spreading corruption on earth—it shall be as though he had slain all mankind…"

Qur'an, 5:32

"Women are inclined often to have tall ambitions, to complain much and… have a blind sense of honor. "

Mansur Abdul Hakim, Women Who Deserve to Go to Hell

DEATH AT DAWN
Kirkstall Road, Leeds: Rania & Faraz Zandi

RANIA ZANDI. Morning child.

She's gone to bed and risen in the dark, her lamp the only one burning along the street—the whole sprawled-out warren of red brick, back-to-back houses hugging the hill that reaches up from Kirkstall Valley.

She tiptoes downstairs. Although dawn is more than an hour away, it's already humid and close. Sitting down at the kitchen table, Rania switches on her laptop. She scans two knockout games—she's in the endgame of both, and it's looking good—uncannily good, because her opponents made precisely the mistakes she dreamed they would, and she's excited about her next moves...

Her face is rapt with a myopic glow of concentration, her chest and forehead moist.

Now she hears big brother Faraz, fresh from his ablutions for morning prayers, come stomping down the poky stairs. That sets the saucers and teacups rattling on the shelf beside her—and the walls shudder, as if the house were stretching itself awake...

Rania's never met her opponents—Cici1413 in Jakarta, and Shannon93 in Ventura—but today, the morning after her fourteenth birthday, she's about to checkmate them both.

She feels like she's flying.

She sees Faraz through the frosted glass of the kitchen door, a dark, blurred silhouette standing in front of the mirror in his wraparound shades, black T-shirt and hoodie.

Poser.

Rania smiles and looks back at her laptop. It was yesterday's star present from her parents... that and the new styling they allowed her. When Faraz came in and saw how she'd done her hair—the sharp short bob, the highlights—he'd given her nothing but a scowl, the icy void of a stare.

Trying to freeze my blood...

She'd stared right back at him, feeling strong in herself.

What a gloit.

But the laptop, now. She's so proud of the thing she wants to hug it, she loves the look of it, loves that she can play whenever she wants, no more trudging off to the internet café.

Faraz can't openly disapprove of that, can he?

Or can he?

He disapproves of pretty much everything else. All these moldy old proverbs he's been laying on her lately... he's got stockpiles of them handy — stiff, ancient sayings, he comes out with them all the time, chucking them at her like verbal mothballs.

Like:

As long as a word is unspoken, you are its master. But once it is spoken, it is your master.

(His way of telling her to shut up the other day. It makes her want to laugh when he says those things. But she never does laugh... He's too twisted up in that scary stuff for it to be funny).

Okay, now Faraz is glaring at her through the frosted glass — she grins and gives him a little wave, but he turns on his heel, and out he stalks without a word.

Off to the mosque for his awareness training class.

The front door slams behind him.

Think of the going out before you enter.

She shakes her head. Shame his class doesn't do awareness of little sisters. Shame they've turned him into this wannabe control-freak, a man-boy from a different age.

It's past five already. Time to get going. A quick shower now.

First off, she's seeing her soulmate, Yass. If they can twist their parents' arms, and the weather stays nice, they're planning a day-trip to Blackpool tomorrow. Just the thing for the Easter holiday.

The Golden Mile. They've never been, but they've heard a fair bit about it, and they think they can wangle it to go.

So, her clothes. Her tightest jeans, her coolest top...

Rania puts on some make-up, and she's looking great, she's feeling better than she has in months, like she's beginning to take charge of her life finally, and *changing*, changing into someone... someone maybe boys might fancy. She thinks she might like that, might like being looked at, like being liked for what she looks like, not just for what she *is*. And whatever Faraz might say when he's ranting at her, she's not jailbait, no way—she hasn't even *kissed* anyone yet, well not really... just a little brush of the lips—nothing, really.

A splash of scent...

And she really wants, really *needs* to be looking good... she's got to be all fresh and cool, because it's not just Yass she's seeing, but Yass' second cousin, who's coming round later for tea...

He's a DJ, stage name *Gorgeous Yahya*, and he's every bit as superawesome as he makes himself out. Yahya likes her, she knows, she caught him checking her out last time. His big brown eyes so intent on her, so *into* her, he was all there, wanting to reach out to her, yet somehow just out of reach, dreamy...

She slips out the house not waking mom and dad. Let them have their beauty sleep. They need it—bone-weary from hours on their feet minding the store, they don't rise till six.

She clicks the door shut as soft as she can.

Strolling out toward Kirkstall Road in her summer clothes, she feels the sun and the wind on her skin, she glances around her, looking forward to the day ahead. Dawn's breaking, but not a curtain twitches, no one else is in sight. She hears nothing out of the ordinary, just a mob of birds squabbling by the soot-black chimney pots.

She walks down the hill, humming a song she loves, *Irreplaceable* by Beyoncé, under her breath, singing snatches of it in the stillness of the morning.

Then, out of the silence behind her, frantic sprinting footfalls drill across the asphalt sidewalk. She turns, looks back. Three guys running down the hill. The one at the front screams *Beauty is for the worms!*

A strangulated, half-broken voice...

His arms raised to the sky, his head thrown back in rapture, he's calling the wrath of heaven down on her head like she's the painted whore of Babylon. An adolescent zealot. And he's waving a cricket bat around, slicing it through the air, like a dervish—a *cricket bat*—and there's two thin-shanked, gangling boys behind him, and they're coming after her now—they're all dashing pell-mell past the back-to-back houses.

In the split second she looks, she's recognized one of them.

But by then, Rania's already running.

In a damp cobbled alley off a side-street, the quickest one—not the shouter with the cricket bat, but a taller, more agile guy—closes in, hurtling on behind her.

She runs on, and she's hearing his breathing, he comes after her, getting closer, his breath ever louder, his footfalls ever more insistent in her ear. Rania redoubles her speed, her vision pixelated in tears and panic. She runs as fast as she can, running along in a blur.

The guy's virtually on her now. His hand shoots out. Like the strike of a buzzard's beak he grabs her by the neck.

His grip tightens around her throat.

With his other hand he swings at her head—but the angle's wrong—his fist just tips her on the chin with a passing *thwack.* She hardly feels it, wards him off with an elbow to his face.

They're still tumbling down the alley.

The guy flings both arms round Rania. A demented tackle, like a psycho's hug. He pulls her down, clenched fists at her neck, strong arms bringing her down like a recalcitrant animal.

He's pushing his thumbs into her throat. Rania trips, her feet falter. She's thrown thudding onto her back.

Rania's head hits the granite.

She's lying there stunned.

FREDDIE OMM

Her hair is black with streaks of hennaed gold. A blob of blood oozes onto it. She's lifeless for a second, then comes to herself.

He's standing above her.

Her eyes brim over in terror. Bracelets clink and clatter on the cobblestones where she sprawls, scrabbling about in the dusty grit. She's broken half her nails. One of her wrists is bleeding.

The other two boys catch up. All out of breath they stand in angry poses around her shouting.

She raises herself up but the big guy forces her down again. Fingers press into her windpipe. He pushes all his weight down on her shoulders. She kneels, trying to push him off, but he's so heavy, his face so close, so livid, his eyes swollen, the wispy beard flecked with spittle, his hot breath all over her face.

The second guy behind him starts filming on his mobile phone.

Rania retches. She twists her body—and, inside her, the last bit of power she's got rises up—she raises herself up again. Half on her feet, half on her knees, her eyes are bleeding and she gulps in great heaving mouthfuls of air, choking like a stranded fish.

She might still make it, might still get away.

Then the third guy steps up, he fumbles in his pocket.

Rania's round eyes fix on the knife he now takes out of its sheath. She looks up at his face. A zomboid expression has warped his features, stamped them into rigid lifelessness.

She hardly recognizes him. But she does recognize him.

The expression in his eyes is glazed, unseeing.

She can't grasp what's happening. Half thinking it must be a joke or something, but she knows it isn't.

"What *is* this, Faraz?" she sobs, trying to break through to him.

Her brother.

"You," he says, cold and harsh. "You've gone too far. And you know it."

Faraz steps up to her. Breathing hard. She draws back. Feels she's been here before—all through their childhood Faraz has been trying to *goad* her to be what he thinks she ought to be—and all through her childhood she's been running away from him.

But now in her blood she knows this may be her last chance to get away.

"Don't be stupid, Faraz!"

She crawls back another few paces. He comes in after her. Quick and thoughtless as a schoolyard game he takes the knife and not meeting her eyes punches it into her chest.

The knife's blocked by a rib—it just tears at her, slips through her skin to scrape at the bone beneath. Rania sobs in shock, she cuts her palm pushing away the blade, little drops of scarlet blood drip from her bosom.

Faraz changes his hold on the knife, his hands shaking. He takes a breath. Then he sticks the knife in at another angle, and it slips cleanly under her left breast.

Rania cries disbelieving, slides down off the blade onto her back in the alley.

The dark starts closing in on Rania where she lies. Her brother holds his bloody knife, staring at it in his bloody hand. She sees him shudder through a blurred film.

His eyes are cloudy and dim, as if he's hearing a faraway call.

Then he leans down over her where she lies half-dead and with a single swipe of the knife he slices it across her throat.

Rania lies half-dead in the bloody grit.

Through closed eyes she senses a flash behind where her brother's standing, and flaming light penetrates her pupils, sets her eyes afloat in her head, her thoughts melting in her mind, everything reeling past, a swarming slideshow of thumbnails, glimpses imprinted like exposures on her brain.

She sees Faraz and the others—they're backing away from her now. Vacant horror on their faces—pale and wan, their eyes wide, rounded like ghouls.

Already haunted by what they've done.

Already haunted by themselves.

Faraz chucks away the knife. He wipes his hands, trembling, on his sleeves—and they're all of them looking half gone, fading away, all of them want to be out of that place.

Only Faraz seems to be holding back. His eyes, red and wet. Unfocused.

Rania hovers, detached, between the warm light whirling her inside out herself, weightless like a spirit, and the street where her broken body is, and where the hill rises up beyond it to the sky.

She's letting go of what's holding her there, she can't hold on, she only senses impulses, flashed from inside her.

Her parents' hurt will break them, if she goes like this. And she senses the hurt they'll feel, and her friends—ripped from them all at the beginning of life, snapped off like a light.

Her brother, even, doesn't want her gone.

Not Faraz. Not truly.

And she doesn't want not to be.

She isn't ready. She shrinks away from that warmth inside her, back out to herself where she lies now alone on those dirty cobbles in Leeds.

LOVERS' TIFF
Bloomsbury, London: Azeem al Din & Shirin Shaarawi

AZEEM, A YOUNG MAN in a kufi, is sitting at the breakfast table with his girlfriend, Shirin. Their flat is airy, with whitewashed walls, jade carvings, and rush matting on the floors—and the dawn floods in through high sash windows, French doors opening out to a balcony where potted herbs and bamboo plants grow.

Shirin is leafing through a pile of glossy magazines. Every so often she discards one, throwing it in the paper basket while reaching for the next, all the while interspersing her reading with sips of tea, and languid, desultory chat with Azeem...

She sees an uncertainty in her lover's eyes this morning. The way he evades her (he's started to avoid looking directly at her) riles her.

She sees it, mirrors it back at him, unsettled by his mood.

Azeem gets up. With lithe, defined movements he walks over to the kitchen, a frown playing on his face, and she's watching him from the corner of her eye.

He always looks good, but he never seems to know how good.

Slim, dark and tall, he's got those manly, aquiline features, clean shaven, full-lipped, with shoulder-length black hair. His breath smells of the *siwak* he uses to sweeten it for his prayer session before daybreak.

He hasn't got the hang of the new toaster yet. He stares down at it where it stands on the counter, a wisp of black smoke streaming from the slits like a message. Couple of pieces of toast come popping up. Burnt to a crisp. More black smoke rises up around them.

Azeem takes them out and, turning, tosses the torched slices one after the other out the window like frisbees. His strong cricket player's arm spins them into the garden square, where they land in the long grass under an ancient plane tree. A scavenging starling flutters down from the branches to peck at a piece.

"Well," says Azeem, "looks like we need a new toaster."

He takes the thing up in his hands and shakes it, peering at it, examining it minutely. It disgorges a patter of charred crumbs.

She laughs.

"Just adjust the setting maybe?"

"No, it's been programmed to burn."

Smiling, Shirin looks at pictures of slingback shoes in *Vogue*.

"I hit a cat doing that frisbee toast thing yesterday."

"On purpose?"

She shakes her head.

"It was that very noisy, yowling cat. From next door. It was funny. Just about jumped out of its skin."

"The ginger tom?"

"The black Persian."

Shirin watches him with a raised eyebrow, still smiling.

He doesn't believe me. He thinks I'm pulling his leg.

As it happens, they're both Persian—well, Anglo-Persian—but he's the dark one... a lot darker than she, tanned, properly dusky. And his looks *are* feline.

He pads around like a cat, prowling.

She's thinking how tasty he is, fit and muscular.

But... naïve. She used to warm to that simplicity in him, almost childlike. He saw everything so clearly. Such purity in his mind.

Now she's not so sure. The world isn't like that, is it?

The early morning news comes on, and it starts to describe an honor attack in Leeds. The lovers stop to take it in.

Girl, 14, knifed on street in Leeds, the subtitles scroll. *Community in shock.*

The reporter reels off his report. He rounds it off with a practised nasal coda:

"As the neighbors start picking up the pieces, the wider world will be asking if this was excessive traditionalist rigor—or part of an undeclared war on westernized women..."

Azeem looks out the window, watching an outlandishly large fly hover round the rosemary bush on the balcony.

Down in the street a car starts up with a ragged roar.

Azeem slots two fresh slices into the toaster and adjusts the knob on the side from five to three.

He takes a deep breath, and shoots a glance over his shoulder at Shirin.

She's got a green face mask on. That emphasizes an alien sadness about her mouth. Her almond eyes are half closed, but... they're watching him right back all right, as if veiled. There's a reserve, a caustic, taxonomical coolness in her expression, as if she's codifying the habitat of a mildly intriguing sub-species.

He *feels* watched. And he senses her coolness, unspoken, like she's drifting slowly away, slowly moving into a world he doesn't share with her anymore.

When she speaks, he's already expecting the question.

Is your mate Ghazan behind this, then?

Azeem stares out at those plane trees in the square, their trunks shaded in splodges of green, their high branches thronging with squawking, speckled birds, yellow beaks catching the sun, a riot of feathers among the leaves.

He goes back to Shirin, sits beside her, puts his arm around her. He pulls her closer and strokes her hair, breathes in the scent of her—and her smell arouses him, he kisses her neck.

But she pulls away from him.

She's waiting... waiting for an answer.

Azeem sits there, and it sinks in, with a certain chilly knowledge. She's got a point.

As usual.

"You're not sure, are you?"

No, Azeem is not sure.

How can you ever be sure?

How can you ever be sure about anything?

As it happens, Azeem was at training camp together with Ghazan Khattak, out in Afghanistan.

They'd been in the same group of brothers...

Out of all of them, Ghazan was far the most ascetic—always driving himself harder, harder, harder... In the training, he was always going off for extra practice, pushing himself to the utmost, stretching at his physical and mental limits—always brooding, and only ever at peace when, in his few spare moments, he was sitting by himself, intently studying the Qur'an.

Even then, even there, in that atmosphere of visceral commitment, Ghazan's fervency stood out from the rest, and even then, it had bothered Azeem, bothered him big time.

Ghazan was respected, not popular, but looked up to.

Everyone always deferred to him. Always holding himself aloof, he hardly ever opened his mouth to speak. And when he did, he was acerbic, utterly charmless, yet so patently sincere that he somehow oozed out an involuntary charisma. He'd make clear his austere ideas about jihad, there was even a kind of grim, sickly humor clinging to him when he explained it—he was infected, infectious with the virus of fanaticism.

Anyway, people really looked up to him, could see he really meant it. Even Azeem, if he was honest, sort of admired him.

"I'm sure Ghazan wouldn't stoop to a thing like this."

But is that really true?

How can he be sure? Surely Ghazan's still the same? Implacable in a way that makes it impossible to tell where his head is truly at?

He's always said he will fight till the death.

Why not take him at his word?

Azeem leans back, his head on the cushions, his eyes looking outside, where high above, where it's blue, a plane crawls across the sky, like a tiny gleaming insect on a pane of glass.

Unlike most of the guys who came back from the camps, Ghazan Khattak never softened or readjusted a bit, never reintegrated, still a hard man of duty and ideals—just as tough as he ever was. And then, of course, this morning's honor killing had happened in Leeds, and Ghazan's *from* Leeds—his family, his brothers, all his contacts are there, would-be *mujahidin*, shooting their mouths off about this kind of thing... Always going on and on about attacks on apostates, and gays, and Jews, *kafirs* of any kind.

They *boast* about what they'll do to the unbelievers.

When you get right down to it, though, they're just boys, boys brought up in British suburbs, ineffectual, just like millions of others...

"Anyway, Ghazan doesn't live in Leeds anymore. He lives in London now. He's... he's got a big mouth, that's all."

Allah loves not braggarts and boasters.

Or is there more to it? There's always another angle.

A thing about girls.

Yeah, there's always that... *cherchez la femme.*

Ghazan's always going on about women, and not in the way twentysomething guys normally do.

Immoral girls, he'll say, *should be sharply punished.*

That sort of stuff.

They need to be scourged.

Scourged. Not exactly a word you pick up in the British suburbs, in the normal run of things.

Ghazan never specifies what he means, but of course you can tell what he's *thinking*—death by stoning, or crucifixion, or whatever more repellent means are at hand.

The just retribution for those who fight GOD and His messenger, and commit horrendous crimes, is to be killed, or crucified, or to have their hands and feet cut off on alternate sides, or to be banished from the land. This is to humiliate them in this life, then they suffer a far worse retribution in the Hereafter.

"He doesn't have to live in Leeds to be behind it."

Azeem gives Shirin a blank look by way of reply. It's the best he can do. He's cut up. He doesn't know what to think. He doesn't really *want* to think.

Then he remembers something else. Something which momentarily freaked him at the time, but only momentarily... he'd dismissed it soon enough.

But sometimes these things have a way of coming back to you, revealing themselves in a starker light.

The other day, in Ghazan's office, he'd come in late. Ghazan and his colleagues were just finishing up a meeting. Azeem half caught the last bit of it.

Something about *C1, C2.*

At first, he'd thought they were talking about sociological stuff, demographic segments, target audience breakdowns or whatever. Ghazan has always been big on social work, community initiatives.

Speaks that lingo too.

Sociological marketing stuff. Thinking back to it now though, Azeem remembers one of the biggest lessons of his life—the lesson at the training camp about the bombs.

He sees, now—he knows full well the brothers could have been talking about bombs, improvised explosive devices, blowing things up.

His palms go cold. He wishes he could have kept himself clear of Ghazan Khattak and his big mouth. He wishes he'd cut off all ties with him when they'd come back to England.

But most of all, he wishes Shirin wouldn't keep harping on about it.

Fidgeting, aching, uncomfortable in his skin, Azeem bends forward over his plate, his knife flicking Marmite over a fresh slice of toast, his teeth set in a fixed, diminished grin.

"Look, hon. Try and get this clear. Ghazan... well, he's... he's fighting his own brand of jihad. You know that."

"Yeah, right," she jeers. "Not the same jihad you're fighting."

"Well, you know I don't condone that sort of—"

"Yeah, yeah, you don't *condone* it. Sort of. You stop just short of condoning, I know. But... it's all one big bloody war, isn't it?"

He feels like shouting *No! No! No!*

But she's still talking:

"Look what they've just done to that girl! That's *Leeds*, babes, just up the road! It isn't the Middle East, it isn't Africa. It's sunny Yorkshire. Didn't you hear what the man just said?"

Through vivid eyes she watches him eat. He feels on edge, scrutinized.

And feeling caged, Azeem gets up again, stripped to the waist in his dhoti—feeling caged, but noble, too, and trying to be true, trying to stay honorable in a way that makes him mad and tormented.

He keeps wishing he could put everything on hold, press a pause button to freeze the picture, stop the music—create a moment's silence in which to think, commune with the one he loves.

He'd love to do that right now.

Yes. Time to spend with Shirin has gone right out of the window lately. It's beginning to tell.

She's still staring back at him... but then a smile steals the anger from her lips again, and her dark eyes dilate, and her brow seems to clear.

She spoons up some honey and cream with a morsel of *nan-e-gisu*.

"Some people are talking like it's World War IV."

"They're all a couple of camels short of a caravan."

"Unlike the guys in your precious training camp?"

My precious training camp.

He brushes sticky black crumbs from his mouth, his drawn-out sigh of frustration prolonging the space between them.

"We were all equal there, Shirin. *Brothers*. We all had a *voice*. You can't say that about the UK or the USA."

He knows it sounds smug, he knows she won't let him get away with it—he knows it, even as he says it, but he can't stop himself: he loves her, and he just can't let the argument go.

"They were teaching you *jihad*!" she says. "A thousand ways to hate! A thousand ways to kill!"

"We all have a duty to defend ourselves, you know that. *Fard al-kifaya.* Any of us would gladly die for the rest."

"I thought you'd turned your back on all that?"

He looks down.

"I did."

Shirin sits composed, watching him calmly. Her eyes are radiant, but tired. And they are loving, but worried.

He says, "You know how much I long for peace."

"What did your fancy sheikhs say about your longing for peace, when you met them? Did they pat you on the head and tell you to *make it happen*?"

She's needling him about *Islamic Reform*'s higher-ups now. Another sore point. He's beginning to think he is nothing but a collection of sore points. Actually, in the bottom of his heart, he's really proud he met those guys.

Even now.

Hardly anybody ever gets to meet them. Exalted figures of extreme wealth and influence, most of the time they keep fastidiously to themselves, in the shadows, emerging only at moments of extraordinary importance. Azeem's encounter with those fabulously wealthy, powerful men had impressed him, sure, he won't deny it, even if Shirin thinks him a nutcase. It had been formal, fleeting... more like a royal reception. Azeem's eyes dilate.

Shirin tries to tickle him but he brushes her hand away.

Yes, like meeting royalty. Azeem had felt very important, very *successful*, that evening. He remembers its every detail vividly.

They'd invited him to the Dorchester. An honor in itself.

They'd just agreed to finance his *Islamic Reform* project and give it their blessing.

A big moment, a thrilling moment...

But Shirin, now. She will not let him be, her fingers are all over him. One hand is tickling his armpits and the other is tweaking at his nipple. He twists his torso free, takes both her hands tightly in his left hand to stop her tickling him again.

He takes a bite of toast.

Distinguished, aristocratic Arabs of a certain age, they were reserved, decorous of conduct, enigmatic of eye, full of the arid dignity of the desert.

He loves to replay the scene...

Sitting at a polished table in that opulent room, they murmured some kind words in Arabic, words which the translator put into a kind of purposely-pidgin English for Azeem's benefit.

Almighty Allah be praised, said the translator in a sing-song voice. *When the master frowns, the servant should bestir his diligence, redouble his labors. When the master smiles, the servant can complete his tasks, light of heart.*

Today, the master smiles. Tomorrow, we shall see.

The translator wore a sickly smile. He had a jet black mustache. All that was weeks ago, but it seems like another world.

So Azeem stares out the window, then back at her, blue eyes glowering, nostrils flaring, looking her up and down, filled with deep, mute desire.

To see Shirin as she is right now is pretty alluring, even for Azeem, who thinks he knows her, and knows he loves her, and their argument can't touch any of that—he loves her, from the slight touch of morning redness in her eyes, to the tips of her long, mussed-up black hair, which is all over her face, her milky-brown shoulders, the thighs she thinks are getting too chubby, her dainty toes—he can never get enough of her, and he's never come close to feeling he *possesses* her.

He takes another bite of toast and stays silent.

He knows he should allow her some space. Her people, too, have suffered. He can't lecture her, doesn't know enough about those things.

And Shirin sits beside him, a shawl half covering her shoulders and breasts. The smudge of her dark belly-button peeks out over short black silk pyjama-bottoms. Her little tummy. A smear of honey on her lip.

And in turn, a ripple of tenderness wells up in Azeem, he reaches a hand to stroke her, his heart fills with longing, fresh stirrings of desire.

Time to let it be.

He rubs her stomach, reverently, very amorously, and she smiles at him through her dreamy eyes...

He's loved her so long, his love for her's the only thing he knows is real. He leans down and kisses her softly on her belly-button.

She ruffles his hair.

Jangling cacophony—the doorbell. *"Delivery for Miss Shaarawi!"* crackles the intercom in a croak of white noise.

Azeem wakes from his reverie, lets her go. Shirin gives him a playful cuff and goes to the door, wrapping herself in her slinky pashmina scarf as she goes.

So supple and smooth, her body, he sees her afresh, he licks his lips, wants to be with her, to hold her to him.

When Shirin comes in again, the scarf trails round her ankles—a huge bunch of flowers is spilling out of her arms. Azeem deplores the vulgar profusion with a look. Flowers enough for a palace, far too many for their tiny flat!

"It's *him* again, isn't it?"

He speaks, straining with patience, and he resents his own tone, resents his own resentment...

Shirin bends down and hands him the message.

Sender: Office of Sheikh Faisal ibn Shabbir.

"Fucking Shabby."

Azeem scrunches up the card.

"He just can't leave it, can he?"

Shirin shakes her head, starts stuffing the stems into the bin. Azeem watches her gloomily. He supposes Shabby's pesky floral tributes vex her as much as him.

"Let's not waste them," he says. "Flowers can't help it, coming from a creep."

Shirin smiles and he feels warm again. She loves flowers. And they do add something—they crowd the place out, sure, but so what? Soon, Shirin's arranging them in vases dotted about the room, dispensing little splashes of water over them.

The florid colors bounce off the stuccoed walls, offset the golden green woodwork.

No more arguing. The lovers finish breakfast in peace, savor the moment.

Got to be gone in a minute.

Gaudy scents—orchids, fuchsias and freesias—waft round, mix in with the raucous smells of early-morning London, merge together in the loaded air, mingling at the open windows, and Azeem's breathing it all in with gladness now. As to their spent-out argument, he still clings to the illusion of being right, for what it's worth.

But what's it worth?

He only knows he doesn't know.

Sunlight pours in through the windows, throwing jagged shadows on the kitchen table between them—the vast old plane trees in the square, the clematis tendrils spreading over the balcony trellis.

Azeem and Shirin sit half-listening to the TV.

The honor killing is already history, a single murder sunk into the background babble of a thousand more, and the endless chat on the screen diffuses their consciousness, makes them weary to be gone.

But Azeem knows the morning's brought him a warning.

There's murderers among them. Killers. He's always known it in the abstract. But he's never felt it in his gut, so near, so close to him, as if the killers were sitting in the next room, ready to burst in on them at any moment.

Islamic Reform has a struggle on its hands, and he's in the front line. He's got to find out if Ghazan's directly involved. If Ghazan is, he'll have to sort it out somehow, find proof, track him down, flush him out, purge *Islamic Reform* of his crimes.

In his heart, Azeem is strangely relieved. He thinks he knows what he has to do.

There's always hope.

And this morning, there's more. For the first time in weeks, Azeem thinks he can get Shirin back onside. The two of them might even win back their old intimacy, that camaraderie they used to have.

If I work on it.

So strange that this is coming right at the same time as his realization about Ghazan and getting things clear and sorted, but there it is. Sometimes clarity washes over you all at once, like a big refreshing wave.

He feels good about Shirin in a way he hasn't done in months. It was that thing with the tickling, and then with Shabby's wretched flowers—she'd been about to bin them, just out of consideration for his feelings—that was what told him.

Knowing it makes him feel better able to deal with the other stuff too. The heavier stuff. The bloody stuff.

And so they dress and go off to their places of work, a long make-up kiss having smoothed away their differences and made their parting sweeter.

THE ONLY END
Edgware Road, London: Ghazan Khattak

EDGWARE ROAD, London—smoggy, loud and dirty, is right on his doorstep, and outside, a crazily interflowing stream of humanity teems and spills along the curb—buses and cabs and all the people, tired and grubby, and all the faces with their endless variations—stern and vacuous, carefree, absent, in-your-face and mad—bustling figures in burqas, tipsy party animals nursing hangovers, salarypeople, artists, hookers and rent boys calling it a night—all of them flickering past his store window.

Ghazan Khattak, a scraggy, gaunt-eyed man, is peering out through the grimy glass, watching the street like it's a speeded up film.

But he's not really watching.

He's gobsmacked. His haggard eyes are haunted. He looks unkempt—unshowered, unshaven, very male and rough. Sweaty, musclebound, with a big, jutting chin from which his prodigious beard protrudes. His large, piercing round eyes stare out under eyelashes whose length and general exquisiteness are the only facets of him you could say were less than wholly masculine.

Just a few minutes after it's over, and he's already picked up the fatal call, telling him what's happened up in Leeds, and he's been getting the whole story, gabbled to him in disjointed phrases like sobs—how they chased her, how they filmed it, how they've left Rania lying there... left her there for dead.

He's been getting more and more irate as the story unfolds.

To start with, he's disturbed by the fear muddling up the boy's voice. It sounds ever more sunken, listless, as the lad goes on, the eagerness of the chase wrung out of him by the kill.

Ghazan Khattak turns away from the window, fists clenched.

"Why didn't you warn me you were doing it today, you daft fuckwits!"

Ghazan walks into his office, a brown, dust-filled room. His home-town, Leeds, is two hundred miles away—and Ghazan knows he should be up there, now.

"Are you getting out of there, man?" he says.

"She's dead, Ghazan, dead."

The lad muffles his words. His voice breaks, catches. He sounds like he's got a scarf wrapped around his face, as if he wants to hide himself away from the world, speak only in whispers.

Faraz, the brother, the knifeman, now comes on the line. He's throaty, smothered.

"Ghazan, it's me..."

Faraz is strangulated, he's swallowing down his agitation like a sudden reflux. He forces out his deep voice with all the self-control he can muster, trying to sound cool and collected—but out it comes panicked, lost...

He's scarcely a man... but it's time he woke up to the fact that he ought to be a man, and he should behave like one, talk like one... But he's not, he's unsure about everything, is Faraz... full of fear.

Ghazan knows too much about him.. Someone he's helped grow, right on to the very threshold of manhood, someone he's helped, in every way, to get where he is... but now, he's someone Ghazan knows he doesn't need around, not anymore...

And just listen *to him this morning... He comes over like a whingeing woman, whining like a whipped dog.*

He doesn't sound anything like what he's meant to be, a warrior fighting jihad.

"Don't feel good about this," Faraz is telling Ghazan in that strange, fraught, subdued tone, vocal cords thick.

He sounds like his voice never properly broke.

"My own sister, man. I shouldn't have done it, man... she didn't deserve this."

"It was the right thing you did," Ghazan says, sharp, but all quiet and brotherly... almost whispering. "You *know* it was right. I told you time and again... It was the only thing left for you to do. It was your duty, man, in response to the decree of Allah. You just... you just did it the wrong time...

"Keep yourself together, man," he tells Faraz. "I'm sending someone."

And without wasting any more words Ghazan ends their conversation.

Soon after, Ghazan Khattak hears three shrill beeps from his phone. The video clip.

He watches it dispassionately. A job well done. Even if it seems a waste... a pity it had to be this way... but it was the only way, it was for her own good. Her own good, ultimately, as much as her family, the whole community...

Rania Zandi. Apostate child.

She'd gone too far. And now, she'd gone as far as she would ever go... She was with Almighty Allah.

Only Allah knows where she is now.

It was better for her, better for her family's honor, better for the honor of all.

We will raise you into a form of which you have not the slightest knowledge.

Burning in hellfire, most likely, *Jahannam*, with dregs of oil boiling in her belly. That's how it ends for her sort. It wasn't just her morals, her lips were loose too, dripping in lipstick, filthy and brazen, always smiling, always speaking disrespectfully. She'd gone beyond what was proper, that girl—she had to be stopped.

Faraz her brother had done his duty, no more, no less. Done the will of Allah, in the spirit of *the Great One, the Vanquisher.*

Ghazan's sombre face feels heavy on his skull as he struggles to come to terms with the killing, his sallow eyelids laden, drooping. And he feels heavy inside, his compassion muted. His passing pity for this unclean female, regret for her necessary disposal, is tempered by the realization that it's now up to him to get the aftermath sorted.

He wants to make sure this killing has a wider effect. Make sure the act isn't wasted, let the rebuke ripple out, let it wash over as many of the guilty as possible.

People must take heed, listen to the warning.

As to Faraz, the brother, he will lose his home, lose it forever... He'll have to flee Leeds—flee, like a thug, like a thief, for the security of Pakistan.

That's what happens when you live on the frontline and you lose your nerve. When you are in a corrupted land, enslaved by perverted western priorities. When you do right, you do something those people cannot forgive. It's the price you pay for daring to face down these idolaters in their own kingdom.

Ghazan reflects on those things.

He looks around his office with a scowl, the accumulated clutter annoying him. In the corner stands his dusty old cello, an instrument he hasn't touched since his teens. Its black case is dented and battered. There's a Leeds United sticker on it. He's been planning to sell the thing on eBay, but never gets round to it—hasn't the heart, really.

He takes a sip of tea and wipes his hand across his mouth. His lips are chapped, raw and itching, his beard matted with sweat, his skin moist with the grime of the morning, his eyes puffed and sore with tiredness. His temples throb, and the throbbing threatens to take over his head. His familiar frustrations rise up in him, deep, elemental frustrations made keener by a lifetime of living in the United Kingdom. He's already looking forward to the hypocritical howls of outrage which will come simmering up in the media when news of this gets out.

A people without understanding.

They value the life of a single immoral girl more than the honor of an entire family, the standing of our whole community!

Ghazan drinks more tea, and washes down a couple of paracetamol, closing his eyes to take stock of things. A minute passes before he forces himself to open his eyes and get a grip.

He grabs the phone, connects it to his laptop, and his stained, nimble fingers start to tap away at the keys. He loses himself in his work for a few minutes.

Having encrypted the clip, he sends it to a secure file-sharing site.

He clicks on the icon and watches the clip again. The film is grainy, and the hand holding the camera, a bit shaky, but the message is clear enough.

He's staring at the final, frozen frame. Rania lies motionless.

Every soul shall have a taste of death: And only on the Day of Judgment shall you be paid your full recompense.

An ambulance passes outside and he comes to himself again. He takes out his cellphone's chipcard, throws it away.

There comes a time when words have to stop—when to carry on talking becomes not merely wanton and useless, but deadly dangerous, dishonorable. Enough people have spread enough rumors about Rania Zandi, her shameless intercourse with an infidel, her lewdness, her looseness of tongue. Words, too, as well as girls, get infested by the uncleanness of the culture, they must be purged, cleansed in a pool of silence.

There comes a time when death is the only end to a dispute.

Leeds: Rania Zandi

Rania is in that sleepless, dreamless state of limbo, suspended in the place people go when they're about to die, when the body is on the verge of shutting down, and the mind wanders in mindlessness, unhinged, and time is absent, meaningless. Visions are flashing through her brain, unmonitored, like disconnected movie frames, visions she will later recall in fragmented shards of memory.

She sees bright light at the end of a dark tunnel. Although it feels warm and beckoning, she knows she must resist its pull. She half sees her parents in the shadows behind her, as if projected onto her retina from inside her, she hears their gentle voices.

All of a sudden she is injected with coldness, and she shivers, feverish and sweating.

Her brother is standing in front of her. Faraz's face is not his, it is a demon's face, it bears the twisted features of a fallen jinn. He has with him his knife, and it is bloody, but not with her blood, and he lifts this knife above his head.

She is trapped in space, unable to shift herself free.

Then time freezes still and she sinks into the black silence of her coma.

HIGHER REALMS
West End, London: Rupert Wythenshawe, Myles Lyall

TWO MEN IN SHIRTSLEEVES are conferring at an oval wooden table in a bright long room in central London. A shiny black plastic jug stands between them, and from it they pour coffee into creamy white china cups.

"When it comes to the higher realms of bullshit," the older one's saying with an air of easy, focused expertise, "you can't beat him, Klinker's definitely your man."

They've been talking about a big project just assigned to their advertising agency, Wythenshawe & Lyall—the story is splashed across the front page of that week's edition of *Campaign.* A fresh copy of the paper lies before each of the men.

Both of them are deliciously aware, in that state of anticipation which dwells close to fantasy, that the way they handle the account as of today will shape their futures, not just professionally, not just financially (the sky's the limit here, they know), but holistically—affecting their whole lives, and everyone who shares in their lives, from their wives and families, to their employees—executives, creatives, producers, media planners, art buyers and traffic controllers—to their accountants, lawyers, and bankers—their suppliers, photographers, hairdressers, directors, wholesalers, printers, company car dealers, office management experts, right down to the man who comes to rinse the coffee-making machines without which the whole ad agency operation would grind to an unceremonious, grumpy halt.

All of these people will look at them with new eyes, if this takes off, eyes informed by respect and gratitude. There will arise a widespread wish to partake of their newfound riches and success.

It's that big a deal for them. They can't afford to fuck it up.

And on its own terms—as a piece of advertising, PR, and marketing—it's a difficult one, a real communications conundrum. A campaign called *Islamic Reform,* it's being set up by their newest client, Azeem al Din, Communications Director of the *Islamic Reform Organization.*

Azeem has asked them to do something radical. Something no one's attempted before—a pan-European campaign to introduce indigenous Europeans to the beauties of Islam, Islam's power to better the modern world. In Rupert Wythenshawe's view, it's a venture that is beyond the capacity of their agency on its own. They can lead it, and run it, but they'll need some outside help.

That's why he's seized on the name of Dr Klinker. He utters the name in a whisper charged with reverence, like a holy name.

"Klinker's a legend, old boy. And not just in his own lunchtime either (though I hear he's quite the stout trencherman). He's a genius, a true European research guru. Some of his intuitions verge on the godlike... And we're going to need that brand of expertise."

Wythenshawe, a tall, blond, fortysomething man, has got a growl in his voice.

"Now, Klinker and his partner are hot on this whole cultural integration thing—Muslim consumers—the torments of exile in your own culture—cross-border, inter-community perceptions. You name the ethnic footprint, they'll know its size. And we are literally crying out for their insight! They'll help make *Islamic Reform* a going concern."

He reckons that, to expedite this, Wythenshawe & Lyall should take a significant step—merge with Klinker's German agency.

"Face it," he continues, "we need allies, old chap. Sooner or later we'll be looking at a major-league PR disaster... this *Islamic Reform* game is pre-programmed to self-destruct.. I know a bit about the financing of these capers. Sure as eggs is eggs, there'll be links to terrorists somewhere along the line—Al-Qaeda, or Hamas, Lashkar-e-Taiba, or LeT, or Hizbollah—God knows who else... and that's when we'll be needing some fall-guys, people to scapegoat when solids start hitting fans."

Wythenshawe sits back, brooding, staring at the ceiling, his expression restless, Machiavellian. His reverie's interrupted by the entrance of the PA, who smiles apologetically at her bosses, a slim, blonde creature tottering on unfeasible heels. She hands Wythenshawe a small package and slips out again.

Wythenshawe starts ripping it open.

Myles Lyall watches him restively. A short, dark-haired rugby player, he has red cheeks and worried eyes.

He says, "The big question for me, in regard to Klinker, is whether we're in the market for bullshit, or beef."

"Bull and blarney... they can be highly persuasive *tools*," growls Wythenshawe, appreciatively contemplating the occult powers of obfuscatory lore.

"That might be so if Klinker knew what he was talking about," says Myles, "or if he had the decency to stick to simple honest bullshit."

Inside Wythenshawe's package is a small, tightly-rolled up cellophane bag. Wythenshawe pulls it out.

Myles keeps his eyes on him, tight-lipped. Wythenshawe and he are fond of each other, as business partners often are, with a fondness born of familiarity and mutual interest. Seasoned with a few tart pinches of wariness and, in Wythenshawe's case, liberal intakes of cocaine. That Wythenshawe does rather go to town with their pretty receptionists is generally seen as forgivable folly on his part.

Another knock on the door.

A hapless copywriter sticks his head into the room and asks about the timing of a meeting. Myles stares at him, his mouth tight.

"Fuck off out of here. *Now!*"

"Is it being postponed, then?" the copywriter says.

"*Out!*"

"It's just, I have some new copy I want to share—"

"Are you being purposely obstructive or just fucking obtuse?"

The door closes.

Wythenshawe's still busy with his sachet, oblivious to this little contretemps. As far as Myles can tell, Wythenshawe has never had any discernible professional talent, aside from a certain sharp, dogged bluntness, but Wythenshawe enjoys himself, and his enjoyment is infectious. He's endearing. Daft as a brush sometimes. He charms people.

"The problem I've got with the Klinker gambit," continues Myles, "is this whole, wretchedly bogus Kraut habit of *Vorsprung durch Bullshit* and all that sort of claptrap. That jargon and pseudo-science. I don't think it's really down our alley."

Wythenshawe is busy transferring the contents of his plastic bag into an antique silver snuff box.

Cuts himself a long line of coke on the conference table.

"It's time you got with the programme, old chap," he murmurs in between sniffs. "What we want is respectability. Especially now we're in the business of selling something that's frankly unsellable!"

Wythenshawe's vulpine eyes beam a kindly, paternal light toward Myles. Wythenshawe is good at projecting such vibes, whose calming effect on people's insecurities is detached from his own essential insincerity.

"If we can get some cutting edge scientific schtick on our side," he says in an hypnotic, snaky whisper, all soft-eyed, insinuating, and soothing, "who's counting? Klinker's Bochy old multi-culti bollocks might push the right buttons."

"Well, maybe," Myles concedes.

Wythenshawe paces the room.

"And Klinker's got a doctorate *and* an MBA, which is incredibly credibility-enhancing!"

Wythenshawe is smiling with irrepressible enthusiasm. At times like this, he is quite the thing, a joy to behold. Myles feels cheered despite himself. Wythenshawe holds forth, enthusing, "I do *love* a title and a bit of intellectual distinction. I am thoroughly in love with the idea of this Dr Klinker altogether."

He sniffs deeply, and swallows, savoring the drug, and his jaw's working away, chewing at nothing, and he's licking his lips, rubbing his hands with a glee so effusive it borders on the demented.

"What about his partner—Rinky, is it?"

"Rincke."

"Rincke and Klinker. Got a ring to it."

"When I met them, Udo Rincke seemed more your bog-standard type of smarm merchant," says Myles not making this sound like unblemished praise. "He's good-looking... but he doesn't really care for the business he's in."

"Which of us does? They're making money, aren't they?"

"By the skin of their teeth."

Wythenshawe muses for a minute.

"Sounds to me these guys have been sent to us as a gift from heaven."

"But no-one can understand a word Klinker says!"

"All to the good, my boy, all to the good."

The older man shoots his partner a wolfish grin.

"I've often thought an excess of understanding undermines communication."

Now, twelve floors below them, their new client, Azeem al Din, walks into the foyer wearing a splendid olive-green kufi. He slowly approaches the young receptionist.

It's just after nine... The girl is nursing a hangover and a mug of coffee behind her desk.

She arches a sculpted, perhaps sceptical eyebrow at him.

"My name is Azeem al Din."

His voice sounds surprisingly gentle in that empty post-modernist space, that expanse of cool cloistered marble.

"I'd like to see Rupert and Myles. It's about *Islamic Reform*."

She's nonplussed. "What was the name again?" she needs to know.

He repeats his name and his business.

"Just a moment, Mr Din," the girl says gravely, gamely, perplexed by the way he sounds quite posh but, aside from his obvious cleanliness, looks like some sort of a street Arab in his kufi and his long flowing cloak. "Let me see if I can locate them for you."

She makes it sound as if they're holed up somewhere in Equatorial Guinea.

ROAD MAP TO PEACE
West End, London: Azeem al Din

SHE'S A DELICATE, close-cropped redhead with a long, elegant neck. She sits perched behind a large, glass-topped desk. Through it, Azeem can see her white slacks, her black laced-up boots.

When he looks into her pretty face he sees she's all but *gaping*, her eyes crawling all over him as though he were some freakish interplanetary visitor, freshly beamed into her orbit, dripping alien slime onto her pristine tabletop, and he feels that familiar flush of resentment.

"Rupert and Myles are in a meeting. They weren't expecting you, ah, Mr Din. You're not actually in the diary."

She peers at Azeem through her thick black eyelashes.

"Are you sure your meeting was slated for today?"

She's wearing a clingy lowcut blouse. Azeem stares at her with enough involvement to render his reflex disapproval—*they should draw veils over their bosoms*—specious and silly, and he blushes, prickled by self-reflexive shame.

"No!" he says. "It wasn't slated at all. Rupert told me to drop by whenever I wanted, so I'm basically here on the offchance. I'm a new client... *Islamic Reform*?"

"I see."

She looks at him coolly appraising his likely importance, an impossible calculation.

"Just a moment."

She gives Azeem a polite smile as she speaks to her colleague upstairs, Myles and Wythenshawe's PA.

So shapely.

Soft cupped tops of her breasts. Azeem does his best not to stare.

Even so, even so...

She's dressed to inflame the loins of the lecherous.

Dutiful, his thoughts. He feels ashamed, ashamed and uncomfortable in his own skin.

To offer up your breasts like this—on a platter, as it were. Just a step away from outright whorishness.

Isn't it?

Well, is it?

Azeem knows he lacks the righteous conviction such judgments require to sit easily in a man's heart. Since pimply adolescence, right up to and including today—*especially* today—he's always been keen on girls and their bodies, there's no point pretending otherwise, he's much too keen on them to think showing them is a sin.

He recalls the nakedness of his own Shirin earlier that morning, how she'd walked under that diaphanous scarf to answer the door, beautiful breasts bobbing up and down, jiggling as she walked.

When she'd come back, the scarf was gone—her breasts barely covered among the profusion of the flowers. He half closes his eyes, picturing it again, her nipples peeping at him puffily through the blooms...

"If you could just wait a few minutes, Mr, ah, Din," trills the pretty receptionist, basking in Azeem's gaze. "I'm sure we can arrange something for you... if you'd just care to sit, Mr Din."

Rising from her seat—spreading a delicious scent around her, intoxicating, she shoos handsome Azeem in the direction of a groovy sitting space.

Here, tinted glass walls look out on the busy street scene.

Azeem wanders over. It's all very Seventies, or Gothic, punky swathes of purple and oatmeal fabrics imprinted with bold Japanese patterns, that kind of thing... beige leather sofas, edgy perspex tables positioned stylishly around.

In this intimidatingly casual atmosphere Azeem plops himself down.

A widescreen plasma TV screen is hovering above his head. Audiovisual anaesthetic: long stretches of commercials interspersed with tasters of news.

Azeem sits back.

Rain or shine, you're breathing easy, he hears. Unpleasant upheavals, bacteria lurking in the alimentary tract, is the gist of it, like unblocking a drain.

Al-Qaeda regroups in the Tribal Lands.

Fulsome tributes are paid to some kind of energy-boosting snack. *The pick-you-up that won't let you down,* it works *with* your body not *against* it.

Road map to peace reopened. A glum, plump man in beige from the UN comes on to denounce the men of war without whom, he complains, the map wouldn't be necessary in the first place.

Don't leave home without it.

Azeem's mind wanders upside itself. In that diffident, airless space, he feels stuck in a glob of amber. He picks up a virgin copy of *Cosmopolitan*, settles down to wait for Rupert Wythenshawe and Myles Lyall.

But then a newsflash concentrates his mind, zaps him right back into the here and now.

"The victim of a would-be honor killing has been named as Rania Zandi, fourteen.

"Ms Zandi's fourteenth birthday was only yesterday — but this morning, she's fighting for her life in intensive care in Leeds..."

Rania's picture comes on screen. Bright-eyed, cheeky — great looking kid, cheerful and fresh. Azeem feels sad at once, and angry. He muses for a minute.

And then something crystallizes in his head.

The attack on that girl — the barbarity of it... the insane zealotry of it — that's exactly what we have to confront, that's exactly what Islamic Reform is for.

Rania Zandi.

That's it!

He's never seen it so clearly, so simply.

"Doctors are keeping her in intensive care until, they hope, her condition stabilizes."

A home video is shown. Scenes of a summery park, Rania mucking about with friends, playing soccer, chasing a big red ball.

Azeem intuits she's going to make it.

"Police are appealing for witnesses to come forward."

Azeem nods his head.

This is it, he knows. It is right, it is fate, it is timing... *serendipity.*

His heart is pounding.

I'll brief Wythenshawe & Lyall to contact her as soon as she's better...

Rania Zandi will become the face of *Islamic Reform...* the new face of a Muslim survivor.

Azeem is re-energized.

Just like the adverts promised.

FIXING THINGS
Edgware Road, London: Ghazan Khattak

GHAZAN KHATTAK, having put a new chipcard in his cell, is frantically making calls.

He's still in the same place, in his office behind the mobile phone store, waterpipe emporium and internet café. He's moved into his private space, which is tucked behind a locked wooden door and a frosted window to the rear of the twelve scruffy workstations up front, where a few students are intently doing their stuff, watched by the manager, another man Ghazan trusts, called Abdul.

Ghazan Khattak keeps half an eye on the store as he talks, but his attention's on his emergency.

He's been trying to get hold of a man he can rely on in Leeds, to pick those impulsive hotheads off the streets before the police catch up with them.

Ghazan's even more furious now—he's heard the news: the girl isn't even dead.

Why couldn't they wait, like he told them?

Maybe she'll still die of her injuries... They're described as critical. That would be the easiest outcome now.

If not, someone will have to finish the job...

More urgently, the lads need to be spirited away somehow. Ghazan hasn't got anyone lined up for the getaway drive—the man he'd normally have called is away on holiday.

Ghazan takes a swig of tea and rings one of his cousins, called Inzamam, in Leeds.

He needs a man, he tells Inzamam. He needs a man to make a *collection*. Can he do it? Just off Belle Isle Circus, a pre-arranged drop-off point. Can he do it, Ghazan asks Inzamam. *Can he do it?* No, says Inzamam, agitated. No he can't, he's all tied up.

He must've already have heard, and guessed what's up, and decided to stay well out of it. A bit of pressure might change his mind...

Inzamam sounds put out, stammering out in response to Ghazan's spitting vehemence, that furious spate of words, which is designed to stop him getting any of his questions out, all those questions he'll be wanting to ask.

Why now, why so quick—who are these bloody people—what have they done?

Dangerous questions. Pointless questions. Questions whose answers can only be lies. Inzamam should know better than to want the whole story.

Ghazan rejects out of hand the names suggested by his wary, apologetic cousin, taxicab drivers who might be called upon.

Ghazan has to have someone he knows really well—well enough to trust with his life.

Because this really is a matter of life and death.

Now, Ghazan says things like that all the time, it's his manner of speech, like his calling card. But this morning he means it.

Ghazan's plan—the bit he's not telling Inzamam—is about covering his tracks, keeping the lads at arm's length while getting them safely out of the country. He wants them to be driven from Belle Isle to a safe house he runs in Tower Hamlets. From there, his London-based dogsbody Kudrat can drive them in a borrowed van to Paris.

In Paris, they can hole up for a while before they hop on a flight to Pakistan. After that—they're on home turf—they're out of Ghazan's hands.

Let them lie low, let them lie low forever.

They're finished here. They can't come back. Let them get on with their lives. Let me get on with mine, let me fix things here.

His nervous, stammering cousin Inzamam doesn't have anyone who fits the bill. They ring off.

Ghazan Khattak's mind is tensed up as he works the phone, calling up his contacts one after the other. Ghazan's been jolted but he isn't about to panic. He's always well prepared for contingencies, even an honor killing he's prescribed, but hasn't approved as to the timing, and whose botched outcome he can only deplore. Ghazan jabs at the digits on the Nokia like an automaton, speaking tersely, cleaning up a mess others have dumped on his plate.

To calm himself, he takes a mental step back, looks at the bigger picture. Sure, the lads were too quick off the mark, Ghazan thinks, pausing for another gulp of tea. Sure, they rushed off too impetuously anticipating his desires.

But the aims he inculcated in them were right, he knows it... He knows it, yet he feels harder hit than he'd ever thought, and that frustration rises in him again...

She'd showed her uncovered shoulders, her head, her hair... She'd spent her purity, shared her beauty with infidels.

Rania Zandi. Defiled child. Defiled her body with makeup, depraved her mind with intoxicants; she was a harlot, a standing rebuke to her family, a blot on the conscience of the faithful. She deserved death.

And if death hasn't come for her yet, it soon will. Ghazan will find someone to finish the job, if Allah doesn't send *Malakul-Maut*, the Angel of Death, to take her first.

It doesn't take Ghazan long, nor much in the way of mental effort, to organize his men. He calms down. But then the phone rings again.

And this call is even more incendiary.

MORE VICTIMS
Soho, London: Azeem al Din, Myles Lyall, Rupert Wythenshawe, Abu Jaffar & Co

MYLES LYALL puts down the phone. "Azeem is downstairs," he says.

"A little earlier than we were expecting," Rupert Wythenshawe remarks drily.

"A week earlier. It's really rather awkward, we're not remotely prepared yet... no ideas to share about directions... What can have got into him?"

A sly look passes over Wythenshawe's wolfish face, so swift it's gone before Myles sees it.

"Not to worry old chap," Wythenshawe is saying affably. "We can just tell him we're finalizing things with our partners."

"*Finalizing*? It all feels so rushed," Myles complains. "It makes me think we're being bounced into this wretched German merger."

"Trust me, Myles. It's for the best, old boy. *Trust me.* We don't want to *overthink* things. And if it goes well with Azeem today we'll get the Krauts round next week and put some paw-prints on paper."

"Well, I suppose we shall have to see him."

Something's still bugging Myles. "What should we call him?"

"I'm tempted to just call him Azzie, like we used to when he worked here."

"But he's a client now. He may not care to be reminded of his humbler days."

"Shall we just call him Azeem to his face, and the full Azeem al Din when we're introducing him to new people?"

And that is what they do in the meeting which ensues.

This is a key meeting for all of them, and they're feeling buzzed. Azeem shares his idea about a campaign centring on victims of hardline Islamist violence.

"It'll be a big campaign," he tells them. "I want a campaign which focuses on a single tragedy—hopefully it'll turn into an inspiring tragedy. A tragedy to put an end to tragedies. The case of Rania Zandi..."

Just as they're wrapping the meeting up, the office walls shake — a dull thud like a detonation. A block or so away, it feels like.

The reverberations recede. Dust sprinkles down on them from the ceiling.

"What in the name of Christ was that?" says Wythenshawe, with a quick look at his watch as if wishing to pinpoint the happening in time.

"It came from the direction of the parking lot," says Myles, peering out at the window.

The air outside is tinged with dust, pregnant with swelling smog, black clouds blowing past their window and rolling down the street.

"Whose offices are there?"

"Nobody's... it's just the courtyard and the parking lot."

A siren sounds below.

"Turn on the TV so we can see who it was."

Just then the phone buzzes. Myles flicks it onto loudspeaker. The receptionist's breathless voice comes on.

"Sorry to disturb," she says, all flustered, "but a man's just come in off the street and he's standing here inside the main entrance..."

"Is he a client?" Myles asks with an apologetic glance at Azeem.

New girls can be so clueless. Any little thing throws them into a panic.

"He didn't give a name," she says, "but... but—"

The line goes dead. Myles stares at the phone.

"Sorry about that," he says. "We were wrapping up, weren't we?"

"Yeah, gotta go," says Azeem. "See if I can find out what's going on out there."

"We'll meet again next week, won't we?" says Wythenshawe. He's peering out the window, straining to see what's going on.

Azeem, standing at the door, nods.

"It's all clear," he says. "Let's see how quickly you guys can get hold of the Zandi family, without intruding of course... Work out what kind of campaign message we can put together. It should all revolve around Rania... Something hard-hitting... traumatic... but *hopeful*."

Wythenshawe and Myles shake hands with Azeem in the corridor.

He steps into the lift, presses the button to go down to the lobby. For some reason, as he's standing there behind those buffed metal doors, he remembers the last time he was in New York, in one of those elevators which make your ears pop as you go up, and where the view as the doors slide back is a vast vista of sky and cloud, and the city spreads below like an endlessly layered maze of skyscrapers and alleys, a disjointed grid system, hazy, and it's silent aside from the wind buffeting at the windows.

When the doors slide open the memory fades at once.

He's confronted with what he's been half expecting— complete bloody chaos.

The receptionist's being dragged back by a big dark man. He's Middle Eastern—an Iranian or an Iraqi maybe. Well-built, wearing a floppy hat and sunglasses like a tourist, and he's got her by the neck.

He's got a fixed, overexcited grin, he's holding a gun to her temple. He's shaking as he covers her mouth with his thick-gloved hand. The heels of the girl's boots scrape along digging trails on the rug.

Her eyes are wild.

As soon as the man sees Azeem he stops. He raises the girl up, then shoves her in the back. She shoots forward, stumbles, falls to the floor crying.

"Shut your trap!" shouts the man. His gun's pointed at Azeem. "I've seen *you* somewhere before," he says. "Glad… *glad* I was told to come here... Ghazan said we were... *working* together with this... these people... "

The gunman looks around the fancy lobby with a sneer.

"I'm Abu Jaffar."

Azeem knows the name. It isn't the gunman's real name. It's his *nom de guerre*. The man is staring at him with a lopsided grin, like a demented clown. He's deranged.

His gun is pointing right at Azeem.

"You're one of Ghazan's buddies, aren't you?"

Azeem's heartbeat is frantic. He slowly raises his hands. This mad clown-like man, Abu Jaffar, is nervous, unhinged—his eyes are all over the place.

He's speaking disjointedly.

"That fucking bastard's landed me in all this... nearly copped it out there... crappy old car blew up before I got out the parking lot... I'm probably all over the closed circuit cameras...complete fuck-up."

He's breathing hard, waving the gun to punctuate his points. Every time he does this, Azeem and the girl shrink back.

"Don't want to end up a martyr... not my scene... I'm just a nobody... you, now, you better get me out of here or you're dead meat, okay?... You're coming with me, matey! Going upstairs... I'm taking some hostages!"

The gunman takes a step toward Azeem. Then he stops. He's distracted, looks up at the ceiling as if frantic for a way out.

Then he looks down.

Glares down at the receptionist. She's still lying at his feet, whimpering.

He aims the gun at her. Seems to be considering his options. Azeem's looking at him. Calculating the odds.

Can he risk a move for the gun?

Don't do it.

Abu Jaffar looks over at Azeem. Azeem shakes his head.

Don't do it.

"Don't go telling anyone what you've seen," Abu Jaffar tells the girl. His voice is hoarse.

The girl just whimpers, her eyes dissolve. Now he's poking his gun in her face.

"Where's the stairs?"

The girl points blindly to a door beside the elevator. The man turns. Pushes Azeem through the doorway.

They go down a long, dimly lit corridor. Azeem's in front, the man's got the gun muzzle stuck into the small of his back. They get to another door at the end of the passage.

"Open it!"

Azeem does so. They step out into the light.

"Police!"

The shout comes from behind them, inside the building.

The gunman stiffens and sticks the gun into the back of Azeem's skull.

"Hold your fire or I'll shoot this fucker's brains out!" he shouts. "He's my hostage! Stay where you are!"

He shoulders the door shut behind them. It slams closed with a metallic thud which rings and echoes off the walls.

They're in a long, narrow, terraced mews-type side street that's jam-packed with parked cars, but no moving traffic. Azeem looks around. It's dingy, garbage everywhere, overflowing dumpsters. There's an office across the street. It's full of zombie-like people huddled into computer booths, speaking nineteen to the dozen into headsets as though to themselves.

No one even glances out into the street.

"Shit!" says Abu Jaffar, looking up, looking around, lost.

He pushes Azeem towards a yellow truck. A burly man's sitting inside, at the wheel, eating a gyros.

"Out!"

The man jumps out and scuttles to one side, holding his lunch to his chest as if in self-defence. Abu Jaffar shoves Azeem into the driver's seat.

"You're driving! Move it!"

Azeem starts the engine.

The truck jerks forward. They're wheezing towards Tottenham Court Road where it is teeming with people in the sunshine.

"Put your foot down!"

They're approaching the corner at speed. A woman with a buggy is halfway across. Azeem slows down.

"Don't stop!" shouts Abu Jaffar, hitting the horn. The truck ploughs on ahead. With a scream the woman jumps out the way. The van just misses the baby-carrier. Azeem sees uncomprehending hatred flashing out from the woman's face.

They come shooting out onto the road and squeeze between two stationary cars. They skid to a halt, almost immediately, behind a bus.

Nothing's moving. They're stuck.

"Get out!"

Azeem steps out onto the road. Cars behind them honk. Azeem thinks about making a run for it. Abu Jaffar is already beside him.

"Move!"

He pushes Azeem along the road in the direction of Oxford Street. They're walking among the idling cars. A man with his head stuck out the window of an old red Renault smiles when he sees Azeem coming.

"Had enough, have you, mate?"

His smile fades when he sees the gun. He pulls his head back inside the car.

Azeem's mind is churning.

The gunman doesn't have a plan.

How's he think he can get away? They're exposed on all sides. The police must be pouring out of the building by now. Radioing each other for reinforcements. Closing in.

Abu Jaffar must know that. But maybe not. Obviously an amateur—the most dangerous type to be with in a situation like this.

They're approaching Tottenham Court Road underground station.

Is he going down there? That's what I'd do. But I probably would've headed north to Warren Street, not here.

"Soho Square!" says Abu Jaffar.

They turn right down Oxford Street. They're on the sidewalk now. It's packed. People spread to either side when they see the gun. Their eyes go round, they step away, cowering. Faces freeze or twist in terror. Some of them scuttle off, some of them just melt away, cover their faces, seem to cry.

Azeem sees all this in slow-mo. He feels like he's watching himself walk, watching himself walk to his death.

No sign of the police.

They turn left off Oxford Street. Not so many people now as they approach the square. It's just thirty yards ahead when Azeem hears a shout.

"Hey! Where you going?"

Azeem turns round. Big tall man in the distance sprinting toward them. All in black and he's got a long knife in his hand. He's running right at them. A knifeman!

"Stop or I shoot!"

The knifeman's closing in. His right arm's stretched straight in front of him. He's rushing right at Abu Jaffar.

The gun goes off. The knifeman's still running. The gun fires again. Now he's half stopped in his tracks by the impact. He rocks and stumbles, clutching his chest.

He falls three yards away from their feet.

"Fuck!" says Abu Jaffar. "Another of Ghazan's guys! He wants me dead, man!"

He looks over at Azeem, his face full of dread, horrible.

"He wants me dead... 'cos of what I know."

All the people have melted to the sides of the streets, there's some shouting and screaming in the middle distance, people scrambling to get away.

Azeem knows the gunman is thinking about killing him too. The man's eyes are so scared now, he looks more witless than ruthless.

"Come on!"

They head on to Soho Square. Cross the street, go into the park, toward the little half-timbered house.

"Sit down!"

Azeem sits down under the crumbling statue of Charles II. The gunman crouches beside him, pointing the gun at his temple.

"Are you ready to die?"

Azeem stays still.

"Because I'm not. You need to start talking, mate. Start shouting, let everyone know..."

The gunman starts to call out at the top of his voice.

"I want to talk!" he hollers, his voice oddly high, shrieking. "I've got information! I want to talk to the police. Or I'll shoot this man—" he pokes his gun into Azeem's neck— "shoot him like a dog!"

Abu Jaffar withdraws into the shade of the little house, his whole body shaking, his hands wild, his gun wobbling, but still covering Azeem. He's trying to take a leak, Azeem sees, a dark stain spreads from his crotch down his leg.

Azeem cannot bear to watch him, dissolving into his own fear, and he shouts out, "Is there a policeman here!?"

Abu Jaffar comes back out and puts the gun to Azeem's head.

"If they start shooting at me, I'll kill you, man!"

Azeem shouts, "He doesn't want to shoot! Hold your fire! He's got information!"

A police car comes in off Oxford Street. It stops just before the square.

A cop steps out. He's got a loudhailer. He's crouching down beside the car door.

Azeem shouts, "Don't shoot! He wants to talk!"

The cop with the loudhailer says, "Drop your weapon! Drop your weapon now!"

"He wants to talk!"

There's maybe ten seconds' silence. There is no sound in the square, the birds in the trees, the people at the corners, everything is still. Only the traffic beyond the square rustles as if nothing is wrong.

A single shot echoes from somewhere above, somewhere behind them.

Azeem feels the gun barrel slide down his temple. Abu Jaffar's falling. Another shot. Then another.

Abu Jaffar collapses beside Azeem. He slumps down letting the gun go. The left side of his skull's been blown away.

Azeem's face is wet. He wipes away moisture. His hand is red, speckled with little lumpy blobs of gray.

He falls back, overcome with nausea.

The dark grass under him is spattered with red and gray matter. He falls down as if onto a blanket and it receives him like a bed.

There's a ringing noise in Azeem's ear, a metallic tang in his nose. He's lying on the grass among the soggy bits of brain and flesh.

The statue's shattered head lies beside him, the white marble pocked with blood.

Azeem blacks out.

ISLAMIC FEMINISTS
Islington, London: Shirin Shaarawi & Mamida Hanif

HAVING SURVIVED a sweltering transit by underground—a single stop on the Piccadilly line from Russell Square, all squashed-together, standing-room-only, squeezed-up, in sweaty closeness with strangers—Shirin Shaarawi switches to the Victoria line to continue to Highbury & Islington.

The carriage she boards is even fuller. She's got her back to the door, sandwiched against it by an old man in a grubby blue pin-stripe suit. His eyes are bloodshot and vague, watery; he keeps them well away from her face, but she can smell last night's brandy on his breath, which he appears to have been drinking with garlicky grappa chasers, and washed down with cheap sparkling wine—all the drinks most noxious to Shirin's stomach at this time of the morning, it is like being dragged face first through a sewer.

His body is right up close to hers, hemmed in by the press of passengers behind and, as the train clatters along the bumpy tracks, the motion of his lower belly and groin becomes one with hers.

We're like two puppets stuck together, being made to dance.

She looks down, tries not to breathe too deep. It seems involuntary, this uncomfortable intimacy with the stranger, and for a while she accepts it, silently suffering the rolling and rubbing of the man's flesh, and his warmth, and his smell. That lasts about a minute. It ends when she sees his mouth, now spread into a luxurious leer, and she feels him getting stiff.

She slaps him hard across his face. He recoils, his body writhes free of her, as if she is the aggressor.

"Stop that, you pervert!"

The train is already slowing down and the platform lights are flashing past the window.

"This man was rubbing himself up against me!"

The other commuters avert their eyes. The man is wriggling away. The train stops and as the passengers escape through the doors, he slips off, quickly dissolved into the crowd.

Shirin goes up the moving staircase, shaking, bustling herself past the people, her eyes wide, unseeing, her ribcage thumping, throat constricted in embarrassment and disgust. She steps into the fresh air of the street and stands still for a moment to catch her breath.

Great start to the day.

She pulls herself together and sets off for work. After a couple of minutes, she walks into a dingy house off Holloway Road, Islington, home to a gang of Islamic feminists.

They monitor the media here, keep an eye on all forms of hate-speech.

"You look tired this morning, Shirin love," says her colleague Mamida Hanif, a well turned-out widow in her mid fifties.

"Couldn't sleep," sighs Shirin. "Then on the way in I got hassled on the tube."

"You mustn't overdo things," is all Mamida will say as she shifts her attention momentarily away from Shirin to mark her place in the report she's reading, called *She Who Disputes.*

Shirin leans against the door-jamb, smiles at her.

Her colleague Mamida is newish in the office. She came up to London last fall, after her husband died. She'd lived in Leeds. Her previous job, with the Muslim Women's Hotline, ended through lack of funding last April.

She and her husband were originally from Baluchistan, but when Mamida speaks, she sounds Yorkshire. She knows a lot of people up in Leeds and—her manner implies—a lot of their secrets.

Shirin, unwrapping her scarf, clicks on her computer.

"Sheikh Faisal ibn Shabbir's office was in touch again," says Mamida. She gives the name the kind of stiff emphasis a lackey at Buckingham Palace might give it. "They called just a minute ago..."

She glances at Shirin. Shirin is standing at her desk, blinking, as if hypnotized by her computer monitor.

"They were calling to express their *concern* about you, love."

Shirin's non-reaction is a reaction Mamida seems to recognize, and she goes back to reading her report.

Shirin stays silent. Her energies are wound up inside her, she breathes in tense sighs.

"They don't give up, do they?"

Mamida peers at her. She sees a spark flaming up, then fading, in Shirin's eyes.

"They're paid not to, love."

"I'm just so not interested! I've got better things to do than... than *pandering...* to the delusions of some pampered sheikh!"

"He does seem a classic example of the outmoded patriarch model," says Mamida, smiling. "Forget him, ignore him while he forgets about you..."

For a moment they're silent.

Mamida senses Shirin's tension, how coiled up she's feeling this morning.

"So what's up, love?" Mamida asks gently. "What's bugging you aside from all that?"

Shirin can't put it into words, though she realizes what it is. She thinks she wants to talk, or that she ought to want to, and she knows she'll feel better for it, seeing as it's Mamida, who always cheers her up. So she relaxes.

She sits down.

Azeem comes to.

"Where am I?"

"You're in the resuscitation bay... stay still for a bit."

The male nurse looking down at him is about his age, a serious-faced Indian.

"Did I get hit?"

"No... no, we thought you did. You looked a lot worse than you are... covered in... blood. The gunman's dead."

No shit. Didn't survive losing half his head then.

"You're going to be fine... there might be some trauma."

Azeem slips away again.

He knows he's lucky—somewhere in his mind he knows it. But somewhere else, nightmarish visions tell him he's still in danger.

Everything's mixed together in his head. And he sees Ghazan's face in everything he dreams.

The dead gunman's face—half of it blown away—transmogrifies, assumes Ghazan's features, becomes Ghazan's face.

Azeem sees himself from above, from a sniper's perspective, being pushed into Soho Square. He hears Ghazan's voice behind him.

Scourge him with bullets!

Ghazan runs to the little house, the gun poking out from his flies like a black metal cock. Blood spurts from the muzzle like urine. Then Ghazan twists it in his hand, wrenching it out until it starts spewing blood out like a hose. There's a spray of red matter.

Ghazan turns it on himself, showering his face in blood.

There's another explosion behind them, muffled in the wind, and then the whoosh of the statue's head flying through the air.

A dull thud on the grass, where it lands beside Azeem.

The head is smiling at him with a creepy, bloody grin.

Ghazan's head.

Kiss me, it says. *Kiss my bloody lips.*

As this is happening a few blocks away, Shirin and Mamida sit with their cookies and coffee at Mamida's desk.

"You know this communications project Azeem's been setting up?" says Shirin.

"*Islamic Reform*? Yes, you told me all about that, love."

"It's getting him so worked up. Hence the lack of sleep."

Shirin is tired, red-rimmed eyes, skin somewhat parched. She dunks her cookie in the milky tea, bites it in half, then she puts the rest away for later.

"We've been arguing all night," she says, poking a crumb into her mouth. "Then just after dawn we heard about that honor killing in Leeds..."

"What was that?"

"That girl who got knifed in Leeds this morning?"

"What girl?"

"Some young girl, a teenager they said. Didn't you hear?"

Mamida shakes her head.

"I hadn't," she says. "No. I've been here since six." She shifts in her seat, rubs her sore back. "Oh, no. *Another one...* it'll never end, will it? *Killed?* Oh, Shirin, this is bad."

"They didn't say she was dead. I think she may have survived."

"We'll have to get hold of the full story. I'll make some calls in a minute... some interviews maybe. We shouldn't let one of these pass without comment. It needs to be publicized."

Mamida is worked up, but sombre.

Shirin looks down, down at her hands, her lap. She feels Mamida's eyes on her. She half wants, half doesn't want to talk.

"So, whatever are those extremists of Azeem's cooking up now?" Mamida is saying caustically.

"The usual. I don't really know. He says they're moderates, and that all they're cooking up is a network of advertising agencies."

"Good heavens! Another network! Whatever next? Haven't they got enough networks to be getting on with? Can't they leave well alone?"

Shirin smiles despite herself at Mamida's disgruntled, flustered tone. She always speaks like that, she sounds like a proper misery-guts, but isn't, at heart.

"Who knows what they'll find to advertise," says Shirin, "the mind boggles... it's way beyond me. I mean, it's not as if they've got anything to *sell* to anybody."

"He should be careful, your boy. He's *naïve*. Those extremists eat people like Azeem for breakfast."

"It's marketing communications, Mamida," says Shirin, still playing down her colleague's foreboding. "That's what Azeem knows about."

"That's as may be, love, but I know some of those people of old. They used to call themselves the Beeston Boys. Beeston Beasts, more like. *Baraderi*. Associated with the Mullah Boys, Mohammad Sidiq Khan's lot. 7/7."

"You think they're the same people?"

"An unsavory bunch of psychopathic Pashtuns, every last one of them. Extremist to their eyeballs, psychotic in the very marrow of their bones."

Shirin smiles. "You told me about Ghazan... Azeem's mate."

"Yes I did. Ghazan Khattak's the worst of all of them, love. The dregs."

Again Shirin laughs. "The way you describe him, he sounds like some kind of incarnation of evil," she says. "The whole thing does to me sometimes."

Shirin shakes her head. "You know, the only one I actually know — know in the flesh, if that's the right word — is toxic and repulsive, but aside from that perfectly harmless. A guy called Samir Muhsi, he used to be a tacky drug addict playboy."

Mamida says, "I don't know about your toxic playboys, love, but you couldn't get an envelope between the ones I do know and the jihadis. They're lawless Pashtuns, Shirin.

"Imagine," Mamida continues, "they used to push *heroin*. Now they're pushing jihad. Go figure that one out if you can."

With a portentous look Mamida goes back to her report. Shirin sits down and so continues her working day.

MEDIA RABBI
Edgware Road, London: Ghazan Khattak & Co

OUTSIDE GHAZAN'S office, out of earshot, a group of brothers have been waiting patiently for him to finish.

He feels trapped…

He knows he isn't remotely finished with his mopping up of the morning's messes. This emergency—this *live* emergency—is still hanging over his head, waiting for him to deal with it… The car-bomb, planned for that morning in London. The problem with the man who said he'd prime it. The man who backed out when everything else was set.

That lost, faithless traitor… he's committed treason against the cause of jihad. He'll pay for it, pay for it dearly…

To rescue the situation, Ghazan had had to strong-arm another brother—Abu Jaffar, a far less technically gifted brother—into taking over the task of resetting the timer in the car. Abu Jaffar has always *seemed* solid enough, but he would never have been Ghazan's first choice…

And then, what was absolutely the worst thing, the radio connection between them had broken. Ghazan sent out another back-up, another guy to try and see if he could find out what was going on. The other guy… well, he was a bit of a hothead, a bit of a thug when he got wound up about anything.

Handy with a knife, and likes to use it.

No news yet on that front… And no news, in this kind of situation, is bad news.

Still.

Probably best carry on with the day, just make it look like everything's normal. Don't want to be panicked into showing your hand.

Ghazan nods at all those men waiting for him outside his office. They get to their feet and file in. Ghazan rises to greet them.

New recruits.

He looks them up and down, and they begin to exchange the conventional greetings.

"*As-salamu 'alaykum*. May Allah's peace be upon you."

"*Wa 'alaykum as-salam wa rahmatullahi wa barakatuhu*."

He looks each man in the eye, unsmiling, as they pass, and bumps his chest and shoulder against each of theirs, one after the other, in line. The mujahidin greeting.

Ghazan's problem has never been finding keen young men with the right attitudes. Far from it. It's sorting out the committed from the dilettantes, the *doers* from the *posers*. The group now gathered in his office off Edgware Road are men he has high hopes for. Men with excellent references from the training camps, proven men, men with plenty of potential. Men who have steeled themselves abroad, risking their lives, men whose real names are already written on the lists of the spies always circling around us, watching, spies who try and fail to watch those things, those righteous things which have been decreed, and which they should not watch…

They sip mugs of filter coffee, glasses of sweet tea. After some inconsequential chit-chat, Ghazan starts knocking around ideas for good targets. He's feeling mounting frustration on this subject, he wants to energize himself, and not just himself but also these new brothers, these men looking for leadership, he wants to show them what it means, to submit your life to jihad in the way of Allah.

There's so many targets, so many in need of chastisement. Who should they go for next?

The oldest enemy of all… men whose malice and enmity is aimed at the Apostle of God…

"Next up for us I think… is killing a rabbi," he says. His voice is so soft that the others lean forward to catch his words.

"Killing a rabbi?"

The men grin. They're excited. Ghazan nods slowly.

"Yes, killing a rabbi," he says. "And not just *any* rabbi… I want to hit the headlines… front page splashes… all day rolling coverage on the box… I want the head of a *well-known* rabbi…"

"Does it *have* to be a rabbi?" asks the youngest, a spotty boy called Abu Arshed. "I don't know that many rabbis... People today are more into *celebrities* than... than men of God... Couldn't we just kill a famous Jew?"

"A rabbi would be better for our purposes... far better... But I'm not... unpersuadable," Ghazan concedes. "You got anyone in mind?"

"Bob Monkhouse?"

"Nah," says everyone else, laughing. "He's long dead."

"Allah be praised."

"What about one of the Saatchis?"

"Nah," choruses the group.

"What about that Nigella Lawson?"

"Nah..."

"What about that sex doctor, what's her name, Dr Leah?"

"Nah..."

"Rachel Weisz?"

"Sam Mendes?"

Ghazan shakes his head. "A rabbi would be better."

"What about a *media* rabbi?"

"What media rabbi?"

"Of course!"

Ghazan starts nodding his head, and as he thinks, his nods get more pronounced. "Yes of course man," he says, "a media rabbi..."

Ghazan smiles to himself, and as he looks down at the coffee table, his smile broadens into a big happy grin of pleasure. He points to the friendly, Semitic face on the cover of a copy of the *TV Times* lying there—a face which, but for the amiability and the kippah, bears an uncanny resemblance to himself.

One of the guys leans forward, picks it up—and laughs aloud. He hands the mag round to the others.

The toughest, cockiest man among them, Sohail, a stocky butcher in his mid twenties, takes it in both hands. He looks for a minute at the man on the cover picture with a mixture of mockery and distaste. Then he rips the cover off. He hawks his throat, spits on it, covering the picture with runny phlegm.

He scrunches it into a ball and throws it into the wastepaper basket by the door.

"He'll do," Sohail growls.

Ghazan's still smiling. Sometimes you really don't have far to look to find what you need. Your victims present themselves to you, actively *beseeching* to be your targets.

IN THE VAN
Southbound Carriageway, M1: Faraz Zandi

THE BEATEN UP white van is barreling down the M1.

It's an old Bedford Blitz, a type which hasn't been in production these twenty years.

It is a rust bucket, and it rattles thunderously as it rolls south.

Inside sit the three youths from Leeds, and the driver Ghazan has found for them. This is a nervous-looking, thin man, leaning forward short-sightedly, his eyes fixed on the freeway, his long bony fingers trembling on the wheel. He is Ghazan's fourth cousin.

The lads don't have a lot to say to each other. Two of them are hunched over their phones, texting goodbye messages. They're doing it fast, their thumbs flying on autopilot. The driver's told them Ghazan wants all the phones dumped next time they stop.

The third lad, Faraz Zandi, Rania's big, gangling brother, lolls desultorily in his seat. He looks as if he might keel over any minute.

He is ghostly pale.

He's strapped in his seat, his eyes puffed and bleary behind his shades. His body sitting limp, wrapped in his black hoodie—its sleeves stiff with dried blood—he wrestles with abstract things which have come to life in this alien way.

Honor.

Death.

He stares blankly out the window, not seeing the dreary suburbs, the thin spread of anonymous lives. Slumped back, his head against the glass, his limbs and muscles twitch in ceaseless little convulsions, and the van hurtles down the motorway, ever further from the scene of the crime. He tries to compose his mind to the implications of the morning. Can't really take it all in. His mind races, unfamiliar emotions seethe and roil around inside him.

He'd dropped his knife beside lifeless Rania's body, left it there, shiny with blood. And it's the knife he keeps seeing when he closes his eyes, and the blood he keeps feeling, warm and sticky between his fingers.

Her blood. *His* blood.

His mind keeps bringing it back to him, and his *honor*, the concept of honor echoes in his mind, as it has been echoing, echoing so loud, so long, the past month or so.

His vision keeps superimposing the knife. His knife was his honor's tool, its *instrument*, he keeps thinking to himself.

He sees the knife still there beside her lifeless body.

The bloody knife, lying in the gutter where his sister bleeds. So, is her dishonor gone now? Has his knife cut more than just her chest and her throat?

Even now he burns with jealousy and love, mortified, as he remembers watching little sister Rania slipping up the hill. The *shame*—his mates watching her too, watching her *defy* him. Their envious eyes on her hair and her neck, and her long legs in those tight, tight jeans, all of it on show.

And her smile, just as she'd always smiled.

His little sister Rania—just a few years ago so submissive, so sweet... How she'd adored him, admired him, hung onto everything he said, copied everything he did... Now she'd started turning into a whore, nursing a crush—planning to have sex, when you got down to it—planning sex with an infidel.

Ghazan had kept telling him about those rumors, kept telling him he had to put a stop to it, end it before it was too late.

Faraz had been well pumped up with awareness that morning, fresh out of the class where they pump you up and inject your consciousness full of steroids. There had been a guest speaker, a holy man from the *madrasa* in Pakistan where Faraz had been. A great community man, burning with charisma, fired up with righteous pride. Such an inspiring speaker. He had talked less of the Qur'an than usual, more about the traditions of honor and respect in the community. He'd spoken of *zan, zar, zameen* (women, gold and land) and their value for honor. It was a really short talk, maybe twenty minutes, but all the more powerful for it. Fervent eyes blazing with passion, he had spoken of the duty of the individual to uphold the community's honor, to preserve it from corruption.

That is the custom, the holy custom, hallowed by belief, the honor of the tribe and long usage.

And some of the other men who were there, the older ones, they'd whispered things about Rania after the talk was over, he knew it was her because they made it so obvious, whispering some of their words with hissing ferocity, bad, gross stuff, things no brother would ever want to hear.

(Things no brother should ever *have* to hear.)

A rotten finger should be amputated.

Afterwards, trying to put it out of his mind, Faraz was keen to impress his mates, remind them who's the boss. He knew they were envious of his closeness to Ghazan, and really envious of his time at the *madrasa.*

None of his friends had been there yet. That trip had earned him respect all right, he only had to make sure they showed it.

But there was more to it than that, more working away inside him. He was full of anger, seething really, and he had been for a while. The whole week had been bad, he'd had a hard time of it.

There had been some bad, bad stuff with his girlfriend. She'd been acting up, saying she didn't like his attitude of late. She wanted shot of him. And his sister was pissing him off about that too, dissing him like she was always doing these days.

He didn't rightly know what had set it off. Something one of those men in the mosque had said was still running through his mind.

The man had taken him aside, spoken with pity, with a bullying pity, close to contempt: *If you don't make her feel the shame, man, the shame she's bringing on you, just think of what she'll have done to you—not just to your dad, but both of you... it's like you're less than men, like you're letting her turn you into eunuchs... You know it's true, men who don't control their women have no honor, bring dishonor onto all of us...*

They're not men any more. They're eunuchs... And those kinds of eunuchs who let their women pursue their desires—even if they're

*virtuous men, constant at salah, fasting, Hajj, and righteous deeds —
their women will pull them down into hell behind them...*

Maybe... maybe (but he didn't know why he'd done it really)
Faraz had hoped to shame Rania with his rebuke, make her feel,
make her *share* in the shame he felt.

Maybe he hoped she'd turn back, filled with that shame, run
back into the house, cover herself...

But she hadn't done that... and something in him just flipped.

Some switch thrown inside, and he'd seen red, his eyes filled
up with fury. When she smiled over her shoulder with that
dismissive, that immodest wave of her hand, his face flushed
with instant rage.

In the van, now, Faraz leans against the window watching the
endless asphalt unfurl beside him. The drab bedraggled weeds
in the strips of dirt beside the freeway, the dull faded browns
and greens of the trees, the hedgerows and the fields. None of
that registers. None of that matters.

He thinks of his parents.

*They weren't watchful enough, but they know now... they'll know I
had to do it, for their sake, for everyone's sake, for the sake of all our
honor. Those rumors, those wagging tongues, they had to be stopped,
had to be silenced.*

Faraz has always gravitated into commitments bigger than
himself. Bigger than the petty needs of his family.

For the good of the whole community.

And not just the community in Leeds. Reaching right out
across the ocean, to their tribe in Pakistan, reaching right back in
time, to their ancestors, people of their blood. He's seeing now —
now he's running away from them — how he's only got the
haziest impressions of his actual family, of the people closest to
him. And he feels he knows them only insofar as they've entered
his day to day concerns.

So now, he takes in what he's done to his little sister Rania —
it's only beginning to soak into his consciousness, but it's doing

so with bloody-minded insistence—he begins to see the image of her face, her overall presence, more and more clearly.

He keeps seeing that little wave she made and that smile she sent over her shoulder, the gestures which angered him so a couple of hours ago.

And as his parents recede behind him in the distance, they too—and the whole living outline of their lives together—assume a clearer, sharper image, sharper and more distinct with each passing minute.

He knows he's killed his former life just as effectively as he killed his sister.

You die with the person you kill.

When they get to Tibshelf service station, they all dash out for a pee and to change and to clean themselves up. Having re-emerged into the cold sunlight, Faraz's mate Jamshad calls up Ghazan Khattak, to ask about that connection in Paris.

He puts the loudspeaker on so they can all hear.

Ghazan answers their questions with an impatient air, absent. His voice on the little speaker sounds tinny and detached, he sounds like he's already *moved on...* He's cut himself off from them.

Two of the lads are standing on the curb by the van smoking cigarettes. In their T-shirts and trainers, they look like young scallywags out on a spree.

Only Faraz stands to one side—squirming inside, full of queasy regret. And as they stand there with their smokes, a police patrol car rolls slowly in their direction.

They're very paranoid.

They all bundle into the van, keep their heads down and let the police pass by. They carry on smoking when the patrol car has passed, and they watch it go as it speeds up and shoots onto the freeway.

Then the thin nervous driver finishes his sandwich. He throws the bag out of the window and wipes his mouth, watching them with his watery eyes. Jamshad nods back at him and he clicks on his seatbelt and starts the engine and pulls that wheezing van out into the lane.

They're off again.

Faraz is feeling giddy and sick and alone.

He pictures Ghazan back in London—once Ghazan knows they've got safely away—Faraz can just imagine Ghazan *moving on*, consigning him to the back of his mind.

Deleting him from his memory.

Let him make the best of his fate, Faraz can hear Ghazan thinking. *Let me make the best of mine... I've made everything possible for him.*

He'd said exactly that to him once: *I've made it all possible for you, man.*

That's what he'll be thinking now: *I made him scourge his sister, his sister who dishonored us all, and now he can see inside the gates of paradise...*

Ghazan will be congratulating himself.

Faraz feels ever more nauseous as the van drives on south.

They make it to the safe house in Tower Hamlets without further incident. And Faraz is in a kind of zombified state.

He's hardly aware of the tunnel, the crossing to Paris. He's hardly awake. His mind has gone AWOL.

He lets everything flow over him.

LIFE-SUPPORT
Leeds: Rania Zandi, Mr & Mrs Zandi, Dr Khan

RANIA ZANDI. Damaged child.

She lies in the bed so pale and slight, her breathing shallow.

Outside the room her mom is weeping, her dad looking washed out, as they sit and wait to hear, as the hospital staff bustle back and forth around them.

She's on the life-support machine.

"Patients *have* recovered from injuries this severe," says Dr Khan. He looks uncomfortable, non-committal. "I can't promise anything."

Rania lies in the room. And her pulse is weak, so worn out by trauma and the loss of blood.

Her mom and dad slump in plastic seats. Remembering how the morning started for her, the mother is dazed.

She remembers Faraz rushing upstairs, unexpectedly early after his awareness class, jolting them awake.

"Where's Rania off to dressed like a slut?" Faraz was shouting.

She looking at him—bleary and startled, already a little scared.

"I don't know..."

Telling him in her grumpiest voice, grouching and cracked in her throat, "She's probably seeing Bousseh and Yass."

"Not looking like that she's not."

"Let her be."

"She'll be picked up by a curb-crawler before she gets there!"

"Don't get overexcited, Faraz love."

Mrs Zandi sitting up, wiping the sleep from her eyes, mightily scared, now, by her son's hot head. She thought she knew what he was going through. He just learned that his girlfriend had started going out with his best friend.

Close to distraction, poor lad, he's going through hell.

"I'm not standing for any more of this!" Faraz was saying. "She's a disgrace... she just goes off where she likes, doesn't tell her family anything, going off... to sell her body to an infidel, *dishonoring* us, making us all look bad... We've got to put a stop to it."

Mrs Zandi tried to calm him, she plucked at his arm to restrain him. But not stopping to hear his mother's soothing words Faraz was out of there.

His manner that morning had flipped over into mania, she thought. He went down the stairs making enough noise for a man twice his size. On the way down, he smashed the mirrors hanging there, the mirrors where Rania always put on her last touches of make-up, smashed them into a thousand pieces.

Mrs Zandi and her husband glanced at each other, appalled, over the crumpled bedsheets, dislocated, listening to the din of the shattering glass—and even then, neither guessed what was coming, the stuff of nightmares everlasting.

An eternity's worth of bad luck...

So now in the hospital glare they sit together. She looks at her husband and sees the shock, cowering in his usually stoic eyes. She feels anger rise within her.

How often has she begged her son to take up a hobby, to do something other boys his age enjoy, normal boys with their girls and guitars, their bikes and their skateboards?

How often?

And how many times has she asked her husband to talk to him man to man, try to reach him, try to muzzle those violent, bullying words, rein in that crazed religious obsessiveness of his, which has been threatening to run away with him, turning him into a full-scale maniac?

None of that worked.

He's been out of their reach a while now, too far sunk in his rebellion, wrapped up, carried away in his runaway, fundamentalist whirlwind. His parents might have been puddles, potholes in the street, or trees, statues, birds in the sky, invisible spirits, for all the attention he paid them...

Irrelevant.

And look at him now. On the run, like a common criminal.

It's terrible, a trial no parent deserves.

We've failed. Failed him. Failed ourselves.

Their son is gone. Their daughter is close to them, here in her hospital bed, but she's damaged, close to dying, she lies there beside them, not really with them anymore.

All of them silent as the night passes by outside. And the only thing waiting for all of them, out there somewhere, the only thing they can be sure of, now, is death.

Paris: Faraz Zandi

Faraz wakes. He is lying under a sheet on a sagging mattress in a dim, scruffy room. It smells of dust and socks. His comrades, snoring in their bunks, all seem to be asleep. The drapes are drawn, but through their flimsy moth-eaten fabric the first light gleams. Rain drizzles onto the street, he hears it pattering softly outside, and the air is heavy and thick, damp in his nose.

He rises. He's still wearing the clothes they gave him when he arrived, gray slacks, beige polo-neck. He looks at his hands, grimy, sticky.

He lets himself out of the room and walks down the corridor. The floorboards, covered by unraveling pieces of rug, creak under his feet. A single door leads on to a landing, a rickety staircase.

There's no one in the hall downstairs. On the desk stands the TV. It's switched on with the volume down. A 1990s soft-porn film is showing.

Faraz goes to the door. He looks through the window, out into the empty street, slick with rain. He wants to go out there, get a taste of Paris, his first foreign city.

He pulls the door open and steps outside. Looking up and down the street, he sees nobody, hears nothing but the dripping rain, buses passing a block away.

He heads down the street.

As he walks off, a white Renault pulls away from the curb.

DEATH AND COMPROMISE

Düsseldorf and London: Udo Rincke, Dr Norbert Klinker, Rupert Wythenshawe & Myles Lyall

THE RHINE IS FLOWING low between the embankment on the south side of the city and the long green meadows on the north, snaking sluggishly through a Düsseldorf whose skyline is sharp against the brilliant blue, pocked here and there with a cloud, a white smudge where a solitary jet is circling in to land, and the air above it all hangs heavy, replete with high summery listlessness.

Herr Doktor Norbert Klinker, a tall Byronic man with flowing curly locks, sits behind his antique partners' desk, looking contemplatively out the window through his half-moon spectacles. He has the lordly manner and aquiline nose of the Romantic poet, the crazy eyes, and tangled facial hair, of a foppish goat.

But anyone who knows him can see how ripped apart he feels, derailed.

He's torn up about his company's future. Are they ready to merge with that upstart English agency? It means an end to the proud independence of their company, Rincke & Klinker.

The choice before them is stark—to merge or go bankrupt.

He turns his back on the view and says, "*Jetzt versteh' ich es.* I can see you've already made up your mind about these Englishmen."

Dr Klinker has full lips, which he uses to great effect when smiling to seduce a client, or a female, or himself in the mirror, but they are parched dry this morning, chapped and peeling, and a small piece has flaked off, exposing a patch of blood, and he licks at this obsessively, his tongue protruding from his mouth like a livid serpent emerging from a basket of figs, wormlike in color and length. His partner, Herr Udo Rincke, watches him with a mixture of admiration and disgust, utterly fascinated by Dr Klinker's charismatic repulsiveness.

Udo Rincke, for his part, is every inch the thrusting strategic communications consultant. He sports a perma-tan and blond floppy hair like a romantic movie-star. He's wearing tight black trousers and a white, open-necked shirt. He looks keen as mustard.

"There's two of them," goes this dashing Udo Rincke, exuding a confidence he doesn't quite feel. "The younger one is called Myles Lyall... He has no intellect, no political principles, but a lot of that very British pragmatism about him."

"Pragmatism is another word for defeat. It has a smell of death and compromise."

Dr Klinker stares at the ceiling as he drawls, employing a languid pomposity nobody has known him long enough to tell is affected or genetic.

"Myles is very effective about getting things done."

Udo sounds very brisk, very together, but his briskness is certainly bogus, and he is less together than he sounds, too. Maybe because he chooses not to externalize it, he is, if anything, even more uptight than his partner.

"When a man prides himself on being pragmatic," sniffs Dr Klinker, "you can be sure it's because he believes in nothing."

Klinker tightens his lips and the knot of his bow-tie. It is one of his mannerisms signalling disapproval. He is like a human patchwork made up of many such physical tics.

Udo smiles cheerfully. How hard his business partner finds it to unwind, constantly coiled up as he is within abstruse cogitative processes. Klinker shoots him a grim look back.

"Tell me about the other one... tell me about Wythenshawe."

"*Rupert* Wythenshawe, *ich bitte Sie*... They will want us on first-name terms immediately, like all Anglo-Saxons. Wythenshawe is far more experienced. Supine. Alcoholic. Hopeless. He's an old school kind of English advertising man, very laid-back... brandy and cigars, aristocratic... The name Rupert alone is enough to tell you that."

Klinker lets out a snort. And then he lets out another one, even louder, and a third, each successive snort an intensification of disapproval.

"So, to summarize," he says, "we're getting into bed here with a cynical pragmatist, a man called Lyall, a man who loves death and compromise."

Klinker shakes his head sadly.

"And as if that is not enough, we clutch to our breast a lazy, drunken snob, this reprobate named Wythenshawe—a Rupert— a noble debauchee, an anachronism, completely sidelined by the 21st century."

Dr Klinker draws out the final phrase, *einundzwanzigste Jahrhunderten*, as far as the syllables will bear. His eyes are rheumy. He snorts twice more.

He places his head in his hands. His trembling eyelids flutter closed. He manages, visibly, to contain his grief, but it seems quite a struggle. Udo Rincke watches him patiently.

"*Meine Güte*," Dr Klinker now laments, in a broken, lachrymose whisper. "Is this really to be the fate of Rincke and Klinker?"

His eyes seem to liquefy in their sockets, and he sucks in his cheeks, wheezing, as if his head were imploding into the black hole of his self-absorption. Shaking his head slowly from side to side, he let out a croak of primal despair.

Klinker puts his head on his desk and quietly begins to sob.

Herr Rincke watches him with an expression of polite concern. Dr Klinker's partiality to theatrical display is notorious in the trade, a silly, occasionally tiresome affectation, but either way, part and parcel of the man. And today, somewhere behind all the posing, some of the display is sincere.

"Come come, this could be our way out, Herr Dr Klinker!" insists Udo Rincke. "This new *Islamic Reform* project gives us the chance to silence our critics once and for all...

"It's virgin territory," he says. "Untouched. *Verboten*. Taboo. This whole Islam versus the west conflict isn't just what it often gets passed off for—a mere clash of civilizations. It's more...

much more. It's a whole new world of untapped opportunity for the marketing communications sector! We can have a huge effect on the industry, make a big splash!

"Believe me!" Udo Rincke urges. "The dream isn't over. There is another chapter to be written in the book of Rincke and Klinker. A glorious chapter!"

"We don't have much choice, do we?" Klinker snorts, balefully lifting his head.

Udo Rincke's bleached teeth grin and glimmer vacantly, and his whole face shines. He breezily brushes his hand across that bland unwrinkled brow.

"None whatsoever."

And so, a week later, Rupert Wythenshawe, Myles Lyall, Dr Klinker and Herr Udo Rincke meet in London.

"Welcome to Wythenshawe and Lyall, gentlemen," says Rupert Wythenshawe.

They all stand in a semicircle awkwardly figuring each other out. The room is subtly lit with spots of halogen on the walls. Udo Rincke, the gallant young German, is so bright-eyed and bushy-tailed that Myles takes against him at once.

Not another fucking druggie, thinks Myles. *These guys, they just don't know what throwbacks they are. They should just go back to the Eighties. That's where they left their souls.*

In quickstep staccato, sprucely turned-out Udo Rincke now barks out, "I have a good feeling!" His lips form a grisly kind of smile. "More than just good. Much more than good. A very good feeling!"

"So do I, my boy, so do I!" Wythenshawe oozes, clapping him on the back.

Turning to the goat-like Herr Dr Klinker, Wythenshawe exclaims, "Well, well, Dr Klinker, we meet at last! How do you *do*, my dear sir, how *do* you do?"

"I am very good, thank you," bleats Dr Klinker with a sniff and a stiff sort of bow.

"This is an... ah... historic moment," Myles observes.

"Indeed it is, it is, indeed it is," says Udo Rincke, blinking like a mole. His jaw chomps. Rincke's rictus smile infuses his face with robotic rigor. *It's the drugs*, thinks Myles.

"The hand of history is on our shoulders," Dr Klinker declaims through clenched teeth. His eyes have a faraway glint, as if seeing rosy sunkissed vistas of glory in the ethereal plane. "We must beware it doesn't push us the wrong way."

Klinker's expression is mystic and glassy.

"Above all," he says, "we must beware it doesn't strangle us."

Everyone except Klinker himself laughs hard and loud at his little sally of wit. Wythenhawe especially roars, throwing back his head in an obsequious excess of mirth. He seems altogether delighted to have the goat-like Dr Klinker for his prospective colleague and partner, his mentor and friend.

Myles' irritation grows.

"But, to be serious for a change," Dr Klinker continues, capitalizing on his involuntary joke, "these are times... when what appears to be mere *pragmatism* is also the ideal *strategic solution*." Dr Klinker snorts, purses his lips and fiddles at his bow-tie.

"Quite, quite," Wythenshawe booms, full of *bonhomie*, looking uncertain whether another joke has been intended.

"Shall we sit down gentlemen?" Myles suggests as the merriment dies down.

They sit down at the conference table and start to thrash out the details of their merger deal.

That evening, in the car, Wythenshawe calls his wife but she's out. In the West End, driving slowly along, he sees Azeem walking toward Starbucks across the way.

Azeem's all alone. Under the street lights he looks lonely and down. Wythenshawe wonders whether he should join him for a coffee. He's tempted to do so.

But then he sees he's late for the call he's expecting. He accelerates, the Bentley pulls away. Wythenshawe drives toward Chelsea, where his mistress is waiting for him.

His mobile rings.

"All right, Mr Wythenshawe?" says the reliable-sounding Scottish voice, oozing an unctuous bonhomie. "It's good to connect. Always good to connect. I've got the information you asked for about your wife. My, my, she has been a busy girl... If I didn't know you were a man of the world, Mr Wythenshawe, I'd say it could prove a major embarrassment for you... and your *reputation*, if even a fraction of this saw the light of day. I'd like to knock around a few ideas to make sure that doesn't happen, Mr Wythenshawe..."

MEMORIES OF THE HUNT BALL
West End: Azeem al Din, Samir Muhsi

AZEEM WENT INTO Starbucks, got himself a drink and sat down. He was waiting for the man he supposed was his boss, although it didn't really feel that way. How should it? Everything was so informal, deliberately kept vague.

He sipped at his tea, checked his watch.

A tiny, tipsy-looking girl happened at that moment to sidle past him. She was giggling loudly, half-recumbent on her boyfriend's arm, and she looked Azeem up and down with a lewd eye. Azeem, fairly striking with his dark, aquiline looks, was modestly dressed, as always, but wearing western clothes for a change, jeans and a T-shirt. He remembered, now, why he had started to prefer his kufi and his salwar kameez. His T-shirt was tight across his pectorals. He'd been getting the odd female look throughout the evening, but this girl was squinting at him with especial intensity.

"Haven't we met somewhere before," she slurred, her boyfriend meanwhile attempting to move her on.

"I don't think so," said Azeem in his melodious voice.

"I'm sure we have... was it at Exeter? Or was it... the East Devon Hunt Ball?" she insisted, drawling drunkenly.

She seemed used to getting her way, even when semi-paralytic from drink, and Azeem smelled fumes of gin on her breath, and the fragrant odor of her sweat. Her smell agitated him, succulent, fermenting in his nose. Now she shrugged her boyfriend off—even as that man put his hand on her arm, she freed herself from his grip with a toss of her spoiled, pretty head.

"Yes, it was that Hunt Ball, I'm sure it was!"

"No, no."

Azeem maintained a polite demeanor.

"I'm very sorry," murmured the boyfriend, his face embarrassed, dragging the girl away.

"See you later then, Osama," she giggled as they went.

She had one of those loud, tinkling laughs which make people look up, startled, irritated.

Azeem blushed to his roots. He hated nothing more than this blanket contempt, this *racism*, all the more when coming from an attractive girl, who did in fact look as familiar to him as he had to her. Fenella something was her name, he seemed to remember. But that was all so long ago... he couldn't be bothered with it now. Running into old acquaintances, whether you wanted to or not, was part of living in London.

The past few days had been busy for Azeem. First, getting himself patched up after the shooting. He hadn't been hit by anything really lethal. Just fragments of skull, and a sharp stray shard of statue which had inscribed a bloody scar on his forehead.

He was treated for shock.

The police questioned him in the hospital. There was no suspicion, after they'd been told who he was. Wythenshawe and Lyall vouched for him, told the police about their meeting in the agency. It was probably just a coincidence that the gunman had come in there after the explosion and taken Azeem hostage.

By now, Azeem was far from sure that was true.

He kept quiet about what the gunman, Abu Jaffar, had said. That stuff about Ghazan.

You're one of Ghazan's buddies, aren't you?

He wasn't sure what to believe in that connection. Abu Jaffar had been quite adamant that Ghazan was behind the bomb. He'd also said that the knifeman who'd come after him, in Soho Square, must have been sent by Ghazan, to silence him...

But Ghazan is a common enough name...

It might have been misinformation. And Abu Jaffar had been rambling, mad. Even so, in his gut, Azeem felt pretty sure Ghazan *was* involved.

No proof, though.

He really needed proof. If he told the police what he'd heard, they would surely interrogate Ghazan. If Ghazan then turned out to be innocent, or they couldn't bring any charges, Ghazan would get his own back on him for talking. At minimum, he'd see to it Azeem never had anything to do with *Islamic Reform* again. He might even decide to get rid of Azeem, have him killed.

It wasn't worth risking such unpredictable, deadly consequences.

As it happened, Ghazan was joining their meeting here in Starbucks too. Azeem tried to banish the uneasiness, the vague unsettling fear which was making him sweat.

Ghazan hardly ever came to meetings, and when he did, he said little. He was usually content to just spread his atmosphere around.

None of these feelings were new for Azeem.

Because even before the Leeds honor killing and the episode with the gunman, Ghazan had scared him. Right from the start, Ghazan had made a big, indelible impression on him. Nobody Azeem had ever met unsettled him so. In the training camp, Ghazan often spoke about death in Allah's cause as if it were the sublimest thing this planet had to offer.

The Hereafter is far better for you than this life.

Luckily, since *Islamic Reform* had started, Ghazan was happy to leave what he called the artsy-fartsy advertising stuff to Azeem and Samir. He conveyed his disapproval of their doings by his surly, openly dismissive attitude.

After leaving hospital, Azeem had been busy developing the advertising campaign. At least here there was good news. It looked as if Rania's family were open to the idea of doing something for *Islamic Reform*. Assuming Rania made a good recovery. The odds on that were getting better every hour. Azeem was really encouraged, and he was planning to go up to Leeds tomorrow to meet the Zandis, maybe even look in on Rania in hospital, if that were appropriate.

At this point, though, his thoughts are interrupted, and a man sits down next to him at his table.

A chubby, slightly florid fellow who could pass himself off as perhaps twenty-nine, he is dressed in designer jeans, buffed up boots, some clanking jewellery, and a smart kufi. With a floating hand he smoothes his exquisitely trimmed facial hair. His eyes, disconcertingly blue, peer around him dubiously as he sidles onto the seat next to Azeem.

Like a man in disguise trying too hard to be inconspicuous, Azeem thinks.

Azeem has known Samir Muhsi since university. These days, their link is purely professional. *Islamic Reform*, nothing else, brought them together.

Ghazan isn't coming till later, says Samir, much to Azeem's relief. Samir sips at his coffee and looks around, letting his eyes rest on a particularly striking blonde a couple of tables away.

"So... what progress have you made on the communications front?" he asks.

HE KNOWS YOU WELL
London: Ghazan Khattak

GHAZAN KHATTAK is patiently instructing a young lad, the brother of a friend, an orphan now, in the ways of the suicide belt. With great tenderness and care Ghazan shows him how best to arrange the straps to secure the explosives and shrapnel-plates. The aim is to leave your silhouette looking neither bulky nor too corpulent.

"Never leave big gaps between the plates," says Ghazan softly, patting the boy on the stomach. "Because then some of the targets may escape injury."

The boy looks up to Ghazan. They've known each other since the boy was a baby. Ghazan has always been solicitous of the boy's spiritual and physical wellbeing. Intergenerational conflicts of the sort Ghazan intimately knows have left the lad psychologically vulnerable, lost.

The boy looks uncertain now, he's not sure about this latest lesson. He looks a little sick.

"Don't think that those who die in Allah's way are dead," says Ghazan Khattak quietly. "No, they live... they find their sustenance in the presence of their Lord. Remember what the Surah Al-Ankabut tells us: *What is the life of this world but amusement and play? But verily the Home in the Hereafter, that is life indeed, if they but knew.* That is a truth acknowledged by all. Even Christians believe that!"

"I don't think I'm ready to die," says the boy.

"I won't ask you to die if you're not ready," says Ghazan with tender patience. He ruffles the lad's hair and smiles.

"Don't worry, don't worry. Remember that Allah has always known you, always supported you: *He knows you well when He brings you out of the earth, And when you are hidden in your mother's womb.*"

Ghazan gives the boy a piece of liquorice candy. He pops a piece into his own mouth. The liquorice reminds him of his own mother. She used to buy this brand for him.

"Those who fight in Allah's cause sell life in this world for life in the hereafter," says Ghazan, chewing. "If you fight in Allah's cause, no matter whether you kill or whether you get killed, you'll receive a gift of priceless value!"

"I'm not ready for that, Ghazan."

"You don't know what you're ready for yet," says Ghazan indulgently chewing his liquorice, and smiling with the forbearing wisdom of experience. "You're still young. Don't worry, I'd never ask you to do something you're not ready to do."

They sit quietly together at the window for a while, enjoying their sweets. They contemplate the puffy clouds rolling in from the west. The sky beneath is a rich intense hue and beneath it the city lights are beginning to come on, spreading a yellowish neon glow upwards.

When Ghazan Khattak's finished with his liquorice, he takes up his instruction where he left off.

Ghazan is unrushed, his voice gentle and loving. The boy takes it all in as best he's able. Ghazan puts his arm around him to reassure him with an almost paternal warmth.

MAMIDA'S TEARS
Peckham, London: Mamida Hanif

IN PECKHAM, the night air is close. The discombobulated sounds of the city seep in through the open windows of the apartment where Mamida lives by herself.

She's been sitting there, sitting there in her old upholstered armchair, nursing her stiff back, and a further array of ailments, and thinking—something she's been doing increasingly often of late, trying to get her restless mind into a meditative groove. She can't seem to come to terms with things which bother her anymore. Something stops her from letting it all out the way she used to. Something prevents her feelings from welling up to be washed away, like tears washed away in the wider current of the world.

After the call came through, confirming the attack (a friend of the Zandi family broke it to her), Mamida's tears were slow in coming. Willing it to be untrue, but seeing it all so clearly, it sharpened the hurt. She was alone in her apartment in Peckham, a small, smartly kept-up place full of knickknacks and reminders of home.

Close to Rania over the years, Mamida had watched her growing up in Leeds. She knew her pretty well.

Rania Zandi. Beautiful child.

Mamida babysat many times when Rania was still small. Then later on, they stayed in touch. Mamida was like a gran to the girl who'd lost her own.

Mamida always looked forward to seeing her. When Rania came round to her spotless little terraced house, with its immaculately kept garden, they always had bags of fun. A bright kid with such a lovely, quick smile and a good warm heart, Rania knew her own mind, was used to getting her own way. So now, hearing the news from Leeds came as a shock, and still somehow unreal—the way happenings in far-off places which were once your home can seem unreal when you first hear.

Then, as Mamida sits thinking things over, her memories drag her back into her old familiar intimacy with the place, and her closeness to all those people she'd left behind. Her memories crowd in on her like a hubbub, jostling for her attention, and she remembers one tiny event, how once Rania hurt her arm in the garden.

Racing up and down the lawn in an old potato sack—she keeled over, gashed her elbow on the concrete edge of the patio. The fallen child screamed fit to burst, at first, and her husky voice was loud with pain and shock. There was some blood, which when she saw it made things worse. So Mamida cleaned and patched her up, put an icepack on the wound, and then stuck a colorful plaster with laughing hippopotami on.

The brave girl was quick to recover her cheerful mood. Soon they were joking again. Drinking down her fruit juice Rania spluttered and laughed when Mamida said, "Good job the arm hasn't come off altogether, eh? There's nothing worse than a useless spare arm lying around the place."

"I could get a new one."

"I doubt it, love. Arms don't grow on trees."

"They don't need to grow on trees," said little Rania, with a serene smile of reproof, "they just should grow on me!"

"No need for that now though eh? The hippopotamus will hold it on for you while Faraz comes to pick you up," said Mamida prodding the girl playfully to make her laugh again.

Well, Faraz had come all right, Mamida reflects bitterly, and her tears finally began to flow. That afternoon, Faraz came round to Mamida's house to collect his sister, brandishing his flute case, he was on his way back from his weekly lesson. Noting his sister's scratch, Faraz let fall some remark, in a soft tone, about it maybe not being so good for her to run around like a tomboy and hurt herself.

Faraz himself couldn't have been more than about ten at the time. Mamida had warmed to him, to see how much he cared for his sister, how open he was about showing his concern

But she'd been wrong there too, Mamida realizes. Her tears broke now, they pour down her cheeks as she sobs, thinking of the girl lying there dying for no reason, so young and full of life.

Mamida's thoughts are black—soon, she thinks, that lovely child would be forgotten—her family forgetting her for shame— and for the rest, she'd be *just another one*, disposed of like an unwelcome statistic. A child who'd been so bright and warm wiped out, wiped away like a stain.

Rania Zandi. Beautiful child.

Mamida sits for an hour or so crying in her old armchair, and never once do her tears dry out, her sadness never stops.

When the neighbors, hearing, call on the telephone, Mamida lets it ring. They don't call again. They know her tears have snatched her out of their reach. They hear her crying; it makes them still in their hearts, as they watch TV on the other side of the hall.

And so the evening falls and surrounds Mamida in her sitting room, wrapping her in darkness and near-silence, where she cries until she falls asleep.

The telephone rings again. Mamida is shaken out of her sullen stupor.

She recognizes the voice at once. It's a woman she'd never really known, never much liked, a neighbor from Leeds, louder than life in all things except those which matter. A very practical woman, very traditional, very involved and committed—very sceptical in her manner about Mamida's feminism, but never opening her mouth to say anything one way or another.

"You've heard about Rania Zandi?"

"Of course I've heard."

"She's still alive, Mamida."

"Yes, I know... still..."

"She might still make it."

"Maybe," says Mamida, a strange impulse of optimism lifting her heart, and making her willing to lift some of her reserve. "Maybe Faraz couldn't quite bring himself to do it."

"Maybe. But I've heard... there's talk of not allowing her to..."

"What do you mean?"

"There's people saying they want... they want to finish off the job. They're planning to go to the hospital and kill her."

Mamida hears her out, the warning of this practical woman.

No more tears now. Enough of the crying.

They say good bye and hang up.

Mamida runs it through in her mind. She'll get a message through to Shirin, she decides. Shirin would warn Azeem.

And Azeem might be naïve, politically out his depth, but with the training he's received he could take care of something like this.

Azeem has to be told.

He has to see where his duty lies.

Leeds: Rania Zandi

Rania Zandi. Deathbed child.

In Leeds, Rania's eyes open, and she thinks she's alone in the night. She breathes. A tang of formaldehyde irritates her nose.

She hears a nurse laughing in the corridor, footsteps, a gurney rolling by. Blinking lights, a shadowy machine standing beside her bed like some solicitous robot. Bleeping, the ghastly breathing of the pump, her mouth covered with a mask....

A flush of panic invades her veins, the moment of unknowing. But then she falls into unconsciousness again, she lies back in the bed, motionless, wrapped up tight under crisply ironed covers.

Her eyes close.

She's dreaming she's back at home. She's in the kitchen at her laptop, playing chess with Faraz. The pieces blur, a seamless progression of moves.

In a corner of the room, a nurse sits in the shadows, crying softly to herself. The nurse wipes her eyes, gets up, and walks quietly out of the door.

Paris: Faraz Zandi

Faraz got as far as he could on foot.

It was late evening. He'd ventured out again after everyone else had gone back up to bed.

The day had been endless. There was a problem getting the right tickets for the right flight to Karachi. And getting their papers sorted was taking far longer than expected. So they sat around all day.

A day punctuated only by prayers.

Faraz stares out of the window. Clouds are closing in, darkening the sky, yellowish at first but then livid and black, so that it seems night had fallen in the afternoon.

The others play cards. Faraz is preoccupied with himself, he doesn't join them, although they try to make him.

Then it was evening, and they left him alone. He thought he'd go out again, try to go further than he had that morning, when paranoia had overtaken him. He'd turned back without having seen anything more than a kebab restaurant.

It is later now, sultry, with a heavy moistness hanging in the air, a smell of mold and sodden earth. The rain has passed, the sky is gray, but the roads and sidewalks are still steaming, stained and damp.

When he gets to the corner of the second block, Faraz notices the white Renault behind him, thirty yards away.

He crosses the road and walks on. Halfway down the block he turns and looks over his shoulder.

The car is tailing him, thirty yards behind.

Faraz quickens his pace. When he gets to the next corner he looks right and left, sees the coast is clear, and starts running full tilt ahead.

The sidewalks are deserted. There is a man walking his dog in the shadows ahead, but nobody else. The blunted noise of the city seems miles away. All of a sudden, it starts to rain again. Fat droplets spit around him, in isolation at first, spilling onto the sidewalk, into gutters. The downpour grows thicker, clouds merging into a dark greenish haze, unloading themselves ever more relentlessly. The man and his dog begin to jog off down a side street. Faraz carries on running ahead, he runs on for a hundred yards.

The wind picks up, sends the moisture lashing horizontally between the trees and buildings onto Faraz' sprinting form. He is half blinded. Neon lights, lamp posts reflect garish flashes at him from the deepening puddles. His face is wet. Big salty drops of water slop from the tip of his nose into his mouth. The soggy clothes cling close to his skin, his coat hanging heavy from his shoulders, his jeans clasping tightly round his hips.

He stops by a lamp post, grasping the cold metal for support, and breathing hard. As the wind blows through his lank hair, he starts to shiver convulsively. He turns round.

The car is just coming to a stop thirty yards behind.

Faraz's heart is thumping away, he feels chilly and faint, can hardly see, he is that distracted. He stands there leaning against the lamp post wondering whether to carry on running or just stop.

The Renault's passenger door opens. A uniformed *gendarme* emerges.

ORGANIZED ATHEISM
London: Azeem, Samir Muhsi, Ghazan Khattak

"WHAT PROGRESS have you made on the communications front?" Samir Muhsi is asking.

Azeem wants to show how well things are progressing. That way, Samir might leave him alone to get on with things. He begins to tell about his meeting with Wythenshawe and Lyall.

"You're sure they're not Jews?" asks Samir. "Don't want to sound prejudiced, but advertising men often are."

"Oh, yes, Sam, yes, I'm absolutely certain."

It was the first thing Azeem had done, check Wythenshawe and Lyall's religious affiliations. Both turned out to be Church of England men.

"They're not Jewish. It's hard to describe precisely what they are. The C of E? A sort of watered down new-agey ecological Christianity. Certainly not Jews."

Samir, listening, smiles across at Ghazan Khattak who was now coming over to join them, earlier than expected.

"I know about the C of E," jeers Samir, with a derisive roll of the eyes. "It's organized atheism, basically, run by a load of clueless crazy Nancy-boys. Happy-clappy, all-inclusive..."

"They don't know what it means to believe," Ghazan interjects, with a sour smile. "They used to believe in three gods, the idolaters..." His smile faded. "But two of those died, and they've ended up half believing in a ghost."

Samir laughs.

"*There is no god but God*," says Ghazan. "*He is One. He has no associate.* Certainly not a ghost."

Ghazan is out of place here, deeply uncomfortable. He knows how he stands out among those surroundings—the orange walls, the late-night atmosphere with its over-groomed heterodox groups. He skulks, silently watchful, beside his colleagues. With his bushy eyebrows, his shaggy unkempt beard, he looks like a huge, ill-tempered Schnauzer. His sulky mouth is hidden, mostly, behind his beard, his beard cupped between folded hands, his hands wringing themselves with tiny impulses of furious, nervous intensity as he soaks everything in, giving nothing away...

Infidel *kafirs* to a man, Ghazan sees at once. Lewd crusaders, junglies, Asiatics and sodomites infesting the place, a jumble of faithless scum.

Not to speak of those shameless women, brides of Shaytan, with their naked, painted faces.

Ghazan drinks them all in, the women, group by group, enjoying that sense of superiority felt by the predator.

He isn't indifferent to them; he *pities* them. Pities them for the lust they arouse. He itches to end their suffering for them.

Some of them, he sees, sit mournfully slurping coffee, deserted by their Lord. Large, immodest eyes, shifting liquidly between the mirrors (in which they constantly ogle themselves, as if afraid they'll vanish) and the men (they always stare, shamelessly, at the men), sparking off indecent thoughts, ever more lustful urges.

Corrupters, corrupting men only too happy to be corrupted.

How can men escape?

Great blonde manes of uncovered hair they toss up in the air, glittering, golden fountains of lubriciousness and temptation. *Girls who refuse to submit, reject the way of Allah*, profane, extrovert and loud—obscenities, oblivious to the doom of their destruction, their looming annihilation.

Ghazan Khattak sees them sitting there in Starbucks, children of darkness, desecrating the temple of their bodies, disbelievers, drinking to their own shameful reckoning.

He remembers the warning of Rumi:

Like water, you may outwardly dominate woman, but inwardly you are dominated by her and seek her.

But he knows he can escape those juicy temptations. And he knows the reckoning will come for them, as surely as the bill for their drinks. It will come, and release them from their shameless consumption of self.

He pictures the filthy place engulfed in flames, rivers of blood, with swarms of flying creatures—Gog and Magog let loose, the people burning, their last blasphemous words bubbling up in spurts of blood, oozing out from black holes in melting faces.

Azeem is watching him. He feels a dread inside when he thinks back to what Abu Jaffar, the gunman, had said. Azeem is dying to ask Ghazan to his face whether he'd been involved in it. His wariness inhibits him, stopping his mouth and the words he yearns to ask.

"So what are your admen doing for us?" Samir now asks, with a businesslike aspect.

"In organizational terms, Wythenshawe and Lyall are setting up a partnership with an agency in Germany, setting it up especially for us."

"Excellent," says Samir, beaming from ear to ear. "The bosses will be pleased. They are eager for progress in Germany. They tell me, *Germany is ripe for reformation.*"

"Yes, you told me."

"Sometimes you really have to laugh," says Samir, his eyes hard and cold. "The Christian Reformation started in Germany didn't it?"

"Of course. Martin Luther."

"But now it's the target for *our* reformation. It's our turn to reform *them!*"

Samir Muhsi pauses.

"There is of course an added affinity with Germany, what with the whole Jewish thing."

"Yes, Sam, they've got form."

"*Form* is good!" Samir says coldly.

"The best thing about Germany in my mind," Ghazan remarks. "Shame they didn't finish it... Western liberals, slaves of Jews, got them first. The next time there are gas chambers in Europe, I know who will be in them."

"The Nazis aren't doing particularly well in Germany at the moment," says Azeem.

"No, Nazis never do well in democracies, do they?" says Samir. "One reason for the symbiosis between democracy and Zionism, although Zionism is intrinsically Nazi in its methods."

Azeem lets it pass.

Ideology is for idiots, he thinks.

"Rincke and Klinker, the German agency's called."

"Those names have a Yiddish ring to them," says Samir dubiously. "Don't you think, Ghazan?"

Azeem sighs. He hates the constant preoccupation with Jewishness and the injunction to *kill them wherever you find them.*

Not his idea of jihad. Not his idea of the noble Qur'an.

"I can assure you they're Aryans of the purest pedigree, whiter than white," he says. "I checked Rincke and Klinker. Free of any stigma of Jewish blood, at least unto the third generation. If they weren't—let's face it, Sam—it's unlikely they'd be alive and well in Germany today."

"Allah be praised. Okay."

Samir still sounds unconvinced.

"Do they know the sort of thing we want them to do?"

"Of course. I've been very clear. They understand, Sam. The media climate's better for us in Germany. There's a healthy scepticism about western capitalist values. The socialists denounce Jewish capitalist locusts and the Christian Democrats attack cardinals for saying Catholic things."

"May Allah think well of their discernment."

"The media there will be receptive to our aims."

"Allah knows best," says Samir lugubriously. "Jihad is often twisted, misunderstood by the media."

"Jihad is not always an easy concept."

Ghazan Khattak seethes.

"Jihad is crystal clear," he says, bristling. "I keep hearing that *jihad is a difficult concept.* But I say, what could be easier to understand than killing the brothers of pigs and apes?"

Ghazan's sunken eyes brood around suspiciously.

"Jihad gets misinterpreted and defiled," he complains, "when the media is in the hands of the wrong people, the *kafirs*. See what the Zionist Entity and their running dogs in the media do to make out our Palestinian brothers are terrorists."

"That's true," concedes Azeem. "But no one believes those lies in Germany. They can see the Zionist Entity for what it is, a puppet of American imperialism."

Now Ghazan explodes, smashing his fist onto the table with such force that some of the other customers set their coffees aside and peered over at the three of them as they huddled there—scarred, turbanned and intense—with more than a soupcon of suspicion.

"It isn't the puppet! It's the hand in the glove, Azeem al Din! *Everywhere* the Zionists are in control. Just remember, we are *obliged* to wage jihad until all fall down and worship Allah. That is our holiest duty. Because until that day, the unbelievers dwell in hell, man... bear that in mind! Dwell in hell for all eternity! We wage jihad against them for their own benefit, Azeem al Din!"

Ghazan glowers at Azeem as he spoke. Samir Muhsi smiles savvily.

"But what we *tell* them," Samir now says, wiping his mouth, "of course... it must strike a different tune..."

"Yes, I do see."

"We have to be very careful who we associate with. We have to proceed carefully, watchfully, like a cat in the night."

Azeem nods.

"And I must ask you, my friend and brother, to invite me to your next meeting with these communications people. And any other contact you may have with them, I *need* to know, Azeem."

Now Azeem is mortified. The communications campaign had been his idea from the start. He'd expected he could run it as he saw fit. Even the choice of advertising agency had been made on the basis of his being connected to one of the partners.

So he says, "Don't you trust me?"

"Of course I do," says Samir in a soft chilly voice. "You are my brother, and unity between us is all. It's just, I've been asked to oversee and coordinate your labors personally. I must obey. You know that. Remember, we are but cats in the night, and we must heed our master's bidding."

There is still that vaguely hostile smile playing on Samir's lips. His suspicious, watery blue eyes watch Azeem. He watches him, hawklike, until Azeem spreads out his hands in a gesture of acceptance.

Azeem now tells them about his plan to go north to meet Rania Zandi's family. He explains the direction he thinks he might go with the advertising campaign. He says he hoped Rania would play a central role—if Allah were willing—to star in the campaign, as the spokesperson for resilient Muslim women.

Ghazan hears all of it out with his usual, unreadable face.

He takes deep swigs of tea, lets it warm the hollow of his stomach. His mind is wandering, uneasy, as he listens, not really listening, but then lights on the man behind the words, Azeem al Din, sitting opposite him, but so far away, so far away these days…

Azeem has turned into a vain and foolish prattler.

Azeem had been one of the *baraderi,* a brother in days past.

But Azeem had changed. Not in his starry-eyed idealism, no, that had always been part of him. And he was still a brother. He was still a believer.

Sure, sure. Whatever that means.

But not the way he was before. He'd been unquestioning then, filled with certainty. He had been *real.* He'd been like a rock, whereas now he was just air. Azeem and he, back then, had shared everything, their tent, their food, their water. They'd gone together on those endless barefoot marches through the snow, supporting each other all through that pain and discomfort in Afghanistan.

That made me, *for sure. Made* me. *But what did it make Azeem?*

These days, Azeem seemed to be withdrawing himself, cutting himself off from his brothers, dissociating himself from the struggle.

Losing himself, as he lost his commitment to jihad.

Maybe it's time for Azeem to feel some pain again.

That head-in-the-clouds pacifist hadn't known a thing about the car bomb—hadn't even known Ghazan was planning it—and maybe that was for the best, but he needed to share some more in the struggle.

He needed to be reminded that you cannot disengage yourself from the struggle.

It is *one* jihad. Unity is all.

You do not turn your back on your brothers. To do so is to lose your honor, and if you lose yours, your brothers lose theirs.

They finish their drinks. Nothing more of interest is said.

Azeem goes home.

When he lets himself in, the place is dark. He clicks on the light in the bedroom. The bed is empty.

No sign of Shirin. She hasn't left a note, nor is there a message on the machine.

He sits down on the sofa. Although past midnight, it is still hot in the flat. His scalp itches, at once dry and damp. He lies back and stares into space, rubbing his forehead.

He calls Shirin's number, hangs up without leaving a message when she doesn't answer. Desperately wanting to know what she is up to, hardly daring to guess what it might be.

Azeem had prepared himself for great difficulties to come, in the wake of his new mission. He was fully prepared to bear whatever sacrifices were required. If he had to, he'd have to bear the price of losing Shirin. And he'd make himself bear the price of working *for* Samir, rather than with him.

Unity is all.

Dispute not one with another lest ye falter and your strength depart from you.

He lies there in the dark silence, no longer focusing on anything.

FINISHING THE JOB
Leeds: Azeem, Mr & Mrs Zandi, Dr Khan

NEXT AFTERNOON, in the hospital up in Leeds, Azeem sits in a waiting room with Mr and Mrs Zandi. It's crowded and hot. They are huddled together in a corner. A smell of boiled cabbage and formaldehyde wafts around, although the window stands wide open.

Mr Zandi, a tall man, has a compact belly which protrudes, like a family-size Christmas pudding, over his belt. Despite a tendency to twitch and blink alarmingly, he seems to be holding himself together. A wispy gray mustache grows under his thick, bulbous nose, and a set of yellowing teeth protrude from his mouth.

You can tell that, if you met him on a normal day, you'd see the chirpy, avuncular store owner he really is. But now, twitching and blinking in that scary way, he's a cartoonlike character, trying to take a bite out of his own face—as if wanting to rip out the misery that resides there.

Mrs Zandi, red-eyed, dishevelled, looks vague. Disoriented by grief, she appears to be ebbing away in front of them, wishing herself anywhere else.

The other visitors waiting in that room are aware, somehow, something terrible has happened. It's unspoken, but there is a kind of *cordon sanitaire* around the Zandis and, for all the lack of space, a few empty seats separate them from the others, where no one sits, but only glances across.

"I worry about Rania being here," whispers Mrs Zandi, casting her big wet eyes around the waiting room.

"I'm sure the staff here will do all they can," says Azeem.

"I am not referring to the commitment of the staff."

"We have no complaints about the staff," Mr Zandi says in a precise voice. "Dr Khan is an exemplary doctor. He has left no stone unturned in his search for a cure."

"What is worrying is her being here in Leeds," says Mrs Zandi. "People here... people here want her dead."

A chill came over Azeem as she said it.

Later, like a sinister hallucination unrolling across his eyes, Azeem sits alone, watching, in that same waiting room, empty now apart from him. It's 3:30 AM. The temperature has dropped and he's shivering. He's looking at the door to Rania's room. His eyes are feverish with irritation and tiredness.

He's been fighting off sleep for hours. Occasionally he dips off for a moment, then once his head droops down, he starts up again, with a shock, remembers why he's there.

He's agreed with the Zandis that Rania should be taken to the London Clinic just as soon as the doctors say she's allowed to be transported. He's promised he'll cover the costs.

In the meantime, from all he's heard, from everything he *imagines* being plotted, he's decided to assume the worst possible scenario, and so he's staying here to watch over her door. He's told the police about his fears. A constable has been round to check him out and talk with the hospital security team.

"I'm trained for this sort of thing," Azeem has told the Zandis. "Surveillance. Unarmed combat."

He senses their scepticism. He doesn't blame them—he's lean and ascetic, looks like a pacifist, a thinker. He doesn't have the air of a fighter, a warrior who can kill with his bare hands. He has a natural humility about him, and he eats frugally. His clothes aren't designed to show off his muscles.

But he stands before them, knowing he can deliver his promises. The toughest training camps in Pakistan and Afghanistan have given him the skills.

And fighting to defend an unconscious girl is not against his principles.

"Trust me, I'll see to it nobody does anything to her."

It's his vigil.

Room 1122. Restricted access. There's a nurse in there round the clock.

His phone rings in his pocket. It's Shirin.

Her voice, soft in his ears. "How you doing, darling?"

"Oh, fine, I guess. All the better now you've called. Very sleepy. What about you?"

"Listen, I just got another call from Mamida. She says it definitely looks like they're planning something for tonight."

"That's why I'm here, hon."

Azeem gets up to stretch his legs. He walks over to the window, spreads his arms out to either side, yawning. He looks down at the parking lot. Cold light below illuminates a haze of mist around the lamp-posts.

The roofs of the parked cars are shiny with damp. Nothing is moving down there.

Azeem sits down.

An hour later. He's pacing up and down again. Out of the corner of his eye he sees a small white car pulling up some two hundred yards away. For half a minute he stands looking out of the window, his body out of sight behind the wall.

Three big men get out. Their shapes are indistinguishable. Two of them are huddled close together, and in the obscurity they look like a two-headed man. The third walks a few yards behind them. They're marching quickly towards the hospital entrance, with swift steps, intent and smooth, hardly touching the ground. It's a way of walking Azeem recognizes, the mujahid way of walking.

Azeem runs over to Rania's door. It's ajar. He peers inside. Rania's lying there, surrounded by the blinking machinery that's keeping her alive.

But the chair in the corner is empty. The nurse is gone.

Dr Khan sees the situation at once. A trim, serious-looking man with large black glasses, he hears Azeem out in silence. He looks as tired as Azeem. He doesn't say anything right away. He's holding a polystyrene cup, and slowly lifts it to take a sip of steaming coffee.

"The duty nurse is gone," Azeem tells him.

"She's blown?"

"Yes, gone."

"That is strange. Very strange, and bloody unusual. You think maybe she was a plant? I'll call security and warn them about these men you saw. You could be right... they could be ringers, wrong numbers."

When he comes back, Dr Khan looks apologetic.

"It's okay," he says. "You can relax. The house dicks say it's only some extra cleaners just come in for the morning shift."

But Azeem says, "It doesn't feel right. It's too much of a coincidence, the nurse gone, and those guys marching in... and they didn't look anything like cleaners, I can tell you. And if the nurse is in on it, she'll tell them where Rania is. She'll give them the code to the door."

Dr Khan, fatherly, sixtysomething, has been troubled and outraged by the whole aftermath of the attack on Rania. He's met the parents, and he likes them. And when he first saw Rania, when she was first wheeled in, he thought she looked a lot like his favorite niece, his sister's little daughter, a girl back in Kurdistan he hasn't seen for four years, whose photo he keeps on his desk, as though she were his own daughter.

Dr Khan has treated plenty of girls in a similar state over the years. He's seen how horrifically these questions of honor get settled. His duty, always to help such girls, he knows, and in his heart he wants to do it.

Surely God loves those who are careful in their duty.

And he's sure Azeem is right about the danger Rania is in.

His instinct tells him that Azeem's right, there's something bad going on inside the hospital this evening. He feels threatened, and on his guard, and he knows he has to rise above himself if he wants to help.

If they find Rania, those men will kill her, rub her out like a human mistake. They will disfigure her face as a warning.

God makes the Signs clear to you.

It's the way. Hideous, barbaric. He has to do what he can to prevent it. He has to do the right thing.

Khan thinks of the old gangster movies he loves. They were his first real encounters with English, and he still lapses into the lingo sometimes, especially when he's stressed. For a passing moment he imagines himself in a scene from one of those films... How he wishes he were packing heat, wearing iron, so that he could burn some powder, blow the bad guys away...

But then he pulls himself together. This isn't a movie. It's happening right here, right on his doorstep.

Rania's in room 1122. In room 1137, just down the corridor, there is a cancer patient, an old widow, who died earlier that night.

God has taken her.

Her body is awaiting a porter to take her down to the morgue.

It doesn't have to stay in that room.

He summons a new nurse. Occasionally looking over at Azeem as he speaks, he explains the situation to her.

"We're switching the beds around."

The nurse starts to protest. Dr Khan raises his hand. He knows he has to get her onside. She's got to want to help them to do this.

"I know this isn't orthodox procedure. But if this gentleman here is right, there's some... some crazy men on their way here, you savvy? They already tried to kill Ms Zandi once, nurse. And now... now they want to finish it off... this bloody honor killing. But if we make the switch, and those... fanatics come into room 1122, they'll see Mrs Winthrop lying there instead. She's already dead, so there will be nothing for them to do. Their racket will flop, and they will have to leave, fade, with their tails between their legs."

He looks at her gravely. A charged moment. She nods. And with that Dr Khan squeezes her arm, and goes into Rania's room. Azeem and the nurse follow him.

Twenty minutes later, Azeem is standing in an alcove to one side in the shadows of the corridor. His tiredness has gone, he is psyched up to the eyeballs with expectation.

Soft, confident footsteps, swishing towards him. His chest pounds in time with those footsteps approaching. His temples throb.

The footsteps get closer.

Three shapes go past, looking neither left nor right. Azeem steals a glimpse. Three shapes. They're wearing blue orderly outfits and surgical masks.

They head straight to the door of room 1122. The first man leans down and punches a number into the keypad on the code lock.

The door clicks open and they slip into that dark room.

A few seconds' silence. Azeem's pounding heart fills him with a sick claustrophobic fear. He's still as can be, listening.

Then the terrible sound begins. Dull, slapping thumps, as of a cricket bat being driven, sloppily, into an overripe watermelon.

A CONVIVIAL SPORTSMAN
Twinnington: Laetitia Wythenshawe, Dave Page

DAWN—A HUNDRED MILES to the north, in Twinnington. Up in the Borders this time of year, early mornings are still fresh and nippy. The dew on the lush grass glistens in the rising sun, and banks of mist like sultry smoke rise from the meadows and the hollows of the hills, far in the distance, swirling between the ancient oaks dotted like tea cosies on the fields.

The Twinnington estate spreads across some few thousand undulating acres, and at its heart lies the House, home to the Twinningtons. The House, once grand, is slightly down at heel, due to the relative poverty of the family in comparison with more affluent days.

The last of the Twinningtons, slim, fit Mrs Wythenshawe, was pulling on riding boots when her mobile rang. She glanced at the display. Her husband.

Oh fuck him.

She tossed the telephone away with a petulant laugh.

Typical of Rupert to call at just the wrong moment. She couldn't remember the last time her husband had done *anything* at the right moment. His whole existence had become a calculated affront to her peace of mind.

Her companion, already booted and helmeted, was waiting, watching her from a small distance. He held her helmet in his hands. Hovering there like some valet, Laetitia thought. But, she couldn't deny, a handsome valet.

He leaned down to unpick the phone from the flattened lumps of dung into which she'd flung it. Something about the young man irked her today. He was bending slowly down, his buttocks so firm and neat in his tight white jodhpurs, bending down so patiently, so *selflessly* picking up her shitty phone. He raised himself and proffered the phone and the scruffy old helmet as though it were the Blessed Casket of Nature's Marvels.

Without even looking at him full frontally Laetitia sensed how aware he was of his own manly attractions. What bothered her was the *showiness* of his self-effacement: it drew attention to the flattering light in which he cast himself—he was dazzled by the marvel of *him*.

Dave Page, her lover these past nine months, a diminutive, well-built, ingratiating man, was the son of one of her late father's cronies, Ben Page. Years before Laetitia herself had even been thought of, back in the nineteen fifties, Ben Page had stumbled into a job on the estate. Started out as a stable hand. Done that for a bit, then got himself promoted to stud groom.

Ben Page was a pungent, foul-mouthed old codger, no matter the job he was supposed to be doing. And precisely what it was that drew Ben and her father together was a source of bafflement to anyone who gave it any thought. Sure, both of them were great drinkers. But the county was plentifully stocked with drinkers—topers, dipsos, fall-down drunks and sots were two a penny in these parts, alcoholism virtually a way of life. With few other traits to bind the two men, there must have been some deeper, subconscious bond, beyond the scope of rational observation.

Laetitia still remembered the stink Ben carried about with him, a rank, gamy redolence which preceded his appearance on the scene, and lingered in the air after he left, tickling inside your nostrils and at the top of the throat.

Even now the memory made her feel sick.

Allowed a grace and favor cottage on the estate, Ben had seldom turned his hand to anything so onerous as actual work.

In his later years this indulged, ageing, drunken soak, to general amazement, somehow begot a son, out of a village girl who'd knocked about plenty herself, a girl called Babs.

The Twinnington Trollop, the villagers called Babs. She'd been with half the men on the estate.

Dave Page was only one by-product of Babs' jolly, careless, long-buried affairs, and Twinnington only the least broken of his many homes. When things got too hot for her in Twinnington,

Dave's mother bolted to Essex. So Dave had an unsettled childhood, split between that county (where he made loads of unsuitable druggy friends) and the edges of the Twinnington estate. As the years went by, an unspecified number of half-brothers and -sisters were born to Babs.

Laetitia asked Dave about them once.

"How many are there, then?"

"Dunno."

"Didn't you ever think to ask her?"

"I don't think she ever counted. She wouldn't have remembered."

Laetitia imagined a sad litter of his siblings, scattered across the country, each of them ignorant of the others.

It made her feel vaguely sorry for them.

True to his vocation, old Ben Page drank himself to death in the end. He'd never seemed to enjoy anything very much, a man as contemptuous of social norms as Lord Twinnington himself, and he left this life, paralytic in a frozen ditch, with nothing to spare for his heir.

"You look really hit today," said Dave, holding out Laetitia's helmet and phone. "Don't let your old man put you off your stride."

"Not on your nelly."

"Can't let him spoil your fun."

"As if."

Dave had always been ignored by his dear old drunk dad on the whole. But Laetitia's own father, Lord Twinnington, a convivial sportsman, stepped in, gave Dave a fair crack of the whip. As a kid, Laetitia hardly noticed it, but later she realized just how much her papa had done to see Dave got through school, an education he paid for.

Dave grew up personable. A compact, muscle-bound hulk to look at, but there was something more to him. A little sniff of something maybe a little sneaky, something a little low-down and dirty, which excited her.

Laetitia always got on with him well enough. They'd a fair amount to do with each other what with the horses, but nothing aside from that—they got *on*, but never *off* with each other, and she'd certainly not allowed him anywhere near her bed.

That only changed last year, when circumstances concatenated, one sweaty Sunday afternoon, her twenty-ninth birthday, to make it an irresistible proposition. The tumbling breathlessness of that roll in the hay made up for its disconcerting speed. Since then they'd been carrying on regularly, fairly discreetly.

He started calling her *his piece of totty*, which made her laugh. Later, in a play on her name, he adapted it to *Titty*.

"I used to love *Swallows and Amazons*," said Laetitia. "Did you?"

Dave had a sheepish air.

"Yeah," he said.

When she probed him on this unlikely affinity, it turned out he didn't know the book at all. He thought she meant a porn DVD he'd taken out recently, *Cum-Swallowing Amazons*. That made her laugh, and she joshed him about it. His bashful smile made it easy to forgive him.

By and by, though, Dave's hunky simplicity was overshadowed by a kind of *preening* which sickened Laetitia. He was getting far too forward and familiar for her liking.

Only the other week, she'd heard him talking to the spotty young maid—he obviously thought he was alone with her.

"Go on!" he said, coaxing, wheedling.

"I don't want to," she said.

"It's only a bit of fun."

"You're doing Lady Laetitia..."

"What Titty don't see, Titty won't mind."

"It doesn't feel right. I don't like to—"

"Her ladyship likes what I tell her to like."

There was a muffled giggle, then a silence.

Dave and the girl smooching. Laetitia visualized it, his calloused hands, kneading the girl's white, floury flat chest. She shuddered, and walked away.

Not at all enamored of such sordid shenanigans, she'd show him who was boss. His skills at pleasuring her were in any case well below par, after the initial excitement it was just *wham bang thank you ma'am*, like a riggy gelding trying to cover a mare. And so, as Laetitia had done before with lovers whenever they looked like turning into bores, she planned to eject Dave.

She was in no mood to dwell on it just now though. She gave Dave a bored smile as he handed her back her phone. Suavely, with a slickly conspiratorial smirk, Dave beckoned her to come outside.

Here the horses waited.

Laetitia adjusted her helmet's headliner and followed him out.

As she comes out to him, Dave cups his arm around Laetitia's midriff and gives her a squeeze. No one there to see. He leans over and sticks his tongue down her ear.

Drives her wild, that.

He's felt better about himself ever since the day he first had her... he'd fucked her brains out like a good 'un, did it so well there'd never be any going back.

Lady Laetitia Twinnington, his stuck-up, toffee-nosed patron's daughter!

A crackpot family, sure, but then aristos normally are. A couple dozen generations of inbreeding may gentrify your genes, but they don't keep them steady.

And her, all cool and offhand always. Always such a cold, snotty, superior bitch.

Now she's my bitch.

He lets her go and they walk on over to their horses. Dave shoots her a sidelong glance. So self-contained, so sure of herself, sultry and pretty... They're dynamite in bed together. She loves his frantic but efficient thrusts, it's always fast and furious, explosive, no lovey-dovey nonsense.

He's proud of his skills—a sure touch, a kind of second sight when it comes to divining what turns women on. He knows he's a phenomenon in bed, his first girlfriend told him so.

"How was I?" he'd asked.

"Phenomenal."

"Phenomenal? What's that? Good or bad?"

"Oh, *good*... as in... phenomenally well-endowed. Phenomenal staying power. Phenomenal sensitivity."

Any woman lucky enough to lure him into her bed got mounted by a real maestro, an artist, a demon—multiple orgasms, the lot.

But Titty's not as grateful as he'd like... she doesn't always show him the proper appreciation. She needs to be jolted from time to time, make her know which side her bread's buttered on.

A good beating from my love truncheon always makes her see sense!

He nurtures his resentment of her like a festering sore, like one of those sores you get when you scrape your knee, half-healed, with a thick bit of hard reddish-brown skin growing over part of it, which still sort of tickles when you press it.

If I work on her... if I'm canny...

He *loves* thinking this one through... He could work things to his best advantage...

The sky's the limit... if I play my cards right...

He might get her to divorce her husband. That Wythenshawe spiv is all wrong for her anyway. Just a jumped up social climber. Anyone can see that. Not in her league by a long shot. She'd be better off dumping the old fart. Then, Dave thinks, she might shack up with him instead.

Things would really fall into place for him then.

Married! That'd do them both a power of good. Strong set of shoulders to stand at her side. And as for him, well, he wouldn't be complaining. He looks around him at the spreading acres of the estate where they stretch out beyond the fences on the horizon.

He'd be as good a lord of Twinnington as anybody else.

HANDCUFFS
Paris: Faraz Zandi, Commissioner Ducoux

"Monsieur Faraz Zandi"—it was Commissioner Ducoux talking—"you're being held on suspicion of terrorism."

Faraz sat, handcuffed, at a small gray table. Commissioner Ducoux stooped above him, a tall, limp-looking man with rounded shoulders and sleepily inquisitive eyes.

"I'm no terrorist."

Faraz's face was bruised. There was a fresh scar on his upper lip. The Commissioner sighed.

"You attempted to murder."

"You've no proof of anything!"

"Believe me, Monsieur Zandi, we know that we say."

"I've got no reason to speak to you."

"No, perhaps not. But we can incarcerate you... for a long time, if you do not... That's not something I want to do. I'm sure you don't want it, either."

Faraz was silent. His face had turned anemic in the days he'd been kept here. He felt weak and sick.

"I'm sure we can come to an accommodation," said Commissioner Ducoux quietly. "I'm sure of it."

Faraz clenched his fist.

"I'll get the embassy lawyer onto you. You can't pick up British citizens from the street, torture them, and think you'll get away with it. There's human rights even in France."

The Commissioner smiled.

"You've been treated well so far. We do not have the intention to harm you. And we are in close contact with your government, believe me. They know all about you, too."

Faraz just shook his head.

"We know all about your associates in Leeds. Maybe we should talk about them a little. It is not solely for you that we have picked you up, Monsieur Zandi... We're much more interested in the people you're with, the people behind your organization. People a little higher-up, with bigger ambitions than clearing up your family honor."

Faraz was weary and scared. His eyes were empty.

"I can help you get out of this, Monsieur Zandi. But you have to help me, too. Otherwise it is I who shall be in handcuffs. If you do not help me, I am powerless to help you."

Faraz wanted nothing more than sleep. His eyelids were heavy, despite the pain his mind felt dull.

But the Commissioner always had another question to ask, another observation to drop into his mind.

He kept him always on edge, constantly shifting his footings of consciousness. Faraz didn't know how long he'd been in here, how long they'd been questioning him. He didn't know how his head managed to stay upright so long.

He didn't know where he was anymore, what he'd told them, what it was they wanted to know, before they finally stopped shaking him and he drifted off into sleep.

NATIONAL STEREOTYPES
Soho, London: Myles Lyall, Dr Norbert Klinker

ONE HUNDRED AND FIFTY miles west of Paris, the Channel was choppy, mud-gray waves in a queasy turmoil. A storm was spiralling in from the Atlantic. The air was wet, whipped by strong winds, empty of birds. The sky loomed dark above all of southern England, from Lizard Point to the white cliffs of Dover, from Maidstone to Bath, black clouds running swiftly up from the coast.

It was getting just as dark some seventy miles further north, above central London, as the front crept steadily north.

Here, Myles Lyall, of Wythenshawe and Lyall, was lunching Dr Klinker (or Norbert as this gentleman now insisted Myles should call him). They were in an expensive Japanese restaurant in Soho, surrounded by likeminded media men.

It had begun to rain. A great clap of thunder came crashing down just at the moment they surrendered their coats to the kimonoed girl at the door. The restaurant was rather hushed as the heavens opened onto the slushy bustle of the streets outside.

"I don't like to stick to formalities, Myles," said Herr Dr Klinker, while they clinked together long tinkling glasses of Kirin Fukuoka beer.

Klinker looked tanned and vital, his face and forehead were full of color.

"*Prost!*" cried the doctor, with a deep, faucal bleat, and Myles chimed in, "*Prost!*"

"We Germans can be sticklers for these things. I know it, I know it... But not me!"

Klinker laughed ferociously, wiping lager foam from his beard.

"National stereotypes cannot pacify me! The freedom of the self only can commence when one liberates oneself, and vomits forth the country of one's birth."

"It was a good meeting, today, I think."

"*Kommt Zeit, kommt Rat*," said Klinker. "Time will tell what we have done. We are learning to know each another... it is like when the dog sniffs at the other dog," said Klinker.

Myles laughed.

"I'm sure we did more than just sniff."

"*Ein blindes Huhn findet auch mal ein Korn*... The blind chicken... well, that is a difficult one to put over."

"*Every dog has its day* comes close," said Myles.

"*In der Tat.* Tell me about Wythenshawe. He is every inch the noble English aristocrat, I marked that at once. The work with such a man cannot be easy."

Myles looked down, uncomfortable.

"Rupert's not so bad."

He wondered how Klinker had formed this ludicrous notion about Wythenshawe.

"Is he a stickler, your fine English lord?"

Klinker's voice sounded jovial.

"A *stickler*? Absolutely not." Myles laughed. "He'd be delighted to hear you say it."

"Old fashion etiquette, elaborated courtesies, these are the first things I mark when I meet Rupert Wythenshawe."

"Well, I suppose maybe he does have fairly... polished manners. When he feels like it."

"*Polished*!"

Dr Klinker exploded in a mad ejaculation of mirth, beer spewing like blood from his mouth. "*Der Witz ist gut!* Does he polish his manners like medals!? Are manners the reward for the lord's bravery in social strife?"

Myles was baffled by Klinker's exuberant whimsy. Maybe the doctor had misunderstood what Myles meant. There was no way of knowing. Myles wiped his hand.

"I think you mistake Rupert's perhaps slightly old-fashioned courtesy for something it's not," he said.

"Perhaps, perhaps," chortled Dr Klinker. "It doesn't matter. I am sure our Arab Sheikhs will love him and those polished lordly manners of his."

Dr Klinker sighed, licking his lips.

Commonplace men like Myles, he was thinking, *are easily dazzled by unexpected twists of conversational brilliance.* "Tell me, Myles, does Rupert also share the Arab... *penchant* for buggery and pederasty?"

Myles now choked, a mouthful of the Kirin Fukuoka going down the wrong way.

"I'm sorry?"

Dr Klinker was looking beyond him, keenly observing where a little waiter was approaching, bearing aloft, at shoulder height, a tray crammed with piles of steaming dishes. As the waiter spread the food before them on the table, the two men kept silent.

"What did you ask just then?"

"I said it doesn't matter."

"You said something about buggery and pederasty I think," Myles insisted.

Dr Norbert Klinker stared at him shamelessly.

"I did."

"Let me assure you Rupert has no interest in either."

"Myles, my dear Myles, I have only asked."

Klinker placed his hand on Myles's.

Myles freed his hand from Norbert's grip.

"And I slightly resent you imputing those tastes to Arabs as a whole if I may say so, Norbert."

Klinker raised his hands equably, as if surrendering an indefensible point.

"Arab males, Myles, are notorious for this. It is their cultural context of desexualized nubility, for females—combined with polygamy for rich and successful males. It leaves a lot of Arab men dangerously frustrated... Everyone knows that."

"I don't," Myles said primly.

Klinker gave him a good natured smile.

"Never mind, don't bother, let's forget it."

Repressed British schoolboys of Myles's stripe, he was thinking, *use prudishness to cover their depravity.*

Myles persisted.

"As it happens, Rupert's been married quite a while. I wouldn't say the marriage is perfect, she's a bit of a handful. But they're still together. It's a credit to him, I'd say."

"A good credit to him indeed."

Klinker was pleased to have discovered something useful about his new partner Rupert Wythenshawe.

There's no information so promising as compromising information. An imperfect marriage, a frustrated wife...

Soon their talk moved on. Myles began to tell Dr Klinker about something called a "Lean Six Sigma Master Black Belt" certificate, which some of his clients were raving about.

Klinker laughed loud and long.

"Cretinous nonsense," he boomed, his eyes aglow with mischief. "*Der reinste Quatsch.*" He proceeded to bleat pithy put-downs about the Lean Six Sigma programme (of whose content he was blissfully ignorant). Myles began to enjoy himself. Klinker was endearing in his way of combining off-puttingly intense intellectuality with the clumsiest imaginable use of English. Myles had to bite his lip a few times to stop himself laughing.

"I am a philosopher of marketing," said Klinker. "I look deep, deep into the motivations of human beings, deeper than any man has dared to explore. *Das lässt tief blicken.* That lets deep looking."

The lunch proceeded uneventfully enough after this, and Dr Norbert Klinker and Myles parted each feeling he'd spent a worthwhile couple of hours.

A FRESH FACE
Soho, London: Lad from Leeds, bar owner & partygoers

A BLOCK AND A HALF from where Myles and Klinker are finishing their lunch, a popular gay bar is doing brisk lunchtime business.

All at once the owner notices a very young Asian teenager, in a bulky coat, standing shyly at the door.

The boy just stands there looking very lost and awkward. Now the bar's owner, who prides himself on his memory for faces, is sure he hasn't seen him before. So when the boy comes up to the counter, the owner murmurs, quite friendly, "There's a fresh face. This is your first time here, isn't it?"

The boy shakes his head, looking at his shoelaces. He mumbles out an order for a lager. He sounds northern. The owner's hovering, calm and still, behind the bar, but a sixth sense or something makes him suddenly cautious.

"It's just you do look very young," slowly says the owner, looking at the downy fluff on the lad's chin. "I don't serve underage drinkers here, you know, no matter how sweet you might look. They're cracking down on it. Left, right and center."

The young lad flushes. He doesn't say anything else, he just goes red in the face and turns round, walks out the bar. The owner watches him go.

The boy's got a slightly ungainly gait, strangely stiff, coated and corseted, for one so elfin and young. But he was a pretty customer, and when the owner turns back to attend to his regulars at the bar, they give him a range of such wonderfully reproachful looks it makes him laugh.

AN ENERGETIC AFTERNOON
Sussex: Laetitia Wythenshawe, Dave Page

A FEW DAYS LATER, Mrs Wythenshawe stood in a row of stables permeated with the sweet aroma of horse sweat and dung, right by the elegant Regency house in Sussex which she'd shared with her husband since their marriage. This place, far more accessible from London than Twinnington (the family's big ancestral place up in the Borders), was her *bolthole.*

It was a lot smaller than Twinnington, almost cosy. Laetitia spent most weekdays here, visiting friends, going up to London, but mostly staying here and riding. In the summer, she was sometimes here for longer periods, periods when she needed her peace, needed to unwind.

Today, Laetitia had been having one of her more energetic afternoons. She'd gone riding out a couple of hours across the heath, then sprinted along the twelve furlong gallop. Her man friend had come south from Twinnington with her. Dave Page had a body she was still addicted to, but he was beginning to seriously get on her nerves.

They led their mounts back to the boxes, where now a stable-girl took the steeds in hand, leading them off to be rubbed down.

"I had a great time," said the muscular Dave, taking off his helmet and shaking the hair from his moist, ruddy face.

"Me too."

Her mobile chirped in her pocket.

"Let me just take this call, Dave... Who's that? ... ah, Mr Twynne, how good to hear your voice. Thank you for calling back so quickly. It was just, I wanted to talk to you about this fly-tipping craze or whatever it is."

She listened for a while to a slow, burr-edged voice holding forth at a volume which could be distinctly heard even at three paces distance.

Dave grew restless. This Mr Twynne was a man he knew only too well. The factor up at Twinnington was a proper pain in the butt, a man with a face like a dog licking piss off a nettle, a dickweed who'd never shown him nothing but contempt.

Dave tried to clasp Laetitia's waist from behind, to detach her from this long-winded bore. She eluded him with a shimmy of her behind, and a pretty step to one side, still chattering away.

"You'd heard about that, Mr Twynne? Well, of course... thank you... thank you so much... yes I'm sure you're right... I'll be coming up next week."

Laetitia rang off. She was silent for a minute, thinking of Mr Twynne, and what he'd told her about goings-on at Twinnington.

"I always seem to enjoy myself when I come here," Dave was saying.

He spoke in his wheedling tone, fingering the sweat out of his eyes as she turned to face him again. "It must be something in the air, Titty."

"I'm always delighted to have you, Dave."

He stepped up to her and put his hands up her front, pushing her bra up over her breasts. She thrilled to this impulsive roughness of his, she loved it when he went all masterful. As he rubbed her nipples in his palms, she kissed him wetly on the mouth.

She'd wanted to tell him how much she hated being called *Titty*, she'd always hated it, but she'd do that later. Stifling a moan, she let her lazy randiness have its head, her frisky lover his way.

Rupert Wythenshawe was just then trying to get through to Laetitia again. The ringing continued for an age and when finally there came a curt hello, his wife's tone of voice put him on guard at once.

She was breathing hard, he thought.

"It's me," said Wythenshawe uneasily.

"Oh," she said, indifference dripping from her voice.

"I'm just calling to say I'll be working late again."

"Right."

"Something's cropped up and I can't get away."

"It's okay, Rupert," she sighed. "I know the feeling. Something always crops up, doesn't it? I can keep myself busy... oh, yes, that's it... D'you want me to keep some supper warm for you?"

There was a catch in her voice as she asked.

"No, no need," said her husband. "We'll probably send out for something."

They hung up and each returned to what they had been doing before.

OUR NOBLE MASTER'S WEALTH
Bloomsbury, London: Shirin Shaarawi

THE CLOUDS HAD long lifted and the sky was clear above the city, whose warmth and vitality radiated up into the sky.

Shirin had the windows open. She was home alone when the telephone rang.

"This is *The Office of Sheikh Faisal ibn Shabbir.*"

"Oh, not Shabby's lot. How'd you get my home number?"

"You are not difficult to track down, Ms Shaarawi. You may think you lead an ordinary and anonymous life... but you are a remarkably striking woman and, both clothed and unclothed, you leave a trail wherever you go. It is like virtual DNA, Ms Shaarawi... electronic mail... credit card transactions, mobile telephony... all the trails and trials of social intercourse... Trails of perfume, and the imprint of your bosoms, even, on the scented flowers you place in your gracious home..."

"You're spying on me in my flat!"

"We are diligent."

"Impotent peeping toms, more like. Why don't you go see to your erectile dysfunction?"

"We have no trouble picking up such trails... no matter who or where the person might be."

"What a disgusting idea."

"We assure you *The Office of Sheikh Faisal ibn Shabbir* wishes to be only of service."

"I've told you I'm not interested in Sheikh Shabby. Kindly tell him to stop stalking me."

"We want to help you. As the Office of a wealthy interested party, we can afford to take a generous view..."

"I don't want the help of a load of halfwits who call themselves an office. You're just wannabe pimps."

"You may be in need of us sooner than you think, Ms Shaarawi. The Office will be watching out for you, in the days and weeks to come."

"What'd you want to do that for?"

"We are acting under the personal instructions of Sheikh Faisal ibn Shabbir, whose Office we are."

"Is he there now, listening in to your pathetic drivel in the background?"

"No. He employs us to conduct these conversations on his behalf, Ms Shaarawi."

"This isn't a conversation, it's harassment! Do you stalk lots of girls like this?" A random thought now entered Shirin's mind. "Are you behind this honor killing in Leeds?"

The voice was still for a second, then laughed softly.

"So many questions, Ms Shaarawi! Those are confidential informations. Our master's wealth is put to the service of others in many ways. He is unlike other busy men. He doesn't bury himself only in his work, chasing after impossible dreams. Sheikh Faisal ibn Shabbir *cares* about those who attract his concern. As is written in the book, *God hath preferred those who are strenuous with their wealth.* He is strenuously concerned about you and, as his Office, we convert the sheikh's noble concern into caring commercial action."

The voice was still. Shirin took a deep breath.

"Well, I'd much prefer it if Shabby were strenuous elsewhere. Tell him from me I've had it up to the back teeth, speaking to his drivelling flunkeys."

"The Office will convey your feelings to the sheikh, Ms Shaarawi," said the unctuous voice. "If we may say so on our own account, you are a rash and foolish young woman to reject our noble master's wealth, and his wisdom, Ms Shaarawi. As you are aware, Sheikh Faisal ibn Shabbir is a very busy man, with many important and useful projects to lead. Allah be praised for the diligence of the just. The sheikh cannot attend to everything personally. In the meantime, despite your rashness, please be assured of our continued concern."

Shirin cut off the connection.

NIGHTMARE
Bloomsbury, London: Azeem al Din

LATER.

Shirin has gone, the flat is empty until Azeem gets back.

Alone when he goes to bed, Azeem's sleep is soon deranged by nightmares.

He's in the hospital again, listening to that awful sound. The bat smashing relentlessly into the dead woman's face, the dull sound of smashed bone enmeshing with flesh.

He cries out, and no sound comes. Approaches the door, disembodied. The first of the men appears. He's got a gun and aims it at Azeem.

The man moves his lips, but the words come out like bubbles, a jumble of nothingness. The two other men appear behind him. They're wearing surgical masks. The last of the men has bloody hands, and the red droplets deliquesce into the air as if they're underwater.

The bloodied bat floats just above the floor.

The men start running at him. Azeem crouches down, braced for the impact, but they sweep straight through him. He doesn't feel a thing.

As if he's not there.

As if he's a ghost.

The next morning Azeem calls up the hospital in Leeds and asks to speak to Dr Khan.

"Which Dr Khan do you mean, sir?"

"The doctor who saved that girl in the attack the other day."

"Oh, him. He's not available. There's an inquiry underway. Are you from the press?"

Azeem identifies himself and explains he needs to know whether Rania Zandi is ready to be moved out of the hospital yet.

"Dr Khan told me she'd probably be ready today," he says.

"You'll have to take it up with the family, sir. I can't help you."

THE MEDIA RABBI

North London: Rabbi Stark

IT'S GETTING WARMER in town. It's almost hot.

Outside the synagogue, Rabbi Stark puts on his fedora and steps out into the street. He takes a long breath. He soaks in the warmth rising up from the soft asphalt and the mellow buildings of the neighborhood.

He feels momentarily uplifted to glimpse a corner of blue among the office blocks crowding the sky a few blocks away. There's not a lot of folks about at ground level.

Mid afternoon. Everyone's at work, or at home, hiding from the heat in cool, shuttered rooms.

Just a small bunch of ragged men hanging out on the corner. They cast furtive glances his way, before huddling together to confer.

Could be *Ba'al Tshuvas*, thinks the rabbi. That is the tricky theme of the class he's just given.

The newly repented. *Ba'al Tshuvas*.

It's been playing on his mind a lot lately, the difficulties of returning to the fold. He looks over at the men with open encouragement. He wants them to come to him with their questions.

Ugly, untended men, but *neshamos*, precious souls, for all that. They want to approach him, he knows, but they're just too *shy* to do it.

It happens.

He looks straight at them with the frank no-nonsense friendliness that makes him so popular in the area, and on late-night TV chat shows where he peddles a charming, self-deprecatory humor.

But the rabbi's forehead goes cold when he sees the men gazing at him again. They have straightened themselves up, and are approaching now, strutting his way in a macho march, staring directly at him with dead eyes. All are big and bearded, but otherwise nondescript—apart from the knives they're brandishing in front of them, blades catching the light.

Rabbi Stark realizes they've already got the answer to their questions.

Death is their answer. *His* death.

He breaks into a run. The moment he does so the knived thugs speed up and go after him. He's heading for his car. It's a few hundred yards west, parked outside the kosher grocery.

He sprints off, not looking behind him. His eyes are fixed ahead of him, he's aiming for the straightest line from here to the corner. The good thing is he's been getting himself fit over the last year. The bad thing is that the grimmest of his pursuers, the one way out in front, looked only twenty, musclebound like Samson.

Rabbi Stark doesn't give himself good odds on getting to his car.

He reaches the end of the street, where there's an intersection. He can hear the men behind him, their breathing, the soles of their heavy boots slapping across the paving. Sweat has broken out all over his body.

He turns to the right, and there are two girls approaching. They're pushing a pram between them. The baby inside it is crying. One of the girls is leaning over making clucking noises.

"Call the police!" says the rabbi shooting past them.

His car's in the distance, standing under a plane tree. There's no-one else anywhere. The sounds of the men's feet are closing in on him.

He grabs his keys as he runs and unclicks the car locks just as he gets to the curb next to the driver's door. Slipping across the curb, he almost falls over. He gets his fingers round the car's antenna just in time. It snaps off in his hand—but he's still standing.

He pulls the door open. Throws himself in, his heart thumping. He pulls himself up behind the wheel just as the gang comes.

They surround the car and, as he fires the ignition, they engulf him in a flurry of fists and curses. The car doesn't let Rabbi Stark down. It pulls off with a jolt. One of the men, a toothy type with a domed bald head, tries to slash at the tyres, but he's too late.

The car swerves off down the street and the rabbi looks in the mirror to see how the bald man, losing his balance, falls over into the gutter, seething with impious imprecations.

The others pick him up. They put their knives away. The rabbi sees them there in a flurry of shouting and cursing, all but shaking their fists at him, like thwarted villains in a comic-book. As the men diminish in the rear-view mirror, they turn round and start off in the other direction.

The rabbi drives on for ten minutes. He stops the car and takes off his hat. His hands are shaking. He wipes his forehead with his handkerchief.

Comes to himself.

He takes a deep breath, shaking his head. Then Rabbi Stark starts to laugh.

Just remembering how he thought they were *Ba'al Tshuvas* makes him laugh and laugh—thinking of their twisted-up faces as they came after him, brandishing their knives, and then remembering how the bald one had fallen over—he laughs till the tears start from his eyes.

DARK AGE
Bloomsbury, London: Azeem al Din

A WORRY DISTURBED Azeem—his mind fixated on what had happened at the hospital, and on another live story of horror which had been running on CNN that morning. Azeem thought it unfair that all these stories were breaking at the same time, as if designed to screw up his plans.

There had been yet another honor killing, this time not in England, but in Berlin. An especially lurid case, the story had been receiving loads of coverage, with much loose talk about *Dark Age standards of morality,* none of it apt to cast a favorable light on Islam.

There was no knowing which way the media would jump, spawning hysterical features about *Pan-European outbreaks of murder, the resurgent specter of pre-feminist repression* and all that sort of hysterical garbage, poisonous hostile propaganda...

Later, when the day has merged into night, Azeem's worries skulk like sinister shadows in his mind.

He sits alone, brooding, with the lights off, the television turned low in the corner.

Shirin's away, working late in her office. Azeem's frustrated. He wants to discuss things with her, but whenever he tries, he senses her impatience.

Azeem can't relax and watch the news, he's distracted by the unending *hype,* this *hyper-reality,* these dull flickers and reflections flittering over the screen.

So he switches it off, starts readying himself for an early night. He tosses aside his work papers.

He performs his ablutions. He steadies himself to say his prayers.

Finally, he goes to the bedroom. He takes a sheaf of poetry with him to bed. But even as he lies there and tries to read, his eyes swim unseeing, and he can't keep frustrations from curdling all those thoughts, fermenting in his head. The motor of his frustration has been turning over, idling, for too long now, and he's accepted a lot of the shit that's been thrown at him—too much of it, really—but suddenly now the engines rev up, he is filled with burning rage.

In the back of his mind he knows he's got to break free from the struggle that's engulfed him, this quagmire of compromises.

But then again, he's part of it now. Having succeeded in getting Rania down to the London Clinic, he feels part of her story, her story a part of his.

He'd tried to stop the men who'd gone into Rania's room. Just after they'd started smashing the bat into that corpse's head, turning its dead face into pulp. He'd gone in. They broke off as soon as they saw him.

But there was no showdown. Because those men were armed with more than cricket bats.

They'd had guns, they'd knocked him down and pushed past him, surged right out the door. They'd run right out of the hospital before police reinforcements arrived.

At least Rania was safely in the London Clinic now. Her parents had been eager to help and everything had been arranged without fuss.

There was a 24-hour guard on her.

LUCRATIVE LOVE
Chelsea, London: Rupert Wythenshawe & Xenia

TO THE WEST, in Chelsea now, the deep mellow evening is falling, as night dissolves the fading debris of dusk—and the air holding it all so surprisingly hot and quiet, with the busy city noise floating up to the troposphere for the night, leaving something close to silence, something close to peace, where all can relax, can come together in the darkening warmth.

Rupert Wythenshawe is sitting in his mistress's abode. It is financed by Wythenshawe, and his mistress shares this splendidly-located if not specially well-appointed place with a number of cats. The neighborhood outside is still fading, all mingling up in the evening—here tall windows reflect the street lights, and some show glimpses of apartment interiors, like candid shots from a lifestyle magazine. It is an intimate, borderline time, uncommitted to day or night. Low-lying gray clouds droop in the sky.

"Work is fairly getting to me just now," Wythenshawe complains.

"Never mind, dear, you should relax more."

Xenia's massaging his shoulders. He surrenders to it a bit. He lets his head loll to the left. She's caressing and pressing the flesh between long, practiced fingers. She loves to rub his lean, knotted muscles, making them tender. She loves the effect on him of her loving touch, kneading his body to respond to hers.

She thinks she loves him just a little.

She says, "Good to let it all go once in a while."

"Yes... that is good."

"No need to worry twenty-four seven."

"No... no need at all," he says absently.

The television is on in a corner of the room, pumping out its bullets of sensational news.

Wythenshawe's weary already. The news doesn't help.

In a bizarre twist to the spiral of violence, the body of Audrey Winthrop, who had died in the hospital aged 83 the previous day, was horribly disfigured. This horrific desecration was the work of attackers who'd intruded into the hospital, looking for honor attack victim Rania Zandi. Due to a mix-up, currently being investigated by the hospital, the attackers are thought to have mutilated the corpse in the belief that it was Ms Zandi. Mrs Winthrop, a war widow, was much loved in the community. Her relatives are taking legal advice and will be suing the hospital trust for negligence...

A doctor employed at the hospital, who saved the life of the honor attack victim Rania Zandi, has been suspended.

Just then Wythenshawe's phone tinkles to say a text message has come in.

"Never mind what Mrs W is up to," his lover murmurs, light teasing in her voice. Her hand mischievously fumbles his buttock.

That brings him up short.

"I do wish you wouldn't be bringing Laetitia up all the time."

"*All the time?*" she says. "It's hardly *all the time*. Anyway, you can't expect me to always just skirt around the issue of your marriage. Lady L is the elephant in the room!"

"There's no call for bitchiness, Xenia. Laetitia isn't remotely elephant-like. And besides, the idea about elephants in rooms is that people never ever mention them."

Wythenshawe's restive in his heart.

"She's *in* the room, and I'll mention her if I feel like it," says Xenia.

Wythenshawe decides he'll have to tell Xenia.

"The point is… well, that main source of money is about to dry up on me," he says blearily.

Her head leaps up from his lap. "Laetitia's cutting you off?"

"Yes, I think she might… I think she's found a man."

"Isn't she *always* finding a man?"

"Yes, but this one… this one seems to be a bit of a superman. The perfect combination of metrosexual and he-man, the fucker. Full of muscles, fit, good cheekbones, the works. But the worst part of it is he's also good with horses, I'm told… Did I ever tell you what Laetitia's father told me when I asked for... her *hand* — "

"You asked for her hand? Very unlike you to have shown such regard for protocol!"

"He tried his damnedest to put me off! Dead set against me marrying her, he was... And I'll never forget the reason. *If a man's into the gee-gees,* he told me—he was a very crusty sort of huntin' man, just like you'd expect—*if a man's into the gee-gees, Laetitia'll like as not go for the man.* That was sterling, the best advice he ever gave me... I ignored it, of course, with the effects we now see. Anyhow, this bloke she's got now, he's really into the gee-gees— as I say, a real superman, way beyond the ken of the sort of smoothychops gigolos she normally goes with."

"You poor darling. Ouch. That must hurt. But really, how mean, how *selfish* of her!"

"I suspect she'll be thinking of divorce."

"No! The spiteful bitch!"

"Yes, and I can't see me squeezing any alimony out of her family trust... It was bad enough when we were happily married. We'll have to have a radical rethink about everything, darling..."

Wythenshawe's kindly eyes watch Xenia as she wriggles on the horns of this dilemma, and confusions play delightfully on her face.

"It looks as though we'll have to make some adjustments, my dear," he says, relishing the effect of his masterful directness on his lover's expression.

"Adjustments!" she cries. "Whatever can you mean?"

"I'm really not sure I know myself. A lack of ready money will make itself felt soon enough."

She makes a terrible look of woe.

"Oh don't take it so hard, dear. I'll find a way out. I always do."

Wythenshawe's agitated. He's confused about his feelings, unable to formulate why. Matrimonially, Laetitia and he have been polite and civilized to each other for years now, with no desire nor expectation of intimacy. That way of doing things started soon after her miscarriage. It wasn't exactly close nor even remotely passionate, but it was comfortable enough, and neither of them ever thought to discommode the other's extramarital comforts.

Until now.

His wife's *betrayal* of this unspoken agreement, as Wythenshawe sees it, puts him in an impossible position. He's been used for so long to the comfort of having married into money that his first impulse is to think how he might angle himself a lucrative new wife.

The trouble is that Wythenshawe now also sees, never having given it any conscious thought before, that he's more than just fond of Xenia. His wife's actions have brought home his feelings for his mistress.

Laetitia leaving him—this appears to be her plan. She's forcing him to make a false choice. He can either subside into... well, *poverty*, near enough, with Xenia, or he can *dump* Xenia, and find himself a new source of money... *Uxory*, as he fancies such an arrangement ought to be called. Neither option easy, and both downright inconvenient. Wythenshawe's not been obliged to think in such terms before. He resents having it thrust on him now.

So he detaches himself from his mistress's rummaging fingers, turns round to look at her. Xenia is a beautiful woman, and her face is ardent with a melancholy smile. He wants to kiss her melancholic mouth but when he leans over to do so she's reluctant. She pulls back, putting her hand on his chest.

"Not now, dear," she says.

"What not now?"

"Wrong time of month," she lies.

"Rubbish. What's wrong with a little cuddle?"

"*Cuddles* have a way of turning into *shags*," she says.

Wythenshawe's heart beats wildly under her fingers.

The injustice of it. His mind closes in on his own misfortunes. When sex is denied him, it can release pent-up vexations. DSBU—dangerous semen build-up, he's always called it. Resentments now grow within him, where normally feelings of lust should grow.

Xenia gives Wythenshawe a smile, mournful.

"I've been thinking," she says. His heart sinks. When women think, a nagging cannot be far behind. "If Laetitia leaves you and you're poor—"

"I won't be so poor as all that."

"Then you'll be able to do what you really want to do."

"Well, yes. What of it?"

"Well... what would it be?"

"It wouldn't be so different from what I'm doing now. I'd still have my equity in the agency. I'd still have you…"

He's staring up into space as he speaks.

"… wouldn't I?"

Sharp Xenia says, "I thought Laetitia owned most of your agency's shares."

"I'm sure I can regularize that."

"That would be important, I think."

"I'd swing it."

"How can you be so sure?"

"I know me," Wythenshawe says. "I know what I want, I know how to get it."

Xenia laughs in his face. She's remembering an ancient punk song she heard on the radio that afternoon, *Anarchy in the UK*, in which these words had been sneered to great effect, in a way to now light up her memory.

"You've got a big mouth on you, that's what you've got, Johnny Rotten."

At this moment Wythenshawe's lust floods back into his loins and in a fit of irrepressible energy he throws himself on her, an action which is rewarded with gratifying success.

Later, limbs entwined in a messy bundle, they melt within a moment, spooned together, his arm under her breast—kissing, half tired, half aroused, a moment where they're one mind and body—they're unspooled, rested and spent.

But when even later that evening they finally fall asleep, Wythenshawe's forgotten about the text message, he lies there in an uneasy sleep until, early, the new dawn breaks and with it his fitful, fretting dreams.

A MIXED BAG

West End, London: Azeem al Din, Myles Lyall, Samir Muhsi, Rupert Wythenshawe

NEXT MORNING.

As Azeem and Samir Muhsi come marching into the meeting room, 9:30 sharp, Myles is sitting there alone. He's dark-suited, tieless, drawn. Looking at his watch.

"Let's get started while we're waiting," says Myles, after Azeem's made introductions. "Wythenshawe must be stuck in traffic somewhere."

Pouring out the coffee, Myles goes through the agenda he's prepared—Overall Strategic Brief—Communications Platform—Image Campaign—Targeted Recruitment—Loyalty Programme.

The new man, Samir, stays silent the while, brooding. He's elsewhere. His glance doesn't meet Myles', but he's listening very carefully to everything being said, and his absent eyes absorb it all with tiny flickers of interest. He watches the walls and the windows and then the other men, as if waiting to pounce, a sly fat man with the nose of a hawk.

Myles and Azeem settle into intense talk about the need to *address negatives*.

Samir shifts in his seat. He's still looking away.

"You're talking about addressing negatives."

Finally his eyes lock into Myles's.

"Would you mind explaining that?"

"Sure," says Myles. "When we research how people currently think of Islam, we find a mixed bag of positive and negative perceptions."

"A *mixed bag*? Negative perceptions? When I hear you say that, I hear a lot of alarm bells. A lot of questions come into my mind, questions which sit up and beg me for an answer! What would these perceptions of yours be? The product of repressive capitalist marketing mechanisms? Have you been asking presumptuous leading questions? You sound like a hangover of empire, Mr Lyall... domination not by gunboat, but by focus group normatives!"

Myles doesn't miss a beat, but he's rattled. This riff of Samir's about negative perceptions shows he's eager to rock the conceptual boat.

He's hacking away at the basis of the brief.

After all, it had been agreed—right from the outset of the project—that whole hosts of negative perceptions were waiting to be dealt with. In a way, the whole project has been predicated on a superfluity of negative perceptions.

It's not as if any of this is controversial.

Myles looks over at Azeem. Azeem is sitting quietly, he takes a sip of coffee, nods vaguely.

Azeem looks distracted. Azeem looks puzzled.

Azeem seems unhappy with the turn things are taking, but he's unwilling to stick his neck out at this point in the meeting. *Azeem's cowed*, thinks Myles, *now Samir Muhsi's here.*

Myles goes on: "If you ask a cross-section of white C1C2Ds, you'll find they think Muslims aren't as in touch with the modern world as westerners. Muslims in the same demographic won't tell you any different."

Samir Muhsi is silent. His body shakes. Whether with anger, or amusement, or withdrawal, or a strange new medical condition, Myles cannot tell.

"The *position of women* is another problem," Myles proceeds.

Samir seems to swallow a snigger. Myles pretends not to notice, carries on.

"A lot of respondents perceive women as disadvantaged in Muslim societies. Of course, some would argue that material subservience aids spiritual exaltation... Others would relativize... Oppression is a double-edged sword, they'd say. It cuts both ways. They'd say... they'd say western women suffer worse oppression under the yoke of consumerism."

Myles clears his throat. Samir's ongoing physical tic has put him off his stride. Myles is a pro. He shows no outward sign of anything much. He takes another sip of coffee. Azeem's avoiding his eye. Samir in his corner is still twitching, giving off unspecified vibes.

The room is cool, the air-conditioning's on full. It's too cool for comfort.

"And then of course there's the whole terrorism angle," says Myles. "There's no getting round that as a... well, as a big negative."

Myles pauses to let that one sink in.

Samir Muhsi's squat body has stopped shaking. He's sitting in his chair, quite rigidly now. He holds himself immobile, like a Pharaoh's statue in stone.

He stares at Myles. His beady birdlike eyes are cold. He opens his mouth to speak.

"I understand what you're saying," he says, slowly, as if speaking to a moron. "And I have to say, we Muslims don't need lessons in democracy from you, Mr Lyall. We invented democracy. Second, I really think you need to *raise your game*, Mr Lyall, if you get my meaning. I'm not totally unversed in the vocabulary of your beloved *marketingspeak*. You have no grounds to patronize me, Mr Lyall, no grounds whatsoever."

Samir grins briefly, discomfitingly. His cup of coffee stands, cold, untasted, on its saucer.

"Some of the issues you mention are not negatives, to my mind. The ones you wish to *address*, as you so quaintly put it, as if you knew where to send them."

Samir smiles to himself, a smile that cuts off both Myles and Azeem, letting him savor the high humor of the two of them, their manifest futility. It seems to tickle him. The twitch is back.

"I cannot agree with you on any of that, Mr Lyall," he says, still smiling broadly. "I would see all that as playing into the hands of infidels and apostates."

"All we're trying to do is kick off a debate—"

"With respect," Samir breaks in with a dead smile, "we're not trying to kick off any debates, Mr Lyall. We're trying to kick off an ideological war—a *war of the pen*, perhaps, but a war nevertheless—a war directed at the enemies of Islam."

Now Myles is flummoxed, so much he's scarcely able to disguise it. He darts another glance across at Azeem. But Azeem's looking at his shoes, quiet, down in the mouth. His shoulders droop down as though he's wilting into his own misery.

"A *war*?"

Myles starts calmly. He wants to defuse Samir's hostility.

"I wouldn't put it that way. I think *war* carries too much negative baggage. We're aiming to *persuade* people to see things our way, to *convert* them if you like. To persuade people, we need to remove their doubts, wage a jihad of peace... as you say, a jihad of the pen. Because you can't remove doubts by denying they exist. That's no way to convert anybody."

"I would prefer a much more positive, aggressive approach to this *conversion* you speak about," says Samir.

His words tremble with restraint as he goes on.

"You're setting the bar far, far too low, Mr Lyall. I think advertising should be used to *attack and flay* the enemies of Islam. We should *flay* the kafirs, the crusaders and the apostates.

"Tell the people of their doom and the deaths they will die," says Samir, his blue eyes gleaming, "when Allah brings them to account, should they refuse to bow to Islam, should they refuse to stop oppressing our people, persecuting them all over the world!"

While Myles digests this, the door's abruptly flung open and in lopes Wythenshawe, not looking best pleased.

"Apologies for my tardiness," he drawls. "I wasn't informed this meeting was happening."

Wythenshawe scowls across at Myles, who mouths at him, "Didn't you get my message?"

Wythenshawe remembers it perfectly having read it not an hour before, just after extracting himself, bleary, from Xenia's bedclothes, but in a spirit of self-preserving bloodymindedness he prefers to embarrass his partner.

"It must have gone astray, Myles."

He lets out a tight satiric laugh.

"Organizational detail is one of my bugbears," Wythenshawe blathers on pompously, with a smile for Azeem and the new, important-looking client he hasn't met yet. "I give everyone hell in this office, simply to ensure a smooth and efficient transfer of data. It doesn't win me any friends... but you can see how necessary it is!"

Samir Muhsi is now introduced to Wythenshawe and he nods with fellow-feeling at the latecoming interloper.

"The difference between success and failure is often concealed in the smallest, least significant detail," proceeds Wythenshawe. He shakes Samir earnestly by the hand and locks eyes with him in the most trustworthy bonding way. Myles watches, sidelined.

"It's like the tiny granule of sand which turns into the priceless pearl," says Wythenshawe, holding up his hand and pinching thumb and index finger together like a man grasping something very fine, very precious. "I always say, we have to be on top of every last little detail if we want to turn sand into pearls."

Samir smiles. "We have a saying," he says. "*Trust in God, but tie your camel.*"

Wythenshawe gives a shout of delight and mimes the act of tying Myles up with a rope. Samir is richly amused. Myles says, *sotto voce*, "Calm down for God's sake, Rupert."

The meeting continues and Wythenshawe, having found his new soulmate, takes Samir's viewpoint on things very much to heart.

AGE OF ENLIGHTENMENT
Sussex: Laetitia Wythenshawe, Dave Page

BAREFOOT, IN HER dressing gown, Mrs Wythenshawe descended the staircase, the cool breeze fanning her legs, her skin still warm and moist after her shower. She walked into the drawing room where she was proposing to pour herself a cup of tea prior to sipping it out on the terrace in the sunshine.

The sun dappled invitingly on the marble underfoot. She needed some quiet time.

But her lover Dave was already outside waiting for her.

"Lovely afternoon," said hunky Dave, smiling out at the park's mellow lawns, which seemed to evaporate into effulgent countryside behind the house. She glanced over his shoulder. A vista unchanged since the Age of Enlightenment, when Laetitia's ancestors had first laid it out, to designs drawn up by Humphry Repton.

"Are you staying for tea?" asked Laetitia as if offended by something or other.

"Well I was thinking more along the lines of a gin and tonic."

Dave was pawing at her dressing gown with his hands, rough, inescapably uncouth.

"Really darling, I am rather tired," said Mrs Wythenshawe in a small birdlike voice when he was done.

"Just the one?" pleaded Dave.

He wanted that gin and tonic with his post-coital ciggie.

"Honestly darling, I really don't feel too brilliant."

Finally he saw that imposing himself on her wasn't a good plan.

Not long after, Dave was on his way to his own home in Finchley, a suburb of London, leaving Laetitia Wythenshawe exulting in the luxury of tea on the terrace by herself.

Alone at last.

But Dave didn't get the message.

The next day, Laetitia spent the afternoon riding. She'd been looking forward to being by herself some more, but her man friend insisted on joining her. She hadn't been able to think of an excuse fast enough to put him off. And so he tipped up, all spruce again and well-scrubbed and obviously *wanting* her.

She wished sometimes he wouldn't be so predictable, so saddle-horned with his perpetual urges.

In her annoyance she'd started thinking of him as *the Dave.*

She sighed. She'd been so taken by him, at first. Dave and she were perfectly-matched—as riders. His self-confidence was winning enough, and so too his muscles, his attentiveness, his old-fashioned masculinity, mannered but manly. He had a lot going for him.

But now she saw it wasn't enough. It just wasn't enough.

She'd let the relationship drag on so long, far longer really than Dave deserved, taking into account his glaringly lackluster performance in other areas.

Today though, as Dave took their things off, Laetitia came to the conclusion she'd had it. It was time to draw a line under these sessions.

Lackluster was the right word. Her lust for him, once so natural and happy and horny, was entirely lacking now.

It came to that moment when he would clench her in his arms, from behind, undoing her. Laetitia stopped him unclasping her bra, the usual start-signal for one of their tumbles in the hay. It took her rather more force than she'd expected to stop him.

"What's up?" he said, eventually seeing the futility of carrying on fumbling and wrestling with her.

She told him.

"You think *what?*"

She told him again.

"But we only just started a few months ago!"

"I don't think it's going anywhere, Dave."

He stared at her, dumbfounded.

"Sorry," she said softly. "It's not you."

"We're just beginning to get to know each other!"

His resentment shimmered, briefly, from his fogged-up eyes—a fleeting reflection of hurt, like a swift-passing headlight in the misty distance, which you only half see before it's gone.

Then that spark simmered down within him.

"I don't think we've got a future, Dave. It's not you... It's me... It's my marriage...

"I'm in a difficult phase," said Laetitia. "It's all my fault. I shouldn't have encouraged you. You don't know how difficult it is for me... I'm so sorry, Dave."

Dave was still too shocked to make a scene then and there in the stables.

This finale was the last thing he'd been expecting: he'd flattered himself he was fully involved with Laetitia. That, perhaps, had been his single greatest mistake.

Dave Page left quietly, having accepted, with great good grace, a check Laetitia made out in his name for five hundred pounds.

To Laetitia this was no more than a gesture, a means of reimbursing him for the few times he'd paid for their meals and drinks—he'd insisted on that in their early days. Of course five hundred was far more than the rounds of pizzas and gin and tonics had ever cost—but she felt it was a nice round amount maybe to make him remember her fondly.

She wanted to be shot of him cleanly and quickly, not nastily.

Driving alone back to Finchley, Dave didn't see things quite the same rosy way.

He'd pocketed the check happily enough, never one to turn up his nose at an offer of ready money. Dave was pumped full of pride, but Titty wasn't the first woman to have paid for his well-trained attentions—even if it was only her husband's money.

It always is the husband's money.

As he drove back he began to ruminate on the details of his sudden dismissal.

What had been especially stinging, bitter stuff, was Laetitia's manner. Admittedly she'd been more offhand than she would have if she hadn't been feeling so obviously ratty that afternoon. He'd sensed that. He knew her and her little mood swings inside out. He'd tried to take her in his arms a few times during the afternoon. But she always stood aside, cold, rubbing his nose in her cold, cold, stuck-up self-possession. Putting on that marish, spooky act, maybe just to try and make him bolt.

But I ain't the one for bolting.

It ate away at Dave's sorest spot, what Titty, back in the day, once called his thin-skinned *amour-propre*.

She used all her fancy words on me back then, buttering me up, making me think I was on her level...

The longer Dave drove, the more he dwelt on the *injustice* of it all. Having been sent packing so unceremoniously, with such seasoned ease, by that saucy, sultry *strumpet*, it wasn't many miles before Dave saw that Titty, in addition to her beauty—her upper-class breeding—her wealthy husband—her bland, above the bit ways, was a thoroughbred bitch.

She'd been leading him on all the time. She'd encouraged him to think they could be together as a proper married couple...

Dave's ears were burning as he approached his little apartment in Finchley. By the time he'd parked and locked his car in the leafy street, he'd resolved to take his revenge.

Titty had it coming to her, the stuck-up slut.

The tart with no heart.

Dave threw the front door aside and with a swagger he walked to his telephone. He'd show Titty. He wasn't the type to take things lying down. He had his contacts.

If Laetitia wanted to bomb off and fuck him around, just let her try, he'd fuck her up right back.

JIHAD HOTLINE
West End, London: Myles Lyall, Rupert Wythenshawe

"WAS IT REALLY NECESSARY to be quite so slavish?"

Myles sounds peevish. Wythenshawe bristles.

"I was just mollifying a client who seemed uncommonly down in the mouth!"

Having seen their clients, Azeem and Samir, on their way, ushering them into a chauffeured agency car, Wythenshawe and Lyall have gone back to the conference room to chew things over. Wythenshawe is bullish about his performance, Myles appalled.

"You were merrily agreeing with him that the 7/7 London bombings were staged by British security forces!"

Myles is incensed, not merely peeved—even if an outsider, listening in, wouldn't suspect anything amiss between the two partners. Native restraint and diplomacy, as always, have rendered Myles' tone more reasonable than true to his real feelings. To Wythenshawe, though, Myles's undertone is unmistakeable.

Wythenshawe doesn't bat an eyelid. His untroubled brow exudes bland self-possession.

"One in four Muslims say 7/7 was staged," he says. "Many more think it but they button up their lips when they're with the pollsters. Maybe you should get closer to your target audience."

"Then there was that *Jihad Hotline* you and Muhsi were ever so keen on."

"Well, it's a good idea, Myles."

Wythenshawe's voice has turned confidential.

"It's got legs."

"Oh, Christ! What fresh preposterousness is this? The Jihad Hotline is a terrible, *terrible* idea, about as leggy as a paraplegic."

"It could be highly profitable."

The Jihad Hotline had been treated by Samir and Wythenshawe as if it were some very minor, bread-and-butter activity. But, under cover of offering advice to Muslims troubled by social or religious transgressions, the Jihad Hotline was designed to serve as a grooming, recruitment, and exchange-center, a matchmaker between lost souls and the acts of jihad most compatible with them. That was how Myles interpreted Samir's significant evasions, his looks of complicity to Wythenshawe, although the man hadn't spelled it out. *Jihad*, in this connection, referred to the committed, fullblown psychopathic option, rather than the struggle-against-sin one.

"Jihad is an individual duty for every Muslim in every country," Samir had said. "It is a personal obligation for all."

"In what sense?" Myles asked.

Samir assumed a very righteous posture, his mouth, a reproving primness about the lips. His eyes were hooded, cold.

"The first essential is to know your enemies, those who obstruct you on the way of God. Then, you have to remove those obstructions. Affirmative action is essential."

"Quite so," Wythenshawe chimed in blandly. "The Jihad Hotline will be a tool to empower individuals, allowing them to define their own, personal life-goals, via dialogue, within an outreach community of likeminded individuals. This must be a central plank as the *Islamic Reform* project gets underway."

"Jargon contortion," Myles now says. "PC blah."

Wythenshawe slowly shakes his head.

"*Jargon-contortion* and *PC blah* are very belittling terms, Myles. You mustn't mock our clients. You shouldn't patronize the people who pay our wages."

Wythenshawe looks at Myles as if challenging him to try it on again. Wythenshawe's full of beans. His face is bland and expressionless, but a wicked spark dances deep in the depths of his kindly eyes.

He says, "More power to Samir's elbow, that's what I say."

"I'd picked up on your approval of Samir," Myles remarks as they leave the room. "But we've now got a client who doesn't know what he wants."

They walk up to their own offices.

"Wrong."

Wythenshawe smiles.

"We've got *two* clients. Azeem and Samir. And both of them know exactly what they want."

"Well, one wants peace, the other wants a bloody jihad."

"Yes, but you're missing the bigger picture, Myles. A client in two minds can be a godsend, properly handled. It means we can do twice the work, pocket twice the money...

"You cultivate Azeem, I'll stick close to Samir," Wythenshawe continues intently. "Think of the fees! The bottom line—the bottom line you're so rightly worried about—will benefit no end!"

Despite all his misgivings, Myles can see the potential in Wythenshawe's approach.

SELF-REFERENTIAL PATTERNS
Twinnington, Scotland: Laetitia Wythenshawe, Dr Norbert Klinker

A WEEK AFTER Dave Page's dismissal, Laetitia had gone up to Twinnington. She and Dr Norbert Klinker were now sitting out on her terrace sipping tea. It was a glowing afternoon, the sun melding with a misty green line of trees in the west. Light bounced off yellow globeflowers, spotlighted clusters of bright red poppies, and a russet glow seeped across the horizon.

They were discussing Laetitia's husband in no very complimentary terms.

"I think of him as a dead white man," Dr Klinker began.

Mrs Wythenshawe giggled. "Oh yes, he's certainly *that.*"

She looked fetching, her nose prettily crinkled, her eyes lit up, and this was exciting for Dr Klinker.

"The very type of decadent English lord—"

Mrs Wythenshawe was now spluttering with laughter.

When she'd recovered herself, she said, occasionally interrupting herself with fresh gales of giggles, "I'm not entirely sure about this lord thing... The Wythenshawes... a perfectly *respectable* family as far as anyone can tell. Salt of the earth, I'm sure. But they're not exactly members of the upper ten thousand—"

"Yes, yes," Klinker broke in, not at all getting her point—confused by her laughter—and in any case unwilling to alter the image he'd burnished up for Wythenshawe. "He is the *type*, no? That famous type of English lord, I think—with charm, umbrella and melon."

Mystified, Mrs Wythenshawe hadn't the energy to disagree. Her head spun, her brains felt wrung out.

Dr Klinker had mentally exhausted her already.

When Klinker first tipped up that afternoon she'd been suspicious, also a little intrigued. She hadn't a clue who he was. A tall, handsome man she'd never set eyes on before. When he told her—*Dr Klinker, a colleague of your dear husband*—her first instinct was to tell him to go hang, discuss anything he might want with her husband.

"I am interested, by your leave," Dr Klinker had said, soft and insistent, lifting her hand to his lips, to press it with a kiss.

And when still she looked reluctant after the hand kiss, he persisted, "It is you, specifically, I desire to see, my dear Lady Wythenshawe. I am only come here for that purpose."

Something about him—his tenacious expression, his accent and word choice—enchanted Laetitia. He had his comic side, and charmed her, even if it was unwitting. She found his high brow, with the long, swept-back locks around it, rather distinguished and attractive.

Laetitia was at a loose end that day. She decided to let him in and see what developed.

They'd gone on to the terrace and soon Dr Klinker was holding forth.

"What for a gentlemanly view!" he exclaimed, blinking out over the lush lawns with a dazed expression. "You really do have a splendid living room."

He delineated for some time the effects of landscape on human wellbeing. Laetitia had never come across anyone like Dr Klinker, loaded as he was with gifts of prophecy and insight a lesser man might have wished to keep under wraps out of office hours.

She soaked it up. She knew what she liked, and she was taking a decided fancy to him.

"To me, it is not enough to converse," Klinker explained. "*Klatsch und Tratsch*—how do you say it, clash and trash? Social tits and tattle? This means nothing to a man of my passions, I want all my intercourse to throb with the vital spark... I can see you agree with me... I can see that you too are throbbing with the vital spark. People such as we need to *grapple* with each other's souls."

Dr Klinker had looked over and seen a pretty woman beaming back—well, to him she was little more than a girl, really, but she seemed to have focused her whole self onto him.

She is definitely intrigued, he thought, *by my mystery, by my profundity.*

He saw her smiles, and was turned on. He thought he might impress himself on this girlish *Lady* and extract some more of her tinkling throwaway laughter, so soft and delightful in the ear.

Klinker was an excellent listener when he wanted to be. Good at that *olde worlde Mitteleuropean* courtesy, he piled it on pretty thick. He determined to show himself tolerant of Laetitia's artless confidences, to overlook her girlish airhead piffle and treat her as if she had a mind worth cultivating. It was hard, for him, but he wanted to penetrate her reserve.

When she admitted how bored to tears she was with her own company, he told her—putting into good practice those ponderous phrases to which he was addicted—that the boredom of a lady as lively as Lady Wythenshawe was more intriguing than the *Geistesblitze*—the ghost lightning—the brainwaves—of a thousand *Blaustrümpfe* bluestockings.

Laetitia found the foreign clumsiness of his gallantry no less welcome than its harsh, Teutonic expression, starved as she was of stimulating social intercourse. It was fun to chat with a bona fide intellectual, her Daves and Petes for all their charms not having been any great shakes in that regard.

Laetitia had seen a man—a good-looking, slightly preposterous figure—a man whose soft heart seemed tormented by the sharpness of his mind. Norbert (how she loved that name!) struck her as vulnerable, almost childishly so. His earnestness. His puffed-up verbosity. All that dissolved if you made the effort see through it. And if you couldn't, you could always console yourself with the knowledge that this good German doctor was your husband's colleague, well placed to spill some beans about Wythenshawe's increasingly arcane doings.

And being hunky didn't harm him in her eyes.

All in all, Norbert was well placed to wound Wythenshawe with a spot of calculated infidelity, mixed up with indiscretion, should the need arise.

"I'm going through a difficult phase," Laetitia was now saying, in an effort to equal Dr Klinker's earnestness. "I don't know whether I'm coming or going half the time."

"What is any state but a relative one?" Klinker replied in his deep, booming voice. His words came out in a bassy sort of bleat.

"You're *so* right. I hardly know what to do with myself."

"What is the *self*?" Klinker gently mused. He stood at the balustrade and surveyed Laetitia's acres. He looked straight through the flowery meadow—not even noticing the startled swoops of two red-rumped swallows, sailing directly into his field of vision—his eyes were glazed as if reflecting his own vision back, intervolved, deep within himself.

"What, indeed, *is* the self?" he repeated, to himself.

Klinker answered himself, gazing with visionary sightlessness across the silver meadow, "It's an *abstract self-referential pattern*, Lady Wythenshawe, that arised out of the bouts of neural activity, a looping epiphenomenon generated by the brain. When we analyse us, as we must, Lady Wythenshawe, it can be no wonder we end up going a little loopy!"

Klinker turned back and twinkled at her.

"And you, my exquisite Lady Wythenshawe, it befalls me, can be a woman who's going a little loopy!"

Klinker intertwined his arms with hers. Slowly, he began to dance with her on the terrace.

"Loop the loop!" he gaily sang as he twirled her round him.

Laetitia laughed. Despite the doctor's zany impulsiveness of manner, he so clearly grasped the nature of her frustrations.

So it struck her as they twirled and twinkled together on the terrace, as the night fell on the fields, and the birds fell silent.

"I have the feeling, my dear Lady Wythenshawe—"

"Please call me Laetitia, Norbert," Laetitia protested. "I'm not, strictly speaking, called *Lady* Wythenshawe. It's Lady Laetitia, if you like, though I'd prefer plain Laetitia."

"*Plain Laetitia* is an insufficient appellation... for a creature of your luminosity," said Klinker, twinkling at her in mock rebuke.

He clicked his heels, perhaps ironically.

"Let it be," he said, "Lady Laetitia it is."

Klinker's reproachful glance, Laetitia saw, with his slightly protruding eyes, made him look slightly like a goat—a handsome, romantic goat.

Laetitia giggled.

Klinker didn't hear. "I have the feeling your husband, under pressure perhaps of some alternative emerging proposition, is neglecting you. Am I right?"

Laetitia stared into his eyes, alive with concern.

It was impossible not to open up to such a man, she thought. So full of vitality, so charged with fellow-feeling, so replete with wit and wisdom. He was so intoxicated with himself that she too was intoxicated. And in his flowing-locked, Byronic way, he was, to her, in her present state, by no means unattractive...

She said, "To tell you the truth—"

"I will hear *only* truth!"

"When it comes to fucking up my marriage, I'm not entirely innocent myself," she confessed. "Only last week did I get round to giving my latest lover his marching orders."

Laetitia smiled sadly, thinking of The Dave's departure.

Now Dr Klinker laughs merrily then seeing a tear in her eye he turns serious.

"I am a true *lover of truth*," he says very quiet, his hands folded humbly in front of him like a caring man of God.

He contemplates her for a second, cherishing his luck, sizing up his window of opportunity.

How easy these upper class Englishwomen are to seduce.

Through her tears, she's smiling back fondly his way.

"I will tell you another truth," says Klinker, slightly louder. "I feel for you what we in Germany call a *Wahlverwandschaft*—a whale relationship. Do you feel it? Do you feel it too?"

"With all my heart," says Laetitia, with all her native tact. Her shoulders tremulous, she's still sobbing, Klinker sees.

Klinker at length launches himself bodily onto the sofa beside her, taking her in his arms to offer solace. After a minute or so of that, they're on their way up to her bedroom, where they will spend the rest of the evening together.

The next morning Dr Klinker wakes in a daze in Laetitia's bed. He's dizzy, delirious with the memory of her. What a woman! He stretches himself and turns over with the intention of fondling her awake, but she's already gone. There's a piece of paper on her pillow.

Gone riding! Back at around 9.

He squints at the alarm clock. 9:47.

Lying back, he lets his mind empty, absorbing the silence. His cock is hard. His nose is full of the scent of her. He feels himself slipping away...

Coming to again, he looks at the clock and sees it's gone ten.

Muffled clatter of hooves on the cobbles outside the stable block. He hears her voice, she's shouting at somebody whose replies are indistinct, subservient-sounding, one of the stable girls presumably.

He gets out of bed and walks to the window to take a look. She's down there, still scolding the girl as she walks into the stables. Her hair is in disarray, her jodhpurs have got a rip down the left leg, there's some blood stains.

"*Guten Morgen!*" he shouts down. "What happened?"

She turns, sees him and smiles. Her face is sweaty.

"My fucking jodhpurs got snagged in some brambles! It's fucking agony!"

"I'll come right down!"

"Don't bother! I'll just get changed and come up!"

He decides to ignore that and, not bothering to put anything on, walks down the stairs to find her. Goes down the stairs into the vast marble hall, portraits of her ancestors glaring down on him with condescending sneers. They look at him from their canvasses, in their frozen postures, as if they want to call him out, throw him to their slavering hounds, horsewhip him for what he's done to the heiress of their estate, and for what he still plans to do.

In der Tat.

He's smiling to himself. How he loves this place! The delicious irony of being here, all his senses aroused! The stone is cool underfoot. He walks on, sneering right back at the ancestors, naked and proud. A gallery of fops and popinjays, dyspeptic gallants, corpulent from the profits of coalmining and slavery. One or two of them have the drooling mouths, the hangdog, sheepish air of men who mate with quadrupeds... men who loved their prize pigs, their marrows and their cricket pitches more than their wives—ladies constrained by their lords' perverted preferences to fornicate with underlings—pages, grooms and whippers-in, huntsmen, ploughboys, valets, lackeys, ostlers, oddjob men and gamekeepers.

He pictures the great hall full of writhing limbs, orgiastic excess, venery, and his arousal perks him up.

But how glad Dr Klinker is not to have lived in those decades of inglorious pomp, that age of grotesque inequity, an age when he—he, Dr Klinker!—would have been required to bow, scrape and kowtow, to tug his forelock at these snobbish, inbred imbeciles!

Not now. No longer. Now I am the master here.

He slips down the corridor to the right, it leads to a side entrance. There's nobody about, but in his present state, he doesn't care either way.

He steps out into the yard. It's a fine, balmy morning, and a soft breeze wafts across his skin. Into the stables, he walks past a couple of empty boxes before he sees her. She's sitting there in the hay, pulling off her jodhpurs, looking as delicious and vulnerable as an oyster out of its shell, and he wants nothing more than to gobble her up, to sate his priapic hunger between her firm young milky thighs.

A rough clump of hay has embedded itself between the cheeks of her bottom. Her bloody left leg is still sore where the brambles ripped through the jodhpurs, and she's rubbing at the spot. Only a scratch, she needs to go up and have a shower.

She sees him. He looks so obscene, so out of place there, it shocks her. He's brandishing his hard-on proudly, and he's got this dazed expression on his face, half leering at her as he walks in. She sits back and covers her legs with a blanket.

I must look an absolute mess.

She sits back, sees his excitement all over him.

"Couldn't you wait?"

"No, of course not. I need you now."

Kneeling down before her, he rips the blanket away and feasts his eyes on her. His hands are on her legs, caressing them while pulling them apart. She feels so exposed and helpless, but she doesn't struggle, she lets him, she just lets him. He's licking his lips, utterly shameless! And now she feels shameless too. Whatever will the stable girls think? She smiles, and he smiles back, then lowering himself down, puts his head between her thighs.

His tongue warm and wet inside her, she lies back in the straw, closing her eyes, and everything is blurring—that pesky piece of straw between her buttocks like a needle, the rich honeyed smell of the dung, his tongue darting in and out making her all squishy—it all melts and merges until she arches her back and gives herself up to the muddy, squelching moment.

IN MY TRIBE
Mayfair, London: Rupert Wythenshawe, Samir Muhsi

WHILST ALL THIS WAS unfolding in his marital home, Wythenshawe, the husband, was up to no good on his own account. He'd hit it off so well with Samir Muhsi at the meeting that he now determined to strike home his advantage where he could.

Wythenshawe arranged for them to meet privately, for an informal evening consultation. Samir Muhsi was amenable.

"We might take in a *show* of some sort," suggested the urbane holy warrior, and Wythenshawe wasn't shy about ascertaining the kind of show Samir had in mind.

"It's good to talk man to man," said Samir that evening as they toasted one another with expensively-branded sparkling wine.

"It's *essential*, Samir, essential," Wythenshawe replied. "Get away from our jargon-contortionist colleagues for an evening."

"*Jargon-contortionist* is good! But this," Samir said, placing a twenty pound note into a dancer's thong-strap, "this is a highly preferable form of contortion. It would not be to the taste of your very prim and proper Mr Lyall, I suspect."

"Lord, no. I've known him for years, but I still can't get rid of the suspicion he plays for the other team."

"It is most valuable that you place me in your confidence like this," said Samir. He smiled oleaginously. He was wearing a dark pinstripe of distinctly distinguished cut. "I think you are a man I can do business with."

And Samir proceeded, as the evening progressed, to share some highly sensitive information—relating to *Islamic Reform*, Azeem, and the financial side of things. The latter subject was not altogether kosher, in fact Samir was proposing...

"... if you're up for it, the accounting of fees and income could be done on a more *informal* basis than Mr Lyall might prefer..."

This opened up a potentially lucrative sideline which was music to Wythenshawe's ears.

"You're just like me," said Wythenshawe sucking on a fat cigar. "You like to have fun. And you love to make money!"

The two men were bonding with a mutual sycophancy which clung round them like pungent aftershave. A great many refreshments and private entertainments having been enjoyed, Wythenshawe, rather red in the face, and leaning closely against Samir, outlined at length his worries about his wife, and the likelihood that her unfaithfulness might embarrass him in various ways.

"In my tribe she would be subjected to the lash," said Samir, casting a sidelong look at Wythenshawe. Samir's face was a little uncertain. "Then would come death by stoning."

"Unfortunately that's not possible over here."

Wythenshawe gave vent to a sigh.

Samir, by now, was inclined to grandiosity. "Perhaps I can help you with that," he suggested, stuffing another note into yet another dancer's thong. "Because from tonight... I call you my brother, and you *are* my brother, one of my tribe. And in my tribe, the men... the men keep their women... in perfect order."

Samir leaned back, surveying, in his mind's eye, the edifying rigor of his *tribe* as he watched the nubile dancers writhe, snakily servicing their poles.

Samir seemed satisfied with what he saw.

"In my tribe, we bury homosexuals alive, under walls," Samir said.

As he spoke, Samir justified his lurid lies to himself. He thought of his "brother" Ghazan Khattak, and of Ghazan's casual, brotherly fatalities.

He remembered how Ghazan's talk, in its stony-hearted callousness, was full of brutal swagger about his *tribe.* But Ghazan's tribe, such as it was, was based on loyalty to Ghazan Khattak, rather than any ethnic link. Anyone prepared to submit to Ghazan Khattak's will could join Ghazan's tribe... So Samir himself, if he chose, could count himself one of Ghazan's tribe.

"Adulterers we hurl from high buildings," Samir continued, "so they are crushed to a pulp when they fall... it blots out the stain of their sin."

So Samir Muhsi spoke, intending to curdle Wythenshawe's blood, as the contemplation of these things curdled his own, filling him with a guilty thrill.

All in all, it turned into a memorable night, with neither of them remotely clear how it ended.

LEFT FOR DEAD
Paris, France: Faraz Zandi

FARAZ IN HIS CELL with his cellmate eked out a life of disgusting, enforced intimacy—cheek by jowl, yet detached, as much from each other, except bodily, as from the world outside—the walls and fences between them and the rest of the planet having invisible counterparts inside their minds. Faraz thought a lot about such things as he lay on his bed and his cellmate above him tried to engage him in talk, talk which circled ever closer around the topic his cellmate went on and on about—the necessity of jihad.

But Faraz couldn't stop an apathetic tone from creeping into his desultory replies whenever they spoke of it.

The only jihad he was fighting now was in himself.

The only life he wanted to live had been killed, left for dead on a cobbled alley in his memory.

He wasn't even sure he wasn't better off in this prison cell than outside it, although he wished nothing more than to be gone.

There was an open toilet in a corner of the cell. One thundery night, as Faraz tossed restlessly on his bed, he dreamed of diving into it, swimming through the clogged, stinking pipes to break out to the other side and start a new life, to start afresh.

QUIT
Bloomsbury, London: Azeem al Din, Shirin Shaarawi, Dr Khan

AZEEM WAS TALKING to Dr Khan on the telephone.

"I decided to quit my position at the hospital," said Dr Khan.

"Why?"

"A lot of reasons. You know they're investigating... It would be pretty strange if they didn't, I suppose. It's a bad scene. The news-hawks are circling the place like vultures, there'll be an inquiry... and me? Well, I was guilty of irregular conduct all right, moving the Winthrop dame into Rania's room."

"But that saved Rania's life! Without you, she'd be dead!"

"That's correct. But it isn't what concerns the hospital. There are questions of procedure, standards and protocols to be observed. And poor old Mrs Winthrop's relations have let legal eagles and mobsters muscle in on the action. They want to sue the hospital's asses."

"Sue? For what?"

There was a pause before Dr Khan replied.

"Listen, this whole thing is baloney," he said, his voice trembling. "It's lousy... crawling with crazy, jingle-brained angles. Originally, the relatives wanted to sue for negligence. But then they found out the body didn't technically belong to them... or to anyone else, for that matter. So now they've decided to sue the hospital's asses for the psychiatric distress they've been caused."

"That's... terrible."

"It's the law, sunshine." Dr Khan's voice was on edge. "It is not clear if they can win their case. The legal considerations aren't cut and dried, they'll be beating their gums on it for months. However, I thought it would be better to cut my ties to the hospital, to deflect some of the crappy publicity raining down upon them like... like shit from the sky."

"I feel bad about it," said Azeem. "Maybe I shouldn't have pressurized you."

"Oh no, don't be a bunny, Mr al Din, you didn't!" There was suddenly a reckless ring to Dr Khan's words. He sounded younger, careless, full of swagger. "I would have done the same thing, even if you hadn't been there."

"I hope it works out for the best."

"I'm spry, Mr al Din... spry as a raccoon on dope! Hell, I've even been sent some abusive messages to speed me on my way. Threats... threats from the happiness squad, our friends the *baraderi*. Wrong numbers. They said they would return to the hospital, take some steps, teach me not to interfere again in future. Well, I wish them luck with that. Because I'm not getting trampled on... like a daisy. I'm hightailing out of here, Mr al Din."

"How horrible."

"Yeah, well, it's okay, jakeloo, I got no kick. I thought I'd let you know. Don't worry yourself about me. I shall find my way."

"You have done everything right, and nothing wrong," said Azeem.

"Well, I haven't done jack to date," Dr Khan said cheerfully. "I need to get a wiggle on. I'm sick and tired of seeing people who call themselves Muslims... *stuffing* other Muslims, and nobody lifting a finger to help. I think I shall go back home to Kurdistan, go to read and write, and see what I can do there."

"Back to Palookaville, eh?"

Another pause. Then Dr Khan laughed, a pleasant soft baritone laugh.

"My version of Palookaville, Mr al Din."

They said their goodbyes and hung up, promising to stay in touch.

Azeem felt bad, responsible for what had happened. He felt guilty too, knowing Dr Khan's life—if not utterly ruined—had been utterly reconfigured, metamorphosed into something more dangerous and risky, way beyond his control.

And all for saving the life of a girl he didn't know.

Azeem was chopping away, making quite a noise as he worked. His hands looked like they were moving on autopilot. Standing at the kitchen counter, his posture was as random and lethargic as a sleepwalker's, a man slumping out of control.

He suddenly stopped. Stared out the window, his eyes listless, blank.

She knew he wanted to speak, and she knew what it would be about, and she didn't think she wanted to hear it, although she knew she must.

Nothing in today's world is more pathetic and useless than good intentions, thought Shirin. For a while, she'd been watching Azeem struggle to come to terms with the cruel new realities of his job. Hard things had happened, and he'd taken them hard — the attack in the hospital, what had happened to Dr Khan, and now...

He'd tried to open his heart to Shirin.

They were standing in the kitchen preparing a salad.

"Samir... oh boy, Samir's *changed*. You know, these days he sees himself as... as a hero. Sees himself as the man, the man who rips the masks off hypocrites," said Azeem as he skinned an avocado. "He wants to rub western noses into the dreck of their own decadence. *Decadence.* The one area he's got real expertise."

"Don't take it to heart," said Shirin. "*Quit.*"

Shirin was out of patience with this aspect of Azeem's troubles, this elbowing-in of Samir Muhsi. Because she, too, knew more than she wanted to remember of Samir and his playboy ways. She considered Azeem an idiot to have gotten mixed up with that morally depraved vulgarian.

Shirin tore apart a head of lettuce, rinsed it in the colander, and let the cold water spray her warm hands.

She couldn't begin to believe, not for a second, that a lost soul like Samir Muhsi would turn penitent. Her memory heaved with stories of Samir's exploits, stories which were laughable when they weren't actively stomach-turning. Tales of that sort had been a staple of gossip during their time at university. Back then, Samir had thrown away fortunes on the commonest, flashiest whores.

Azeem told her how one morning he'd seen three of them teetering down the stairs in their high-heeled latex boots, wired-looking eyes.

"All tits and lips, puffed up and stuffed... not a turn-on in any shape or form," he explained. "Strange to think that's the kind of thing Samir likes."

Rumors of drug-fuelled orgies on rubber mats were assiduously spread among the undergraduates.

And gambling. Samir ran an account at his bookies, placed thousand pound bets on the outcome of *Big Brother* episodes he didn't even watch.

And drugs. His dealer, a Ferrari-driving pimp of a man, was a personal friend of Samir's.

And Samir Muhsi didn't just *do* all that tacky junk, he flaunted it, paraded it with *nouveau riche* brashness. If you went to the source of those disgusting and graphic myths about him, you'd find it was Samir himself half the time—no-one else could have known it all—who spread the slime of scandal, spread it to all and sundry via the scoffing lips of his scurrilous, upstart pals.

Shirin hated Samir—the mere idea of him—to a degree she didn't understand herself, it made her mind seethe and overflow with random epithets of loathing. He was low down and shifty, a sponge of booze and drugs and sex, a rabid sack of delusions stuffed with appetites he couldn't control, soaking up and swallowing the souls of those who loved him, repaying them by pulling them down to his level, forcing them to join him in his festivals of self-indulgence, tawdry self-abuse, self-immolation.

Remembering it, and letting her knowledge of his moral turpitude swim into her consciousness again, Shirin felt ill. She really wished Azeem would ditch Samir and his gang and return to a proper job.

But this didn't appeal to Azeem. For one thing, he'd convinced himself Samir had repented his errors. It was a curious, unworldly conviction, and somewhere inside, Azeem knew that, but he clung to it all the same. He reckoned Samir's filthy explorations of the wild side must have turned bad on him—festering away in his conscience like bad meat rotting, unseen, behind a cupboard. Samir surely burned with shame, remembering those university antics, it must spur him to remorse... He only harped on about them because of an unreal, horrible—but ultimately wholesome—fascination they held.

Memories of when he'd hit rock bottom.

And as to professional matters, Azeem still thought he could steer Samir away from that brutal martinet-like way of running things. He believed he could get Samir to run the *Islamic Reform* project along gentler pathways, collegiate and civilized, more congenial to Azeem.

The campaign focusing on Rania was coming together nicely.

Wythenshawe & Lyall's creative team had come up with an idea called *Voices.*

It opened with Rania in closeup, her throat wrapped in bandages, saying through a voice box, "They tried to end my life, but my life hasn't ended."

Intercut images of a knife slashing at something fleshly, pulpy.

"They tried to stop my voice, but my voice will not be silenced."

Shot of a bloody gag being bundled together and thrust into the camera, blocking the picture.

"They hid my skin from the sun, but I cannot live in darkness."

Camera pulls back to show Rania sitting in the sun, surrounded by a large group of supporters, who hold hands and lift their voices together to chant,

"Join your voice to ours, and we'll never be silenced."

(The Islamic Reform *logo flashes onto the screen.)*

Azeem put the avocado pit to one side. Sliced his knife through the buttery green flesh, thinking of the commercial, thinking that maybe it could do some good, that his work would lead to something positive coming out of the attack on Rania, help bring on a change of heart.

Shirin was watching him, absent. She cast her mind back to Mamida's warnings about the Beeston Boys—or whatever they were called—and how those warnings had borne fruit, with the attempt to kill Rania in the hospital only being foiled by Azeem's presence, and the alertness of the medical man in Leeds, Dr Khan.

Mamida had been right about that.

Shirin replayed the calls she kept getting from Sheikh Faisal's Office, with their sickmaking, lickspittle expressions of "concern". Not for the first time, she aired her disquiet to Azeem.

She spoke for some time, letting her words wrap up her feelings and her fears without over-thinking things, just letting him know where she stood. He cut up vegetables for the salad as she spoke, silently slicing his knife through peppers and onions, sun-dried tomatoes and coriander.

"They're not worthy of you, Azeem," she said, towards the end. "They do all this... underhand stuff. It's *murky*, Azeem... *You don't know the half of it*, Mamida would say... I mean..."

She took a breath before forcing herself to go on.

"They *pretend* they want to communicate—but there's something dark and shifty about their whole set-up. They're shitty people. They blot out the light..."

She was thinking of a documentary she'd watched—a documentary about something called *Red Tide*, whereby patches of phytoplankton, containing photosynthetic pigments, discolor great surfaces of water, busily poisoning marine life, spreading brevetoxins and toxic aerosols... algal bloom, red tide on a crimson sea... and she was thinking that Samir and Faisal, and all the rest of them, were like that, insidiously creeping into their lives, turning everything more sinister, darker, slimier, shittier.

"It'd be so much better for both of us if we could cut ourselves loose from them and all the crappy baggage they bring with them."

Azeem wouldn't be persuaded. He'd put too much into the project, too many hours, too much of his heart, personally and professionally, he couldn't back out of it now, he refused to contemplate it. Success had become just too graspable and solid in his mind to surrender it to the shimmering appeal of Shirin's reason.

Azeem drizzled dressing onto the salad in the big green bowl, then started to mix it all up.

CONVERGING
Düsseldorf, North Rhine-Westphalia, Germany: Myles Lyall, Udo Rincke, Dr Klinker

MYLES LYALL and Udo Rincke strolled along the river promenade in Düsseldorf, Myles having flown over to settle a few financial details and forge a closer connection with his German partners.

The changing nature of the *Islamic Reform* project still played on his mind. It was a sunny day, with a stiff breeze blowing in from the Rhine, messing up his hair, and occasionally splashing his face with a drizzle of water.

"Samir Muhsi's gotten it into his head to play hardball with perceptions," Myles was explaining. "He's got it into his head to show Islam as a harsh and aggressive faith."

He hunched his broad shoulders against the wind. His voice had a disconsolate tinge.

"For the life of me I can't see why... Advertising doesn't work that way."

"Maybe he thinks honesty is—how do you say it?"

"Honesty is the best policy?"

"Precisely. Honesty is the best policy."

"Well, the honesty of this is moot, but even if it were, honesty can be ruinous to the prospects of perfectly good products," said Myles.

Udo Rincke laughed and Myles was glad—he'd been dreading Udo might turn out very dull and proper, or too coked up to converse satisfyingly. So far, though, Udo seemed on pretty good form.

"And I don't buy the honesty spiel, anyway. Is it really honest to dwell so much on aggression and punishment? Only a tiny minority of Muslims see Islam the way Samir does!"

Myles watched a cloud of gulls come flurrying down. The birds settled down awkwardly before scattering along the gray concrete wall, emitting great raucous craws.

"There is such a thing as a Muslim Mainstream," said Myles. "Isn't there?"

"Our research has discovered there is... The broad middle. The median. Mediocre. It's not so different from normal consumers."

"It must be full of people who'd be *scandalized* by Samir's assumptions?"

"Maybe, maybe... but they don't count. Remember, Samir's paying the budget."

"It's still crazy..."

"We have a saying in German: *He who pays, decides.*"

"We have a similar one: *He who pays the piper calls the tune.*"

"It is the same. Samir is the piper. He pays, he decides. We do the dancing. If he wants... well, strong imagery, he can have it."

"It's unsettling."

"You're seeing ghosts, Myles. Really. Just remember this is Samir's campaign now. You must only answer to him. Leave your conscience out of it."

"Well, at least *Voices* could turn into a good campaign."

"If *Voices* goes on the air. I get the feeling they're not going to run it."

"You never can tell."

"I think they are more interested in setting up a network to facilitate other things."

"Well, that's doubly unsettling," said Myles Lyall. "It could even be *dangerous*, if it turns out Samir's group is involved in terrorism."

"I don't think that'll be a worry," said Udo. "Terrorism... it's... it's a shadowy concept. Utopian. Escapist. One man's terrorist is another man's freedom fighter. And a touch of terror always adds glamor to a cause."

Udo was looking up at the telecoms tower a few hundred yards ahead. A single white cloud passed in front of the sun above them, momentarily altering the light.

"In Germany there is a great sympathy with the enemies of globalization," said Udo, as they continued along the river walk. "Most of the Baader-Meinhoff murderers are free today, even the ones who don't regret killing innocent people, and they still want to overthrow capitalism. In France, if you read our reports, it's the same, maybe even more. The peasants are always revolting at McDonald's. They drive there in their tractors, they dump down their piles of shit. I wouldn't worry myself about terrorism, Myles, it's *salonfähig* these days. Fit for the salon."

"Perhaps you're right," said Myles, far from convinced.

A sturdy blonde girl on rollerblades whizzed by. Her thick brown legs swayed from left to right, strong thighs gliding, in mesmeric, rhythmic repetition.

"What is truly tricky for us right now," said Udo, "is this question of honor killings."

Myles Lyall pricked up his ears. "Oh man, that's so sick, brothers and fathers killing their own sisters and daughters..."

"Yes, it's a growing trend—the *last cry*—all the rage here at the moment. When a girl wants to marry a non-Muslim, or if she's just looking too westernized, then she's marked out as *ridda*, turning back, fit to be killed. This can lead to her being eliminated."

"That's why our *Voices* campaign is right on the money. "

"No. It's why our *Voices* will never go on the air. "

Just then, out on the promenade, Myles didn't want to tell Udo about it, but it so happened he had been discussing this very thing with an old university friend that previous Sunday afternoon.

The subject had been preoccupying Myles ever since the meeting in which Samir Muhsi had told him to *raise his game*. Myles—often overflowing with anxiety, and occasionally subject to lacerating, self-abnegating depressions—thought Samir might have a point, that the whole caboodle of *negative perceptions* he and Azeem had identified was no more than western prejudice and aggression.

Janice Primrose, the friend he'd thrashed the matter out with, was a pale, scatty rebel. Tall and youthful, impulsive, abrasive in her manner, in everything she did. She threw herself into torrid affairs with all sexes, and was cheerfully open about them. Myles, monogamous himself, loved getting the lowdown on her latest sexual conquests.

"I've become a Vagina Warrior," Janice recently told him. What it meant Myles couldn't have told you, even after her explanation—a flurry of right-on jargon—beyond the fact that she flaunted, as she put it, her *cunnilicious appetites,* and put herself about in clever feminist circles.

Myles had known Janice since they were kids.

"Men can be Vagina Warriors too," she told him. "Not that you'd be cut out for it. Rugger buggers don't count. You know what they say — *You can be a man or a human being, but you can't be both…*"

She was laughing at him now. She abused him, and his opinions, in a way he secretly enjoyed, not out of any sense of masochism but, somewhere in his mind, her upfront brash openness turned him on, and her long lean limbs, her bee-stung lips, somewhere in his loins. That Janice was aware, now and then, of her absurdities—she happily smiled at them—more than made up for her rudely acid tongue.

So last Sunday Janice and he met up and sitting after lunch in his garden fell to discussing yet another real-life horror story in the news—the case where a twenty year old Muslim girl's body was found buried ten feet under a patio, strangled and stuffed in a suitcase. She'd been disposed of at the instigation of her own father—who *disapproved of her lifestyle.* The newspapers listed a number of girls killed or gone missing in similar contexts of familial disapproval. It upset Myles—himself the proud father of a daughter, and mindboggled by such evil—but Janice hadn't shown especial surprise or sympathy.

"Yeah sure that's oppression, Myles," she'd conceded flatly. "But is it the most widespread sort of oppression women suffer? How much of it goes on? How many does it really touch? You're talking dozens, maybe hundreds of girls in the UK... In numbers, that's peanuts. I'd say the cosmetics industry is doing a *lot* more harm to a *lot* more women, Myles, they're just doing it more *subtly.*"

Janice grudged him a wan smile.

"And they're doing it with the help of lowlife scumbags like you in advertising."

Myles smiled at the memory of Janice's absurd opinions and her sweet, truculent face. He wished she were there with him now.

"Is there a lot of honor killing going on in Germany?" Myles asked Udo.

"No, I don't think there's so much honor killing. Maybe a few hundred cases. But that's enough to give cause to bad publicity. It's something we need to take into reckoning."

"What do the German authorities think about it? Are they doing anything to help these women?"

"The German authorities are not big thinkers, Myles. They're like authorities anywhere, their chief commandment is to protect their authority... They always prefer to avoid difficult areas of cultural controversy... nobody can make a good career there... Some of our judges think it's classy to let Muslim men beat their wives. There was a judgment a couple of months ago. It gave a female judge... She wouldn't let a Moroccan wife a quick divorce, even though her husband beat her, threatened killing her. That was *normal* in their *culture*, the judge ruled. She cited even the Qur'an to justify it, this German judge, taking her judgment from what it says in the Qur'an! With such judges the psychopaths aren't having anything to fear. With honor killings it is the same. Our judges wish it could be a matter for Muslims to deal with among themselves."

"I'm beginning to suspect Samir will ask us to communicate honor killings as a measure of the strength of Muslim faith."

Myles spoke ironically, but Udo looked thoughtful.

"Would he? Well, maybe there's something in that, now you say it. It's sounding counter-intuitive at first, but when you are thinking about it, you are seeing its attractive side. We must be discussing this with Dr Klinker over lunch."

Myles and Udo wandered on among the gulls, and the gusts of wind, and the inline-skating girls, toward the restaurant. For those few minutes, they were silent. They walked on through the passing scene like *boulevardiers* without comment, without a care. Even so, Myles was beginning to think something *was* wrong, not just with the project, but in the wider world which allowed these things...

Dr Klinker was waiting for them in a trendy fish restaurant in the Düsseldorf docklands.

He looked decidedly chipper. Myles watched him where he sat ruminatively clutching a cup of herbal tea, his swept-back locks making him look even more Byronic than usual.

"It is good to welcome you on my green home grass, Myles," Klinker said in English when he felt he was being watched. "Especially now... I have been playing away from home a little."

After a spate of introductory badinage Myles, who spoke reasonable German—well enough to be made impatient by Udo and Norbert's incessant string of solecisms whenever they ventured into colloquial English—began to express his unease about the turn things were taking in that language.

"*Es gibt Sachen, wo ich das Gefühl habe, wir verlieren die Kontrolle,*" he began.

Klinker raised a hand and smiled.

"Let us not concern ourselves with matters we cannot control," he said. "Our job is to do as our Client wishes, no more, no less."

Udo had gone to the restaurant's bathroom facilities. A quick in and out for a line of coke. He stood in a cubicle, cutting a fat line on the cold porcelain surface, breathing the bland deodorized air, permeated with a whiff of urinal cakes.

He came out again, ambling deliberately back, feeling afloat and self-propelled, like a bathyscaphe in the deep—swimming past the diners—the groupers, the plankton and the krill—like an alien, spinning randomly through the seventh supernova behind the sun—feeling infused with the simple principles of science, he observed these paltry people, like bacilli on a petri dish, bathing them in his microscopic gaze.

Returning to the table, he was amazed to hear his old partner sounding so reasonable and service-oriented a note. He sat back and wondered, savoring the moment, reassessing Dr Klinker with a fresh appreciation of his qualities.

The coke may have had some influence on his sudden enthusiasm for Klinker. Udo didn't know. Didn't care. Just enjoying himself in the feeling while he could.

Throughout his and Klinker's long association, the doctor had been irksome in one respect. He showed nothing but contempt for the aspirations of mere clients.

Obstacles in the way of intellectually-satisfying work and creative excellence, Klinker liked to say.

It made things hellishly hard for Udo—who felt it best to do what clients wanted without question. Something, now, appeared to be rearranging Klinker's priorities.

"My worry is that we shall be associated with terrorism," Myles Lyall was saying, interrupting Udo's thoughts with his tedious drone, his obsessional fixation on the non-existent terrorist threat.

"Your worry is irrelevant, Myles," Klinker replied. "Our Muslim brothers have a very noble, very pure commitment to the defence of their lifestyle. To worry about that is patronizing. It won't change it a single iota. The very least we can do is respect it."

"Respect murder?" Myles began.

Klinker again interrupted, raising his hand, saying with some gravitas, "You must never judge other cultures with the standards of ours. A very insightful man, Franz Werfel, once said, *Nicht der Mörder, der Ermordete ist schuldig.* Not the murderer, but the murderee is guilty. It may be worth reflecting on that."

"Isn't that a sort of… moral blankness… being too clever by half?"

"A prime task of our business is to push things as far out, as extreme as they can possibly be pushed. You have to break the eggs to make the omelettes. The great creatives have always agreed with that, Myles!"

"What about the law?"

"The law!" snorted Klinker, as if no more needed to be said.

And now to Myles, even in his own ears as he spoke, his next remark sounded like the blatherings of a wimp.

"We're undermining our own deepest convictions."

Klinker reeled back in his chair. He grunted. He let out a snort, like a goat whose tether has been tweaked once too often.

"*Convictions*? I spit on convictions!" said Dr Klinker. "Convictions are hypocrisy cloaked in self-delusion." He stressed the word *Selbsttäuschung*, with a hiss of sibilant spittle, his leery eyes fixed on Myles Lyall.

Udo was nodding with fervor.

"The important thing," Udo now said, "is that profit can be combined with cutting-edge communications. *This* is what Rincke and Klinker are all about."

He picked at his mixed salad. He stuck a leaf of lettuce into his mouth, chewed at it vaguely. He took a sip of mineral water.

Myles was taken aback, at first, to hear his concerns so blithely dismissed. Clearly none of his partners, either side of the Channel, saw the slightest drawback to working for an organization devoted to killing people like them, to wiping out their way of life.

Myles looked round the restaurant. Its tall walls were battleship gray. Maritime paraphernalia hanging around—nets, sea-shells, large mounted swordfish, buoys. Fellow diners, soberly darksuited business people, emitted mellow hums and haws, purring out their discreet conversations like a congregation of sleek, satisfied cats.

It was he who was wrong, and his colleagues were right on the money.

Maybe Samir Muhsi's Islamist poster-boy posturing was no more than a common species of heady anti-western invective, with only the vaguest connection to reality. Samir was certainly a world class poser, Myles thought. He enjoyed *shocking* them so. Maybe it was best to look beyond all the rhetoric, see the profits beckoning there.

As Myles considered this, he began to feel that, if he were the only one to have qualms, his qualms might be baseless—all smoke and no Semtex.

He was disoriented by it all.

They continued to eat their lunch. Conversation moved on.

"Did I mention I have been playing away from home recently?" Dr Klinker wanted to be reminded.

"You did indeed, Norbert. What exactly do you mean by it, if I may ask?"

"You may, Myles, you may," sang Dr Klinker in a merry sing-song voice. "Listen! I have always found that travel broadens the mind."

His eyes faraway, he pondered this insight.

"I have discovered that it expands other areas of life, too. Bodily... as well as spiritually."

Klinker looked down, now, and focused his whole attention on tackling a bothersome lobster claw with his pincer. Myles gave Udo a quizzical look, signalling *what on earth is he going on about*? But Udo, abstracted, mind on another plane, perhaps not wishing to supply any further details, merely smiled back, vacuously, across the table.

Nothing. Nobody. Nowhere.

It's those drugs again, thought Myles. *Maybe I'd feel better if I joined him in a line...*

"I have been converging with a delightful creature," Klinker confided. "Our souls have grappled and intertwined. Our bodies have mingled vital fluids. I can honestly say that I am a new man."

"Tell me more," said Myles with a weak smile, "about this happy transformation."

"That would be inapposite just now. Suffice it to say that it's something with which our friend Wythenshawe, our fine English lord, would do well to acquaint himself. He should pass up on his wife. *Sie geht fremd*—she's going strange."

Klinker gave a bark of laughter. He was wearing the lazy-eyed, dribbling look of a demented goat, or one of the ancestors whose proclivities he had so unerringly diagnosed on seeing them displayed in all their glory in the hall of Laetitia's house. He wore the blurred and random look of a man who might, at any second, jump from his chair, cartwheel between the tables, and grab the nearest bartender to perform the tango. His eyes were darting around the room as if in search of victims.

Now he let his mouth fall open to cram in a heaped forkful of crustacean. He wiped his lips with the back of his hand as his jaws began to grind and crush the food. Looking at Myles Lyall with a benign, slightly insane expression, he continued to laugh as he masticated the decapod shell and all.

"Don't worry, dear Myles," he spluttered. "I shall make everything clear soon enough. But first, let me finish eating."

Later, when Myles has left to fly back to London, Dr Klinker and Udo Rincke sit in their office contemplating the sunset over the river. Dr Klinker is in a fine state of excitement.

"This will have serious repercussions," he says. "Wythenshawe could besmirch the good name of Rincke and Klinker. He'll regret this to his dying day, if I have anything to do with it!"

Udo sniffs and says, "I took him out to the clubs the first time he was here. I must admit I thought he was the criminal type that night. Plied him with coke. Got through at least a gramme. A gramme! A crate of champagne. A crate! Tequila. Cocktails. Introduced him to some very expensive call girls. His appetites for all three were disgusting. And prodigious. Insatiable. His priapism is a close-to-certifiable mania."

"I saw the expenses claim, Herr Rincke."

"I think he's formed a more permanent liaison with one of the whores. A Russian girl. Svetlana, I think she's called. He told me about her, it was very touching. He subsidizes a place for her, a home away from home here in Düsseldorf."

"That is good to know."

"The man's an animal. Insatiable. Depraved. Base."

"I, too, have confirmed my basest suspicions."

Klinker is speaking in a smug tone.

"Who? When? Why?"

"I went to his wife, the Lady Laetitia, to see if she could help me."

He smiles.

"What do you suppose occurred, Herr Rincke?"

"I have no idea, Herr Dr Klinker."

"I manipulated her mammaries. She came... she came up trumps."

Klinker now regales Udo with a blow-by-blow account of Laetitia's "coming up trumps". Rincke feels no shock or disgust—a little surprise, perhaps, at Mrs Wythenshawe's supine compliance.

Dr Klinker makes an absolute meal of Laetitia's abandon, her profligate, horny enthusiasm. He omits to tell Udo about the swings and roundabouts—the later limits of Laetitia's consensuality, her moodiness—her unaccountable rejection of him, perverse fruit of female hysteria. So, hypnotized by the Doctor's deranged vim, Udo gets the sluttiest possible impression of Laetitia, an impression whose veracity he isn't especially inclined to query. Those couplings with Lady Laetitia Wythenshawe have certainly put a spring into the Doctor's step, that much is clear to Udo. The lady has sharpened his partner's sense of potency.

"I gave Mrs Wythenshawe the seeing-to of her life... *Der Fick ihres Lebens*," says Klinker, his little twitchy hands groping the air like two manic octopuses on heat. "I then inspected Wythenshawe's secret files, while Lady Laetitia lay back, exhausted, on the *chaise longue,* where our love was so memorably consummated. Some of these files," Klinker recounts with relish, "were kept locked in a chest... under the cuckold Wythenshawe's marital bed."

In them, Klinker says, he'd found the passwords to Wythenshawe's private email addresses, *noms de plume* which the Englishman used for his murkier dealings.

"I have read and photographed enough incriminating words to be quite sure Wythenshawe's cooking the books. Kickbacks and sweeteners, inflated media figures, it's easy to read between the lines...

"He's skimming off a cool half a million in sterling, by my reckoning," Klinker says.

"Du meine Güte," says Udo.

"Just in this financial year."

"Unthinkable. Insane. Degrading." Udo takes a deep sniff. "What shall we do? Go to the police?"

"No, no, no. That is a decidedly ill-conceived plan. It'll get us splashed all over the trade press. Destroy our reputations. The client will depart, *auf Wiedersehen.* No, far the best thing is to approach this criminal Lord Wythenshawe direct. Confront him. He'll have to cut us in on the deal."

"This is not the outcome we hoped for when we set off on this merger," Udo Rincke remarks. "Disappointing. Dysfunctional. Lamentable."

"Wythenshawe always seemed every inch the British lord of legend, all stiff upper lip, ladies first," says Dr Klinker. "For the ordinary man, there was no way of telling he'd turn out to be a con man. Thank God I followed up my suspicions! I have begun to have suspicions about Myles Lyall, too. At first, I suspected a flaccid erectile syndrome, but then I diagnosed its psychological source. Lyall is psychiatrically *kaputt. Er ist am Ende.*"

"Quite probable. They are playing a dirty game together."

"Lyall is weak. His eyes have a weakness in them when you look at him."

"Is that a fact?"

"His lip trembles when he's challenged."

"Really?"

"His personality is cracked. He is a boot-licker. He has submissive, self-abasing inclinations. He projected his filthy fantasies around my person."

"Really?"

"He wanted me to cover his hand with mine."

"How opportunistic. And rotten. Decayed."

"These Englishmen are often flawed like this, they suffer from pathological compulsions caused by loss of Empire. They're charming and normal enough on the surface, when you first get to know them..."

"But then they turn," says Dr Klinker. "They're diseased on the inside. They're dangerous liars, lunatics who have lost touch with reality."

Udo nods thoughtfully.

"Yes," he observes. "But that insanity, that barking English intemperance, is our big opportunity. We can turn them into *betrogene Betrüger* — get them to pay us back in their own coin!"

CULTURE
Holborn, London: Dave Page, Rupert Wythenshawe

LAETITIA WYTHENSHAWE'S last lover, Dave Page, has given the matter of his revenge on her some serious thought. Not that he's normally the kind of guy for analysis. He's never claimed to be a big thinker. He loves riding, and he likes horses well enough, but he doesn't bet, so the study of form, and the infinite mysteries of the turf, are closed books to him. But once in a way a matter crops up important enough to warrant giving the Page brain a thorough canter round the paddock. Being dumped by Lady Laetitia Wythenshawe, just at the moment he thought she and him were shaping up to be a proper item, with thoughts of maybe even getting hitched, is one of them.

He's decided the best first step would be to confront her husband, confront him with the bare facts of the betrayal... spring it on him, then carefully watch his reaction, eke out any weak spots.

Dave has found that approach profitable before. It's netted him useful money. And in all sorts of situations. Husbands are a funny lot. No two alike. And husbands married to two-timing sluts are often wimps, soft touches, limp dicks, geldings. Last year, a couple of husbands ended up paying him to *go away*, to leave their errant wives alone and stop the shagging. But it takes all sorts. An even more submissive husband, for his part, paid Dave to *continue* seeing his wife.

All one to Dave. He'd have let the man watch, if the money was right.

At the other extreme, there'd been another one who didn't pay Dave a penny. *Outraged*, he was. What a joke. If he'd been man enough to give his wife competent sexual stimulation one of this hassle would have cropped up in the first place. Outraged! But he threw his wife out on her ear instead.

You never could tell in this game.

But, *even stevens*, any reprisal along such lines would be a *result*. The first thing to do was check out this Wythenshawe for himself, then figure out the painfullest, most eye-watering way to put the squeeze on.

One evening at half seven they meet in a pub in Holborn. Dave starts his spiel pronto, no time to lose.

"It was... *abuse*... I was *abused*, Mr Wythenshawe," says Dave, gasping as he sits with his pint by the bar—his mouth down, his face sad, heartsore, as if wounded—next to the betrayed husband. "I was *molested*. Used for her pleasure, then tossed away like an unwanted toy. I mean. If that's not abuse, what is? It's been doing my head in, I can tell you...

"I've... I've got to get it off my chest," he says. "I've got to... let out my pain. You see, I had no idea at first your missus was even married. I hadn't seen or heard of her for ages, after I left the estate... Laetitia... made herself out to be an orphan."

He pauses, looks stricken, gulps.

"She said she'd become a single mom. And that she lost the baby."

Dave's face goes red. He now chokes abruptly then lets out a harsh retching sound. He retches long and loud, sending phlegm shooting either side of him. Worried, Wythenshawe slaps him on the back, as if congratulating him.

Dave's choking and belching—it appears to have been an overambitious gulp of beer. A final, extended retch clears his throat.

"She appealed... to my nurturing nature," says Dave in a choked voice, wiping at the wetness on his chin. "Then, when I found out the truth, it was too late... Too late! I was shattered. There was no way I could ever tear myself away from her, Mr Wythenshawe... I was in love."

Dave Page gazes soulfully at an ornate mirror on the wall of the Edwardian gin-palace they're sitting in. He can see how redfaced and tearful he looks. He feels sorry for himself. It's crowded in there. Wythenshawe buys them another round of drinks.

"I tried my hardest, Mr Wythenshawe, I tried everything to free myself from her clutches. The guilt was unbearable. I felt I was defiling your marital bed—it felt worse with every stain I left. But whenever I tried to leave for good, she'd bribe me to stay."

"She *bribed* you?"

"She bribed me, Mr Wythenshawe."

"How?"

"She paid me... to—to—*make love*—to her. And the money made the guilt even worse."

Dave and Wythenshawe look each other in the eye. Neither man is particularly impressed by the other, but Dave gives his attempt to wound Wythenshawe his very best effort.

"It was a living hell, Mr Wythenshawe," Dave says.

He stuffs a fistful of pork rinds into his mouth. Chews with relish. His stuffed face drooping with feigned regret, he checks his profile in the mirror he can't keep his eyes away from, to verify the credibility of his performance.

He's looking good, and he's on a roll.

"My guilt felt worse, Mr Wythenshawe, for knowing she was using your money to keep me," Dave complains. "She was dipping into your account twice a week... to *betray* you, Mr Wythenshawe."

Dave's eye holds Wythenshawe's in its fishy gaze. Wythenshawe takes a breath.

"Was she paying you well, Dave, to fuck her—a little extra, perhaps, to assuage the horrific guilt?"

Wythenshawe speaks with a frank, man-to-man smile.

Dave can't fathom the geezer's calm. Dave's spellbound by Wythenshawe, his polished vowels, that unhurried manner, the bland tranquil smile. An almost convincing wannabe gent. But... totally without pride. He just doesn't give a monkey's. Weird one, the calm of a compliant... what's the word? Cockhold? Yeah, *cockhold*...

But a better word would be tosser. Fucking tosser. Fucking sissy tosser who let his wife turn herself into a fucking fuckdoll.

Not that Dave's complaining. He's enjoyed himself with Lady Laetitia. Maybe not as much as she enjoyed him, but that was her problem, she was always gagging for it, she was insatiable, couldn't keep her hands off of him. Girls get like that when he's around.

Even so, this whole bloody performance is getting Dave nowhere. Stung, he asks, "Don't you feel nothing for her then, Mr Wythenshawe?"

"Oh, I do, I do, dear boy."

"You're not showing it. You're not showing nothing. Not even the smallest sign of jealousy. It's like you've got no feelings left inside of you!"

"It's bad form to show jealousy of one's spouse," Wythenshawe vouchsafes.

"But she's *sponging* off you and you're not getting anything back!"

"Good God no, you've got that arse over tit, my dear boy. She's the rich one in this marriage. I don't pay her a penny for her fancy men."

While Dave digests this, Wythenshawe gets in another round.

"I've never been fussed about Laetitia's extracurricular bonking activities," Wythenshawe says, as the drinks are placed on the bar by the landlord—a vast, parrot-mouthed, red-cheeked figure with a walrus mustache—like a revenant from those Edwardian days of yore. "She doesn't get fussed up about mine. I asked someone to investigate her affairs for me, once. Shouldn't have. They ended up trying to blackmail me too."

"A detective agency?"

Dave figures that if he can't get Wythenshawe to pay him, he might as well pump him for information.

"No, some Scottish sleazeball called Sholto McClintlock."

"Sholto? Sholto McClintlock? I'll bet he didn't thank his mom and dad for a naff name like that!"

Dave shakes his head in wonderment and pity. Wythenshawe smiles.

"There was a touch of bitterness about McClintlock, now you mention it. Anyway, he came back with a whole list of men Laetitia was allegedly rogering. Threatened to go to the papers. I told him I didn't care a fig about the men. And that I didn't have the money in the marriage. He should go public with it if he wanted. Never heard from him again."

"I see," says Dave, stunned. "So you're a kept man, just like I was, Mr Wythenshawe."

"Well, not quite. Do call me Rupert, by the way."

Wythenshawe worries that they might be overheard and gossip spread. All this *Mr Wythenshawing* makes him nervous even if the chances of someone there knowing him are remote.

Dave laughs.

"She paid me to stay, *Rupert*, and fuck her tiny little brains out... but she'd have to pay you to get *rid* of you!"

Dave's laughing, draining his mug to the dregs.

"There's nothing I could teach you, Rupie!"

"It isn't quite as black and white as all that, Dave," Wythenshawe says. "Laetitia has been very helpful to my business over the years."

Wythenshawe's eyes focus on the middle distance, contemplating past spousal favors done.

"I'd be the first to admit it... No point denying a thing like that. But I'm successful enough myself these days, if not remotely as rich as you seem to think I am, or as Laetitia actually is. I'm well enough off not to have to be subsidized by her. As to my feelings, well, suffice to say I'm properly grateful for what she's done."

"I've known the Twinningtons since I was a nipper," says Dave. "Her old man was quite good to me back in the day. But I always thought they was poor. That's what old Twinnington always said, *we're poor as church mice, my dear boy, have been these past two hundred years...*"

"That's often the way with these old families. Terrible liars... especially when it comes to money."

"Brought you in some juicy business contacts, has she?" says Dave with brazen cockiness accepting another drink.

"Our newest client came in via a family connection of Laetitia's, as it happens."

"Anyone I'd know?"

"*Islamic Reform.*"

"Islamic Reform? What, Muslims and things? Towelheads? You live and learn. I'd never had Laetitia down as a towelhead-fancier."

"She isn't, as far as I know. Although there's a mystic Muslim cousin in her family somewhere."

Dave takes this in with a frown. It jolts him off topic. "What, one of the Twinningtons…? Never heard that one before. Doesn't really go together, does it? Those Muslims, they're not exactly liberated, are they, they're not sexually liberated, like those Twinningtons... It's more like Stone Age values they've got. They're not even allowed a pint, for Chrissake, let alone go round chasing skirt."

"Now, now, Dave. It doesn't do to mock. It's an ancient civilization, you know. They have a fascinating culture."

"The only culture they've got is growing between their toes."

The two men have a laugh and another round before going their separate ways.

A LOOSE LADY

Edgware Road, London: Ghazan Khattak, Samir Muhsi

GHAZAN KHATTAK was in his office off Edgware Road. He stared out at the work stations, his eyes empty, his eyelids heavy and slow. He was brooding about his series of recent failures.

He'd never in his life before had a run of setbacks so long, so unwarranted, so unfair. What was he doing wrong to be singled out with ill luck in this way?

Bad luck can be found in houses, women and horses.

Then again, there was no such thing as a bad omen. It was wrong to read too much into mere accidents and hapless circumstance. Idolatry, it was, and much better to respond to setbacks with patience.

So difficult to stick to, though.

There is no avenging spirit, and the most truthful of omens is the good omen.

The Evil Eye is a reality.

He decided to stop overthinking about the ultimate cause, which he could never hope to know, and focus on what had actually happened instead.

The West End car bomb had been a disaster. His runner, Abu Jaffar, a man he'd trusted, had done everything possible to make matters worse, started shooting like a trigger-happy psychopath.

Ghazan sat back in his chair, sighed, and looked down at his hands. He had come close to losing his grip that morning. He'd been in radio contact with Abu Jaffar until the bomb went off. He'd ordered him to go to Azeem's communications agency, just down the road, to stir things up, create a scene there, try and cause an incident, something to make those admen sit up... reconsider what they were doing, getting themselves mixed up in matters which were none of their business, sensitive things, dangerous things—things important to men of faith whose sincerity they would never, ever understand.

Ghazan was sure none of those agency people had ever thought anything through. It wasn't in their nature to think deeply. Like children, they only ever got excited about glossy surfaces—image, gossip, PR flim-flam, throwaway stuff. They were full of sickness, those people, and they thought only about the symptoms of things.

They did not fear God in their brothers' business. They were addicted to the business of speaking and spreading idle slanders.

Rubbing their noses into reality might make them reconsider what they were doing, bloody their stuck-up noses, make them recoil from the stench and gore of the gutter. Yes, that would be a healthful corrective. It would stop their tongues.

Man's evil is from the tongue, he remembered. *The faith of man is not straightened until his heart is straightened, and his heart is not straightened until his tongue is straightened.*

He remembered an old Arab saying he'd picked up in Afghanistan:

Your tongue is your horse. If you preserve it, it will preserve you.

Azeem al Din had probably only ever told them about the non-controversial aspects of *Islamic Reform*, the kiddy stuff about building bridges and holding hands and breaking down borders. All that useless crappy claptrap. Empty words without faith, words without seriousness, echoing emptily in the ear of God.

And at the same time, Ghazan had calculated, a controlled incident, with a police-hold-off, a siege with hostages and a certain amount of bloodshed, right in the heart of London, in the flashiest part of the West End, would prove fascinating to the media and the chattering classes and anyone in fact who ever watched the news, and make them all see how powerful an organization was growing among them, and not just plotting, but performing acts to dazzle and amaze the world.

Make them think. Make them show some respect. Make then change their behavior, be wary of dissing the brothers in future.

Without any serious risk to himself (he was sure Abu Jaffar would have gotten himself silenced before getting the chance to speak) Ghazan would have orchestrated a worthwhile outrage, with plenty of media coverage.

But instead, of course, none of that came to pass.

Soon after getting into the agency, Abu Jaffar must have ripped off his microphone, he must have gone running back outside again, running out with his hostage, trying to get away.

Instead of that, he had run into the arms of death.

A disaster.

But all told, a lucky escape. Ghazan realized it now. Abu Jaffar, even though he was only a runner, and didn't know much, could have given the cops some extremely dangerous live leads once they'd got him on the waterboards. Good that evidence had been destroyed. If Abu Jaffar had been taken alive, Ghazan would likely have been forced to follow Faraz and all the others to Pakistan—something he knew would happen to him sooner or later, if he lived, but he was hoping for another few years' active service in the UK. He knew he could serve the *Ummah* best here.

All in all, Abu Jaffar getting himself shot had been the best outcome to a bad business.

But of course that wasn't all.

The attack on the charismatic media-rabbi in London had also come to nothing—the rabbi too fleet of foot, the lads too slow off the mark. Were they less fit than they looked? Or did they lack the killer instinct? It was beyond Ghazan, what had happened there.

And now that bagel-guzzling rabbi knew the *baraderi* were after him, he was behaving in a much more circumspect way. He was no longer flaunting himself in public, the way he'd done before, like some kind of *hebe* Yiddish superstar. So something had been achieved, if not precisely the execution Ghazan had hoped for. As a result of the setback, Ghazan was now looking to find a suitable new rabbi to chastise—or what might be better, a fresh opportunity to chastise the same rabbi.

To add insult to injury, the attack on the filthy *qaum Lut* shirtlifters' bar in Soho had likewise fizzled out. The young lad he'd sent had panicked, and fled, before setting off his bomb. The sexual degenerates had escaped scot-free, unaware their perversions had even been targeted for reprimand.

Ghazan knew he'd need to give that lad some extra attention, to bring him back on track.

Finally, even the simplest job, finishing off Rania Zandi in the hospital, had been botched. The lads in charge had been disturbed and had to make a run for it. Rania herself appeared to have been spirited away from Leeds. Ghazan was still trying to establish where she was.

All in all, the past few weeks had brought Ghazan no satisfaction. He'd lost his winning streak—all his painstaking efforts, in the cause of jihad, were just producing duds, letting deviants off the hook, his campaign going nowhere fast. It was a test of his strength, he knew it.

He would not fail, would not be weak-hearted. He would strive and struggle in Allah's cause.

The telephone rang. It was Samir Muhsi. Ghazan shook his head. This did not bode well.

"What's up, man?"

Samir was silent for a long while before answering.

"I need a favor, Ghazan."

"Not another one."

"Well, it's not exactly a favor, it's an opportunity... a *project* basically, with a couple of dimensions you might find intriguing."

Ghazan could hear Samir taking a long breath, turning the subject over in his mind. He knew that was Samir's way, to think of all things as though he were in the souk, preparing his pitch like a merchant, and seeing his request as a jewel, calculating which angle he should cast it, whatever would be most likely to catch Ghazan's eye and close the sale in Samir's favor. Ghazan well knew how Samir's mind worked. He was a typical Jeddah merchant, when you got to the bottom of it, nothing more than a salesman, the son and grandson of salesmen, the spirit of money-grubbing mercantilism infecting every gene in his body.

"There's another instance of immodesty," Samir was saying, "another loose lady in the case... This is one immoral little floozy, Ghazan... virtually a prostitute. But... very, *very* high profile. One interesting dimension is that she's married to one of those admen Azeem is working with. It's actually the husband's idea, what I'm calling about, he wants her chastised. She needs to pay, Ghazan... it's time for some retribution."

Samir began to explain about Wythenshawe's problems with his wife, Lady Laetitia—her betrayal of all marital rights, her standing as a pillar of society, her subversion of the very idea of female subservience.

"Remember what the Prophet said, that the world is like a ship, and mankind its passengers. If anyone tries to damage the ship, they must be stopped. Now, Ghazan, if you imagine being on the ship here, sailing through the rancid oceans of western decadence, this woman, this *Lady*, she's like the rotting bowsprit of that ship, a symbol of sexual immorality in the flesh..."

Ghazan had to stop himself cutting Samir off—it felt all wrong, laughable, really, to be lectured like this by a mangy dog like Samir—but he wanted to hear where it was leading.

"Just imagine the impact it'd have, if you could hack that bowsprit off the ship! Remember the hadith, Ghazan: *Whoever amongst you sees an evil should change it with his hand.*"

At first, as Samir rattled on in this way, talking about chastising the woman, Ghazan felt only mildly intrigued. He picked up how Samir was trying to speak to him using his own kind of language... He felt good about his acuity at picking that up, but also, despite himself, flattered. Samir's normal language was different. When trying to be serious, not in full-on Jeddah merchant-salesman mode, he usually sounded more like a social worker. Today, though, Ghazan could see he was showing respect. But Ghazan couldn't see the point of beating up some woman in the middle of nowhere, a woman who wasn't even a Muslim—hadn't even lain hands on one.

And so he thought he'd fob Samir off.

"I'll think about it, man."

But then, as Samir droned on, in his would-be cunning way, about crusader arrogance, inappropriate and immodest nonconformist conduct, red flags to decency and so forth, Ghazan contemplated his empty appointments book, and reconsidered.

Samir said this Lady Laetitia was morally off the rails. That she did what she did very much by her own choice. Her shameless whoring, even Ghazan knew, was now and again portrayed in glamorous magazines like *Tatler*, a standing rebuke to modesty and good example. She was one of those women who flaunt themselves shamelessly, oblivious to the very existence of such a thing as shame. There was surely merit in showing a woman like that her *boundaries*, the *limits of acceptable behavior*. If her way of life was offensive to purity, if it was being held up as something the naïve should emulate, it would surely be worthwhile to show that such degeneracy was no longer acceptable, in a society no longer ruled solely by decadence and self-indulgence.

Ghazan pondered some more. The other advantage, he saw, was that the harlot lived in the middle of the country. That made her a sitting duck as a target. The lads could go for her at night. She couldn't make a getaway—where'd she run to?—and was unlikely to put up much of a fight. The lads would be sure of getting their hands on her, and giving her the stiff reprimands she needed.

All in all, failure would be difficult.

A final attraction—what with her being a *Lady* and so forth, as Samir had repeatedly emphasized, *a proper aristocratic Lady*—was that there was juicy publicity in it. Aristocrats still meant headlines in England.

Ghazan began to warm to the idea. He interrupted Samir's flow and informed him that maybe there was more to this Lady Wythenshawe than met the eye...

DISTANT COUSINS
Twinnington: Azeem al Din, Laetitia Wythenshawe

"ARE YOU MY SECOND cousin once removed, or my third cousin twice removed?" says Laetitia.

"How should I know?"

"I used to be able to work it out... we share a great-grandfather, don't we?"

"I thought your grandfather was my great-grandfather."

Laetitia laughs.

"Whatever. We both descend from Sir Eustace de Twyningtone, that's for sure."

"The one in the parish church?"

"The crazy crusader, yes."

Laetitia and Azeem are sitting outside. The grand old terrace, with its thick slabbed marble flagstones, catches the sunlight and it's a hot, humid day—both of them sitting glowing in shirtsleeves are getting progressively moister, merely from breathing, from moving their lips to speak.

Laetitia's getting stuck into her third stiff gin and tonic. She's loosened up, lolling in her chair, bare-shouldered, in flipflops, languorous and flippant. Her hair blows in the wind with a wayward, messy charm. Azeem's turned down her offer of a proper drink, as always, in favor of mineral water flavored with lime juice cordial.

"Sir Eustace, eh? Did he have a spiffing mustache?"

"Why yes, he used to twirl it on his lance!"

Although Laetitia and Azeem are only distant cousins they're close in age. Their parents were always friendly. They saw a lot of each other through early childhood. Whenever there was a house party at Twinnington, they'd play rough games of cricket together with everyone on the lawn.

When they hit puberty, ponies and rugby started taking up more of their time, but their friendship revived when Laetitia, at nineteen, abruptly married Wythenshawe. That marriage (a union everyone judged *exceedingly* ill-matched) came about mainly because Laetitia fell pregnant.

Awkward, awkward. And *terrible* timing for her, everyone agreed. Wythenshawe blamed a faulty condom. Laetitia didn't want an abortion, and this, combined with her overwhelming need to leave home (and her fatal fondness for raffish older men, or "bastards," as she herself called them), decided the matter.

Azeem came to the wedding. Catching up with each other breathlessly at the reception, they uncovered a mutual interest in arcane esoteric matters—astrology, alchemy and the Philosopher's Stone... The sixteenth century Danzig alchemist, Alexander von Suchten, was a remote family connection, and that coincidence stimulated them to an ongoing email correspondence which continued even when their interest in Paracelsian alchemy ebbed away.

The other thing they shared was a love of cricket. Laetitia's father let the village team play on his lawn, and Laetitia often played alongside the men, one of only three women who regularly got chosen for the side.

"Do you still play cricket?"

"Yes, of course, there was a great game here only the other week. You should try to come up and play sometimes."

Azeem had been a regular guest player at Twinnington. He was a pretty adept spin bowler, a useful enough batsman. Everyone assumed he was Indian.

"I spent some of my best years on the sub-continent," a florid, tweedy man once told him.

"Is that a fact?"

"It was a beautiful life. And the people—*your* people—always so friendly, welcoming, so grateful..."

"Sounds like heaven," Azeem politely observed.

"Where are you from, if I may ask?"

"My father is from Iran. My mother is from Gloucestershire."

"Ah... *Persia*."

Later, Azeem had worked briefly, and quite brilliantly, at Wythenshawe's advertising agency, in between taking A-levels and going on to university.

Laetitia and he made a good pair, physically, intellectually and temperamentally. If they'd lived in an epoch when marriages were arranged according to family interests, they might have made an excellent match.

After a matter of years, when Azeem was constructing his first ideas for the *Islamic Reform* project, he at once thought of asking Rupert Wythenshawe's advice on the branding and communications aspects. The kin-connection in due course led to the appointment of Wythenshawe and Lyall to the *Islamic Reform* account, as it had by then become.

Today, all that feels eons behind them.

"It's like it's slipping out of my control, the whole project, really," Azeem is telling Laetitia. "It's drifting... dangerously."

When Azeem fixed up the visit, he assumed Wythenshawe himself would be on hand for a talk. But now he's here, Azeem is happy enough to share his worries with his charming, tipsy cousin. He's easy confiding in her.

"Since Samir Muhsi's elbowed in. I've got the feeling the whole thing's losing its way."

"I must say Muhsi sounds like more like a Swedish breakfast cereal."

"Not when you pronounce it properly. *Muhsi.*"

"It does seem rather an odd set-up, frankly," says Laetitia. "I happen to know one of the people working on your project in Germany. Dr Norbert Klinker?"

"Oh, yes."

"He came here a week ago. He's quite all right in small doses, if you like that sort of thing. He was sniffing around trying to get information."

"He's not everyone's cup of tea."

Laetitia holds Azeem's eye levelly for a few seconds.

"He's not most normal people's cup of tea," says Azeem.

Laetitia sits silent. She punches his arm.

"Hey!" he says, rubbing the spot. She gives him a vivacious look, a look of gleeful shame.

"He's *your* cup of tea," says Azeem knowing his cousin's ways.

"We'll see. Dr Norbert Klinker. Quite a mouthful. He does go on rather. Quite a handful too, I can tell you! He comes out with the most screamingly funny stuff, really *intense*—it's all I can do to stop peeing myself sometimes... I call him Nobby... but nomen isn't especially omen in that regard."

"I see."

"He more than makes up for it, though..."

"How?"

She holds his gaze levelly for some seconds, as if wondering whether to tell.

"He's got an incredibly long tongue."

"I don't think I want to hear more."

"Really! It's eighteen inches long!"

"What!? That's the size of a camel's tongue!"

"Is it? Maybe he meant eighteen centimetres."

"That sounds more like it."

"And he's funny. Makes me laugh."

"I've never come across that side of him."

"Well, you have to look for it. Just between ourselves, I do think he's got a few screws loose... I mean, he does take that freedom intellectuals have of being frightful a little too far. You know who he reminds me of—that German with the funny mustache, I forget the name—the one who went on and on so terrifically."

"Could be any number of people, really."

"No, you must remember, it was all about Superman, *Lebensraum*, the will to power and so on. Or maybe it was an Italian. A futurist, or a surrealist or something. Or a nihilist. Nobby's rather reminiscent of one of them, anyway."

"I see."

187

"One of the things that happened when he came here again has utterly put me off him, though. I caught him going through my things."

"Your things?"

"Well, you know, my underwear and so on."

"God how sordid. Going through your drawers."

"Well, yes. And then he showed me where he'd been going through Rupie's drawers in the study."

"Rupert's drawers! *Kinky* Klinker!"

"Well, Rupert's papers which were in Rupert's drawers."

"In his underpants?"

"Well, wherever Rupie keeps his things."

"Oh, yuck. Does Rupert know?"

"Don't be silly. Don't breathe a word to him either!"

"No, no, of course not."

"I don't want to be *surreptitious*, but there's no pressing need for Rupie to know anything about Nobby."

"No, I do understand, Laetitia."

"Do you?"

"Yes."

"It's not really your thing, is it, marital trouble and strife? You and Shirin always come over so romantic. *So* deeply in love. It's fairly stomach-turning, actually..."

"We've had our moments."

"*Moments!* You're the kitschiest, *sickliest* incarnation of lovebirds alive."

"Once upon a time, maybe. But now it's got to the stage where even Shirin's telling me I was naïve to have started this thing."

"D'you fancy another drink?"

As Laetitia busies herself with her glass, Azeem explains some of the back-story about Samir, Ghazan, and the Beeston Boys. Although Azeem smiles when he mentions the Beeston Boys, as if thinking of them as a loveable bunch of scallywags, his smile feels forced, his tone far from jolly.

The Beeston Boys had struck him as a bit of a joke before. Now they seem more sinister. They seem to have mixed up their jihad with a brand of low-life gangsterism. Where's the brotherhood in that?

Azeem had told Laetitia about the episode with the gunman in London soon after he returned home from the hospital. But he played down any possibility that his partners might have been involved in that. He hadn't been sure himself, for all that the gunman had kept repeating Ghazan's name.

Now, Azeem tells her about the attack on Rania in Leeds.

"I can see all that might disconcert poor Shirin," says Laetitia. "There does seem to be absolutely masses of murder going on right now. You Muslim chaps are rather at the center of it all. Then again... I suppose in your position you don't have much choice, do you? You have to confront it, don't you? It's sort of the whole point of what you're trying to do? Isn't it?"

Azeem lets his cousin burble on, half amused, half irritated by her blithe daffiness. He's watching some hares in the distance. There's two of them, and they are going at each other some, running around in big semicircles, then dashing at each other as though jousting.

Laetitia brings him back to himself.

"Isn't that the idea?" she's saying. "Your whole idea of *Islamic Reform*... it's propping up nice reasonable Muslims against mad murdering ones, isn't it? Or have I got it all wrong again?"

He nods.

"That's what I always hoped it would be. But Shirin, oh, Shirin... she's not against it as such, but she's scared of *Islamic Reform* ending up as just a front organization for the mujahid."

"Moo what—I mean honestly?"

"*Mujahid*."

"Christ, Azeem. You've really taken to the lingo, haven't you?"

"Comes with the territory. Jihad is *struggle*. The Mujahid are *those who struggle*."

"Oh, the headhackers. I see. And then if your lot are linked to it you'll end up being accused of terrorism."

"Something like that."

"You'll end up naked in Abu Ghraib, with that fetching little Lynndie England and her randy pack of hounds."

"That is my fervent wish. But fancy your knowing about that."

"Comes with *my* territory, darling."

Laetitia has fetched herself another goblet of gin. Azeem marvels that she can walk as steadily as she does, but she does, very self-possessed, stately, an aristocrat in her very intoxication.

She plonks her glass down on the table.

"Do you suppose Rupie's aware of all this?" she says.

No hint of a slur in her voice.

Azeem considers what Wythenshawe might know. He always comes over as pretty sharp, but he's fixated more on the financial side. Money drives him. Always has. So this situation is only likely to interest him insofar as it has pecuniary ramifications. Aside from that, does Wythenshawe know what's really going on? Does he care?

"Only up to a point."

"And what about my not-so-nobby Dr Klinker?"

Good question, thinks Azeem. Klinker has more than a touch of the mad boffin about him. Mental. Full of intellectual brio, but ultimately harmless... probably.

"God knows what he knows," Azeem laughs.

Laetitia smiles back at him.

"I'll find out what I can, Zimmie."

PURITY

Norfolk Crescent, London: Ghazan Khattak, Lad from Leeds

GHAZAN KHATTAK sits with the young lad. The weather's sunny and fresh, and they're out on a park bench, going over what went wrong in Soho.

"It put me off my stride, those men all staring at me," says the lad, looking bashful, "and the owner standing there, asking how old I was."

"We can fix that. We can fix them."

A crowd of schoolkids comes ambling past. Some of them recognize the lad, say hi. They're slouching, mumbling, scruffy boys with their shirt-tails hanging out, and they're loud, gum-chewing girls in short skirts and heavy make-up.

The lad smiles back at them shyly. Ghazan ruffles his hair. The lad pulls his head away—he's too old for that kind of mollycoddling. Ghazan at once picks up on his seriousness.

"Look around you," says Ghazan, his voice almost too quiet to hear, "and all you see is corruption, *pollution...* indulgence and death. Aimlessness. Nothing left to live for. Westerners *destroy* us, man, they destroy everything we really are, what we are... in our hearts, our souls. For they have turned their back on Allah. They *deny* Allah. Where there is no faith, oppression reigns, corruption arises, there is no security... a life without faith is annihilation, because it makes nothingness equal with life. Their society is dead, man, dead! But we are not like that. *Oh Allah! Lord of Power! Thou bringest the Living out of the dead, and Thou bringest the dead out of the Living; and Thou givest sustenance to whom Thou pleasest, without measure.* There's more, so much more in us than these *kafirs* will ever understand. Polluting our minds with their sexual jungly music, their magazines stuffed full of corruption. They corrupt our bodies with their shameless temptations. They corrupt our hearts with their materialism..."

Ghazan scowls around the dingy park.

"It's time to *stop* the pollution, man! Stop them polluting your body... and your heart... and defiling and shitting on everything you want to be. If you act now, believe me, man, you'll help stop their corruption and you will find true purity! You'll find the real you… You'll find the real man in you!"

PROSPECTS
Peckham, London: Shirin Shaarawi, Mamida Hanif

SOMETIMES, WHEN THEY'RE in their office together, Shirin hears her colleague, Mamida Hanif, speaking to her dead husband. She talks to him under her breath, when she thinks nobody's listening...

Shirin likes Mamida a lot, understands her, despite the difference in age. She guesses it's because both of them have these big parts of them missing, the absences left by their dead—and that missing pulls them together, close and tight, like items in a vacuum pack.

The impression Shirin gets is that Mamida thinks of her husband only and always with a fondness not far removed from passion. That Mamida's spirit feeds off echoes and responses only she can find.

But Shirin understands those things. She's got echoes of her own. Her menfolk back at home—she misses all they shared, even if she also feels gratitude, a strong sense of relief to have escaped the country where so many of them died, to be free.

One child, Mamida's got.

A daughter in her mid-thirties who lives in Leeds. They rarely see each other now. The daughter doesn't like to come up to London, while Mamida has hateful memories, unwelcome in Leeds, never wanted, never wanting to go to back.

Tempted?

Definitely. Of course Mamida had been looking forward to seeing her grandchildren grow up...

But now... it's too late now.

Mamida underwent a strange awakening—already well into her widowhood, she became more and more sensitized to the sufferings she sometimes glimpsed for herself, and constantly heard whispered around her.

She took a young girl who was married to a virulent wife-beater under her wing. She got the Leeds council social services involved.

Mamida lost some friends after that.

By refusing to keep silent about it, she lost more. She made herself the black sheep of her extended family.

Her *community*, even.

She got abused. There were threats. Those were dangerous times. She turned her back on Leeds.

Now, she and Shirin are preparing lunch in Mamida's flat in Peckham.

Shirin's a good cook. She's offered to do most of the cooking and Mamida's assented with a light heart, happy to take the weight off her aching feet.

Shirin empties out a bag of foodstuffs on the kitchen table.

"I'm making you *Khoresht-e Karafs* with some *Borani Esfanaaj*," says Shirin, starting to sort through the pile. Explaining what these dishes are, she plunges bunches of celery and parsley in the sink. Then taking up a knife she starts to slice.

"You can help me cut this spinach."

They begin to chop.

Their talk at first concerns the attack on Rania Zandi, Mamida's friend, knifed for honor. This part of their conversation is more than difficult for them both.

Mamida seems reluctant. Shirin would prefer to skip over it.

"I know this'll sound melodramatic," says Mamida. "But I feel as though death is always around me. Always closing in... Getting closer. My father, my mother, my husband. My daughter is like dead to me, although she's alive. Now this terrible thing, too, this... this travesty with Rania..."

"Rania may still live."

"Yes. She may. Rania may be lucky," Mamida says. "By some miracle, she may survive, may get better... thanks to your Azeem, too. He did a good thing there, your boy, I wasn't sure he had it in him…

She shakes her head.

"I want more than anything for her to live… I even pray for it! I do, I really do, although I don't even know if I believe any more! I wonder if there's any point in praying..."

Mamida's face is sad but somehow cheerful. A small smile, only a few tears in her eyes.

"All this death!"

Shirin takes her hand and looks out the window, notices the waning half-moon among the clouds in the dreary gray daylight, full of smog. Mamida sees it too.

"I've spent so many hours of my life staring at the moon," says Mamida, trying to sound bright. "It may be stupid, but I think it's the only thing which connects me with my dead."

Shirin smiles back at her.

"I see," she says. "Well looked at that way, the moon connects you—doesn't it?—with everyone who's ever lived—and the ones who are still living now, as well as the dead... but surely that's not the only connection you've got?"

Mamida opens her tear-soaked eyes.

"Maybe not. There's memories, I suppose. And other things we shared. But, like, the only permanent thing. The only *visible* thing. The only thing you can point to every day and say, that's something we had in common. I know you think I'm mad."

"No, of course not... I just never looked at it like that, the moon... yes, you're right, it's something kind of permanent, even though it's always changing. Goes, but always comes back."

"It's not the only thing that keeps on coming back," says Mamida. "These... these... *boys*, with their knives... with their bombs... this killing, this death, how many more—how many?"

Shirin takes her friend into her arms to comfort her.

Soon they're back on an even keel again. Mamida pulls herself together. She dabs at her eyes. She smiles. She looks outside. It's clearing up—a blue windy day, small clouds are sailing swiftly across the sky.

"I had a chat with a friend from Leeds. She reckons the Beeston Boys had something to do with the attack. Apparently the nurse who was in Rania's room made off, just disappeared in the night. And the attackers knew the code to Rania's room."

"Azeem told me about the nurse. But why does that mean it's the Beeston Boys?"

"They must have got it off of her. My friend reckons she knows who the nurse was. She's vanished, apparently."

"But what's she got to do with your Beeston Boys?"

"The nurse? She's engaged to one of them."

"If that's true, they must have waited until it was her shift before making the attack."

"Oh, sure. They have a lot of patience. It's how they always work. They wait till the moment's right. There was someone else involved from the hospital, my friend says. One of the security guys, I don't know what the connection was. A brother, or something, she wasn't sure."

Shirin is silent as she takes it in. The wind picks up, it whistles against the window frames.

Their talk resumes. After a while, they're back on the tricky topic of Azeem. Shirin wants to get some things out in the open about her relationship with the man.

Mamida knows about Azeem al Din's starry-eyed, head-in-the-clouds idealism. She knows it's started to alienate Shirin, whose impatience is never slow to express itself.

"But... is there still love?" asks Mamida.

"There is still love," Shirin says. "But I begin to wonder whether love's enough."

Mamida shakes her head. "It's never enough," she says. "It's a start... that's all it is."

"Azeem and I *had* our start already. And a very good start it was too!"

"I know, my love, I know."

"Maybe the sequel can only be an anti-climax."

"No call to think like that."

Shirin walks out onto the balcony. She's never been remotely shy about her early relationship with Azeem, its many felicities. She leans down to snip some mint-leaves from the tall dusty plant in its pot.

She told Mamida how she met Azeem, how they fell in love. And Mamida knows the story's memory is a space of peace in Shirin's bosom, where she hugs her happiness to herself.

Mamida is watching Shirin through the doorway. Shirin turns round to her and says, "Your olives are thriving!"

"Yes, such as they are... Your mother's family had olive plantations didn't they, love?"

"Well... they had quite a few at one point, yes."

Family.

Another tender spot, full of pain. Most of Shirin's own family are now gone, long gone. Gunned down by the committees of the Islamic revolution. A few survived, forced into hiding, into exile, disappearance, during the years after the Shah was forced out.

Her parents are dead, Mamida knows that. Of the family members who made it, only a couple of aunts and uncles managed to hang on in Khuzestan, cradle of their vast and ancient family. A few moved to Teheran, and other parts of Iran, while most of the exiles ended up in Germany.

"So, tell me, love. How'd your family react to Azeem?"

Shirin laughs.

"There were... issues. I don't think it was so much him being a westernized half-Iranian. And a Sunni. Well, he wasn't that religious when we met. Didn't help, of course... and then he's very young, quite poor..."

"Well, he's Oxbridge, isn't he, he has *prospects...*"

"Yes, there's always his prospects. It was more them knowing I'd never be able to marry a man from Khuzestan..."

"Did any of them stir up trouble?"

"There was a bit of... there were some hints..."

"Threats?"

"Well... you know how it goes."

"I suppose they're too far out of range to do anything dangerous," says Mamida. "Probably too poor themselves, these days."

"Pretty poor these days, yes," says Shirin.

Shirin gets up, walks to the window. She looks down on the panorama below, Peckham's gray towers, dirty brick blocks connected by pockets of grass, walkways of concrete.

It's not the prettiest stretch of south London. Not the safest either.

Mamida's voice.

"Was Azeem just as intense in those days?"

"Oh, back then, he was a gentle hippy soul... he was heavily into poetry and playing his guitar..."

"And did he take drugs? That's what hippies do, isn't it?"

"Well, in his early days he was quite into dope and booze. He had this very... *shaggy* head, strummed his guitar... sort of overflowed with verses and songs. Then a while after we met, he stopped all the mind-altering stuff."

The scent of cooking lamb fills the women's nostrils where they sit chatting in the kitchen. They're drinking their glasses of doogh and nibbling at the nan-e lavashi Shirin's brought along, dishes of sabzi and panir and a salad-e shirazi standing nearby. The two women are hungry. They spoon out the steaming pans and fill their plates and then they sit down, knees close together, at the little table.

"Is there no way you can wean him off of this foolish project of his?" asks Mamida, having savored the first mouthfuls, and expressed due appreciation of the minty, lemony lamb.

"I don't rightly see how. It's been me who's encouraged him all along."

"Well, you were a fool to lead him on. He was a bigger fool to believe you. Does he really imagine he can convert people to his way of thinking? You cannot get people into Islam like you can with Christianity. It's not in the head, love... not a mental thing. It's in the blood, *visceral* like. That's where jihad starts too, in the blood and the gut. You're born to it, you don't make a rational decision to *become* it."

Shirin knows how much she had encouraged Azeem, drummed into his mind the positive potentiality of Islam. In those days, she believed it was the way to answer his questions, allay his spiritual conflicts, obviate his distaste of capitalism.

And (when she had it herself) Shirin's faith moved most powerfully through the inner spiritual beauties it awoke in her, vibrating in sympathy with a larger, a deeper being.

She still senses its echo, in her breast, as she sits there with her friend.

And at first, it was the music of her vision which resonated in Azeem's soul, became his.

"After Azeem's first Hajj to Mecca, he began to... *inhabit his name*," says Shirin. "That was how he put it himself. He was much more into who he was, where he came from—Azeem Jamil al Din."

"Which means?"

"Defender of the Beauty of the Faith."

"That's lovely," said Mamida.

She smiled at Shirin.

"What's your name mean?"

"Shirin Amana? As Shirin I am charming. As Amana I am a gift. I am not ownable."

"That's lovely too."

"A lovely idea, isn't it? Anyway, Azeem got really into it. He started learning all about his Persian side, his family ancestry— directly descended from Imam Hassan al-Haskari the eleventh, I think—great Sufi saints among them. He started to see everything through this rosy tunnel-vision... he was like a fresh convert, still unformed."

Shirin begins to tell Mamida about Azeem's devoutness.

"Spirituality changed him for the better at first, brought out something pure in him," she says. "But then he thought he should return to the world of action. He went to that *madrasa* in Afghanistan. At heart, he isn't really a dreamer, he's a doer. That's good, I like it. But when he came back, I thought he'd been brainwashed. He picked up a lot of those mujahidin affectations. A lot of guys do. There was a lot of talk about pre-emptive jihad, and he made some deeply dodgy friends. But then he went to the other *madrasa*, the *tabligh* one. That made him stronger in his faith."

"He was lucky, the *tabligh* is a much healthier approach."

"He now knows that jihad can mean love. To him, jihad is love, bringing the lost back to Allah, saving souls..."

Mamida shakes her head.

"It is. It is."

Her eyes are still full.

"He is a noble soul."

"Well, maybe. He doesn't seem to know it fully yet, but he really does need to do good... and I mean *do* it, not just think it."

Mamida is staring at Shirin's lips as she tells her all this, as if reading them for recollections of her own.

"I was a devout muslima once," says Mamida after a while. "Utterly traditional, you know, the whole thing, the whole *burqa* deal. Never forget that, Shirin. And it was when I most believed that I hated most."

"I can't see you as a hater."

"I don't know about hate. But I became *intolerant*," Mamida says sadly. "I thought I had a divine knowledge unfaithful people didn't. I was so intolerant, Shirin, I was *intolerable*, actually! You know the saying, *there are no jokes in Islam*? Ayatollah Khomeini said that."

Shirin smiles.

FREDDIE OMM

"And there were so many other things. Simple things, like not feeling the sun on my skin. Here in the west, wearing the burqa began to bother me. I felt a big space between me and other people. I felt unhealthy, and I was... I got osteoporosis."

Mamida laughs.

"Vitamin D deficiency. But then I looked back, and I thought, back home, it isn't just the woman who can't feel the sun on her face—but the boy they suspect of being gay: they'll hang him from a crane—people who leave Islam: killed in cold blood on the streets."

"I know, love, I know."

"It depressed me, Shirin. You know, I really wanted to think then like Azeem does now, to believe in jihad as a kind of love, love as a kind of jihad. I still do want that to be true."

Mamida has finished eating. She sits back with a sigh.

"But it's different for a man," she says. "For me, in the end, I just got tired of being a second-class citizen. It depressed me, Shirin, I got tired of all this—all this nonsense—being one of the *Women Who Deserve To Go To Hell*."

Mamida leans back and grabs a pamphlet she's got lying there, which has that title on its cover. She looks at it, shakes her head, and hands it over to Shirin.

Shirin looks over the pamphlet absently. It has a black and yellow cover with a tasteful picture of a flame.

"It's from the public library," says Mamida. Lets out a little sigh.

Another piece of hateful detritus, Shirin thinks to herself. She takes another mouthful and reflects.

Women Who Deserve To Go To Hell.

She glances through it idly, as if it were a copy of *Elle* or something.

"The woman who apes men..." she reads. "The woman who adorns herself... The Grumbler... Women who kill animals and birds. "

Mamida nods.

"That's right, women who grumble and kill birds are earmarked for hell... just as surely as heaven awaits men who murder their sisters and daughters."

Women Who Deserve To Go To Hell.

Shirin reads, "A woman was sent to hell because of a cat."

Suddenly she's overtaken by a giggle... she pictures herself and Mamida being carted off, grumbling, in a tumbril pulled by a cat... *what we deserve, after all*—she savors the preposterousness of the pamphlet's title.

Women Who Deserve To Go To Hell.

She's laughing out loud, knows it's hysterical, she's nearly choking at the pointlessness of it all. Shirin tries and fails to explain, just laughs and points at the cover, and Mamida joins her in laughter, the ridiculous, evil little pamphlet—*Women Who Deserve To Go To Hell*—lies, discarded, between them.

Soon the two women are laughing loud and hard, sitting knee to knee at the kitchen table, cackling like witches, like she-devils cracking up.

"But *Azeem's* case is very different," Shirin tries to explain, when their laughter's subsided, the hysteria gone, and they're recovering themselves.

"By the time he got serious," she says—still finding it hard to talk, until Mamida finally consigns the pamphlet to the bin.

"He'd already decided all religions have their blind spots..."

All religions have their blind spots sets them off again.

"Azeem dreamt up some extra responsibilities for himself, responsibilities which weren't properly his to take on. He got arrogant, I suppose. He should have recognized it as impious. But he didn't. He decided he had a message to tell the world... he decided he'd put his advertising skills at the service of Islam."

Now, Shirin blames herself for Azeem's myopia. The more so because she no longer submits to her faith the way she used to. In the few short years since her graduation she's witnessed too many lives going wrong. The sympathetic vibes she loved have long been drowned in dissonance, discordances in her brain, the crying and screams of girls she's known whose lives have been wronged.

Mamida, meanwhile, is talking in that soothing, slightly sing-song voice, which betrays her anxiety as much as any desire to influence Shirin, masking her worries with cheerfulness, the way people do when their worries really worry them.

"You're right to be concerned, Shirin," she's saying. "It's not just his *inner peace* Azeem needs to watch out for. I've told you many times and I can't say it often enough. Those Beeston Boys Azeem's hanging out with really are *dangerous*. They're not dilettantes, those ones."

Shirin sips some doogh, shakes her head.

"The new guy that's upsetting him now... it's this man called Samir Muhsi," she says, "the guy I mentioned the other day. Azeem and I knew him at university."

"Samir Muhsi? I've come across that name somewhere."

"He's not from Leeds. He's from Saudi Arabia, but very westernized—a playboy, he used to be. *Toxic*. Well, he's Azeem's new boss! Azeem started it all off. But now Samir Muhsi's muscling in on the action."

Mamida picks at her panir.

"You say Azeem started it all off," she says.

"Yes. What of it?"

"That's not how it happened."

"Yes it is."

"Azeem didn't find them. It was them found Azeem."

"No, no, it was all his idea to set up this... communications thing. Spread the message. I know you don't think much of it. But it's what he's good at professionally, Mamida."

Mamida sits back, chewing the bread with an expression of excessive delicacy. When she speaks, she makes the act of utterance look utterly distasteful for her.

"*He* might see it that way," she says. "I think somebody might have planted a seed in his mind."

"Could be Azeem knocked the idea around a bit first."

"Someone knocked him around a bit, more like."

"No, Mamida!"

"They're *using* him, Shirin, using him pure and simple. It's what they do."

Mamida looks exceedingly disgusted. She juts out her lower lip, shakes her head, frowning. Her dyspeptic expression makes Shirin laugh again.

"Well, maybe they *are* using him, sort of. But doesn't *everyone* get used? Nobody is allowed to just *be*. Aren't both of us being used? Don't tell me you don't think so some Monday mornings. But the idea of communicating the positive message of Islam came from him. And... well, he believes in it. So where's the harm?"

"We shall see. Maybe it will all turn out for the best, as you say."

In fact, Shirin thinks no such thing.

Their lunch proceeds more merrily after this. They gossip about workmates. Shirin tells some more about Sheikh Faisal ibn Shabbir and his Office, and the bumptious calls she's been getting. She passes it all off as a farcical sideshow.

But when later the two women part, Mamida's still worried, she squeezes Shirin's arm solicitously at the door. She looks at her colleague in loving empathy, her eyes close to overflowing.

"Take care, my love," she says as Shirin goes. "Take real good care."

And she watches her friend walk away down the corridor with her hand to her mouth, as though unwilling to say something which needs to be said.

PROOF OF IDENTITY
Soho, London

IT'S LUNCHTIME IN SOHO. Sunny and warm, the afternoon, now the rainstorm's passed by.

The young lad wrapped in his bulky coat walks into the bar. He doesn't look left or right but heads straight for the counter. A crowd of people are shooting some pool and the breeze. They don't take much notice of him, they all know each other and they're being loud and hilarious. They're tightly packed at the bar, with all sorts of raucous backchat going on.

The owner is standing to one side, talking to a regular, but when he sees the lad come in he detaches himself and saunters over.

"Hey! You again," he says in his soft friendly voice. "Didn't I tell you we don't serve underage drinkers?"

"It's my birthday today."

The lad is looking him straight in the eye, unflinching.

"I'm legal, as of today."

The owner eyes him up and down.

"Well, happy birthday and welcome," he says. "You wouldn't have some proof of identity I could have a butcher's at, would you?"

"Yes."

The lad reaches inside his coat.

There's a split second where the world freezes.

Then the explosion. It blows the lad's head clean off, chucks it spinning at the ceiling, bouncing it down onto the floor, a spurting bloody mass of flesh and bone and cranial matter.

A ball of fire belches out from the lad's body, shooting sparks and flames like a firework until everything erupts and blazes.

The bar is engulfed in the shock wave, filling the space in a sheet of fire, and the blast like an earthquake rattles the rafters, reverberating the place to its foundations. Shrapnel, scores of nails, screws and steel ball-bearings shoot out like bullets ripping through people's arms and stomachs, embedding themselves into skulls and eyes, bloodily invading each orifice.

The windows blow out into the street. Glass flies in sharp pieces lacerating every surface they reach.

Everything shatters inside.

The people in the bar are blown away. Bodies fly and disintegrate, spatter onto the ceiling and the walls.

A shower of flesh and fat and blood drips down onto the floor.

No one is left alive to see the carnage. No one sees a thing till later, when the security forces come, and the TV teams come prowling in their wake.

VIOLENCE WITH REFINEMENTS
Finchley, London: Dave Page, Mad Mick

LAETITIA'S EX-LOVER, Dave, is at home, stretched out on the sofa with a can of Budweiser in his hand and his phone clamped to his ear. The afternoon is young, and he's talking to his mate, Mad Mick.

"I've got something lined up for you, mate," he says.

"Some*thing*?" said Mad Mick. "Or some*one*?"

Mick's specialty is extortion.

Mick and Dave have worked together a few times. The last husband Dave had *cockholded*, before Wythenshawe, also had a piece of loose, posh totty for a wife. This man also had a public profile he should have taken great care to protect—but he flat out refused to pay.

He turned notably more pliant after a visit from Mad Mick and his pals.

Forcible persuasion. It wasn't so much the broken nose and windows that made him see sense. Mindless violence has its point, but it's never been the only string to Mad Mick's bow. In this case, Mad Mick threatened something far worse than a broken body, a smashed up house, a crippling for life. He threatened to spin the papers a cock and bull story, a story to destroy the husband's reputation, break his life into little bits forever. The cock and bull story he'd fixed on concerned the husband trying to shag a young Bangladeshi lad. The kid brother of one of Mad Mick's musclemen.

"A purported seduction," Mad Mick had told him, "is a very serious, an *heinous* crime, if it involves interfering with a minor."

And so the husband, seeing the lie of the land, and understanding the futility of resistance, and where his interests lay, made ready with the cash.

That was a notable success, but a while back now. Dave smiled, realizing his mate was expecting to be offered another caper like that. Today, though, Dave had a much better idea to share, and he knew Mad Mick was his best hope for putting it into action.

"Yeah, it's a *someone*, Mick, and not just anybody. A real *somebody*. She's called Lady Laetitia Wythenshawe."

"Hang on. Isn't that that posh bird from up north... owns that big old place where you grew up?"

"Could be, yeah. She's living alone up there. In the middle of nowhere, right, out in the country, you know... a scary sort of situation to be in."

"She's looking for protection?"

Dave laughed.

"Not exactly, mate. The opposite, more like."

"If you just want to give her ladyship a *scare*, do it yourself, mate. Just show her your dick or something."

"I don't just want to scare her, Mick."

"We don't run to rape, Dave. We like to keep things consensual. There's some honor left among thieves, you know."

"That's not what I said. She's got money. It's miles from anywhere. I know it like the back of my hand, Mick, I used to live there... And the other thing. She lives the sort of life your towelheads don't fancy."

"My towelheads?"

"You've been using those towelheads of yours a lot lately."

"Don't call them that, mate."

"Call them what you like, it makes no difference. You've been using them a lot lately, right?"

"Well, mate, they're bright and breezy to work with. They do as they're told. And they don't expect the earth when it comes to the dosh, unlike some I could mention..."

"Easy come, easy go. They're doing good men out of a job."

"Maybe good men have priced themselves out of work. Not my problem. So what is it about her my lads wouldn't fancy? What's this all about? What's with this lady?"

"Well, she likes her sex if you get my meaning."

"No... that's way too cryptic, Dave."

"She puts herself about like nobody's business."

"You been in there yourself, have you? You fornicated with her ladyship?"

"Might have, yeah."

"You shagging this bird, Dave?"

"What if I have?"

"It's personal, then."

"Nah, mate, she'll fuck anything. She flaunts herself. She's constantly at it. It's... it's disgusting. She should be setting an example. She's a *lady*, for fuck's sake!"

"I suppose there might be something in that. I wouldn't like it if my old lady got up to stunts like that. And now you mention it, some of my lads are a bit... *prissy* in that regard. Tolerant, open-minded... but a little prissy when it comes to the sex."

"They're well into modesty for women, your towelheads."

"You're not a million miles wrong there, Dave."

"She screws around in public, virtually. It's a big fucking scandal, Mick."

"I see."

"I can get you a list of her sex partners, too... There may be people worth bribing amongst them. There's some famous German guru she's been knocking off. I've got a contact up in Scotland who's been looking into her sex life."

"She sounds like a very naughty lady. Indiscreet. Courting notoriety."

"She is. Very much so. And I thought you'd like it even more because of the towelhead angle. You could get them to maybe make an example out of her, nothing too heavy, just humiliate her a bit, maybe take some pictures, maybe put something up on YouTube... She's rich, Mick. She'll pay you a lot to get left alone."

"You could be right there, Dave," says Mad Mick. "That's good to know. That's information you might call actionable."

They shoot the breeze a bit more, this and that. Dave manages to get Mick interested in the madcap scheme. Come the end of their chat, Mick reckons there's worthwhile action to be had with this Lady. He hangs up with a thoughtful sort of squint at his knuckles.

TOOLS
Florian's, Venice, Italy: Ghazan Khattak, Samir Muhsi, Sheikh Faisal

VENICE WAS PACKED. The ubiquitous year-round tourists had been joined by another heterodox crowd, the international art scene. Rooms which were usually pricy went for triple or quadruple the normal rate. There was an atmosphere of hectic partying in the air. But when Ghazan Khattak, Samir Muhsi, and Sheikh Faisal ibn Shabbir met (they were ostensibly visiting the Biennale), their meeting had nothing festive about it—and it brought into sharper focus a discordance not previously as clear.

Sitting in a side room in Florian's, half-screened from fellow imbibers, the three men drank endless espressi, taking their time about the conversation.

Ghazan Khattak, that scraggy, rangy man, with his splendidly thick, bushy beard, sat in the shadows on the left. He was younger than the others. But somehow he looked older, already graying, his face pitted and drawn, marked with the unending tiredness that etches its furrows in constant vigilance, undeviating effort in the cause of jihad. He was scruffily nondescript as to clothing, trainers, a tatty jumper. A fixated look haunted his eyes, which burned in their sockets, his mind on higher things. In his heart, he was rejoicing over the tactical coup he'd just scored—the bombing of the degenerates' pub—a dozen dead, two dozen injured, a heavy blow to the infidels. Back on form with a vengeance, he was, and he wanted to keep the ball rolling, press home his advantage.

Ghazan's aim now was to crush any pretensions Azeem al Din might still cherish as to the purpose of *Islamic Reform*. He reckoned it wouldn't be so easy. Azeem had been to university with both Samir and Sheikh Faisal. They might feel honor-bound to support their friend. But if it came to it, Ghazan was prepared to take Azeem out for good.

Squat, hawknosed Samir Muhsi sat to Ghazan's right at the table. He looked darker and shorter, and sleeker than usual, wearing rich western clothes just this side of ostentatious.

Ghazan disliked Samir's dress sense, he considered it affected, a way of disguising who he really was. Samir fitted in too well in this effete place for Ghazan's taste, he looked at home here.

Samir smirked at a pretty young tourist, his face all smiles, an ingratiating cringe, eyeing her up with those flattering, subservient eyes. His thick black hair was expensively, shinily styled. He looked like a gigolo.

Sheikh Faisal ibn Shabbir, sitting in the middle, with his back to the wall, was tall and saturnine, conscious of his dignity. He wore traditional Arab clothes, a plain dishdashah, and a ghutra with an ogal on his head.

To start with, the nub was in the discrepancy between Samir Muhsi's deplorably relaxed take on matters, and the more rigorous line taken by Ghazan. Sensing this, Ghazan knew he must try to make an ally of Faisal.

And so he nurtured the root of all the trouble which was about to befall Azeem and Shirin.

Samir Muhsi—flabby of body like a pampered dog, slick in his styling, sharp of face, with the cold, cold eyes of a vulture—had come to manhood in Jeddah, scion of a Saudi family of traders. Ghazan had made it his business to find out about his background. A. H. Muhsi and Brothers, the family broking company, still employed many of Samir's relations, and sent him an allowance of 45,000 riyal a month.

Petted and self-indulgent as a youth, Samir had been packed off to an English boarding school when he was thirteen. Then came a spell at an even more opulent, international college in Switzerland. While at these places Samir was seduced by all sorts of western habits, just like any of his schoolfellows.

Even today, Samir retained positive aspects. It was pointless to deny it. Intelligence, an ingratiating, easy charm—he'd had all that since childhood. His vices, and his relaxed take on things, must have come along with his education, which fitted him out as a well-bred whoremonger and a sot. Now Ghazan thought about it, Samir had many of the uncontrolled, racy qualities of a *Restoration rake*. Ghazan had read about such creatures when he was studying sociology. *The Pathology of Vice,* his paper had been called, with the sub-title, *Sexual Exploitation in 17th Century London.*

The young female tourist was making eyes at him. He froze in his seat.

What is the greater jihad? The servant's struggle against his lust.

Or no... no, it was Samir she was ogling. He glanced at Samir to see how he was taking it. Samir did nothing to repel her lascivious looks. He smiled right back at her. Patted his hair. Vain, but that didn't put women off, Ghazan had noticed. Then, when Samir saw Ghazan observing him he flushed, and turned away, self-conscious.

When a man has no shame he will do as he pleases.

At Cambridge Samir Muhsi led the riotous, cosmopolitan playboy life, as it is led by rich, rootless young men. His red Ferrari burned up the miles to London. Plenty of coke and champagne laid waste to the lining of his nose and his liver.

Enthusiastic sexual decadence...

Ghazan's disapproval had been whetted by the disgusting details he'd dug up. Stories relayed by people who'd known Samir at Cambridge showed how thoroughly vice was spread at that fallen institution—students had eagerly participated in Samir's sordid antics. Samir himself had spoken of these things with him, without showing much in the way of shame.

But others had felt shame, and were filled with remorse.

One night, in the summer of his second year, on Samir's birthday, in his rooms on the first floor of the inner quadrangle, he invited three hookers and fourteen handpicked male friends for an intimate little celebration. Even as the whores stripped, and displayed their tanned, oily bodies, their bleached hair and teeth, a fog of alcohol descended on all, blurring the narrative of what happened.

Samir himself was the only one to stay relatively sober. His eyes gloated as he watched, his eyes sparkled as he rolled between those bodies intertwined, radiant with delight, cherishing the lurid depravity.

Ghazan blushed to remember what the whores had then done to the men. Even Samir had been reticent, referring only to "oral services". Some sort of depraved ritual had then been performed with the semen.

The story about Samir's orgy was well known. Even beyond the confines of Cambridge people heard about it. One of his guests was an aspirant journalist, supplying low-grade gossip to the tabloids. This little episode did the rounds in the red-tops, in toned-up, bowdlerized form, describing the oral services they'd enjoyed as "sexual acts", but taking care to highlight the names of guests from well-known or rich families. That may have been one of the reasons Samir never got himself accepted by those he most hoped would accept him.

The snottiest, raciest circles, especially the females, were what seemed to excite Samir. Ghazan couldn't get to the bottom of it, but Samir was fascinated by these upper class layabouts. It was in such a social context, in fact, that Samir had first met Azeem al Din.

That was one of the many things Ghazan held against those two. That aura of privilege. They'd never had it hard. Ghazan could never work out what had made Samir and Azeem friends.

Cambridge was a closed book to him.

In fact, that first meeting had come about purely by chance.

One day, Azeem had come up to the rooms of an old school friend, at a time in the afternoon when cocktails were being served there. He'd recognized a girl he knew from home, a horsy, charming, not unpretty divinity student. She was deep in communion with a chubby, toothy young Asian.

"Hello, Allegra," said Azeem, approaching her with a smile which the girl returned.

A round-eyed face, somewhat coltish and gamine, with a touch of the twitchy young mare about her. There was this rangy, nervous energy, this litheness in the way she moved her limbs. And Azeem rather fancied that in a girl, in fact he'd decided, years before, that he liked Allegra a lot, and that nostalgic sentiment still tripped him up whenever they met. He knew scatty Allegra well enough to see beyond her nervy frown, and he saw in her look that she was unusually distracted, unusually agitated just then.

In due course she introduced him to her companion.

"Azeem, this is Samir," she said, her eyelids twitching, her voice unwontedly vibrant. Azeem nodded at the well-upholstered Samir.

Samir smiled back toothily, his demeanor guarded. Scared of being caught poaching, Azeem thought.

Allegra said, "Samir's interested in *the colonial context of Victorian theology*."

There was a short silence.

"Isn't that it, Sammy?" said Allegra with a sort of splutter.

"The exploitation of Empire," Samir explained, nodding rather eagerly, like a beaver putting the finishing touches to a dam, "was underpinned by Christian paternalism."

"The white man's burden and all that?" said Azeem.

He didn't like to question Samir about it, dreading earnestness so, and as their talk moved on, he absorbed a wildly misleading impression about Allegra's sallow, unprepossessing beau. Unthinkingly, Azeem bracketed the eager-beaver Samir with *Asian divinity students*, wildly wrong on all possible counts.

By the time Azeem had begun to see what Samir really was (and that took him months), Samir had courted him with enough effect to have made a friend, of sorts, of him.

Poor, pious, twitchy Allegra by that time had long been abandoned for more promising females, in pastures new.

Their friendship continued.

On graduation Azeem went into advertising and thrived.

Samir, watching Azeem's ascent in the business, marked him down as a great success in the making. He scented something useful in Azeem's career.

For Samir, by this time, was beginning to see himself as worthy of being *branded*.

He once told a blonde debutante he'd seduced, "I, Samir Muhsi, am just as much of a *brand* as Louis Vuitton," as he lay beside her, smoking. "Louis Vuitton is *nothing*, just a name on my bags. Chinese coolie-factories make those bags. Louis Vuitton is a fraud, nothing but a frog name and an advertising campaign."

"You pay pretty good money for the frog name," the debutante observed, casting her eye over his wardrobe, which sparkled and flashed with brandnames and logos. "You're the kind of guy who'd pay good money for just about *any* name, just as long as it *is* a name."

"I've been brainwashed," Samir smiled. "Brainwashed, dazzled... I'm in love with names, and things I hate."

And having said it he made love to the girl—descendant of Charles II, from a house glorious in the annals of history—with a passion she couldn't tell from contempt.

"Terrorism," he told his debutante afterwards, a fresh Monte Cristo in his mouth, "is the easiest road I can think to turning myself into a famous brand name... Think Che Guevara."

He waved the cigar under her nose.

"Don't be disgusting," said the debutante with a tolerant smile.

"Think of Nelson Mandela."

"No!"

In line with all of that, Samir Muhsi had become a jihadist of convenience, when in due course jihad became his career-path of choice. He was intelligent enough to know how cynical and self-serving his mask of jihad was.

But he didn't admit it to himself. Like most playboys, he saw his life—life itself—through the most extravagantly romantic shades.

"We've now got two agencies working for us, one in London and one in Düsseldorf," Samir was explaining. His black eyes darted between his two companions busily.

"Had to crack the whip a bit. Azeem al Din, basically, was briefing them to do a soft image campaign, airy-fairy, multi-culti hogwash. So I got involved myself. I insisted he come up with something harder, confrontational, more challenging."

Samir's colleagues received this in silence.

"Azeem is doing his best, but he's too well-meaning. We have to remember he's a modernist, a liberal," Samir continued. "He always has been. He's got hold of the wrong end of the stick, frankly. We can't let him do this communications project on his own, because we'll end up with global feelgood pap no-one'll notice."

This, so far as it went, was the point Samir wished to make in Venice. Azeem could proceed with his communications campaign, as long as he did it under Samir's control. Here, today, in Venice, Samir wanted merely to confirm that he, and nobody else, was calling the shots.

In the shadows, on the sidelines, he was hatching a notion to sideline Ghazan and Sheikh Faisal, when circumstances optimized. By then, he calculated, the whole show would be up and running. He'd get to be the movement's figurehead—his face in the magazines, his voice on the airwaves, his fingers on the purse-strings.

But all that was for later.

There and then, his partners didn't demur. When Samir had finished his piece, they raised no objections.

That, too, was all to come later.

Ghazan gazes at his companions with murderous intensity. His take on things is altogether simpler, more brutal. That of the Salafist radical, the jihadist of the sword.

"I agree with what you say, man, about the uselessness of soft words, soft messages," he tells Samir. "Leave all that bleeding-hearted mush to Shaytan, and his acolytes, the ethnocentric equal opportunity gang, *we* can be much more direct and open in what we say..."

Born into an expatriate Pakistani family, prosperous owners of a dry-cleaning firm, settled in Leeds since he was five, Ghazan has followed a path trodden by many men who were radicalized before him.

"You know me, man," says Ghazan, placing his hand on his chest with a fierce, declamatory look. He holds their attention, looking as though he is on the verge of a baleful species of song.

He stares at them as he speaks on.

"If you tell me, loud and clear, that someone needs a lesson, I'll help you. You know this, to your profit, Samir."

"I do, my brother, I do."

Ghazan's parents are traditionalists. They've always kept to themselves. They're quietly proud of what they've achieved, proud of their kids. At home, Ghazan's always Ghazanrahman— *servant of the most gracious, servant of the merciful.*

"And I do it with a light heart. To kill an infidel is to spare him much suffering."

Ghazan's heavy dark eyes peep over at Samir with a malignant charge. His beard juts out, he seems to brandish it in front of him. He speaks on, full of self-control.

"Let's not *mince words*. I'll admit I have no great expectations advertising'll ever deliver us anything useful of itself. But I'm happy to let you try, Samir."

Again that glance.

"I'm happy to let you try, my brother!"

Ghazan Khattak's eyes shine with hooded malice. He looks briefly at Sheikh Faisal to sense his approval. He feels drawn to the primitive self-belief of the Saudi Arabian prince.

In the dim light of Florian's, Ghazan's beard spreads a broad shadow on his white T-shirt as he talks. He's never made any bones about despising *ads*, irredeemably tainted as they are with all the filth of western consumerism. Advertising, he reckons, is a limp adjunct to Kalashnikovs and suicide bombs. His scorn is partly habit of mind, partly suspicion of Azeem, contempt for Samir.

When it comes to getting the message out, Ghazan knows *ad hoc* videos, posted on the internet, are more potent by far than any paid-for commercial. The Kirkstall Road honor attack, for example, has had great success as a viral, thousands of hits a day.

Ghazan's instinct for using western tools as weapons against the west is the skill that sets him apart from the thousands of similar men across the world, who preceded, and will follow him on his savage pilgrimage.

Aside from that, Ghazan just doesn't like the thought of putting his life's mission on the same level as selling toothpaste and cola. As a rule, weapons should really be, unequivocally, weapons—look like weapons, kill like weapons. He understands weapons, knows them intimately, loves them. The PK and PKM, the RPD, the AK-47, the RPG's and Dushkas—these are the weapons he's cradled in his arms, and they are evocative names for him, conjuring up the happiest stage of his life, in the training camps, where he learned what it is to be a mujahid, how to be a man.

Ghazan is nowhere near as rich as Samir, let alone Sheikh Faisal. And over the years, he's come to despise business, and he totally abominates any form of usury. Usurers, he knows, will abide in the flames of hell, drinking from a boiling spring with the Jews.

Ghazan has no problem with money as such. He needs it. But *money of itself does not give birth to children.* Only if it is put to work will it create profit and good.

Ghazan's contribution in the *Dar al-Harb*—the Domain of War—is buttressed by the ruthless way he deploys his *baraderi*, his gang of thugs. The *baraderi* originated in Leeds, and are the disaffected psychopathic jihadists Mamida tends to refer to as the *Beeston Boys*.

Ghazan used to call them that himself, once. Back in the early days. Come to that, Ghazan knows all about Mamida, too. He knows how she disgraced herself, setting herself against the community, raising herself up above her station, to her shame. The terminology of that shameless woman, like her jaundiced feminist view of the world, is outdated now, and inaccurate. Ghazan's *baraderi* are no longer just boys (nor just from Beeston). They don't confine themselves just to jihad, either. They are flexible in the fights they pick, they move with the times, dabble in nonreligious violence and gangsterism when it suits—an easy way to raise funding for jihadi projects, to poke some bloody gaping gashes into the guts of this rotting society, to stay sharp and in training.

In this way Ghazan channels money through his little private army, always at his beck and call, so that it struggles for the forces of good on many varied fronts.

A tall girl wearing a short red dress and a long black leather coat now stalks in. Her face puffy with *ennui,* she joins an equally jaded-looking businessman who's been sitting, alone, at the table opposite. Having embraced this enervated fellow, the girl shakes her shoulders out of her coat, revealing alabaster skin, elegant curves.

With a glance from beneath impeccable lashes she takes in those three Arab men—a swift practised sweep of the eyes, blanking all of them except for Samir, who's favored with a passing hint of a smile. Upon which, Samir freezes... he looks down at the table, something very gripping seems to be materializing, invisibly, on its surface as he stares down, perhaps seeing something he didn't want to be reminded of.

Then, keeping his head averted, Samir gets up, heads off to the bathroom.

Sheikh Faisal perceives this interchange with a small sad smile of his own. It passes Ghazan completely by. The two men regard each other. It is as if Samir had never been there. They begin to speak of things they couldn't if he were.

"Azeem al Din is well placed to serve us," says Faisal softly, watching Samir walk off, "to create our network of agencies. He will find us many helpers, serve us in the spirit of Islam, weeding out all idolaters, sodomites and Jews."

Obscenely rich, a *sayyid* of well-attested lineage, Sheikh Faisal lacks the vulgar mercantile urges that drive Samir. Nor does he need to create credibly legitimate channels of support and funding, as Ghazan does. Unlike them, he is his own man. He is conscious of this, has always been conscious of it.

"Azeem knows how to brief such shucksters, make them broadcast the messages of our choosing, in the professional western way."

There's a heavy look to Sheikh Faisal, his face hangs down with congenital fatigue, as if his genes were loaded with the weight of a hundred generations' care.

"I share your distaste, Ghazan, for advertising and all its filthy works. But we need something to camouflage our wider plans."

Faisal is keeping a slyly observant eye on that pale-skinned tart in red, who snuggles, cheek to cheek, with her fancy man. Then he turns to Ghazan. He speaks to him in a low, confiding voice. A regal smoothness informs his demeanor, like a monarch reassuring a valued subject on the very points that irk the subject most.

"Listen to me, Ghazan," whispers Sheikh Faisal. "You think those ads Azeem is working on are a futile exercise. That's your view, is it not?"

Ghazan softly assents.

"It is partly that. Although I think... I think it's *worse* than futile. I see Azeem as a Shaytan in human form, and his ads as Shaytan's sneaky whispers."

"I could not agree with you more, my brother! And this is why I will tell you that *there will be no ad campaign, no communication.* I have decided to put an end to it, just before Azeem is ready to put it on the air. What there will be is a network. The network will work on a very different kind of campaign. One that has nothing to do with advertising. Azeem does not know it, and I haven't informed Samir, but Azeem's one and only purpose is to build me this vast construct of contacts. Once that is done, our useful idiot will have outlived his usefulness."

Faisal speaks dismissively, as though granting a minion everything he most desired, the ruin of a rival, the destruction of other men's plans.

"It will be like a spider's web," says Faisal with a grin, "it will all interconnect... It will be infinitely extendable. But it isn't designed to create communications. Far from it."

Faisal smiles. "Azeem will sit in the web, thinking he controls it. But he doesn't control it."

Sheikh Faisal laughs softly enjoying this excellent joke. "*We* control it. Azeem isn't the spider in the web. He is but a fly caught inside it, entrapped in a web he has made himself, to our design."

Faisal is still savoring his joke. Ghazan Khattak, beside him, nods in approval. He feels he and Faisal understand each other well. And so for a second or so the two of them commune over the coffee cups, joining enjoyably together, laughing about Azeem, no longer his own man, no more than their tool.

DECADENCE
Cambridge: Shirin Shaarawi, Sheikh Faisal ibn Shabbir

OF COURSE GHAZAN had had Sheikh Faisal investigated too. He was intimately aware of his new rich friend's weak points. For Sheikh Faisal had passed through university alongside Samir Muhsi. He'd known Samir. Shared interests yoked them together. They attended some of the same Pimm's and punting junkets. Like Samir, Sheikh Faisal at this time was a child of darkness, partial to parties, disdaining neither drink nor drugs, nor denying himself promiscuous intercourse with females. For a time, Samir *pandered* to Faisal's desires—making introductions, connections, and taking a cut himself—fuelling Faisal's drug and whore consumption.

Each man fed the vices of the other, reciprocating favors in cash or in kind.

But Sheikh Faisal changed.

One party, in the Lent term of their first year, proved a life-changing experience for him. It was at this party that he was introduced to Shirin Shaarawi. He took one look at the bright, lippy undergraduate and was instantly intrigued.

"Don't you find it unsettling, being a Sheikh?" said Shirin. She'd been celebrating a girlfriend's birthday. She'd come on to this party out of politeness, not planning on staying, already unusually well charged up. Someone introduced her to Faisal using his title. She picked up on that at once.

"Unsettling? No, not at all," said Faisal, ogling, completely drunk himself. "Why do you say that?"

"Well, the word Sheikh's got such unsettling semantic connotations hasn't it?"

Shirin rambled inconsequentially, her dark golden eyes glowing in playful mischief.

"There's shake rattle 'n roll. There's milkshake. There's Shakespeare. There's even Shakin' Stevens, if you know him. They're all movers and shakers, innit?"

Faisal was nonplussed by Shirin's outburst at first. He had one of his bodyguards, discreetly watching from the shadows, fetch Shirin another drink. His hand felt nervous as he now offered it on to her, ice clunking inside the glass.

In a minute, Sheikh Faisal was loose-lipped and pompous enough to say, "With anyone else, I'd say you were being impertinent."

She looked at him, brown eyes hard.

"You obviously don't know what the word means," she said. "You probably mean *insolent*, which may or may not be true, depending on how much you choose to stand on what is laughably termed your dignity.

"I'm never impertinent," said Shirin. "Never."

From the first, she was well able fight fire with fire when it came to Sheikh Faisal ibn Shabbir.

As the weeks went by, anytime they met, Shirin would deal with him as though he were her cheeky young relation, fun to tease, to be sent running along when he got tiresome.

"Run off now, Shabby," she told him when he came to visit her in her rooms. "I've got work to do."

Faisal wasn't used to being sent packing like this.

So by these and other means Faisal—merely smitten at first by her looks and nonchalant sexual confidence—soon fell under the spell of her spirit. He ended up falling for her hook, line and sinker.

It was never entirely clear whether this had been Shirin's intention all along–consciously or otherwise—nor, at first, was it clear whether she'd even noticed what had been wrought in the heart of her powerful admirer.

Sheikh Faisal went on to cultivate Shirin's friends with a zeal which would have disturbed her, had she seen it first hand. It may have been instinctual, patrician cunning on Sheikh Faisal's part—a congenital condition of the very sort Samir Muhsi, for one, was so strangely keen to admire in people of that caste. But it was also a product of Faisal's passion, which, although spontaneous and sudden, was painstaking.

One summer's afternoon Fenella Fitzgibbon, a spiky-haired girlfriend of Shirin's, was looking out of her window onto the quad below.

"Look what the cat's dragged in," Fenella remarked to the girls with her.

Sheikh Faisal strode along, accompanied by his bodyguards. One of them carried a crate of champagne.

"I wonder who *he's* come to seduce," thought Fenella's friends.

He came up to Fenella's rooms.

"Good evening," he said. There was an awkward sort of silence during which the girls sort of simpered.

"What a lovely evening."

He looked round at Fenella's friends and smiled with a little bow.

"I hope you won't object, but I couldn't resist bringing this, in gratitude for having me round the other day."

As it happened, Shirin had brought him along for tea. They'd only stayed half an hour or so. This second visit was even briefer. Sheikh Faisal ibn Shabbir smiled at Fenella, said goodbye.

"I hope we'll see each other again soon," he said. "I would like that very much."

No one thought to criticize his behavior.

Faisal put into play all the moneyed resources at his disposal. He looked on Shirin as his *prey*. She came to sense his ample appetites, his partiality, with a secret shiver of excitement.

In all this she let him get away with more than was strictly *ladylike* or honest, hugging to her breast the proofs of his honeyed words, his great undeclared love. She thought she was firmly in control of whatever was happening.

He escorted her to a polo match. He showed her his stables, where everything was polished and swept, where horses languished in surroundings of equine luxury. After the eighth chukka, Faisal joshed with the players, most of them well known to him. It revealed another side to the sheikh.

Shirin sensed from the way the men spoke across her that they didn't give her tenure of Faisal's arm a month if that. They seemed used to his *fillies*. They politely patronized, they didn't really see her.

There was a point-to-point near Melton Mowbray where Faisal was riding, not with especial elegance, but competently. Then there were meets at Stratford, Windsor, and Cheltenham where horses paraded and raced in his livery. Copious drinking of champagne in the club enclosure. It was all very horsy and swanky, but suddenly Shirin had enough.

"It's not really my world," she told him as they were driving back to Cambridge in his open-top SLR. The night was closing in and the cool air streamed through across her face, her shoulders, making her shiver.

"It's nobody's world," he said looking straight ahead at the road.

"It's great, Shabby, *grand*, and I love it really... but I don't think it's me."

"If you like it, if you want it to be yours, I can make it so," he said with a high-flown tone that made her smile. She dropped the subject.

Faisal had a gift specially commissioned for her. It was a one-off, gilt-embossed, leather-bound edition of Nizami's great love epic *Khusraw and Shirin*. The choice of poem was as sedulous as so much was about Faisal—he affected to see in its drama an anticipation of his love for her.

He presented the book to Shirin over dinner.

"Paradise," he said, offering it to her, "can be found on the backs of horses, between the breasts of women, and in books."

It was a sumptuous present dripping in gold. Shirin tore off the wrapper and took it out, her eyes shining. She flicked through the pages at once discerning the craftsmanship and care.

"How..." she began.

She paused.

Sheikh Faisal was looking across at her expectantly, juices of anticipation filled his mouth, his eyes betraying his overeager appetite.

"How... *thoughtful*," she said at length. "How very... *kind*."

Sheikh Faisal's hopes were squashed. He got nowhere that night. His rival Azeem, a half-caste Persian of good family, but moderate means, virtually indigent, was playing a better hand.

CAPERS

Paris: Shirin Shaarawi, Azeem al Din, Sheikh Faisal ibn Shabbir

SOON THESE THINGS came to a head.

Shirin, Faisal and Azeem flew off on a jaunt to Paris, a trip for which each of them would pay a price in pain that lasted far beyond its short duration.

Faisal's moods in Paris veered—manically—between exhilaration and despondency. In long, stoned, stretched-out nights at the chic exquisite *boite* they liked, he sank oceans of booze, champagne and Armagnac.

Then he sharked around the dancefloors, going round each girl in turn. He moved his body stiffly, jerking his long thin legs and making stately movements with his neck like a clockwork giraffe. Exhausted at their table afterwards, he'd scatter lines of coke for all within sniffing distance.

At the end of the night, when the flying had to end, he landed facefirst into the bowls of canapés and tapas on the bar. Covered in crumbs, hair sticky with brandy, he staggered away to pass out in some murky corner of the VIP lounge.

Azeem and Shirin dragged him out.

On their penultimate night, these capers come to a suitably shuddering climax. Sad-eyed Faisal, ecstatic and exuberant on the effects of 1990 Cristal, is E'd up, to boot. In such high spirits of excess, Faisal finally proves unable to contain himself. He can't keep the lid on his lustful obsession for Shirin.

With all the embarrassing effusions such obsessions spawn, he spills out his love for her...

It happens like this. On the steps of the Sacré Coeur in Montmartre, with Azeem out of the way on a pretext, Faisal takes Shirin's hand. Though discomfited with guilty excitement, she lets him, if only to see how far he'll go. She too has indulged in some champagne, not as much as Faisal, but enough to make her floaty, slightly rash—as always when tiddly.

Sweating Faisal whispers in her ear Nizami's famous lines -

Your lips flow with sweet sugar,
The sweet sugar that flows in Khuzestan.

At the same moment as those words transfix Shirin with a thrill, one of Faisal's hands cups her breast, her heart beats faster against his hand. His other hand, too eager, clasps her buttock. As his fingers cherish her there, he leans his head toward hers, to whisper honeyed words of love.

"Let me be your slave, I love you so," he whispers in her hot ear.

"Let me be, Shabby," she says, her heart wild. "What will Zimmie think, if he sees us?"

"Forget him, Shirin. He's a loser, he's not good enough for you... my darling, my princess, I worship you."

Shirin let no more than a few seconds pass before she tore herself free.

She saw at once their friendship had ended.

In his eager spillage of love, Faisal had gone far too far, too quickly intruding his body into her private spheres.

Faisal tried to restrain her. His sweaty hands grasped at her shoulders.

She slipped free. He reached out again. His hands were on her—pulling her to him, but she eluded his grasp. He was left pawing at her neck. Clammy with sweat and breathing hard, both of them—and she looked at him with hate. Seeing this wouldn't do, he finally let go. For some moments, he knelt beside her supplicating her with his face and words.

She couldn't deal with it, revulsion filled her.

There and then, Shirin cut Faisal out of her life, did it the sharpest way she could.

She told him, in her most formal tone, "Sheikh Faisal, you have become an embarrassment. An embarrassment to yourself, and an embarrassment to me...

"You have insulted me," she calmly told him, "and betrayed our friend. I wish never to see you again as of now."

And so, when Azeem returned from his pretext errand, clutching the bottle of champagne Faisal wanted, he found Shirin alone on the steps of the Sacré Coeur.

She'd been crying.

She sat looking sad and stricken. Surrounded by a horde of pacific students sitting round her, hanging out and mellow like a drove of droopy angels. Clouds of dopey smoke hung in the air close by.

Shirin's heart was overflowing. Her lips parted slightly, she tried to smile when she saw him coming.

They pulled open the bottle.

Later, when she told Azeem what Faisal had done, he took it a lot more calmly than she'd hoped.

He said, "I've been thinking all along there was something about the way he looks at you."

"It makes me sick!" cried Shirin. "To think how he planned it all, sending you off, then pawing me... wrapping me in his oily arms! His tongue... he tried... it was like being sucked by a greasy octopus!""

"Poor darling," Azeem said. He nestled her in his arms.

As they cuddled, Azeem thought of his false friend Sheikh Faisal, and considered his treachery.

Azeem felt just a pang of pity for the sad-eyed young man whose vast petroleum-based riches had brought him no happiness.

"And poor Shabby," said Azeem in a tone of pious pity, trying his damnedest to forgive.

"*Poor Shabby!*" said Shirin. "How can you say that, Azeem, he virtually tried to rape me!"

"He *loves* you, Shirin," said Azeem thinking of the friend he'd lost. "He's pitiful... he's sad. I love you... but at least—"

"Your love's a funny kind of love," said poignant, smiling Shirin, "I get pawed and licked by a stoned, drunken sheikh, then my lover comes back saying... pretty much saying he *pities* my rapist."

Azeem shook his head slowly.

He said, "I feel the sympathy one victim has for another. Loving someone like you is a kind of torture, really. It's no cakewalk, Shirin."

"Whoever said it was meant to be?"

"I pity Shabby as one whipped dog might pity another."

"Leave it, Zimmie! *Whipped dog* indeed. Believe me, Shabby feels no sympathy for you."

"Do *you*?"

"I thought I did, but it's rapidly receding."

High above the city they finished the champagne and melted into each other's arms.

Faisal flew back that same day. He cut short his studies, returned to Saudi Arabia. He set himself to tasks that might console him, that might restore him to a sense of dignity.

Faisal's departure, and its sordid circumstances, sealed Shirin's long-term preference for Azeem. As the world of their love took shape, the two lovers turned Faisal into their touchstone, the personification of gold-plated vulgarity.

In their minds, he assumed an ever more grotesque, cartoonish persona—the sad-eyed, insatiable, would-be cunning sheikh, whose phallus was at any unwelcome moment apt to be thrust into proceedings. Anything unpleasant that happened after this could always be relativized—*but not as bad as being mauled by Shabby at the Sacré Coeur*. Merely to mention Faisal that way was enough to set the seal of mockery on the awfulness of any awkward social encounter.

So, in their private talk, Faisal became an object of ridicule.

THE HUNTING ZONE
Saudi Arabia: Sheikh Faisal ibn Shabbir

BUT THIS RIDICULE WAS soon shown to be as misplaced as it was unkind…

In Saudi Arabia, Sheikh Faisal ibn Shabbir shielded himself from his failure, and the excesses he blamed for it. It led him down eccentric, exotic byways.

For a while, houbara bustard-breeding became the focus of his life. In the old days, Faisal's father had always kept trained peregrine falcons, but hadn't indulged in much hunting, just an occasional hobby, social excursions into the desert. Bustards hadn't really figured in his life at all.

Faisal took up breeding seriously, wanting to create a success of his own. He wanted to share no credit, personally oversaw every aspect of the breeding game. And so he became more intensely involved with his bustards than anything he'd ever done before.

Learning from the best, most celebrated mentors, training and moulding the skill of his own hands, he learned how best to fit his falcons' beaks and claws with covers, a skill of vital importance, to prevent undue sufferings to the precious wild bustards caught in their talons. Out in the hunting zone, Faisal stuck close to the strike-site. He rode swiftly to capture each fallen bustard, before it could be injured, torn in the falcon's frenzy.

He bought incubators. Burning the midnight oil in his workshops, he made modest but significant improvements to their construction.

He invested in sperm, froze it in liquid nitrogen. He traveled the oceans to sit at the feet of the breeding world's masters. He sought profound insights into all those sort of things.

So Faisal became an expert bustard breeder. He was interviewed on Discovery Channel, where his views were reported with the utmost respect.

And all the while, he brooded corrosively on what had happened between him and Shirin. He spent much time alone in the desert, with only his bustards, his falcons and his servants for company. Whilst he was there, in the middle of infinite sands, he felt complete within his mind—his brain wiped clean of the virals which threatened to delete his sense of self.

In due course, he fell under the spell of Wahhabi words— feeling at home in them, he saw that the Wahhabi way was his way. As he explored the byways of Salafist and Wahhabi philosophy, he became a deep aficionado of the works of Muhammad ibn Abd al Wahhab.

From then on, he absolutely refused to meet women on an equal basis. Even when he returned home, he spurned all efforts on his parents' part to interest him in suitable brides.

Withdrawn into his own world, Faisal's eyes fixed on his falcons as they flew the far shimmering horizon—they'd wheel, then turn, high over his head, to blind him, crossing the path of the sun—he never let go of his love.

Faisal had instructed his private investigators-cum-paparazzi to spy on Shirin Shaarawi's movements in the west, and to report to him, every month, what she was up to. Ghazan knew that. He knew that Faisal watched Shirin with the same obsessive watchfulness Ghazan focused on him, even if the Sheikh had far baser motivations—low personal lust, rather than the high ideals of jihad.

From the shadows, Sheikh Faisal ibn Shabbir was well up on all Shirin did, almost a decade after the sordid disaster of Paris. Faisal's fantasies, Ghazan guessed, were becoming evermore encrypted and encrusted in his brain, while the woman of flesh and blood who'd set them off—that girl he thought he loved— had long since swum away into a new kind of life, evermore detached from him.

CYPHER
Florian's, Venice, Italy: Sheikh Faisal ibn Shabbir, Ghazan Khattak, Samir Muhsi

"AS THE PROVERB SAYS, all mankind is divided into three classes," says Faisal, sitting in the alcove in Florian's in Venice. Samir has rejoined them, and they have ordered another round of *espressi*.

"There are those that are immoveable, those that are moveable, and those that move. As we can see, the west is immoveable, and must be destroyed, swept away. Azeem al Din and his breed of useful idiots are moveable, maybe. But *we*, we are the ones who move."

Faisal stares down at his impassive hands, folded on the table before him. He feels his strength pulsing through his veins.

He takes up his coffee and sips delicately. His large hands enfold the diminutive espresso cup as gently as if he held a precious egg. He looks beyond the tall, thin girl in the red dress and her fancy man, and sees a group of tourists twittering at a distance.

Regarding them *de haut en bas* he smiles with masterful condescension.

"New networks for the mujahid!" he continues grandly. "The *Islamic Reform* project will give us that—and more, if we manage it properly."

Faisal stops and pauses again to sip his coffee.

"In achieving that," he resumes, "the *role* of Azeem al Din, to me, is essential. But the *person*—the person of Azeem al Din is expendable.

"He is but a cypher, he must play only the role we assign him, no more," continues Faisal, shooting a complicit glance at Ghazan. "He must dance to the music we compose. He must dash, obey us to the letter, executing the will of his masters.

"He will do our bidding, a useful servant. But he is also, as you say, Samir, a *liberal*, and so he is not far from being an open foe of our plans, if ever he should discover what they are... Azeem al Din is of use to us only as long as he executes our orders, establishes our network, a diligent slave. As to our true aims, we continue to fulfil God's will. Azeem al Din should never guess what we are about...

"We need now to make his labors harder," says Faisal in a kingly tone. "We need to make Azeem al Din *bleed* for our cause. Now that we have Britain and Germany in place, we should add more countries to our network—Italy, Spain, France, keep adding more infidel lands, keep Azeem al Din trotting about, executing our will...

"If there's ever a sign Azeem al Din is thinking independently," Faisal is concluding, "or suspects what is going on—"

"Then he must die!" Ghazan's interjection is rough.

Sheikh Faisal is still for a moment. Then he nods.

"We should not hesitate to sacrifice him for our higher purpose. It would be a high honor for Azeem al Din, to sacrifice himself for Islam, to be sacrificed for the faith which has saved him, a grateful slave.

"That will be the best end for him, the best end for us."

As he's saying this, Faisal catches Ghazan Khattak's vibe, his imperceptible nod.

And in that moment, they truly do see eye to eye.

The three gentlemen talk on another hour. Then they go out into the city to take in some of the Biennale pavilions where, truth to tell, they find little to their taste.

They are sickened—angered, even, by the decadence on display.

CLOWNING
Venice, Italy: Ghazan Khattak

DAWN DOES NOT *arrive twice to awaken a man*, thinks Ghazan
Khattak as he wakes, bathed in sweat, next morning. He's been
sleeping fitfully, visions of grisly western art keep insinuating
themselves, like hobgoblins, onto his mind's eye. Their effete
conceptual grimaces, like obscene flauntings, merge with the
forms of the immodest tourist women he's been nauseously
eyeing up on the streets of Venice...

Perspiring... half out of their clothes in the heat... their skin
glistening, a smelly miasma of scent and sweat, festooned with
gaudy fabrics, fabrics and bodies melting, gleaming together...

In a blur of arms and legs and thighs, hot impressions of bellies,
and heavy breasts, and buttocks, implant themselves on his eyes.

Ghazan is wrenched from his sweaty dreams with shudders of
disgusted delectation.

He's soaked, sopping. His beard is drenched, dripping in
perspiration. He feels he's been sapping his strength in his sleep,
revisiting those scenes of decadent provocation... those female
bodies which harrowed him so whilst awake. He feels like he's
been molested in his sleep, molested and interfered with by a
host of fallen jinns.

He prepares himself for his morning *salah.*

Ghusl.

The heat of dawn swells into his hot hotel suite. Wafts of
languid air, billowing up the silky, effeminate furnishings.

The three jihadists are not due to leave Venice until that
afternoon. Ghazan can't stand the thought of waiting in that
fancy, effeminate room, its soft silks, its creamy side-tables inlaid
with ebony. Those suffocating swathes of silky brocades... they
squeeze the vitality from him.

He knows he needs to shake himself awake.

He'll hit the streets after his prayers. He *wants* to confront himself with Venice's putrid decadence, to wallow in the spiritual hell of this city of fetid canals and gutters—gird himself, mentally, for action.

Ghazan washes his armpits in the sink. Then he cleans the rest of his pale, scrawny body. All the unclean places. He makes wudu. Three times he pours water over his hair and his beard...

Under every hair is impurity.

He cleans in front, behind; left and right. His feet.

Throws on his nondescript scruffy clothes.

He stares into the mirror and sees a gaunt, hollow-eyed warrior staring back at him. He places his left hand on his chest, covering it with his right.

He starts to recite Al-Fatihah.

Ghazan walks unmolested through dank alleys. He walks with light, soft steps, like a cat, scarcely treading the ground, padding intently forward.

Shadowy vistas recede to either side; slivers of sky bright above his head; his feet quiet on the stone, he crosses over bridges in the early still. Now and then the pungencies of the alleyways, and the whiffy waters below, flood into his nose.

He walks on swiftly, with no sense of where he wants to go.

In Campo Santa Margherita there is more noise and happening. A cluster of loud people are busy at the far end of the square, huddled under the awning of a *caffeteria*.

Ghazan stands for a moment and watches them, wondering which way to go. As he's doing so, a big clown—a wheyfaced harlequin, with a yellow ball fixed to the peak of his cap— catches sight of him, detaches himself from his group. The clown stumbles toward him. He's stumbling like a man in a film who's been shot in the back, he stumbles drunkenly, on his last footsteps, drunk with feigning death, like he's swooning in a drugged haze.

The clown is accompanied by two tall girls in bikinis. One of them is filming the scene on a camcorder. The girl captures every move he makes. She swirls round the clown in a light-toed balletic flurry, aiming for all the best angles, a floating sense of movement. She's lissom and keen, watching closely like a tiger.

The other girl carries nothing but a warily amused look. She walks in nonchalance like a model. She is very tall, paleskinned, looks like a freckled redhaired Scot. Her skin is a blank human canvas, waiting for some artist to scrawl lines on it, or drape her in clothes, and her cheekbones are gaunt with etched worry.

Ghazan can't keep his eyes to himself, he so wants to avoid this seedy trio of performance artists. But his glance keeps returning to the girls' bodies, he feels excited and ashamed.

He steps off in the direction of a ruddy brown bench nearby. In the normal run of things this would keep him well out of harm's way. But before Ghazan can fade into the margin, the clown scurries smartly over, comical haste infusing his limbs, and blocks his way.

"Have you got a smoke?" drawls the clown, elaborately drawling out the vowels, in English.

"No."

"Mind if I smoke?"

Ghazan ignores this bumptious comedian.

"Got a light?"

Ghazan looks the other way. But the wheedling clown contorts himself, he stands there leaning against the bench, hogging his sightline. And the bikini-clad girl with the camera is filming away. Ghazan can't keep his eyes off her, can't tear himself away.

"Would *you* like a light then?" pesters the clown now lighting up a cigarette. He sucks at it with pouting lips, smokes with exaggerated fulfilment. Then suddenly, with a zanily demented movement, he thrusts the flaming lighter at Ghazan's chin.

Ghazan stands flabbergasted. And without warning his bushy beard flares up in a phosphorescent flash of flame.

The clown stares transfixed, drunken eyes filling with terror.

That sudden fire rises up into a spreading beard of flames searing Ghazan's cheeks, singeing his eyebrows. The Scottish model jumps forward, she slaps Ghazan's beard fiercely four or five times. By dint of diligently slapping, she tries to douse the flaming beard.

"I'm so sorry!" she's saying as she pummels Ghazan's face.

"Are you all right?"

She's looking at him intently as she slaps him, she's looking at him fixedly searching his face for remnants of burning. Her own face is animated with concern and horror. The flames are all gone now. Ghazan, trembling, looks down at her breasts in confusion.

Then not pausing he turns from her and, using all his pent-up frustrated force, he punches the clown in the face, with a sickening crunch of fist on bone.

That sends the clown sprawling, like spilling a sack of limbs onto the cobbles. Ghazan jumps after him. He puts the boot into the fallen clown—three times, hard and unremitting, his boot's toecap hits home between those spindly legs.

The clown's cries subside into whimpers and, finally, silence.

Ghazan's standing over him where he cowers, panting. He scrunches his heel into his face feeling the septal cartilage give way, the nasal bridge break.

Then Ghazan leans over to grab camcorder girl's camera. He twists it out of her hands, with a rough wrench of the wrists. He hurls it onto the bleeding clown's head with a curse. It bounces off the broken clown, smashes onto the stones.

Ghazan walks off grimly.

He can hear the reproachful remarks of the bystanders, the grumbles and groans of the broken clown, punctuated by nervous giggling from camcorder girl.

A gentle hand on his shoulder. He wheels round. The palefaced Scottish girl is there. Her eyes shift across his face with concern, her gaze lingers on his beard.

"Are you okay? Do you need a doctor?"

Her voice is so soft. Still panting, he takes in her freckled face, those large translucent eyes. For a split second, he feels vulnerable. Her hand comes up to touch his chin.

His head fills with her dizzying scent. His heart's beating hard. He's watching, half wanting her to touch him, but in the nick of time he steps back.

He looks down, pushes her gently but firmly away.

Turns around again.

He paces off in the direction of his hotel. He feels frazzled, as if some vital part of him has been burned away along with most of his beard. The sounds recede behind him, fade into the background of his consciousness. For a hundred yards or so he's stewing in his anger, walks on, seeing and hearing nothing...

Then, as he strides back through the alleys, and his mental balance recovers and rights itself, his rage begins to refine itself into a cooler mood, his more customary one of fixed and steady hatred.

The only way to cleanse the world of clowning, he thinks, *is to turn the comedy into a tragedy.*

Only then will the stage be cleared, and set for jihad.

TRACEY'S FART
Dulwich, London: Janice Primrose, Myles, Fiona & Sophia Lyall

JANICE PRIMROSE, pert young Vagina Warrior, took back a very different, very positive impression of Venice and its Biennale, the art event enabling the world to showcase works by its most famed, fortunate artists.

Having returned from there the previous week Janice was now sitting with Myles Lyall and his wife, Fiona, in their sunny sitting room in Dulwich, having some afternoon drinks. The room was eggshell-blue with fading prints on the walls.

It so happened that Myles and Fiona Lyall had watched a programme about the Biennale that previous evening. The efforts of Tracey Emin, an English artist representing her country, had come in for especial attention.

Fiona thought it all nonsensical garbage and Myles tended to agree with her.

"It strikes me that modern British art suffers from a poverty of imagination," said Myles, wishing to provoke his pretty, flat-chested, full-lipped friend Janice.

Fiona had seen before how Myles loved to needle Janice, especially with these pseudo-cultural topics, where he knew just enough to bait her tellingly.

"It's obsessed with superficials and making money," said Myles.

He was wearing an open-collar shirt and fawn-colored cords. His face looked drawn from overwork.

"Too many artists think because modern life is superficial its art should be superficial too," he said. "It's the mimetic fallacy."

Janice, in overalls, merely smiled up from where she was squatting on the rug. She seemed to enjoy Myles's teasing. She carried on playing with Sophia, the daughter of the house, an energetic bundle of blonde energy aged five. She lifted the child's stuffed dinosaur above her shoulders, waving it back and forth. Sophia shouted and then lunged at the dinosaur, grabbing it with both hands then hugging it to her chest.

"Hasn't art always been mimetic like that?" said Janice.

She looked down at her lap.

"And phallus-centered too, when you get down to it?"

"Miss Emin does fetch remarkably high prices," briskly volunteered Fiona, nipping in the bud any hint of bawdy badinage.

"It's not just her prices that are interesting," Janice retorted.

Fiona tried a little, but not too hard, to cover up her lack of keenness for Janice.

Fiona, a steady, practical woman, had no time nor use for queer theory, let alone Vagina Warriordom of the sort Janice espoused and flaunted. Fiona's own feminism, such as it was, had started out earnestly enough, but was now an unremarkable, unspoken part of her. She thought some feminist mannerisms quite frivolous.

Janice said, "Tracey is by far the most significant artist alive today."

"Is your Tracey the same Tracey as my Tracey?" asked little Sophia referring to a young woman who helped out at her kindergarten. "My Tracey's a very good drawer."

The dinosaur flew out of her hand toward the window.

"No," said Fiona. "The Tracey daddy means is a famous artist. She is known throughout the world. Showed her bed once as a piece of art."

This impressed Sophia. "Her bed? Was she in it?"

"No."

"Her empty bed?"

"Yes."

"Had she made it up special for the show?"

"She left it specially unmade."

"Cool. I'd like to do that too."

"You will, Sophia, you will," said Janice, pulling at Sophia's legs to drag her along the floor. "You're a work of art yourself, you know that, don't you?"

"No," said the child.

"Your bed's a lot nicer than Tracey's bed," said Myles loyally.

"A lot cleaner, too," said Fiona.

Janice looked up at the married couple with their glasses of cava. The child beside her on the floor made air-pedalling movements rapidly with tireless legs.

"I really doubt you two understand what it's about," said Janice. "Do you know what one of Tracey's paintings said? *Every part of my body is screaming, smashed into a thousand pieces.*"

Janice regarded them truculently. "*That's* how it feels to be Tracey."

Janice spoke with an unsmiling smile whose implied artistic superiority was deftly undercut by Sophia's brisk kick to her solar plexus. Fiona, watching, almost choked on her cashew to see the child kick the woman—she felt a guilty surge of pride.

Janice spluttered, took it like the thoroughly good sport she was. Collapsed dramatically onto Sophia's giggling form.

Janice herself was giggling too, but when she recovered, and picked herself up, she couldn't desist from saying, "Tracey's art is the howl of an oppressed heart."

Fiona scowled. Myles, next to her, bit his lip.

Little Sophia widened her eyes.

"That rhymes!" shouted Sophia. She now set herself to chanting Janice's words, very loud.

"Tracey's art, oh pressed heart! Tracey's art, oh pressed heart!"

Sophia carried on chanting and she danced round the room and she chanted and howled, dancing like a dwarfish dervish. An inventive little girl, full of play, she kept coming up with ever better variations on the theme, and these culminated in something like, "Tracey's fart, oh stressed part!"

She giggled jubilantly, squawked it out a further few times for effect, cackling each time as she watched her elders half-distracted still squabbling about Tracey among themselves.

Suddenly becoming bored of all the adult chat, Sophia ran out into the garden to play on her swing.

Janice Primrose watched the little girl sally forth, and she felt full of affection, yet pissed off too. Sophia jumped onto the swing, still singing out her rhyme about Tracey's fart.

"Tracey's been very successful undermining conventions," stated Janice with her small smile, smoothing down her T-shirt on her chest. "And she's sexy with it."

"Sexy? She's a drunken slob," Myles opined.

"She's rather too fond of her own cleavage," observed Fiona tartly.

"She *uses* her cleavage... to show how it feels to be Tracey," said Janice again.

"Maybe she should spend less time feeling herself," said Myles.

There was a peptic pause as they digested his *double entendre*.

"I wouldn't say no," said Janice at length.

"Is there anybody you *would* say no to, Jan?" Myles wondered.

Janice and Fiona both laughed, with Fiona's laugh being slightly louder than Myles's question strictly warranted.

"You, maybe," said Janice.

But this was the very core of Fiona and Janice's mutual dislike.

Little Sophia was irked by the weighty deliberations of her elders. She demanded they join her outside, in the garden, where it was cool and gray but warm enough to play.

So Myles and Janice went out and swung the sweet child, who was clad in a fetching pink and green dress, swiftly through the air.

"I was at a demo the other day," said Janice, pushing Sophia with a deal more force than her slight build suggested.

"Any good?"

"It was on behalf of Muslim women."

"Uh-huh? I thought that whole Muslim women thing was just... an irrelevant sideshow or something... didn't you say, in the sort of broader sweep of oppression?"

"I was just taking a look. There were some interesting people there as it happens. I met a nice woman called Mamida... she had a friend with her I liked even more: Shirin Shaarawi."

Janice looked dreamy as she articulated that name.

"Great. Hold on tight, Sophia."

"Shirin knows you, Myles."

"Really?"

"Well, she knows *of* you."

"Quite right too."

Myles caught little Sophia in his arms and proceeded to spin the swing around in its own ropes so that she could untwist round and round revolving in tiny circles at great speed. The child loved this motion and hugged the ropes tightly all the while ululating contentedly.

Meanwhile Janice continued to tell about her new friend.

"She's going out with a guy called Azeem, one of your clients."

"Oh right, our *Islamic Reform* man."

"Small world."

"Small world."

"I'm seeing her again."

"What was her name, Charlene Charlie was it?"

"Shirin Shaarawi."

"You clicked?"

"We clicked." Janice sighed. "She's special."

"That sounds like bad news for my client."

"Well, it could be very good news for him if he plays his cards right."

DIRECTORS OF CREATIVE EXECUTIONS
Bloomsbury, London: Azeem al Din, Ghazan Khattak, Shirin Shaarawi

AZEEM'S WORK TOOK on more of an international flavor, precisely as Sheikh Faisal had decreed. And at the same time, his life was disintegrating, falling apart.

Following his new instructions to include more countries in his network, Azeem was constantly on the move. Trips swallowed up his time. They were necessary without bringing up anything in the way of tangible results. He made contacts, he collected names and numbers—but the cause was slipping out of his grasp—some of the people he met came across as shifty, and made him uneasy, wary of what they wanted from the network.

And whenever he added another country to his list, Azeem felt the real world to be shrinking. Azeem felt he was making himself smaller to fit the world he knew. Every time, as soon as he got back, he'd be busily sculpting super-complicated new organograms, whittling away at mountainous lists of contacts and companies, seeing what they looked like in Powerpoint format.

International Consistency Co-ordinators, he wrote. He reflected a bit, then added **Total Work Officers.**

Having given this some more consideration he deleted the **Total Work Officers** and in their place put **Strategic Localization Supervisors.** Azeem stared at his work. He put boxes round the titles and linked them with lines like an inbred family tree. **Creative Excellence Officers**, he wrote, before changing it to **Directors of Creative Executions**.

Each trip he took added to the complexity of these diagrams. More and more new faces and places crowded out his head. They overflowed from his consciousness, like gargoyles in gigabytes. Endlessly filling his mind, overflowing from his brain, his eyes and his ears.

Azeem felt so full of others, he couldn't summon a thought of his own.

Only in one area was he making progress. He'd met Rania Zandi in the hospital. They'd gone through the script of the commercial, *Voices*, together.

She read it, first to herself, then, at his request, out loud. Her voice was scarred and weak, but it thrilled with a power from inside her. He was transfixed. Hearing her, he was no longer as upset as he had been about the putative message of the advertising campaign:

They hid my skin from the sun
But I cannot live in darkness.
They tried to end my life,
But my life has not been ended.
They tried to stop my voice,
But my voice will not be silenced....

He was making progress with *Voices*, but he still felt hemmed in by his partners, and goaded by them, as they sent him on one wild-goose chase after another.

Strange things were going on, too, things Azeem wasn't party to. The episode with the gunman in Soho Square was still not totally clear in his mind. He was surprised that no evidence had yet surfaced to link Ghazan to it. If Ghazan had been connected, surely the police would have questioned him by now? The more time passed by, the less sure Azeem was about it. It could well have been based on a misunderstanding on the gunman's part. Or maybe there really was another Ghazan at work, concealed in the sidelines...

Then he thought again about the attempted hospital attack on Rania. On balance, Azeem didn't believe that everything Shirin had told him could be accurate. That stuff about the Beeston Boys and their contacts inside the hospital rang true—but again, no arrests yet. Mamida, who'd been bending Shirin's ear about it, seemed to be totally obsessed by those Beeston Boys. Seemed to think they were behind everything. Maybe Mamida's obsession was just the ranting of a damaged woman—or maybe she had some deeper, darker agenda of her own...

Ghazan had spoken to him about the Beeston Boys. They no longer existed, he'd said. He'd sounded sincere. So Azeem didn't think Ghazan had had anything to do with that.

But there was other stuff. Last time he'd seen Ghazan, his face looked terrible, burned and singed.

"There was a fire," was all Ghazan would say. "There was a boy I had to drag out of there... else he would have died."

When Azeem asked where it had been, and who the boy was, Ghazan said, "I cannot tell you that. It is sensitive information. You should know better than to ask, brother."

Azeem knew he was being shut out of important decisions. But he also knew Ghazan was right in what he said about knowing better. They'd been trained never to ask too many questions. Unity was all, and questions could harm unity, could be dangerous.

More than all of this, though, Azeem fretted that he hardly ever saw Shirin these days.

One weekend he got home late from the airport to find no Shirin waiting for him, as he'd hoped, but a note saying, *Have gone to Mamida's. Don't wait up. Catch you tomorrow. Shirin.*

Next morning she turned up at ten.

Azeem was sprawled out exhausted on the sofa.

"Welcome back," said Shirin, sitting down next to him. She too looked tired.

"Welcome back to you too," sighed Azeem, his eyes incandescent red, his look long-suffering.

Shirin sat next to him. They kissed. Both of them wanted more, he thought. Shirin was tensed up, though. So was he, far more than he knew, but he felt it, now.

She said, "I had to spend some time with Mamida... She's in a bad way."

"I haven't slept a wink. I was expecting you back any minute."

"I told you I wouldn't be back."

"You didn't, you said don't wait up, which implies coming back."

"Mamida's in a bad way."

Azeem let the silence fade.

Then he said, "This isn't about Mamida, it's about you and me."

Shirin shook her head. "I can't bear everything to be about you and me."

"But this is!"

"No... no, Azeem, there's other people to think about too."

"Like who?"

"Mamida's been threatened by her uncle."

"What uncle?"

"Her father's sister's husband if you must know. This is a man who takes it upon herself to say she's bringing disgrace and dishonor on the family... And so he's threatening her."

"Threatening what?"

"Threatening to kill her."

Again the silence dragged.

He said, "*Why*, exactly, is she disgracing her family?"

"Oh, I wish you wouldn't be so obtuse! Mamida's a committed woman! She risks her own life, she helps girls get out of arranged marriages. She helps beaten wives escape from their abusive fucking husbands. She shelters them, gives them sanctuary."

"Maybe she better stop doing that then."

"Azeem!"

"Well, if it would stop the threats."

"That'd just be *giving up*! It's the last thing Mamida would do."

"Well, this may just be the last thing Mamida does. Maybe Mamida is digging her own grave with her obsessions, all those accusations and denunciations she throws around? It got her booted out of Leeds, maybe now she'll get herself kicked out of London, then England altogether, then—who knows, the world?"

Shirin was silenced. She sat still for a moment.

Then she said, "Mamida won't stop doing what's right just because a few deluded members of her extended family choose to get angry."

"Mamida could be very wrong, Shirin. Dangerously wrong."

"She wants to leave that repressive, medieval way of life behind her. I thought you did too, by the way, Azeem. I thought that's what that precious *project* of yours was all about! The one thing you can't do is surrender to that kind of... knuckledragging backwardness. Surely *you*, of all people, can see that?"

"I may have thought like that once."

"I remember. God, do I remember!"

"Why can't she just stick to her own tribe? Why can't she just accept her own tribe and what they're like?"

"*Tribe?* Do you see the world as nothing but a bunch of tribes?"

"It's a useful term. A lot of people think that way."

"Well, maybe she thinks of her *tribe* as more than the people from some minuscule corner of Pakistan. Maybe she feels she's part of a wider sisterhood."

"Yes, I'm sure she does. But obviously her tribe don't see it the same way. It looks like her tribe don't want to sit out the twenty-first century being... being *tribal* in their miniscule corner of Pakistan. They've got wider horizons too, they've got a global reach, just like anyone else. You shouldn't patronize her tribe, Shirin, they're her people. And you shouldn't sit there and patronize our faith."

Shirin shook her head. "I can't believe this is you speaking!"

She was genuinely astonished. Azeem looked at her. He sensed her bafflement, he shared it.

"Why, do I sound like someone else?"

"Has something happened, Azeem?"

"Just the same old stuff. I'm beginning to think that if only people would stop stirring up trouble, things would get a lot easier."

Shirin laughed. Her laughter, never bitter, was sweet in his ear.

But she said, "That's not very constructive, is it?"

"It would be a lot more constructive from my point of view."

"Anything for an easy life, eh?"

"Anything for an easy life," Azeem said. "Especially at weekends."

His mind no longer felt like his. His thoughts felt like cast-offs others had thrown in there, like stray pieces of garbage. He felt Shirin watching him coolly. She was watching him with a detached air, as of a woman watching out for whatever could possibly have attracted her to a man.

Azeem felt desperate. He fell back again, seething within himself. She seemed to have turned a mental corner just there.

She said, "It's strange how you've changed."

"People don't change," he said. "The world changes."

"No, *people* change. *Some* people change lots."

"I'm still the same me I always was."

"No, I don't think the *you* you used to be would have lied to me the way the *you* you are has lied to me."

"I haven't lied to you."

She looked at him blankly.

Fill in this space, said her face.

Azeem was incredulous, full of apprehensions now.

"When am I meant to have lied to you?"

"Faisal's been in touch."

Azeem's heart felt icy, heavy.

"Faisal's been after me for weeks now. He's been sending me messages."

"What's he say?"

"The truth."

"The *truth*. Difficult to believe."

"It's difficult all right, Azeem."

"I seem to remember Shabby being a—a pretty underhand sort of guy, pretty conniving—well, a fucking lying liar really... I know you remember that's how he was, too, that time in Paris."

"I do, I do, I do," said Shirin unhappily. "That's one reason I no longer associate with him the way you do."

"You're encouraging him, aren't you? I can just picture that... oh, Shirin. The great Sheikh fucking Shabby was already ready to sell his soul for you, that time in Paris, do anything to get his hands all over you."

"Paris... Paris was another world... And you seem to have forgotten... it's not me, it's *you* who's involved with him."

"So what makes him this paragon of truth suddenly?"

"It's not *him* becoming truthful. It's *you* becoming a liar."

"I can't believe I'm getting a moral dressing-down because of Shabby. *Shabby!* The sheikh with the greasy mitts! Who wanted to shake, rattle and roll you all over Montmartre! What exactly is the lie I'm meant to have told?"

"It's not a lie you told."

"Well give me a clue. Is it a lie that's been told about me?"

"It's a lie... in what you haven't told."

"I see."

"Yeah. There's lies of silence."

"I see."

"I can understand why you mightn't want to tell me what you're doing together with Sheikh Faisal."

"Good!"

"It's hugely significant! Not telling me is the equivalent of a lie. Don't pretend you don't know it."

"I thought it would upset you!"

"Well, now it has."

"I wanted to protect you."

"Well, you haven't, have you?"

"You know I need Shabby's money for my project. He's got the money. I do the project. It's as simple as that."

"It's *not* simple, Azeem. There's nothing simple about what you're doing. Your precious project's rotten to the core. The *Jihad*

Hotline, for fuck's sake. You're making a base for terrorists! And your lying complicates everything even more than it was before."

She's staring at him, looking down her nose with a cool gaze, no longer really probing where he's at, but more like judgmental, close to contempt. He can still just about hear a note of concern, soft and warm, in her voice. He yearns to give himself up to it, it's one of the things he loves about her, the way she *minds*, but he can't. He can't.

"Things'll work out for the best," he says. "I always knew you'd disapprove if I told you. You know what I think about jihad, and peace. I didn't want the argument we're having now."

"You wanted a quiet life, I know."

"I'd settle for a quiet evening in."

There was another silence between them. Shirin breathed out a slow sigh. She looked at the ceiling.

He badly wanted to kiss her. He raised himself up again. And he was about to lean over again when she spoke.

"As it happens, this evening I'm preparing for the demo with Mamida and some of the girls."

"The feminists?"

"Yes."

"Then I won't be seeing you this weekend at all then. I'm off again on Sunday evening. Madrid."

"Oh, lucky you. Madrid."

Another silence. Eventually Shirin said, "I'll be tied up doing the preparation today till quite late and obviously all of tomorrow... You could come along."

"Not a good idea."

"Faisal wouldn't approve?"

"Ha bloody ha. Shabby isn't my boss."

"That's not what he thinks."

"What's he think?"

"You're there to 'do his bidding'."

Azeem laughed at the phrase. "Well, I'm not. But I don't think my real bosses would look on it kindly, to put it mildly. Even if it were Shabby's bidding. Also I'm not sure I'd feel comfortable there with you and all those women. I'll just end up doing *your* bidding."

"Suit yourself."

And so the chance of that weekend passed Azeem and Shirin by, lost to them forever.

Ghazan Khattak, on his way home from Venice meanwhile, finds himself in refreshed, resolute mood. The miles are chewed up in the thrust of the jet's smooth engines, and he feels himself regaining something of his wonted strength. Evermore full of zest to do his duty, and to walk upright in the light of his Lord.

That fiasco, the nightmare with the clown earlier, although momentarily shaming, has been salutary, jerking his focus back to what counts.

He sits in his Club Class seat by the window, a newspaper on his knees. A headline catches his eye. He reads the article and it fills him with comfort inside—comfort, and a profound sense of compassion. It's about an important Christian in Germany— Bishop Margot Kaessmann is her name—who has divorced her husband, a male priest called Eckhard. The divorced Bishop is continuing, unabashed, in office, and the article has an admiring slant, seeing the divorce as a positive sign.

The idea of a woman as a priest has always struck Ghazan as curious, alien to tradition and common sense.

A woman's entry into Paradise is dependent on her husband's pleasure.

But growing up in the west has inured him to foolishness of all sorts. He sits back in his chair and considers the tortured plights the Christians put themselves through. And he pities them, with a pity that is distinct from his normal sentiments of repugnance and hate, although compounded and confounded with them.

But that's the thing with the west, he thinks, *that everything sacred is turned into sport, play, a form of clowning, fit only to be trampled on, defiled.*

No-one in the west has protested! No German flags have been trampled by outraged chanting Christians, not even in Rome! Not a single effigy of the mitered heretic has been set alight in any western city square!

And Ghazan remembers his reading of the Qur'an that morning:

We didn't create the heavens, the earth, and all between them, merely in play.

Pondering the *surah*, he feels that seriousness about life is a sign of sincerity. It is a mark of strength. He senses his own strength, his own sincerity, with a pure flush of elation.

Ghazan sits back and remembers his mother. She had been a serious woman. She had instilled a serious cast of mind in him. He has always tried to be true to the values she taught.

He knows she would have been proud of him now.

She, too was sickened by the way western society basks in drunkenness and sexual license, drug taking, fornication. She knew that creeping decadence was immoral, weak, that it sapped the energies of the young.

And unserious.

How right she was.

It's clear that at heart, westerners are indifferent to the health of their society, the health of religion—even if it's only Christianity, they're completely uninvolved in its teachings, *unconcerned* when it is dishonored. They do not embrace their religion. And that may be the greatest proof that it is in error. Westerners are indifferent, uncommitted, lazy and self-satisfied—they don't give a damn about what's made them what they are.

Perhaps they're *ashamed* of it. Ashamed of who they are.

Ashamed of living in torment, and it is no wonder.

Truly, the west is lost, he thinks. He stares at the spread-out, flattened panorama of Europe, watching it pass below, beneath him, crushed, and he feels that strange pity well up within him again, he feels filled with compassion.

To finish off its broken body, Ghazan realizes in sad elation, requires no more than determination and willpower—resolution to put the clowning to an end—to put out of its misery the decadent tomfoolery of a culture that has gone mouldy and septic.

Doing so will put those who live down there, writhing in anguish and suffering, out of their misery, and end their dishonor, their indifference... their absence from God.

And Ghazan whispers, under his breath, what is written in the Qur'an:

God summons humankind to the abode of peace, both in this life and the next.

NEW MAN

Paris: Faraz Zandi, Commissioner Ducoux, Divisional Commissioner Jaqmin

DIRECTLY BELOW THE PLANE at that moment lay Paris, where Faraz, Ghazan's young protégé, was incarcerated.

By now, after over a week in custody, he looked jaundiced. He was in a terrible state, saucer-eyed, paler than he'd ever looked, spottier, waxier of skin.

He was beginning to get used to prison routine.

Every day they questioned him. A succession of interviewers came to see him in the gray room he was always taken to. Aside from Commissioner Ducoux—an almost constant presence, whether in the interview cell itself or just behind the scenes (and behind the mirror Faraz knew concealed an observation room)— there had been others, anonymous men, often in pairs. Once, there had come a female detective. She had smiled at him with a warmth that made him ache, he'd almost cried. She had taken his hand and spoken to him softly. She'd disturbed him. She tried to key into a part of him he didn't use, he wasn't sure was there...

But mostly it was men.

Their faces merged in his mind.

The food he was given made a mess of his stomach. When he squatted to relieve himself, the stools seldom came, and only with difficulty. He felt dirty and exposed and watched in his stinking cell.

He'd lost track of the days.

Today, Commissioner Ducoux, sitting at his usual place opposite, was uptight. He wasn't his usual urbane self, he had a haunted look.

An hour of questions passed.

Another man came in.

Commissioner Ducoux turned round to see. He got up at once. The new man had a buzz-cut, he was younger, smaller, fitter, more brutal of expression than Commissioner Ducoux.

From the way Ducoux greeted him, the new man was clearly of higher rank.

They stood either side of the door, conferring in a rapid French of which Faraz could only understand the *oui's* and *non's.*

This new man had a disk in his hand, and that was the focus of much of their talk. As they spoke, the new policeman looked over at Faraz a few times, a slight smile on his lips.

When they'd done talking, he came over. He put the disk into the laptop on the table.

"Regarde-cela!"

He turned the computer round so Faraz could see the screen. It was a video taken off YouTube, and it opened with a close-up of a manic clown, dancing about with a girl in a bikini...

As Faraz watched, his first reaction, on seeing Ghazan, was a twinge of home sickness. He wished he could be with Ghazan right now. He felt a yearning for home, he wanted to be away from this place...

Then, as the video went on, Faraz was filled with sympathy for his mentor, seeing his beard go up in flames like that, seeing him mocked and traduced for the entertainment of thousands of viewers who didn't know him, didn't care who he was... He was filled with outrage, fellow-feeling.

Concern, almost.

But as the film ended, and he felt the eyes of Ducoux and the short fit guy on him, as he was making his own eyes go blank, avoiding theirs, giving nothing away, he felt loathing rise up in him, rise up from his inner emptiness. He felt alone, and his heart felt cold, and he was sick with himself, he hated Ghazan so at that moment. He knew that if Ghazan were there, he, Faraz would go for him, handcuffs or no, he would launch himself at Ghazan, to attack him any way he could, to butt him with his head, his elbows, bite him to draw blood.

Faraz looked up.

He saw how both Commissioner Ducoux and the other man were staring at him, watching his clenched fists, sizing him up blankly. It was almost as if they were expecting nothing from him.

But he knew they knew he would talk, would tell them about the man with the burning beard of flames.

And he wanted to talk, he wanted to tell them everything, now.

And in London, a few minutes later, Laetitia Wythenshawe's ex-lover, Dave Page, took a call from his friend Mad Mick.

Mad Mick hadn't forgotten about Lady Laetitia.

"Mate," he said, "I've talked to some of my contacts about doing a job on this Lady Wythenshawe slut... There's a guy I've found up in Leeds, he's some kind of a community worker who does extra services. You won't like him, he's what you, with your criminal, prosecutable, highly offensive racism, would call a towelhead. The good news is he's interested in taking it on. You can expect something to happen in the next few weeks."

"What's he got in mind?"

"He reckons to make a big thing out of this, mate," said Mad Mick.

"Right. Did he say *what*?"

"Didn't let on. That's still confidential."

"Right."

"He was dead keen on her being this classy upmarket slag... high society... and he's very taken with the idea of making an example out of her... as a *warning* like."

"Right."

"I wanted you to be the first to know, Dave. We'll be calling on you for some particulars soon. This'll be a finely-tuned, top operation. You can help us fix the layout of the place and so on... tell 'em the lie of the land, so they can get in, do the business, and make their getaway quick."

"Right."

And so Dave's mind reverted for a moment to his ex, Laetitia Wythenshawe, of whose recent doings he remained completely in the dark.

He didn't think about Laetitia so much these days, new chickens in the coop, plenty to keep him occupied. He felt like she belonged to another time. He'd moved on.

But just at that moment, it startled him, how quickly she'd become a virtual nothing to him, her face, her body, and all those things they used to do, all blurred up in his mind. Even so—recalling how his raw mortification had burned inside when she dumped him—it was good to know she'd be getting her comeuppance.

SMELL
Twinnington: Laetitia Wythenshawe

ONE HOT MORNING, the following weekend, as Laetitia is leaving the house to go riding before the weather breaks, she notices a smell wafting from the left corner of the porch.

A lumpy plastic carrier bag from Tesco's is lying there. Not there before. She goes over to take a look. When she opens it, the smell is overpowering, it fills her nose, seems to claw at her throat.

She looks in. The bag is crammed full of dead stuff. Dead birds, offal, entrails. Rotting potatoes, black and green, a ripped-off, eyeless fox-head, with worms pullulating in its sockets, a spillage of innards. All floating about, soaking in a pulpy mess in the bottom of the bag.

The sweet, gamy smell of death seeps into her nostrils. A drop of liquid spills on her shoe. Laetitia drops the bag. It plops down, soggily, at her feet. Her stomach turns liquid, her throat seizes up as if she's swallowed sand. She raises her hand to her mouth, retches.

She runs back inside and shouts for the housekeeper.

CONNECTIONS
M1: Rupert Wythenshawe

MEANWHILE RUPERT Wythenshawe is driving out of London in his new car, a Bentley Brooklands in Venusian gray. He's just left the North Circular and is joining the M1.

It's a lovely morning for it.

Wythenshawe has decided it's time to pay his wife a visit. Myles has told him about the heavy hints Dr Klinker dropped in Düsseldorf. So he thinks he'll have it out with Laetitia about that—that incontinence of hers again—and to check the lie of the land regarding her divorce-plans.

There is also the matter of Dr Klinker and Udo's attempts at bribing him, something Wythenshawe thinks he can put a stop to, quite simply by destroying the information. He's wiped clean the trail in London, but he knows there's still a deal of material up in Twinnington.

Wythenshawe thinks he can make it to the Border country in about five hours, reach Laetitia's family estate in Twinnington by the afternoon.

A brightly-polished silver axe lies on the equally well-toned leather seat beside him. Wythenshawe is keen to clear away all the computerized correspondence, the compromising data Dr Klinker's been casting his eyes over in his absence. Taking an axe to the hard file, he's been told, is the only way to guarantee that it's wiped away for ever.

First, Wythenshawe calls his partner Myles Lyall.

"Myles! It's me! Bad news I'm afraid."

"What's up, Rupert?"

"We're going to have to take you off the *Islamic Reform* account, I'm afraid, Myles, old chap."

"Sorry?"

"*I'm* sorry, Myles. I cannot tell you how sorry I am. It's over."

"Sorry, the line's terrible. What's over?"

"The *Islamic Reform* account, Myles," Rupert shouts. "You're off it. It's over."

"Off it? Says who?"

"It's a client request, my boy. There's nothing I can do! I'm deeply sorry. It's over, Myles."

"This isn't something you can just decide without me, Rupert."

"Ah, but it is. I brought the client into the agency in the first place, do you see? My family connections, you remember."

"I do remember! But I also remember signing the contract, which is with our agency, not just with you. And might I point out that we were floating the idea of *dropping* this particular client."

"With an attitude like that I must say it's hardly surprising the client wants shot of you, Myles... have you been at the sauce this morning, or what? But, whatever the rights and wrongs of your slightly... unhinged paranoia, this client is simply too profitable to sack, Myles."

Wythenshawe can almost hear Myles' thought processes clicking away on the other end.

After a while, Myles says, "You're cooking something up, aren't you? You've become too cosy with that dreadful Samir Muhsi. He's plotting something, isn't he? He's *got* at you... I think I shall—"

"Sorry, Myles, line's breaking up! Don't worry about the account. There may be some implications relating to our equity, of course... We may have to recalibrate our compensation... in line with income responsibility. Fair's only fair, eh Myles? Let's discuss in more depth next week!"

Wythenshawe cuts off the mike.

He smiles into the mirror and checks his teeth as he smiles. He sits at the wheel, smiling like a toothsome, nattily-besuited crocodile.

He's driving as fast as the car will go.

Next, Wythenshawe calls his German colleague Dr Norbert Klinker. The connection is surprisingly fast.

"Klinker!" barks the voice on the other side of the sea. "Klinker here!"

Wythenshawe knows full well what Dr Klinker's up to that morning.

He's participating in an *International Fair Trade Carbon Friendly Marketing Seminar* in Düsseldorf, a happening organized by well-intentioned marketing professionals which will extend throughout the weekend.

Klinker's been booked to speak about the propagation of global justice.

His usual perspicacious pearls of cobblers and bollocks, Wythenshawe thinks.

Klinker's taken up something called Lean Six Sigma doctrine. Wythenshawe snorts, remembering the proud light in Klinker's eyes when he told him about it, how he's implementing Six Sigma metrics across all marketing communications channels, using them to save the planet, and how his face is being splashed all over the posters and flyers advertising the occasion.

So, full of himself and his fame, Dr Klinker strides, straight-backed, hair swept back, through clamorous conference halls. He loves these international carnivals of ideas. They make him feel at the heart of things. He's casting about for new ideas, and is struck by a stand whose branding proclaims: **eth!c@l°:@ud!t°**

"What's this?" asks Dr Klinker.

He feels like a kindly uncle, stumbling on some childish stall someone's little nephews and nieces have made of their shells and their toys. Not normally his field, and he's out of his depth. But then it washes over him, something fresh, a quibbling, quizzical feeling, one with which he's becoming professionally familiar, in the quizzical way of childless middle-age segueing into old bufferdom.

Klinker slightly resents it—his life blood is in being *au fait* with the cutting edge, lean and hungry for the new—but it stimulates him.

eth!c@l°:@ud!t° is tosh, too empty for words. Klinker can judge it before he understands it, he knows that. But he feels mischievously sure that once he's mastered it, there'll be money to be squeezed out of it.

He goes, "Can you tell me what it's all about?"

"Well... it's symbol-writing... for *Ethical Audit*," says the dreadlocked, wispily bearded young man behind the stall.

"Symbol writing I know. The language of signs... But *Ethical Audit*?"

"We offer 360° Ethical Audits for the digital age. That's for clients who want us to check up on their corporate responsibility, their ethics and their ethical perceptions. It's important to keep up with the latest buzz in this arena. Because undetected ethical transgressions can creep up on your company's image before you realize what's happening, and destroy it."

"Undetected ethics? Creeping up behind me?" Klinker shouts excitedly.

He sees the brilliance of the idea at once. And, with the sure instinct of a born plagiarist, he straightaway sets himself to sow a little doubt and discord... with the aim of trampling all over the idea, prior to tweaking it slightly and then presenting it as his own at some convenient later time.

"I *spit* on ethics!" says Klinker, his eye glinting.

The folks standing nearby prick up their ears to hear this excited bearded man, shooting off his mouth at another.

"Ethics are for the weak... the weak of will, the weak of mind!" Klinker declares with demonic energy. "To be ethical is to be *fickle*... to lose sight of rolled throughput yield. And that kind of *fickleness* spells defect density, and failure, no matter what symbolic language you use!"

Just as he is getting into his stride Klinker is distracted by the ringing of his mobile. He fishes it out of his pocket.

"Klinker!" he barks. "Klinker here!"

"Norbert, you old stick! It's me, Rupert," Wythenshawe smoothly says.

"I am enjoying my relaxation session this weekend," Klinker barks, glaring round at the marketing delegates who, disappointed the show's over, have started to drift away.

"I am today's featured speaker," he says, "I have been recognized as the champion of maximizing uptime organizational bandwidth."

"Excellent stuff!" says Wythenshawe. "Maximization's the very thing, I always say."

"I'm a Lean Sigma Master Black Belt, you know!"

"Good God!" Wythenshawe exclaims. "I never knew you were a wrestling man."

"I like to work out at weekends, when I can, to tool the mind, it keeps me in shape!"

"Not to worry," says Wythenshawe, "I won't tie you up in knots, ha ha ha. Straight to business. Did you receive the payment I sent you last week?"

"Yes, I have received it, thank you, Rupert."

"That's the kickback payment I'm talking about, for the *Islamic Reform* project."

"Yes, of course," Klinker replies uncertainly.

"The fee we're sharing between us on an expressly private basis?"

"Precisely. As we have agreed it!"

"Splendid," says Wythenshawe. "That's all I wanted to check. You see, that will be the last payment for you, I'm afraid, Norbert. It's over."

"I'm not understanding you."

"I shan't be transferring any more money to you, my dear Norbert. The transfer market has closed. I'm sorry. Very sorry. It's over."

"But what about our deal?"

"New circumstances have rendered our deal redundant, I'm afraid."

Rupert's eyes take in the motorway as it spreads before him in the distance.

"Oh," he says, "it's only fair to tell you this conversation is being recorded."

"What is the point of this comment?" Klinker asks with a panicky yowl.

"Why, the compromising details you've been kind enough to share with me can easily be shared with others. The taxman cometh, and so on. I believe the authorities your side of the pool are as sensitized about fraudulent characters as ours are. It's what we call an occupational hazard, Norbert. If you look a kickback too closely in the mouth, it may end up kicking you in the teeth, as we say in England."

There is a long silence on the other end, followed by a click signalling that Dr Klinker has hung up.

In the *Messe* halls of Düsseldorf, Klinker can wring little pleasure from the remainder of his Fair Trade Carbon Friendly Marketing Seminar. The Wythenshawe kickback revenue stream's now dried up, he has to face it. He has truly been kneed in the balls with regard to that one.

A few new questions rise up at once to haunt him. How much remains to be squeezed from the *Islamic Reform* account? What value, if any, his closeness to Myles Lyall? How can he use Laetitia? If only he'd spent more time at Twinnington, gathering up his incriminating data on Wythenshawe!

He needs to regroup, Klinker sees, regather his forces. He's sure he can coax Wythenshawe round. He'll force him to see sense. Threatening a course of mutual assured destruction may be the only way — something even crazy Wythenshawe will want to avoid.

Restlessly knocking about the marketing show, ambling, dazed, from stand to stand — brochures and flyers shoved at him every step he makes — Klinker does his best to divert the disappointment from his mind. He mopes round the exhibition hall, halfheartedly checking the form as regards female delegates, but even in that quarter he finds nothing to admire — too earnest and leery for his taste. And so he decides to clear off as soon as he's delivered his keynote speech, *Clustering Cross-Functional Six Sigma Principles To Maximize Fair Trade Payback Outcomes.*

The **eth!c@l°:@ud!t°** concept, however, grows in Klinker's esteem. It has even more uplift potential, he calculates, than his initial instincts indicated. He makes a mental note to claim it for his own.

That is his way, the way of the guru of cutting edge consumer intelligence—the keenest marketing brain of the age! To take half-formed, abortive mental gestations from unschooled, untrained, *undisciplined* minds, and mold them into effective and efficient vehicles of added value and business-model transformation, revolutionizing perceptions, attitudes and intentions to buy. *Jawohl!* That's the Klinker way, and nothing shall deflect him from it, not as long as a sentient cell of trend-spotting cognizance remains in his body.

His meeting with the Zimbabwe Tourism Authority, pencilled in for the coming week, at once suggests itself as a fitting forum to unveil his new idea.

He feels hugely cheered up.

Rupert Wythenshawe blazes up the motorway burning it up at a hundred and fifty. He's roaring with laughter. A heavy thunderstorm has been brewing and is now flying furiously all around him. This inhibits his full enjoyment of the vehicle's potentialities, but it matches his mood of manic exuberance. He's in the highest possible spirits, pulsing with the wideawake zest of the mad.

He's listening to Wagner very loud. A morbid glint lurks in a corner of his eye, as of a man finally getting round to the unfinished business he should really have cleared away much earlier.

The car roars north in its wake of slush. Its headlights cut through the net of raindrops, slicing out great beams of light. It looks like a dragon flying home through stormy skies, flashing eyes and breathing fire.

THE MAP ROOM
Twinnington: Laetitia Wythenshawe, Mrs Williamson

LAETITIA SITS IN the kitchen with her housekeeper, Mrs Williamson, drinking tea. A long high yellow room, with big bay windows overlooking the park, it used to be the Map Room. Here Laetitia's forefathers consulted the pedigrees of stallions and brood-mares, ran large chunks of Empire, dreaming up many a subtle, artful scheme, centuries past, and plotted to make them real.

Laetitia and Mrs Williamson are sitting together at an oval oaken table in the center of the room. Battered Chippendale chairs, on bare creaking floorboards, comfortably faded grandeur. The teapot stands between them, its spout protruding from a blue floral tea cosy.

Laetitia is upset, but Mrs Williamson is upsetter.

The gory carrier bag with the body-parts wasn't the last of the unpleasantness that morning. When Laetitia looked out over the lawn, she noticed something odd on the grass, about halfway to the ha-ha to the south.

Stormclouds were brewing on the far western horizon, but it was still dry on the estate. The air was oppressive, hot and pressing, with a cloying scent of sickly hay. A haze of flies was busy above, and when she and Mrs Williamson got to the spot to look, they found the headless cadaver of a fox. It was splayed out on two crossed wooden stakes, like a crucifixion.

The fox had been eviscerated in a sloppy way. Bits of his guts still stuck to the body, and the odor drove the flies into swarming delirium.

Then, further off, in a large paddock Laetitia used when the horses were stabled at home, two hounds had had their throats slit, and were nailed, upside down, onto the branches of two old beech trees.

It seemed some psychopaths had been on the prowl the night before.

SUCH SICKNESS

Twinnington: Rupert Wythenshawe, Laetitia Wythenshawe, Mrs Williamson

LATER, AS WYTHENSHAWE is arriving at the Twinnington estate's southern gatehouse, the rainstorm whips itself into an apex of violence. Drenching the unmade track in rolling sheets of liquid, it all but drowns out the Wagner blaring from the speakers. Wythenshawe sits there in his Bentley and stares out at the place.

The gatehouse is still owned by Laetitia's family, but it's been let out to a young couple. They have no gatekeeping duties, no employment link to Laetitia or her estate. The gate itself has been kept permanently open since Laetitia's father died. As such, Wythenshawe is astonished to see it's barred today.

He honks his horn and the rain pelts down. A face appears at an aperture directly above the gate. Soon after, a thin man in a short paisley dressing gown emerges from the front door. He stands barelegged on the porch looking cold. This man glances at the gate, padlocked shut, and he shrugs his puny shoulders.

"We don't have the key!" he calls over to Wythenshawe, in a cracked, fruity voice like a broken flute. "It wasn't locked yesterday."

Wythenshawe curses like a proverbial trooper at this circumstance which seems to mock his arrival, prodigal, after so many months not venturing near the place. What is Laetitia playing at, he wonders. In a flash of paranoia he suspects his wife of wanting to bar him from the premises but in his heart he knows that wouldn't be the sort of thing she'd do, so underhand and petty. All the same, he now has to ask the Noel Coward-like man at the gate if he can leave his car at the gatehouse.

A place is found for the Bentley on the earthbank between some sodden rhododendron bushes.

Wythenshawe, accompanied by scary flashes of lightning, insinuates himself inside the grounds through a walkway to the left hand side of the gatehouse.

He tramps up the rivuleted muddy drive, a walk of some one and a half miles, a distance he is destined never to complete under his own steam.

Laetitia stands at the window staring out at the rain. Her sniveling housekeeper, Mrs Williamson, has sort of pulled herself together, and is sitting close behind her, by the fire.

Mrs Williamson still snivels once every other second, as with a heavy head cold. In between, she takes gulps from a tumbler which Laetitia's filled to the brim with hot toddy.

As soon as she's drained it, the faithful retainer refills the tumbler from a bottle of whisky standing within easy reach on the table.

Casting about in her mind, Laetitia reckons Dr Klinker to be the likeliest man behind the sick consignments of offal, the bags of entrails, bodies littering up her grounds. Klinker's the only man she knows with an openly acknowledged dark side, twisted, indulged in word and deed—a dark side of the kind to find its release in such sickness...

Klinker's the only man she's ever met whose language will always revert to death, to decay and evil, the only man so sexually depraved as to have made her sick, physically sick...

And why, she asks herself, looking out over her sodden lawns—aside from giving himself a thrill by making a lady squirm—would any man want to do this?

She's looking through the slanting rain as it pelts down on the lawns.

A figure is walking up the drive, he is walking slowly into the wind and, Laetitia sees, he's carrying an axe.

Wythenshawe walks up the drive, his features screwed up in the face of the spitting storm. Square on, the rain hits him in the face. Sheets of icy water slash through his coat like broadsides cutting into his flesh.

The sky turns a greasy greenish gray, like peasoup gone cold.

Wythenshawe feels so queasy, it's like he's being tossed around by a storm at sea. All at once he feels yawed and rolled, he feels he might fall away into nothingness, that the world's surface has become a mere bubble on the ocean's surface, a membrane unable to bear his weight.

But he sets his face against the storm and all these churning feelings and walks on up the drive.

Sidestepping the glass which her half-drunk housekeeper brandishes at her, Laetitia pops out into the hall. She unlocks the cupboard, takes down the old over-and-under Purdey shotgun. Comes back in, the gun broken open.

"Wait for me here," she says, slotting in the cartridges, then lifting the latch on the outside door.

She steps out. The housekeeper, reeling in her chair, watches her incuriously through bloodshot eyes, and takes another swig of whisky, hardly sure of who she is or where.

Laetitia stands in the doorway and looks out. The rain hits her in the face, runs down her Barbour, her boots, an instant puddle spreads across the black slate porch. Laetitia bends her head down gravely, as if genuflecting in church, and then she starts walking down the hill, into the wind, and toward the man with the axe whom she is convinced must be Dr Klinker out of his silly mind.

The greenish blue-hued nightmare atmosphere around him, which he sees blurred, through filmy eyes, is beginning to smell strange, too, in Wythenshawe's nostrils, as if sulphur were fizzing through the air. He walks on like a maniac, his hair tugs upward of its own accord—his hair is standing on end, so he proceeds along the unmade track looking like a scarecrow come to life, the whiff of hell in his nose.

Out of the corner of his eye he sees his wife dressed for riding carrying her shotgun and cowering down close to the ground, seeming to shout at him—and then at once, like a cut—the noise of the storm shuts out, sucked up into a vacuum above, and a great white light expands around him, it intensifies into a flash, an explosion stunning him beyond all sense or consciousness.

Too late Laetitia sees it's her husband, stumbling there like a loon. She's let off both barrels by now, thinking it's Klinker barking mad, but firing well above his head, wanting only to warn him off like a rabid dog with a scare of gunfire.

Then, in the split instant the pellets scatter above, Wythenshawe is struck by a great bolt from the heavens and a flash of light streams around his body like a blazing cocoon. He's lifted ten feet up bodily into the sky, his long frame pulled out of his shoes and half his clothes shredded, his hand drops his axe which falls like a glinting star—he flies forward hurtling and then comes down hard beside the track, headbutting a skull-sized stone standing there—he's knocked out cold, so Laetitia, discarding her gun, runs to his side.

A trickle of blood seeps from Wythenshawe's mouth where he lies in the mud.

Laetitia smoothes away some strands of hair from his forehead, rubs off the blood with her handkerchief.

Her eyes fill with tears. She's sure he's dead.

His tongue lolls out of his mouth in a canine way. She can't see him breathing. And now a sudden thrill of empathy wakes in her heart, so long since he's aroused any feelings in her at all, save frustrated ones. She strokes his head as though he were a much-loved old dog lying sick beside her.

Then he moans, and his eyelids flicker. Her pity dissolves into an eerie sense of fear which is not physical but detached from her. She sees his eyes struggling to focus on hers.

Finally Wythenshawe seems to recognize her.

"Where am I?" he says.

"You're home, darling," she replies.

"Where's my axe?" asks Wythenshawe.

Somehow supported by his wife Wythenshawe drags himself up the hill and now he's making for the house. On the way, he finds his axe in a shallow puddle by the wayside.

He leans stiffly down and picks it up.

"What's that for, darling?" asks Laetitia, regretting her discarded shotgun lying out of reach in the mud.

"I've got some unfinished business," Wythenshawe says grimly.

She says, "It's not me, is it, darling?"

"No, what... *you?* No, of course not, not at all," Wythenshawe rambles. "It's unfinished business."

He stumbles on up the hill.

"What business is that, darling?"

"That's business I haven't finished!"

Now they've reached the house. He heads for his study, raving and declaiming from his mad contorted mouth.

Laetitia is mightily afraid of him.

"That filthy stinking Hun Dr Nobby Klinker got into my computer, didn't he?"

Wythenshawe growls at her angrily, his voice twisted up in a half-swallowed, howling undertone.

He shouts, "He got in there, didn't he?"

Wythenshawe's clothes have been torn from his body by the rod of lightning. He doesn't look remotely sane.

"Calm down, darling, he's not here," pleads Laetitia.

Mrs Williamson appears at the door.

"Weevilly widdershins!" she shouts raucously, raising a fist at Wythenshawe.

"Klinker's been here!" Wythenshawe howls, ignoring the drunk housekeeper. "Smearing his disgusting paws all over everything—he's got into my computer, and now he's trying to take what he wants. Stinking Nazi blackmailing pervert!

"Out of my way now!" he shouts.

Wythenshawe shoves Laetitia out of the way. She tries to hold on to him but falls to her knees in the corridor, surprised by his strength. The study door slams behind him.

Mrs Williamson, clutching her bottle, withdraws into the kitchen, mumbling to herself sottishly.

Laetitia now hears Wythenshawe raving like a crazed prophet in his study. He's ripping open his drawers, he's pulling things down from the shelves, she hears stuff crashing on the ground, Wythenshawe punctuating these noises with bestial roars of his own.

"I'll fix you, you double-crossing Hun!"

Laetitia peeps in at the door. She watches her husband putting the axe in. He's found his laptop in its drawer. He thrusts it down on his desk ranting at it as though it can hear his crazy execrations.

He smashes the axe down, face full of savage glee.

"Take that, you rancid Kraut!"

Now Laetitia is sure he's gone insane—Wythenshawe thinks Klinker's really holed up inside his laptop, and he thinks these rabid blows, with the axe-blade raining down, will crush Klinker and get him forever out of the way...

As Wythenshawe lays about him like a berserker Laetitia watches, too terrified by far to come and stop him. The man is increasingly erratic in his movements. He's stumbling, now, like a hooligan, a mad yobbish fan in exultation, drunk in some foreign square, the away leg won, riotous, oblivious—and just like a hooligan, the cause of his rage is dissipated, gone.

Wythenshawe stumbles closer to his desk. He lifts up the axe to bring a final swing down on the laptop lying there and he takes a half step back to get a better angle. Now his muddy shoe slips on a pile of discarded documents, his legs buckle, and he mis-hits, badly.

The blade bites into his wrist hitting the bone with a dull thud. It rips an ugly gash in his flesh. The hand is half hanging off by the tendons.

Laetitia screams.

Blood starts to spurt up like a fountain from Wythenshawe's ripped wrist. He looks down, he's all dazed for a second, his eyes horrified by his own blood, spurting from that gash of torn flesh, gushing up, and then he falls, he crashes in a heap on the floor.

DISAFFECTED

United Kingdom: Ghazan Khattak, Beeston Boys, et al

ON JUNE 27TH 2007 by prearranged agreement the Prime Minister of Great Britain Tony Blair stood down and was replaced by his Chancellor, a Scottish man called Gordon Brown. A comically inept series of terrorist outrages was perpetrated that very weekend, to welcome the new man to his desk as it were. Luckily the plots, which had been hatched by disaffected medical men, were foiled or went awry, and nobody was killed.

Even so, they were hardly designed to lift the country's mood.

One result of the commotion was that the police started rounding up terrorist suspects. That same weekend they took one of the Beeston Boys into custody, a man well known to Mamida Hanif, and, more to the point, to Ghazan, who had long been the suspect's counsellor.

Ghazan had recruited him into the ranks of the *baraderi*. He'd recently chosen him, pointed him in the direction of Twinnington, saying,

"Go to that place, my brother, and you will find a harlot, sunk in the ways of lust and lewdness. I have heard it from many witnesses. Remember… remember what we are enjoined to do. If any woman is guilty of lewdness, take the evidence of four witnesses — we have far more than four, my brother! — and if they testify, confine the woman to her house until death claims her — or Allah ordains some other way. We must see what Allah ordains, my brother."

The man had taken these words into his heart. He'd gone out with the *baraderi*, full of conviction to do right. But what they did, out on Laetitia's lawn, sickened him. He went through with it because he was scared, and aside from his fear, he'd have felt foolish backing out, it would have meant loss of face. His comrades would have accused him of dishonoring them with his cowardice, or worse.

So he'd gone along with them. But he did it with a heavy heart, filled with shame. It made him think badly of the people he was getting mixed up with.

If this is what Ghazan's fine words boiled down to—killing animals, immolating their corpses—then there was no connect between words and deeds... Either Ghazan had lost control of his men (which he doubted) or his words had lost control of their meaning.

And so, as chance would have it, when he was arrested, the man proved notably helpful to the police. Lacking any fetish for nihilism or self-destruction, he was easily played on by the police's skilled interrogators.

The police asked him about his controller.

"I only know him as Ghazan," he said. "He never told me his real name."

"Where's he from?"

"Leeds."

"He lives up in Leeds?"

"No, he lives up in London."

"What's he look like?"

The man described Ghazan as best he could. He told them about the internet café in the Edgware Road. He helped an artist put together a photofit on the computer. When it was printed out and circulated to the police team, one of the officers had a spark of recognition.

"Seen that guy somewhere before."

After a few hours of searching, the cop came back, saying he'd found a clip.

"It was put up on YouTube a few weeks ago. It was quite popular, got a few thousand hits, but then there was a stiff complaint and it had to be taken off."

"What did it show?"

"You'll see. I think this may be the man our friend knows as Ghazan."

His colleagues gathered round the screen. The clip opened on Campo Santa Margarita in Venice. The clown, stumbling about inanely. The tall girl in a bikini with him. The camera weaved from the long-legged girl to the drunken clown and then the shot focused on a bearded man in the middle distance.

The cop froze the film just at the moment the clown was putting the lighter under the bearded man's chin.

"Is that him?" asked the cop.

The man looked silently at the screen. His face told the officer what he wanted to know. It was a positive identification, a connection to the man known as Ghazan, and now with his onscreen name and internet address, linking him to the complaint which had led to the clip being taken off YouTube, and all the rest of it.

COMMUNING
East Barnet, London: Shirin Shaarawi, Janice Primrose

MEANWHILE, SHIRIN and Janice Primrose are meeting in Janice's flat in a terraced house in East Barnet, North London. The rain whips against the windows, which are old and single-glazed, rattling in their thin and peeling wooden frames.

The bad weather outside makes the drab little flat cosy and intimate.

Shirin is complaining about her boyfriend Azeem. She speaks about the man in a way which, imperceptibly at first, begins to excite Janice Primrose. For as the complaints accumulate, Janice's eyes focus on Shirin's lips, forming those mournful, pouting vowels.

Beguiled by the beauty of her friend's mouth as she talks blithely on, Janice begins, fondly, to fancy Shirin might be induced to sleep with her, or at least that they might cuddle up together in her bed, as the storm rages on, for mutual comfort.

"Sometimes men are so blind!" Shirin's saying. "It's all work work work... and obsessive pointless work too, never a moment to stop and think, and put things into some kind of perspective."

Janice, her head severely shorn, but pretty in pink like a punky princess, nods.

"I sometimes think men lack a fundamental gene we women have..." says Janice.

She stretches out her trim biceped arms, arching back her fit body in that thin, short tanktop. Shirin can't help but notice how well put together a package Janice is, so neat and slim.

"... The gene we have, that keeps things in their proper proportion."

Janice lies back on the sofa, watching Shirin's lips as she responds.

"Tunnel-vision, that's what Azeem's got. He's being taken for a ride by these Islamist propagandists... they haven't a clue what they want themselves. They take their pig ignorance out on Azeem, so he ends up running round Europe setting up futile meetings with agencies and *helpers* and fellow-travelers and God knows what seedy sort of scum and troublemakers... and what does he get out of it? Nothing... nothing but trouble as far as I can see."

"Men really are *differently-abled*," Janice remarks, resting her chin on her hand. "They exploit their male-bodied privilege and the whole status-quo of paternalistic society, but at bottom, they're differently-abled."

She's still regarding Shirin with a droll, tender look, replete with lust.

"And when we think of male-bodied individuals, that's something we should never forget... not that I ever want to, particularly. Think about them, I mean. The male-bodied too often seem not merely differently-abled but disabled to me."

"Lesser-abled?" Shirin suggests with a smile.

Janice smiles right back at her. "They lack the resources to commune."

"With us?"

"With us. With nature. With—fuck knows, themselves!"

Janice laughs, but Shirin feels lonely suddenly. A small sad pang of guilt, as she thinks of poor Azeem, slaving away. This uneasy pang of conscience comes out in a moue of her lips, so red, so delicious to kiss.

Janice, sensing that as a signal of tenderness for her own sweet self, strokes Shirin's cheek.

Shirin takes the stroking hand. But rather than kissing it, as Janice surely hopes, Shirin gently puts it away. Janice Primrose emits an emollient murmur—a murmur of resistance, or reassurance, or petulance, or a bit of everything, she doesn't seem to know.

Shirin shakes her sad head.

"I'm happy we're friends, Jan."

For the moment they leave it at that.

SHIFTING BOUNDARIES
London, Leeds: Azeem al Din, Samir Muhsi, Rania Zandi, Mrs Zandi,
Shirin Shaarawi

AZEEM WAS MAKING good ground professionally—his organograms quivered with angry arrows, intertwined in such a way as to suggest direction and purpose. From this evidence alone, one would have supposed Azeem relished nothing more than the construction of efficient organizational structures. That this was not so was due to lack of recognition: he was working in a vacuum.

Late one rainy afternoon, Azeem was talking things over with Samir Muhsi in the agency. Their meeting with Myles Lyall had ended a few minutes before, a routine *Jour-Fixe* attended by just the three of them. Myles had said his goodbyes, asked if there were anything else they needed—then left them to themselves.

Samir didn't look satisfied.

"I like some of the pugnacious military terminology," he conceded, perusing a chart bristling with Proactive Execution Officers.

Azeem was gathering up his things. Samir sat in his chair and watched him with an expression of indolent malice.

"Just be sure the intent and the content are equally aggressive, Azeem al Din."

Samir looked especially hawklike that afternoon. His sharp nose, like a hungry, questing beak. His keen glances out of the window, as if seeking signals from on high. A sudden gust whipped across the glass, lashing in its tail a scattering of hail and rain.

The city was invisible behind the grayness of the storm.

"You need to draw up a targeted action plan," said Samir, "to combat Islamophobic injustice... *before it occurs*. When kind words and outreach do not soften the hearts of infidels and Jews, we must denounce all perfidy, all bad faith... Sniff out insults and attacks before they've even been planned."

Samir fixed Azeem with an intent, doggy look. "Conflict resolution is what we seek, at the end of the day," he said. "Seek it proactively, Azeem. *War in a wider way.* What do you think about putting some, shall we say *Tolerance Compliance Officers* and some *Legal Enforcement Provocateurs* into your charts?"

Azeem saw what Samir was driving at. This was about guaranteeing Muslim rights—say, as to not being offended by excessive freedom of speech—as with those direly unfunny Danish cartoons, whose impious provocations had been spreading global anathema earlier in the year.

Azeem remembered them with a shudder.

The wretched Danes had denigrated and desecrated the Prophet (pbuh), and a global response had been organized, to guard against anything so insulting and hateful happening again. There was also the ever-vexed question of being allowed to freely wear the *burqa*, for women who wished to maintain especial modesty and *hijab*.

But surely, Azeem now asked, all that sort of thing was being quite effectively handled already?

"Up to a point it is," agreed Samir as they were leaving the room.

"But in their great zeal to hammer home any advantage, on a local, case-by-case basis, our brothers risk losing sight of the totality, the whole enchilada."

They walked into the lift. Azeem pressed the button.

"We are talking about *war in a wider way...* a new way."

Samir emphasized *war in a wider way*, keen to brand the phrase in Azeem's mind.

"A lot of our people are what we used to call *NEETS*—not in education, employment or training. They're not always self-motivated, we need to make our aims easily accessible to them."

The doors glided shut.

"We have to sniff out post-colonial crusader crimes and beam them around the world, so that our brothers' rage can be expressed, long and loud."

Samir and Azeem walked past the greeting desk. A girl unfamiliar to them was sitting there, a stern, close-cropped brunette, wearing a light brown leather skirt.

Samir stopped to be told her name.

The two men went out into the street. They ran briskly across the road, wet with flying rain. Samir was preoccupied. They slipped into Starbucks to finish their conversation in privacy.

"What about Turkey?" Samir asked after they'd settled down on a sofa clutching their coffees. "On all your charts and maps, I saw no sign of that benighted land."

Samir Muhsi sounded urbane and relaxed, but there was something coiled-up about him. He lifted his cup of Grande Caramel Macchiato to his lips.

"We've never talked about including Turkey."

Petulant impatience clouded Samir's face. His features twisted up, spasms of bitterness.

"Never talked about Turkey?"

Samir smiled, irritably putting down the cup, crashing it down on its saucer. "We're meant to be telling the west home truths about the east, Azeem! In all we do, we must flay these crusading capitalists, slap them cross the face with the hollow reality of their spiritual nullness!"

He took a sip of coffee, wiping his mouth before continuing.

"As we spread our message," he said, "we must interrogate all our ingrained prejudicial responses regarding where the east ends, where the west begins. That's not a trick question, Azeem. It's an absolute requirement."

Azeem was silent. So Samir went on, in a sing-song voice. "And *which* country leaps to our minds first—the interface of east and west, the mix of secular cesspit and holy Islam?"

He nodded, deadpan.

"Where else but Turkey?"

Azeem burned in shame.

"You keep shifting the boundaries," he said, feeling justice entirely on his side.

But Samir was wily enough to appeal to Azeem's professional pride, doing so with the same phrases he used to pull away Azeem's ability to live up to it.

"Shifting boundaries are the nature of the beast," Samir pointed out more quietly, with some show of soothing ruffled feathers. "That's what this business is all about. Your challenge is to anticipate what our masters might want, then act accordingly. There's no point in our employing some servile cipher, a gofer who blindly executes orders. We need you to be *proactive*, Azeem, how often do I have to drum that into you?"

Azeem had to come to terms with his consternation again. "So," he said in a subdued voice. "Turkey too, eh?"

"Yes, Azeem, yes, a thousand times yes," said Samir quietly, patting Azeem's hand as he leaned closer to him, confidential, trusting, inspirational. "But not just Turkey," he went on, his eyes flashing with pitiless compulsion. "Think wider, think more of the boundaries, around the edges, outside the box. Is Istanbul the end of the tale? Or shouldn't we be thinking of Kosovo, Chechnya, the Former Yugoslav Republic of Macedonia, Georgia, everywhere east and west have commingled and fought these past two thousand years? In all these places the lands of Islam are occupied by infidels...

"You lack imagination, sometimes," said Samir thoughtfully. "And confidence. You need to think bigger, be more thorough. We need a bigger network, and you must build it for us."

They finished their coffees, put on their coats, and departed into the wet afternoon, nothing more of substance having been said.

A week passed. Azeem worked hard, putting in calls and setting up meetings with prospects in Turkey and other countries.

At the same time, he wanted to progress the Voices campaign. So one morning he went up to Leeds to see how Rania Zandi was getting on. She'd gone back home, to the Zandi's terraced house off Kirkstall Road. Azeem had arranged for private protection, there was a guard from a security company on duty round the clock.

Mrs Zandi's face, peering suspiciously around the door, lit up when she recognized him.

The windows and the woodwork looked freshly painted. When Azeem remarked on this, Mrs Zandi said,

"That's right, love. We're having everything redone, inside and out. The place needed a good spring cleaning."

Rania was sitting at the kitchen table with her laptop.

Mrs Zandi poured them mugs of tea from the teapot on the sideboard. Setting down a jug of milk and a generous plateful of Custard Creams and Garibaldis, she lifted one of the cookies, took a bite, and said she'd leave them to it. She bustled out giving them a tired look.

Rania seemed tired, too.

"I'm playing a lot of online chess. Do you play?"

"Yes."

"I like playing in the real world more than on the internet."

Her voice was still shaky, distorted. Pushing aside her laptop, she pointed to the chess board leaning against the far wall.

"I'm not much good," said Azeem.

She smiled.

"I might let you win."

They fell to playing.

Azeem was a good enough player to recognize, after the swift succession of opening moves, that he was out of his league. He relaxed into losing mode, and before ten minutes were done, he conceded defeat.

Rania sat back and looked him in the face.

"I've been thinking about *Voices*..."

Despite the odd grumbly twists in her voice, her wounded vocal cords, he heard her hesitation loud and clear.

"... I'm not so sure..."

She looked away.

"I've been in two minds..."

"There's no need to rush into a decision, Rania."

"I know. Everyone's been saying that."

"We've still got plenty of time to work it out... make sure you're a hundred per cent comfortable with it."

"Yeah... Well, I'm really sorry and all that, but I don't really think I can go ahead with it anymore."

She spoke quickly, smiling warily at him the while, her head down, her eyes averted, and his heart sank.

He knew he had no call trying to persuade her otherwise, but heard himself say, "But think of all the good it could do..."

"I just want to get on with my life, really."

"Think of the people you might help."

"I know, I know. Maybe I'm selfish, but I'm not ready to become some big symbol of something I'm not."

He knew she was right, in his heart, but he begrudged his heart for reminding him of it.

"I'm still a muslima, you know."

He nodded. He waited for her to continue.

"Listen," she said. "I'm trying to remember. Something I wanted to tell you..."

She closed her eyes and started to chant.

"*For every sign there is an outward and an inward... a limit and a potential.* It's a tradition of the Prophet, right? If I do what you want, become your spokesperson, do *Voices*, I'll be like a symbol, won't I, an *outward sign?* That's what that means, doesn't it? But if I don't, I'll still be filled with potential. See what I mean?"

"I know, I know, but..."

"I don't want to become a symbol. I still love my brother..."

She looked up, into his eyes, and the appeal in that look pulled at his conscience.

"But he stabbed you!" he said. "He tried to kill you! He slit your throat!"

She shook her head.

"If he'd wanted to kill me, he could have done it easily. Something must have held him back..."

Azeem looked into her eyes, trying to read her.

"The doctors told me... if he'd pressed down the knife just a little harder, I'd have been dead within seconds. He didn't do it. I know he loves me, really. Someone put him up to it. He didn't want to kill me... Anyway, that's not the point anymore. The point is I just want to live my life now, put this behind me. I don't want to become part of some big political thing."

Azeem deplored it. He especially rued that he knew she was right, that didn't make it any easier to take. He took her hand, to let her know he understood, to let her see that his concern for her was much bigger than the disappointment he felt. And she took his hands in hers, smiling at him in simple relief.

He said, "Promise me you'll think about it some more, please... Just think about it, and then, just do what feels right. I'll support you any way I can, whatever you choose."

"Okay. But I don't think I'm going to change my mind about this."

"So be it."

He went to say goodbye to Mrs Zandi. She was in the sitting room on her hands and knees, scrubbing the floor. A green plastic bucket stood beside her. The front windows were open.

The sun was shining in across the rooftops opposite.

When he walked in, Mrs Zandi turned, and raised a finger to her lips. With her other hand she pointed at the sofa which stood in the alcove under the window.

There was a sparrow perched on the headrest.

Mrs Zandi rose to her feet somewhat unsteadily.

"He's been there since I started cleaning this morning."

The bird sat calmly observing the humans. It inclined its head first to the right, then to the left, taking both of them in.

"I can't help it," Mrs Zandi whispered. "But I think it's Faraz, watching us."

Azeem smiled at her whimsy. But something about that self-contained sadness of hers made him hide his smile from her.

"Maybe he wants to say sorry."

The bird watched them. Didn't make a sound.

Azeem took his leave. He went back to London on the train. He felt down, defeated.

Something precious had been lost, something he'd really wanted.

Next evening, when they're in a restaurant back in London, Shirin asks, out of the blue,

"You wouldn't mind if I went off for a girly weekend break with Janice would you?"

He looks at her with blank dazed eyes.

"Who's Janice? What's a girly weekend break?"

Shirin and Azeem are out for dinner for the first time in months. They're in a candlelit booth, in a bistro called La Strega in the Fulham Road. A place Azeem used to go to eons before. He used to eat while watching his best friends get wasted on Valpolicella. It was back in the days when he'd first stopped drinking alcohol, and he remembers how it felt, cut off from his friends as more and more bottles were ordered, and he was left alone with his jug of sparkling water.

"I told you about Janice," says Shirin.

"So what's with the girly weekend break, where's that come in? I thought you'd only just met Janice."

"Oh, come off it, you dork. It's not just a break, anyway, I'm only saying that to provoke you. It's partly work. But, yeah, it's got some aspects of girlishness because it's Janice and me, and we're girls... Well we were last time I looked. We're having a meeting with a feminist group there, *Ni Putes Ni Soumises*."

"Sounds French."

"The name is. It means *Neither Whores Nor Submissives*. It's an international grouping and they're setting up in Turkey."

Shirin lets it sink in.

But all Azeem can think to say is, "Ooh la la."

"We were thinking of going to Istanbul on Thursday. Meet up with the group on Friday. And then stay for a long weekend. We can get really cheap flights out there... No way *you'd* know about that sort of thing, of course. No expenses spared for *you*, swanning around in business class every trip like you do."

Azeem is playing with a piece of pizza bread. He looks around. The restaurant is very red in its decor.

"We hardly have time to see each other anymore."

"Exactly... if you're always going to be away on your travels, why shouldn't I take the opportunity to do something new, go somewhere new? You've just come back from there... you're an old Istanbul hand."

"An old hand, eh?"

"You can tell me what I've got to see."

"Which weekend were you thinking of?"

"Next weekend."

It transpires Azeem is away on the Saturday of that weekend too, he's flying out to Milan. But he starts to raise objections all the same, not happy about his girlfriend going off on her own with this strange, feminist, Janice woman.

He asks her to fill him in on Janice.

Shirin happily does so. Janice is one of those colorful characters whose endearing doings gratefully lend themselves to anecdote.

"Vagina Warrior, eh?"

"Yeah, you've heard about them, haven't you?"

"Is that the people who did the Vagina Monologues?"

"Yeah, maybe, sort of. The Vagina Warriors are about ending violence against women. They're also into exploring sexuality and body image."

"Sounds frivolous."

Shirin giggles.

"Maybe they are."

"I'd rather you didn't go to Istanbul with this woman."

"You can't tell me what I can or cannot do."

"I know. I'm not telling. I'm *asking* you not to go."

"If you knew what I was going through, you'd be glad I was going. I need a break... I desperately need a break from this... desperate city. It's really an awful, desperate time of year to be stuck in London... I need to get out, Azeem, really I do."

He drinks his water, carefully sets down the glass. He dabs at his lips with a napkin.

"I was hoping we might do something together that Sunday," he says.

She looks at him blankly, her eyes round.

"What did you have planned?"

"Oh, nothing. Just hoped we could do something together."

She shakes her head slowly.

"This is something I really want to do, okay? And you won't even be here half the weekend! So don't get in a great big huff!"

Later, when they get home and go to bed, they're scarcely speaking to each other. They read a few pages in their books and then, one after the other, click their bedside lamps off.

GRAND BAZAAR
Istanbul: Shirin Shaarawi, Janice Primrose

THAT WEEKEND, Janice and Shirin are sitting in the lobby of the Ibrahim Pasha Hotel, in Sultanahmet, Istanbul. They are drinking glasses of sweet tea. A polite white Labrador sniffs at their ankles.

Sultry and glowing, Janice smiles across at Shirin, who's sitting there utterly drained and looking, to Janice, utterly delicious, utterly kissable.

In her verging-on-prim, governessy voice, Janice asks, "Tired, darling?"

Shirin nods, raising up her sleepy sulky eyes. She sees above her friend's head where there's a long thin window, tucked into the low ceiling. She looks for a second, expecting to catch somebody lurking up there, watching them.

"I'm exhausted," she sighs. "Wiped. There's simply too much to take in."

Since arriving the previous afternoon the two young women have been busy. First, their meeting with the feminist group, *Ni Putes Ni Soumises*. Janice completely in her element. The Turkish women were somewhat stolid and serious—Janice charmed them with her infectious energy.

Shirin felt like a spare part, not saying a lot.

As soon as their business was finished, they embarked on a relentless programme of touristic exploration. A measure too much of it for Shirin's taste. The Hagia Sophia, Topkapi Palace, the Blue Mosque, the Hippodrome—all and more.

Way, way over the top.

The two of them just got back from rushing through the grasping crowds of the Grand Bazaar. The strange, close obtuseness of the place still clings to her senses.

She feels the otherness of the stallholders, of men milling constantly around. The clamor of sounds and smells assailing her, the shimmerous light from the arched windows and skylights above. The realization that everybody belongs here, in that moment, even Janice and she.

But of course no matter the numerous tourists, Janice and she were the *others* in there.

It reminds her of something Mamida told her, about the differences that come merely from being born somewhere, born who you *are* and not *becoming* it—about some things just being in the blood, just coursing through your veins.

Every time Shirin wanted to linger at a stall, to feed her curiosity, to look over the strange wares—even just to feel her difference, Janice was already five paces ahead, cantering into the middle distance, like a mare given her head.

It would be okay were it not quite so draining. Sometimes, Shirin would rather melt, unobtrusive, into the crowd, flow with its drift, inhaled by the spirit of place.

She's imagined more mingling, meetings by chance, more contemplation, losing oneself in these quiet corners of history that wait here and there in odd spaces, museums and houses of God, sepulchral, empty but thronged with the ghosts of people past, like catacombs.

As it is, she's feeling exhausted.

Shirin gapes at that empty window behind Janice.

Although still miffed and exasperated with her boyfriend, Shirin now feels pangs of missing Azeem, for all his manifold failings. A jolt when she remembers what he told her about Istanbul before she left, when they'd sort of made up with each other again, the morning after she'd told him she was going to to go....

"Don't even *try* and see all the sights," Azeem had been saying, "you'll go crazy. Everything's a sight. Everywhere you look. Nothing's not a sight...

"So... make sure you wind down," Azeem had urged, his concern for her so palpable, touching her. "Take your time, hang out, soak up some atmosphere."

That idea seeded itself in Shirin's mind. But Janice was a merciless taskmistress in this respect, ruthlessly determined to extract her money's worth.

They're now sitting in that lobby, weighing up whether to take a cruise on the Bosphorus offered for next morning, taking in the Princes' Islands and swimming off one of the smaller ones, followed by lunch on Büyükada.

Janice is determined to do all this and then embark on more sightseeing after.

"We must see the Sunken Palace when we get back," she says, licking her lips.

"I don't think I can keep up if you insist on doing completely everything. I'll start to wish I'd stayed at home... I'll need the longest lie-in of my life when we get back."

"Don't be such a wimp, honey. The Sunken Palace is only round the corner."

They sip their tea. Shirin puts down her teacup with her gracious fingers, her soft ginger movements, looking around the room, her eyes wide, taking everything in with that gentle innocence which fills all she does with tenderness. When she purses her lips just so, she pouts the way a lot of people (especially Janice) like to see her pout, thrilling with a sudden sexual charge.

Shirin's hardly conscious how attractive some of those little mannerisms of hers are.

"Janice, have you noticed anything funny since we got here?"

"What do you mean?"

"Do you get the sense we're being watched? Don't you feel we're being followed?"

"No."

"It's funny. I keep thinking there's somebody trailing us. I keep getting the feeling there's three of us, not just you and me. There's a gray-bearded man I keep seeing. In a gray suit."

"A gray-bearded man in a gray suit? Maybe your accountant has followed you out here?"

"Don't be silly, Janice. Don't turn everything into a joke. He looks revoltingly *sinister* actually. He's got one of those lazy slobbery mouths that make it look like he's drooling at you all the time."

"I've always thought accountancy was the most sinister profession."

"He drools and slobbers."

"Someone else who fancies you, Shirin."

"There's definitely a man on our trail. Don't you feel like there's a third presence? Here, with us, now?"

"There's thousands of gray beards and gray suits in this city, hadn't you noticed? It's the patriarchal garb men assume in this culture. The same when they slobber at you. Their slobbering sends out a psychological message... of dominance."

Janice giggles. She loves to tease her delicious friend.

"They slobber the better to keep their thumbs on their womenfolk."

Shirin's eyes are distracted, nervously disconcerted by Janice's views.

"You're spooking yourself," Janice blithely insists. "Strange surroundings. It's culture shock. You're such a romantic, seeing ghosts everywhere."

"Could be."

"Definitely, definitely. Anyway, when we go to the Sunken Palace tomorrow you can indulge that romantic paranoia of yours some more. It's very James Bond apparently. They shot *Diamonds Are Forever* down there."

Janice grins. Doing what she can to cheer Shirin up.

"Appropriate, that Bond connection," says Janice giving Shirin a thin smile. "One outdated imperial sewer playing host to another."

Now it's Shirin whose laughter ripples through the lobby. For all Janice Primrose's Vagina-Warrior convictions, for all her polymorphic polysexuality, Shirin sees that she's bracingly old-fashioned in some of her notions—her prejudices, her sparing attempts at humor.

That set of the mouth and jaw, the spitting image of a brusque, lorgnetted colonial *memsahib*. Well, at a pinch. Janice does come over, just occasionally, like some Victorian colonel's lady wife. A touch more boyish, perhaps. And none of that daintiness and decorum, that vapid Victorian vaporware. But even taking all that into account Janice is quite distinct from the more laddish ladies of today.

Now the two girls finish their tea, pat the dog, generally gather themselves up. They walk out to find somewhere for a drink before dinner.

Janice is wearing a trouser suit, strictly buttoned up, quite tight amidships, padded at the shoulders. It makes her look somehow stiffer than she is. Her face, at this point in her life still pretty, has acquired a set expression, sensible but sensitive, like that of a pointer setter on the scent.

The two young women are standing in the lobby inspecting themselves in the mirror, patting their hair with sidelong looks.

More than a head taller than Shirin, Janice clucks fussily, like a mother-hen—half-solicitous, half impatient.

"Now now, Shirin," she's saying, in her nannying mother-hen tones, "let's not be miserable tonight."

"We *have* come here to enjoy ourselves, haven't we?" says Janice, knowing full well how matronly and maternal she sounds, piling it on rather. "Not to indulge in a huge great sulk..."

She strokes her friend's hand. Then she leans across and tickles her. Janice has some success with this approach, managing for the moment to tickle Shirin out of her sulky scare—for Shirin's affection is aroused by these kind attentions, and a little laughter too.

Janice has a sweet smile. Even when she scolds Shirin gently she smiles at her with warm eyes, drinking her in, liking her lots.

Later, of course, when it's much too late, Janice will curse herself for her unresponsiveness, her wish to tickle Shirin rather than listen.

She wishes she'd been less governessy, less nannyish, less lustful and blithely dismissive of Shirin's worries.

CALLING

Bloomsbury, London: Azeem al Din, Samir Muhsi

AZEEM RECEIVES a call from Samir Muhsi.

"Shirin is gone," he's told. "She's flown."

"Shirin's gone? Yes, I know, Sam, she's in Istanbul."

"When did you last speak to her?"

"She called me last night."

"How was she?"

"She was fine. She's with a friend. Why are you asking?"

"I had a report from our operatives in Turkey last night, basically. They informed me Shirin had been intercepted over there."

"Intercepted?"

"Seen. Observed."

"I know she's there, Samir."

"Sounds like there's trouble brewing."

"It's a girly weekend break."

"That sounds… ominous."

"No it doesn't."

"Whatever. I just thought you should know."

… Azeem al Din, Myles Lyall

Myles Lyall soon got the news about Wythenshawe's unfortunate accident. After that disturbing call Wythenshawe had made from his car, about the client supposedly wanting Myles off the account, he'd known Wythenshawe was in a dangerously frisky state, more than his normal state of friskiness. When he heard what had happened later that afternoon, up in Twinnington with the lightning and so on, Myles knew he would have to deal with it, at least the professional side of it.

So he decided to have it out with Azeem al Din the very next morning.

"Look here, Azeem," said Myles handing him a cup of Earl Grey tea in the agency meeting room. "What with Wythenshawe having been blown up and so forth, I think it's best to speak to you direct."

"But of course, Myles," said Azeem.

"I don't want to mince my words, the way agencies are often tempted to with important clients."

Azeem felt at once flattered and on his guard.

"I always felt you and I worked together extremely well," said Myles.

"Absolutely."

"The latest twists and turns of strategy have left me a little breathless, I'll admit."

"Well..."

"But even with all that going on I really wasn't prepared for the final instalment."

"What instalment was that, Myles?"

"You see, poor Wythenshawe called me just before the lightning struck. He said there was bad news."

"He did?"

"Bad news for me."

"Sounds grim."

"He said you wanted me taken off the account."

"Oh!"

"Is it true or was Wythenshawe suffering from delusions... or even telling porkies?"

"I certainly didn't ask anything like that."

"What about one of the others? Is one of your colleagues queering my pitch? Samir Muhsi perhaps?"

Azeem was astonished to hear this, a strange development. Certainly Samir had told him nothing along these lines.

"Perhaps Wythenshawe was suffering from some kind of... anticipatory stress, relating to his injury," Azeem suggested, rather desperately.

"That is entirely possible. He's been noticeably off color a while now. Acting inappropriately all round, poor old Rupert...

Still, he'll have plenty of time to recuperate now. I suppose it's best forgotten about. Sweep it all under the rug, sort of thing."

"I suppose so."

"So can I take it you're happy for me to carry on running the account as before and it's business as usual?"

"Absolutely," said Azeem.

... Azeem al Din, Samir Muhsi

Presently, Azeem thinks he's hallucinating when that night, in the early hours, about 03:00 AM, he gets another one of those wheedling calls from Samir.

"Azeem, you know Sheikh Faisal's in Istanbul?" whispers Samir's insistent voice in his ear.

Samir sounds cheery, but charged with malevolence.

"No."

"He is."

"What's he doing?"

"Don't ask. I only know he's there."

"Right."

"Just thought you should know."

"Thanks."

"Don't mention it."

... Azeem al Din, Ghazan Khattak

Next morning Azeem has a meeting with Ghazan.

"Have you seen the new video message from Osama bin Laden?" asks Ghazan at one point, referring to a recently-released broadcast from the bin Laden compound.

"Yes I saw it."

"It *surprised* me... Did it surprise you?"

"Not especially."

"It really surprised me. And impressed me too. The whole emphasis he put on martyrdom. Have you thought much about martyrdom, Azeem?"

"Not really, no."

"You might want to think about it some more," says Ghazan. "It might prove fruitful for your personal growth. Especially now that the issue has become so high profile again."

To Azeem's ears he sounds like the employment guidance counselor back at school knocking about a few career-orientation ideas, genially testing the ground with some dead-end job or other.

"I thought *death was too easy?*"

"I used to think within such parameters myself," Ghazan admits.

He scowls, looks uneasy, searching.

"*The suicide bomber takes the easy way,*" he says, "I believed that, once, with all my heart.

"When a man has more to offer," says Ghazan, his voice sonorous, his eyelids heavy, "more to offer merely than his life, then he should focus on those extra things he has to offer. I've always been convinced that was true, in the past. I thought that to choose martyrdom was to choose the instant jackpot. I believed it in my soul, Azeem. The easy ticket to paradise...

"But Osama bin Laden is now re-emphasizing the importance of the martyr. Martyrdom as an objective, a value of itself. The giving of life. The mystical dimension of self-sacrifice. The supreme triumph... *for those who are slain in God's cause, never will He let their deeds go to waste.* It's food for thought...

"The words of our leaders are not like the words of other men, Azeem. They are seeds. Nutrition for our minds. They are signs to be followed, orders to be obeyed. I think about them all the time. I suggest you think about them deeply, Azeem. I suggest you frame your existence to resonate to the call of such words."

NIGHTMARE YEAR
Twinnington: Laetitia Wythenshawe, Xenia, Frank Twynne

WYTHENSHAWE'S AFFLICTION is protracted. Each day, Laetitia comes to visit and, after sitting with him awhile, leaves him to the tender care of the nurses. He keeps slipping in and out of consciousness, suffering from shock and loss of blood.

After the third day has brought no change she calls Xenia, Wythenshawe's mistress. She really doesn't want to, at first, but she feels forced to make the call by an occult form of inner decency which takes her unawares.

"This is Laetitia Wythenshawe," she says. "Am I speaking to my husband's trollop?"

"I am the woman he loves," says Xenia—with admirable aplomb, given the time of morning.

Laetitia's cold clear laugh comes tinkling down the line.

"Where is Rupert?" says Xenia. "What have you done to him?"

Xenia has been expecting Wythenshawe's return for a week now. None of her calls, none of her messages have been answered.

Laetitia Wythenshawe says, "I didn't need to do anything. He did it all by himself."

The thought flits across Xenia's mind that Laetitia might be putting a physical spell on her husband with a view to seducing him back into her arms... That young fit body is one Xenia has seen all too much of in glossy mags, usually wearing boots and jodhpurs, something which never fails to flatter her long-limbed, jolly-hockey-sticks type of beauty.

"Did what himself?"

In her gut, though, Xenia has always felt that she herself is on to a winner with Wythenshawe in the sexual way. She just knows Wythenshawe to be far more at home with her own generous, succulent curves than with his brittle, posh bride, in bed as out of it.

"Cut off his hand."

"Cut off his hand?" says Xenia, her heart all alurch.

"Cut off his hand."

Xenia's mind goes blank. She feels sick and jittery.

"Don't try to scare me, Laetitia."

"It was your idea, wasn't it, you vulgar little tart, this birdbrained visit, to come scaring me, swinging axes about? Is that your idea of *putting the screws on*, you cheap, money-grubbing whore?"

"You're crazy!"

"Your *plan* was crazy, you silly, misguided harlot. The cackhanded idiot hacked off his own wrist!"

"I didn't even want him to go see you!"

"Well, see me he did. Not that he can see me anymore though, the state he's in."

"You're making it up!"

Xenia is close to tears.

"He laid into everything with his axe and made merry havoc, set about destroying everything like a howling madman."

"Tell me what really happened."

"I've been watching over your lover-boy in the hospital. The doctors had a time of it at first, trying to stem all that blood. Gallons, absolute oceans of it. He's been close to death, touch and go all the way."

"Are you shitting me, Laetitia?"

"No I'm not *shitting* you, you commonplace, foulmouthed strumpet. I've been with him the whole time... It's been the most romantic week we've spent together in years."

Laetitia laughs, sounding as tired and hollow as she must feel.

Xenia says, "How is he now?"

"Still in intensive care."

"Can I see him?"

"I really don't know."

"Please!"

"He's absolutely not meant to be disturbed."

"Please... Lady Laetitia!"

"It's hard for me," says Laetitia. "It's not in the nature of things, is it, for a wife to get on well with her husband's concubines and fancy-women, is it, really? Not a wifely duty as such..."

"I've loved him more than ten years now!"

Xenia has a lot of things she feels like saying—Laetitia's own collection of fancy-men, for example, is crowding on the tip of Xenia's tongue, waiting to be dropped into the conversation. How dare this posh bitch patronize her, insult her in those clipped crystal tones!

But now isn't the time for any of that.

So she says, "Lady Laetitia, please! When can I come visit him?"

"I shall let you know in due course," says Laetitia, switching off her telephone in that offhand way she has.

At Laetitia's home farm, in the meantime, broccoli, peas and potatoes are growing, but they're having a hard time of it too.

By this stage of the summer, the year 2007 has already shaped up to be a nightmare year for farmers. It started with hot droughts in early spring. These were soon followed by floods and storms, of which the one that hit Wythenshawe is but one and not the worst by a long way.

As the crops mature and the harvest season looms, the peas rot in the waterlogged fields. The broccoli and potatoes are in a bad way. Little can be harvested because of mud everywhere, sucking down the wheels of the tractors, making it hard to pull the crops up from the greedy suction of the soil.

One morning, immediately after returning from the hospital where Wythenshawe is lying, Laetitia goes down to the home farm to see her factor there.

Frank Twynne, tall and thin, has a shock of white hair that looks blond when it catches the sun. He's 68, and though he never says as much, she can tell he's beginning to feel his age, whenever the dark clouds close in and he's out on the rainswept fields, or mending a post in the morning frost, a fine strong figure of a man.

After expiating for some time about the rotting fields, he says, "And there's worse to come. This fly-tipping you asked about the other day, m'lady."

And Frank fills her in on that, the latest plague to blast the countryside, and more and more of it happening in their corner of the Borders.

"It fair roasts my heart," he says, sounding as cheerful as he always does when relating scandalous disasters. "It's getting worse with every month that passes...

"It started off up on the heath, outwith the north end, where the road comes in close," he says, "but now there's idiots dumping stuff along the woodland, by the east gate, and all along the coverts on the east side too."

Frank chuckles to himself. His eyes are tired.

"We spend over a morning a week collecting it all, lugging it along to the council tip. It's costing us maybe a hundred pound a week aside from the hours."

"Can't we get the police to help?"

"There's not a lot they can do. They won't prosecute on our say so."

He grins at her.

"The one thing we can do... this happens once in a way, you know, when we're lucky, we find an address on the envelopes."

His weatherbeaten face lightens up again.

"Then we just take the bawbag's garbage and dump it outside his door. Give it back to the rightful owner, d'ye ken."

Laetitia laughs.

"Good riddance to bad rubbish," she says. "I'll have a word with the Chief Constable all the same."

"It might be a good idea to dig some more ditches," says Frank. "Plough up some of the land at the edges of the estate, then they can't get their cars so far inside."

"Yes, of course," says Laetitia at once seeing the point. "Let's look at that."

Frank Twynne gives her a contented sort of smile. "I'm already doing it, m'lady," he says. "It's not so much, it's not all that much work."

Frank loves Laetitia, after his fashion. He's been working on the estate forty years, known her all her life. One reason he likes her is he still sees the little girl she used to be. A lovely little kimmer, and she's not changed much, pretty unspoiled, a lass after his heart.

Rumors of her sex life leave Frank cold. The Twinningtons were always funny that way, his own father told him that, and his granddad too. There was even some talk about his great grandfather's dad being half a Twinnington, wrong side of the blanket, but Frank's no desire to pry into any of that.

She asks, "Are you using that advisor, whatsisname?"

"No, I've stopped asking that old tattie-bogle. I learned what I could from him, such as it was. He was always all in a swither about everything. I can deal with the likes of DEFRA and the Rural Payments Agency myself now."

Laetitia says, "I don't envy you, Mr Twynne. It's not exactly farming as we were brought up to understand it, is it?"

"No. They're a bunch o'headcases wi' baws for brains, if you'll pardon my French. Your father wouldn't have stood for it. It's all landscape asset management, rural preservation orders, m'lady."

"If it's any comfort, the government's been fined by Brussels for the payments cock-up."

"Yes, it's a kind of comfort, I suppose," Frank says drily.

He stares at her as though sizing her up. But he's not sizing her up. He's really making up his mind whether to tell her more about his woes.

He decides from the look on her face that he will.

"If I'm honest," he says, "it's no big comfort really. We'll end up paying that fine ourselves anyway. Us, and all the other farmers. You know how it is."

"I do."

"We'll get clobbered other ways too. That's if you count the extra business tax we'll have to pay on top for the farm store in the barn. We're not going to be making any money the next few years."

"I know that, Mr Twynne."

Frank Twynne watches his boots as he stands respectfully beside Laetitia, who's taken a chair by the window.

"It makes me worried for my livelihood," he says with his awkward grin. "There must be a limit to how long you can subsidize everything, all the jobs."

Laetitia smiles. "Don't worry about that, Mr Twynne. As long as I'm here there'll be a job for you, if you want it...

"I'm not turning it into a funpark," she says after a pause.

Frank Twynne grunts.

"Tell me, Mr Twynne," continues Laetitia cutting to the chase. "Who do you suppose was behind all that horrible stuff they did here the other night?"

"I'm sorry about that, m'lady." He colors. "I haven't had the chance to talk to you about it yet. Pretty sure I know who it was. The evening before last I saw a fellow over by the copse halfway down the drive, where it cuts away from the road again. I thought at first he was fly-tipping, went over to nab him but he wasn't. He was a funny bloke."

"Funny in what way?"

"Sounded like he came from Yorkshire or some place like that. He said he was lost. Just having a pee, he said. I didn't believe a word but... I couldn't see anything there, so I let him go, went back to bed. My mistake, m'lady. I only realized it was him when I heard about what happened next day. I'm sorry I left you to find all that keech and all those messy body parts next day... I was off that morning, m'lady."

"I know, Mr Twynne."

"I would've liked to help clear it away if they'd told me."

"I know. It doesn't matter. But did you get a look at his face?"

"Yes, it was dark but I got a good look at him. He was a funny chap as I say. He was dressed casual, jeans, and one of those dark thin windcheaters, and he had the hood up. But he was wearing a turban underneath. You don't see a lot of turbans around the estate, by and large."

DEEPLY
London: Ghazan Khattak, Azeem al Din

GHAZAN KHATTAK has now taken to calling Azeem whenever he feels the urge to do his duty, to have spiritual pep-talks with him, to point him the right way. He makes another of these altruistic calls when Osama bin Laden releases his next video. The bin Laden message is a perfect excuse to chew the fat, Ghazan thinks.

"Did you see it?"

"Yes."

"What did you think?"

"Everyone's saying his beard looks odd. Is he dyeing it?"

"It's quite normal for Arab men to put henna in their beards, Azeem."

"Some people think it's actually fake."

"That is a very superficial reaction."

"Well it's what people are saying. There wasn't anything very dramatic in it was there?"

"No, Azeem, no. That is part of the point. You must remember this about spirituality... it isn't about novelty, it isn't about drama. You must contemplate these things more deeply, my brother. The message of jihad is not new. It was already old at the time of the first crusades. It is the same message, always the same. For the Evil One is always the same. And all that shall stay unchanged until we vanquish the unbelievers. You don't have to go to Iraq to fight our war, Azeem al Din. Jihad is on the march everywhere. For it is written, *I shall terrorize the infidels, wound their bodies and incapacitate them, because they oppose Allah and His Apostle*, peace be upon him."

Ghazan takes a deep breath.

"In the 1930s, Azeem, a time very like today, Hasan al-Banna said it. *The Qur'an is our Constitution. Jihad is our Way. Martyrdom is our Desire.* There is a spiritual dimension to offering your life. It is a timeless, holy dimension. Self-sacrifice. Think of it, Azeem al Din. *Martyrdom is our Desire.* Think of it. Think of it deeply."

"I shall."

... Dave Page, Mad Mick

Many miles away at that very same time, Laetitia's ex-lover, Dave Page, felt a surge of jubilant self-justification as he heard what the lads had done the other night up on Laetitia's estate. His expectations of the "happy event" had been delivered, with more chutzpah and style than he ever dreamed.

Dave had helped prepare things, and had even suggested some of the materials, the offal of death... But then, when all was done, he'd left Mad Mick and his hired men to it. Dave knew that were he to be caught near Twinnington, he'd be recognized, suspected of stalking—or worse—he'd be sure to get fingered by the filth, fitted up for something. So he left the further organization up to his mate Mad Mick and his northern contacts.

Now, a week later, Mad Mick had come back to tell him all about it. Mick even produced some grainy, flash-bleached photos, various locations they'd defiled on Laetitia's estate, the animals crucified. Mick described how a group of Muslim lads, all from Leeds, had done the donkey's work.

Dave Page felt a twinge of regret, to think no Englishman could be found for the job.

"They were up for it, Dave. They wanted to protest Laetitia's lifestyle choice. They were in pretty good physical shape."

He told Dave what they'd done with the offal and the dead animals, leaving it all there for Laetitia to find next morning.

Dave hearing about the carnage quite reconciled himself to the involvement of the Muslims. There was a funny side to that in itself, picturing those towelheads dashing about, doing those revolting things, then scarpering, like something out of a sick version of Sinbad the Sailor, it made him feel altogether pumped.

What made it even better was that this was only the first instalment. Mick promised there was more on the way.

Laetitia would be getting violated again soon.

... Laetitia Wythenshawe, Azeem al Din

"It was like some vision of the judgment of hell," Laetitia was telling Azeem on the phone. "Maggoty skulls... bits of bloody bones everywhere, rotting carcasses scattered all over the estate... Crucifixes."

"How awful. Is that this fly-tipping you were telling me about, then?"

"No, you complete dingbat. Fly-tipping's just dumping ordinary garbage, microwaves and fridges and so on. This was animals they'd tortured close to death then left on my lawn to die. It was deliberately meant to be frightening."

"God," said Azeem. "Who's behind it?"

"Haven't the foggiest. But I was thinking your man Nobby Klinker might have had something to do with it."

"My man Klinker? He's hardly *my man*. He's yours if he's anyone's. And why should he want to scare you?"

"I dumped him, you know."

"Ah."

"It was high time too."

"Yes, he is a tad weird. But so weird as that? I thought he was just very very German."

"Plenty weird, Zimmie."

Laetitia told him some details about Klinker's proclivities. Then she told him how Twynne had heard the visitors speak, in Yorkshire accents.

"That doesn't sound like Klinker."

Laetitia laughed.

"No, I'm not saying silly old Klinker went out and did this himself, in a Yorkshire accent—a highly convincing Yorkshire accent I might add, if Mr Twynne heard it right. I'm just thinking that maybe Nobby got so miffed he got somebody else to do it for him."

"But who?"

"The guys were wearing turbans, according to Twynne. That's why I thought there might be a connection with that awful

Islamist caper of yours. You said there was something fishy going on, didn't you?"

"Yes, there is."

"There you are."

"I'll see what I can find out, Laetitia."

... Azeem al Din, Ghazan Khattak

So when he's rung off Azeem calls Ghazan.

"Did you have anything to do with the attack on my cousin's estate?"

"What is this, Azeem?"

Azeem tells him about Laetitia.

"Muslims from Leeds did it," says Azeem. "They were intercepted."

"Intercepted?"

"They were heard. They were seen. They were talked to. Did Dr Klinker get you to get your boys to do something weird to freak out my cousin?"

"Klinker?"

There is an awkward pause.

"Yes, Klinker."

"What would Klinker have to do with it?"

"You know about it then?"

Ghazan's reaction of silent confusion convinces Azeem he's involved in some way, even if not the way Azeem initially imagined.

Ghazan definitely knows more about it than he's letting on.

LIGHTNING
Dumfries, Border Country, Scotland: Rupert & Laetitia Wythenshawe,
Xenia, Frank Twynne

WYTHENSHAWE WAKES in hospital.
"Am I on set?" he asks. "Did the lights just blow?"
"No, Rupert," says the redheaded nurse.
"Do I know you? Are you from the production company?"
"No. You need to rest."
Wythenshawe subsides back into his coma.
And there's more of that to come later.

The lightning had shot through Wythenshawe's leg and blown off his big toenail.

His eyebrows had been singed off and his hair set on fire.

Laetitia had a big shock herself, when she first saw him. He'd been "cleaned up" in the hospital. That's what they'd told her when she first came to see him. It made her think of the way undertakers "clean up" bodies when they've been mangled and crushed in some horrible accident. Often as not, she thought, with fittingly horrific results, the touch too much of rouge reminding you how much blood must have been lost. And yes, Wythenshawe looked terrible.

He looked a frightful corpse.

His face when she'd last seen him awake, hacking away in his study, had been so blackened and sooty, so flushed with mad, feverish energy, so covered in mud and sweat, that she hadn't properly registered his pallor or just how much damage had been wreaked on her husband's physical condition.

He'd been laid waste to, drained of all vitality, a still unmoving body with a deathmask for a face.

When they wheeled him in, he was in his coma, debilitated. She looked at him closely, more closely than she'd looked in ages. It wasn't a pretty sight, that state of decay. A repulsive stranger. Three days after the accident, there'd been no change, except when Wythenshawe momentarily woke.

He looked into nothingness with his kindly wideawake eyes. He mumbled some indecipherable nothings.

"No, Elsa," he mumbled. "It's over, over now."

Then he fell back extinguished on his pillow. That was supposed to be a good sign.

Next morning, Xenia, the mistress, came fresh off the train, looking distraught, and wearing, if not widow's weeds exactly, sober clothes which made her look anything but mistress-like.

"Oh, Rupert!" wailed Xenia when she saw him lying there with tubes sticking out of him. "What have you done to yourself, you silly bugger?"

Laetitia withdrew. "I'll be back in a bit," she said.

Laetitia decided that to save some money she had to sell a horse. It didn't come easy to her, that decision, but once made she stuck to it. She called Mr Twynne from the hospital lobby and he proposed putting an ad in *Horse and Hound*.

"Any ideas what we should say?" Twynne asked Laetitia.

Laetitia was well-versed in the lingo and briskly shot off some suggestions.

"Cupid, a Dutch Warmblood gelding," she said. "Sixteen hands three, eleven years. Lovely loose, floating paces, with a bold, scopey jump. Impeccable bloodlines, no vices, excellent manners, easy to do, has seen hounds—I could be describing myself," Laetitia said with a sad smile.

Frank Twynne didn't demur. He knew how much Laetitia doted on that horse.

"Six thousand pounds?" Laetitia wondered.

"Maybe as the upset price. Not less," said Twynne. "Maybe six and a half. Let me give that a little think. Haven't been in the market a long while. You might get more. There was an Arab gentleman asking about your horses the other week. I'll have a think, put it all together and maybe you could have a quick look later?"

"Yes, I'll drop by when I'm done here."

She went back into Wythenshawe's sick-room.

Xenia was bent over Wythenshawe looking teary.

"God must have something against him," said Xenia.

"He's not the only one."

"I've heard getting struck by lightning takes it out of you good and proper."

Laetitia was sorely tempted to mock this remark but thought better of it. Now she had Xenia in front of her, she looked a decent enough sort, touchingly homely—and very upset.

"I'm not sure," said Laetitia. "I think lightning affects different people differently. There was a man here on the estate who never actually recovered. He sort of literally lost his mind. Ended up drinking himself to death. You know how men can get. But I've heard of people who carry on as if nothing happened."

"I shouldn't like him being utterly changed."

"Maybe he'll become more relaxed."

"He doesn't look capable of harming a fly, right now, does he?"

Wythenshawe did look docile lying there.

"I wonder if he can hear what we're saying."

"I doubt it."

"He looks so peaceful."

"Don't be so sure," said Laetitia briskly. "There's bound to be reserves of low cunning left."

Xenia wept. Laetitia let her do so. Then having had a moment to put her mental devilry to rest, and seeing Xenia hurting so, she said softly, "You really do love him, don't you?"

"It was just seeing him lying there."

"He looks terrible, doesn't he?"

"Yes, that's just it! He looks a mess! But... he looks helpless, too."

They laughed, a sort of strange relief. Xenia gave up on her crying now.

Wythenshawe lay there in his coma. The two women thought he probably would recover.

EMINÖNÜ EMBARKATION
Istanbul, Turkey: Shirin Shaarawi, Janice Primrose

WHEN SHIRIN AND Janice returned from the Princes' Islands, they were both of them drained and blowsy and feeling frankly irritated. Janice was looking forward to a long bath back in the hotel. She felt ratty. Her skin felt clammy and gritty. She wanted to strip off her clothes, sink down into the embrace of warm soapy suds.

At Eminönü port they disembarked from the large white ferry which had fetched them back from the island. The holiday crowd was packed jostling together with their elbows and huge backpacks, the great unwashed coming back from their day's excursion.

As everyone bustled off the boat Janice and Shirin were separated.

Janice had the impression Shirin got stuck a few people behind her. There was this corpulent wheezing man, and when she turned round, she couldn't see past him. The crowd jostled her on.

When she reached the quay, Janice extricated herself. She put down her bag. Standing to one side, she let all the people flow past her. She waited for Shirin to emerge, hating the delay.

But Shirin never emerged. People slowly melted away. Shirin wasn't to be seen. Janice was left waiting a long time. Then, feeling somewhat sick, she told herself Shirin must somehow have slipped out before her. Maybe she'd gone on ahead, on her own, to the hotel.

The man at the hotel desk was full of charm. He played down Janice's concerns.

"People are always losing each other."

He gave her a worldly smile

"That is life."

He persuaded her to wait a while before involving the police.

"Have a drink, you'll feel better. Wait and see, your friend comes back before you know it."

Janice felt a bit of a fool, a bit ineffectual, taking him up on that drink. But she'd feel still more foolish, she told herself, if she kicked up a fuss. Settled down on the sofa with her lion's milk raki, she sipped it, and felt much worse, focusing on Shirin's disappearance, the whole of that fatal trip, blotting out everything else, ignoring the friendly labrador who came to say hello, the hotel guests floating quietly through the lobby. She knew something had happened.

Something bad had been done to Shirin.

In the event, Shirin enjoyed that day on the islands far more than she expected. It felt good to get outside and be on the water, to get some sun and feel the breeze on her skin.

All through the day she felt attractive. Men were constantly approaching her, flirting. Almost as soon as the ferry pulled out onto the water a tall blond Viking was making passes at her.

"Are you from here? You're so beautiful... can I take a photo?"

The day went on like that. Shirin was finally enjoying herself, Janice getting more and more irritated.

The swimming did nothing to improve things. Shirin looked resplendent when she emerged from the changing room in her swimming things. She was wearing a favorite bikini, a nicely-cut number with a recessive pattern in amethyst and green. It made her skin look really healthy and toned.

That put her in a good mood to play along with harmless flirtations. When they landed, a big handsome Turk came up to her on the dock.

He said, "Hey. There's a space for you in my harem."

"There's even more between your ears."

He held her gaze smiling.

"I can always find room in my harem for a loyal girl, an obedient girl, just like you."

Shirin laughed and walked on. But when she turned to Janice, she saw how little her friend was amused.

Janice, so foxy of face, with her lithe long body, boyish and slim, verged on the bony, so much so she could have been a model. She never felt good in her swimming costume, though. She preferred to be naked.

Today she felt especially uncomfortable. Wearing those clinging textiles, she thought they accentuated her silhouette, accentuated her purely physical attractiveness in a way that nudity, when she was naked among her naturist friends, did not. And part of her, with that generous, sexually-open nature of hers, hated wrapping up her body. What made it worse was selfconsciousness about her English paleness—especially beside Shirin's honeyed complexion—it made her seem even grumpier, more uptight than she really was. She walked along the waterfront with the expression of one who was being led to the stake, consigned to the flames for her beliefs. All in all, Janice exuded this very guarded, stuck-up aura.

It put people off, she knew, while Shirin's sunny open nature attracted them.

After lunch, they boarded the ferry back.

The river floated past. Beside them on the deck, the heads of the tourists bobbed, vacantly, as the boat chugged on its way. Janice and Shirin stood among them, close to each other, and their heads bobbed too, not saying much.

When it came to disembark, they left the boat with everyone else. Shirin was behind Janice. She saw how Janice had the beginnings of sunburn on her neck. She tried to catch up to tell her, but, as always, Janice's brisk pace outstripped hers.

Shirin dawdled along in her wake, turning to direct a polite smile at a young guy who'd stepped smartly aside to let her pass.

An older, redfaced fellow, in a vast suit and a trilby, was waddling slowly, like a big, fat tugboat, in front of her. Shirin called out through the clamor for Janice to wait, but Janice was loping on fast, and too far ahead to hear her.

Then Shirin had the sense of something closing in on her, slowly but surely from behind. There was a sensation like a silent whoosh at her back, she tried to quicken her pace but felt herself getting stuck in the crowd, unable to move forward, as if she were being sucked down into a mushy swamp.

She tried to squeeze through, but the fat man's back blocked her, and the shoulders of other men hemmed her in.

She was about to call out again when a hand from behind came down over her mouth. It was holding a handkerchief which smelled funny. It pressed down hard.

Shirin struggled for a short while, clawing and scratching at the hand over her face before consciousness dissolved. The blackness surrounded her like sinking in a bath of ink, impinging within itself, ever deeper into blank intensity.

Shirin opened her eyes, blind in the saturate blackness.

There was a soggy blanket wrapped round her head. She couldn't breathe properly then again it came wafting into her, that horrible smell.

It seemed like weeks ago, or a second split into a billion pieces.

The darkness came lapping in over her head. She lost herself, enveloped within the clammy darkness.

Then later again, she tasted a sickness on her tongue, a sweet acidic flavor on its tip, a bitter heaviness seeping down the back of her throat.

Her head span round in waves, her eyes were turning loose in their sockets before she subsided again, she fell back fractured into unconsciousness.

She was floating on the water. The speed got faster, she felt as though she were a boat bouncing over the waves.

Next morning finds Janice reporting Shirin's disappearance to the police. The police—two polite, chiselled officers in plain clothes have come to the hotel to meet her—are helpful and sympathetic. They write down everything Janice says.

They promise they'll get onto the case immediately.

"We can't promise you nothing," says one of those handsome policemen taking his leave of Janice in the lobby. "But believe me, we will do everything... everything we can to find your friend. We have the experience to guarantee an outcome. We will call you later today or else tomorrow morning. Don't worry, we are on the case!"

Janice is quite revitalized. She makes some calls, trying to track down Azeem in London, to warn him what's happened. She'd tried and failed to reach him last night. In the end, she leaves a message for Myles, her ad-man friend. He'll be able to help out.

He calls back a few minutes later.

She says, "You know that girl I went to Istanbul with?"

"You can't expect me to keep up with all your girlfriends. That'd be a full-time job."

"I told you about her," said Janice. "I told you she was special, Myles. I even told you her name, Shirin Shaarawi, and that she sort of knows you."

The memory clicks into place in Myles's brain.

"Oh yes, I remember. The one who was going out with my client Azeem."

"Yes. She's disappeared, Myles."

"Disappeared? Where?"

"She just vanished yesterday evening. Here in Istanbul."

Janice fills him in on what's been happening. Myles doesn't sound too concerned, seems to assume Shirin's run off with a man. But Janice keeps insisting until he drops the scepticism.

"Can you tell her boyfriend?" she asks.

He agrees to do so. He wishes her luck.

Then, not knowing what else to do, Janice spends a long day looking over the Archaeology Museum. When she returns she asks the hotel desk to connect her to the police.

"Which department?" asks the girl behind the desk. "What name?"

"The ones who were here this morning?"

The girl behind the desk looks vacant.

"I didn't see any police here this morning," she says.

"Didn't you see me with the two policemen this morning?"

"I saw you with two young guys," the girl laughs, a little flustered. "I didn't know they were police."

"I thought you'd asked them to come."

"Not me."

"Maybe one of your colleagues?"

"Not that I know."

"Please check," says Janice. "They told me the hotel arranged it, asked them to come see me."

"I'll try."

Now Janice panics.

It *was* the police, she insists. She asks the girl to get hold of them at once. The girl opines that it might be better, and save time too, if Janice goes to the police station in person.

AWOL
Aegean Sea: Shirin Shaarawi

WHEN FINALLY SHIRIN wakes she's in a cabin on a boat, just as her body had sensed while her mind had gone AWOL. It's like a nightmare, all tossing like a tortured tethered animal around her.

She's awake now properly. She feels the boat tossing under her, and the ceiling above her coming down at her, she's tossed against the wall and the side of her bunk, and the thick close air seems to furrow her face like a damp net.

The waves now lull the boat back and forth, then judder it in the impact of sudden crashing swells, into which the hull smashes with loud smacks of hollow noise.

She thinks in blurred flashes of violet awfulness which must have woken her before, then faded quickly into the night. Now it is clearer. So she rises and makes for the door. But as soon as her foot touches the floor it totters under her, and melts away.

She collapses. She falls down onto herself.

She knocks her head hard on the side of the bunk and the blackness closes in on her again.

Then Shirin wakes again. Somehow she's gotten back in the bunk. There's someone there with her in the cabin. It is a man she doesn't know, a grinning toothy man with balding gray hair. A smell of mothballs emanates from his beige lounge suit. He tells her to sit up and when she is propped up, dazed among the pillows, he hands her some sweet tea.

"Welcome to the yacht of Sheikh Faisal ibn Shabbir," he says, grinning at her broadly.

"Who are you?"

"I belong to the Office."

Her heart is beating crazily in her chest. She feels as if she's sinking away into nothingness.

The man smirks and says again, "I belong to the Office."

Keep calm... Don't fall apart...

"Oh, another one who thinks he's an Office."

"Not *an* Office."

"*The Office of Sheikh Faisal al Shabbir.*"

"It is my honor."

The man's clearly just some errand boy.

"I told you before, I won't speak to an Office or an Office's flunkey."

"You must speak with me."

"Where is Shabby?"

"Our master is not aboard today. His helicopter is expected on the helipad next week."

"Helipad?"

"Yes."

"What helipad?"

"The helipad is on the foredeck of the yacht."

"You will let me off this boat now."

"That would not be wise."

The man grins.

"You must do it. I've been kidnapped."

Maybe if I make a lot of noise? Scream the place down? Someone might hear me.

The man's just sprawling against the wall, grinning toothily.

"This is a crime," says Shirin. "I want to go home now."

"I cannot do that."

"Let me off this boat at once."

"It is not possible."

"You must do it."

"No, you do not understand. We are in the middle of the sea. You would drown."

The tedium of Shirin's confinement is curdled by fury, biting and acrid like bile. It rises up in her, takes charge of her whole self as the fact of captivity sinks in.

Long days stretch out, vistas of stuffy languor punctuated by mealtimes. Short sharp moments—she spits out her rage at her captors when they bring her food—blunted into flat silence, dragged out into limitless spells of empty time, spells of sweltering solitariness.

The slow shifting trajectory of the sun throws shadows on the bunk's coverlet. Hour after hour those shadows lie there, slowly shifting before they're swallowed up into the darkness, and the night begins.

Shirin is kept to her septic cabin round the clock. The door is locked. Inside, aside from her bunk, nothing, apart from the Qur'an, an i-Pod loaded with Uum Kalthoum's classic Arabic songs.

No computer, no clothes, no books. No distinct voices—but it's never still; no fresh breeze—but always the wind on the waves of the sea.

It does get very stuffy in there during the day. The porthole's bolted shut when the guard isn't there. It's opened up, letting some air in when the guard comes, ladling out his food and drink.

He lets her relieve herself in the portable toilet he also lugs along. He steps back as she pees, watching her intently, not the slightest show of modesty in his eyes, wanting to imprint all of her on his memory.

The boat tosses in the calm waters. The engines are kept switched off for long periods. Occasionally, the yacht glides through amorphous spaces of ocean.

Shirin picks out the sounds of five different men on board. She hears them moving about in different areas of the yacht: the deck, the galley, the cabins and the engine room.

After the second day, she's heard how the rhythm of days pans out on the boat. After the fourth day, she's still seen no sign of shore. She has the sense that land has sunk into sea everywhere.

She fancies the planet has melted into its own vapors.

... Istanbul, Turkey: Janice Primrose

So in the end Janice Primrose, Shirin's severe, pretty friend, went home without Shirin. She finally sorted things out at a police station near the hotel in Istanbul.

Decidedly sinister, it turned out.

The men Janice met in the hotel were not policemen after all. Flirtatious boys, the police aver, feckless, flirtatious boys who thought they could impress Janice. She doesn't think this at all likely, else why haven't those boys been in touch since?

But they're certainly not from the police, the policeman tells her.

She thinks that those helpful, good looking young men she met in the lobby must be connected in some way with Shirin's disappearance. Maybe they were trying to prevent Janice from going to the real police, to gain some more time.

She tells the policeman so.

And he, a tall cadaverous man, says he'll look into it. He doesn't seem motivated by the case. He says, in a voice of infinite, weary cynicism, that it's most likely something to do with some man Shirin met. Maybe Shirin wanted to spend time alone with this man, he tells Janice.

"What man?" she asks. "There was no man."

"She is very pretty from her picture," says the policeman.

Janice had let them print some pictures she'd taken. "She has very polished hair. Girls like that can meet any number of nice men, when they are wanting it."

"She didn't want."

"You don't know that for sure. Listen, Miss Primrose, there's no evidence to investigate either way. We'll do what we can. All. But in cases like this, nine times out of ten? The girl returns... unharmed, having met some nice man whom she likes."

"Shirin was so worried during the days before she disappeared."

The policeman looks mildly interested but, in the end, it doesn't give him any kind of handle.

"Can you tell me why Shirin was having these paranoid feelings?" the policeman asks.

"But it *wasn't* paranoia," says Janice. "It's happened just as she thought! Shirin really is gone now, isn't she? She was *right* to feel threatened."

"We can never be conclusive about circumstances," says the policeman, his unhealthy face taking on an obstinate cast. He's bored by Janice and her pestering questions already.

He says, "She may have been playing an act. We know nothing for sure. So put your mind at rest, if you please... We'll do what we can, I promise it."

When she dwells on this promise hedged with inaction, Janice feels awful about it, and worse than awful to have to leave Istanbul like this, by herself. She knows Shirin might be there, alone, needing her help. Janice feels guilt—especially as she really hasn't a clue what's happened.

Sick as Janice feels, in the end she has no choice but to return.

When she lets herself into her flat Janice puts down her travel bag in the hall. She's overcome, she feels bereft, stuck in her own solitariness. She stands there helpless in her doorway.

She sees the flat just as they'd left it the week before, so happy and carefree when they set off together. Janice bursts into tears. She stands there sobbing, leaning against the doorjamb.

... Aegean Sea, Turkey: Shirin Shaarawi

It's so hot that Shirin, even when she's only sitting in her cabin, motionless and naked on her bath-towel, is bathed in a glow of perspiration.

Next time the guard comes with her food and the portable toilet, Shirin begs him to keep the porthole open when she's done. The first time she asks, the guard ignores the question. He just leers at her silently before leaving, as he always does.

She refuses to eat any food. She leaves it on her plate and puts it to one side.

Next time the guard comes, it's afternoon. He sees she hasn't touched her food. He takes it away without comment. But when he returns next day, there's a changed atmosphere about him. The porthole stays open when he leaves. For some reason the portable toilet is also allowed to remain.

And so they drift away, out at sea. No land in sight, the days stretch on and as they pass, Shirin has more time than she's ever had before to sit and meditate. She withdraws within herself, letting the motion of the sea and the passage of time pass through her unchecked. She eats hardly anything. She does her yoga exercises.

On the seventh day the wind changes.

The sea starts to get choppier. The wind whips against the windows with lashes of spray. Shirin, sitting by the open porthole, is refreshed by drops of seawater on her face.

The engines start humming. The yacht cruises away to find more sheltered waters.

Very early next morning Shirin wakes before anyone on the yacht is stirring. She peers out the open porthole. She exults to see an inch or two of shoreline not merely in sight but not too far off, by the look of the few stunted trees and a blue fishing boat lying upside down on the beach.

Full of adrenalin and without thinking she climbs up, squeezes herself somehow through the porthole. The metal scrapes her skin, breaking it in a few places on her shoulders and hips.

She crawls stiffly across the passage to the railings at the edge. She straightens herself up, stares down into the black waters. She stands stock still for an instant, doesn't stop to calculate the height.

It's greater by far than any length she's ever jumped. She takes a deep breath and leaps, dives naked into the sea.

Shirin sinks down into the cold shock. Her ears and nostrils fill with black salty sea and also in her loins she feels this sudden surge of cold invasive power.

But when she stops sinking she starts swimming underwater in the direction of the shore. Her legs kick out, her arms reach into the dark cold. Her body taut and compact, her eyes firmly shut, she launches herself through the water, six strokes, pouring all her strength into her muscles and her limbs.

She forces herself to stay under for as long as she can. On the seventh stroke her lungs begin to strain. Her head fills full of a sense of bursting. When at last her lungs are about to explode she breaks through surface of the water with a gasp.

She gulps in great deep breaths of air, she lets her lungs fill with sweet oxygen.

She sucks in the air quickly, as deeply and as quietly as she can. The sea swirls around her. She sneaks a quick look at the yacht behind her.

It looks huge. It looks scary.

She doesn't see anyone on board. She dives back down under the surface trying to prevent her feet from kicking up too much of a splash.

She swims on. She's filled with desperate kicking energy. Each time she surfaces again she does all she can to stop her bursting body from breaking the water's surface too explosively.

The water is cold. Her skin tingles with goosebumps. The sea-salt stings in her eyes. Her ribcage aches, her heart pumping against it in great sloppy thumps.

Shirin swims in this desperate way toward her chance of freedom on the shore.

On the deck of the yacht the cook emerges.

He's tired. Hungover. Raki on his breath. He's walking slowly along the side of the boat, trying to clear his head. He stares out unseeing and fills his nose with salty wet air.

He hears a soft splash coming in the mid distance from the direction of shore. A fish? Something he can catch, maybe, and clean, and cook for a nice fresh breakfast.

He scans the sea and all at once he glimpses a fit brown body, with long black hair, gliding through the water. She's swimming fast toward land.

The cook yells and raises the alarm. The crew all come rushing out to see the naked swimmer for themselves. They think they know who it is, but they can't be sure. They check out her cabin in a trice, and finding it empty they curse Shirin for her stubborn will, her refusal to bend to their master's.

The captain sets course full throttle for Shirin's disappearing back.

Within a few minutes they are within hailing distance. They shout down their anger at the swimming girl. The boat's wake floods over her head. She gasps for air. They continue to hurl their curses down on her.

But Shirin ignores them. She continues in a desperate delirium to swim to the shore. Her limbs are seen to flutter and flash in the water.

But now a large blue fishing net appears from below deck, borne by the burly hungover cook. The man reaches the side, he leans over the railings, out of breath, and squints down to get a feel for the distance.

He bunches up the net in his hands. Then with a great heaving movement he casts the spreading net over Shirin's body.

Shirin's still swimming fast, her brown arms and legs thrash through the waves with all her strength undaunted. When she sees it, Shirin tries to dive under again to avoid the encroaching net. She dives about five feet under the surface, each muscle straining. She twists her body in the water, swims to the right, to get beyond the net. But the cook and another crewman are already pulling it in around her, they're hauling it in for all they're worth.

Both of them know full well if Shirin escapes their lives are over. Neither man's in any mood to be made a fool of by this pretty young woman swimming naked into their net below them. They pull it with serious, excited energy.

So it closes in on Shirin and she like a dolphin is caught in the cruel net.

Soon she can't even thrash about any more, the knotted mesh constrains her limbs. The net is pulled out of the water, dripping. It hangs just above the water, swinging back and forth. Now a wave crashes into it, submerging Shirin in a sudden gush of sea.

Shirin screams as the mesh cuts into her soft flesh and squeezes it out like human putty. Two of the crew dive into the water, they help to manhandle her up to the other men waiting to pull her on deck, their hands rough on Shirin's dimpled skin.

The net's winched up. It dangles in the air above the deck. It showers everything beneath with salty spray.

Then the net is lowered. It's spread out on the deck, unfurling its thrashing catch. Shirin lies trapped there screaming abuse while the crew stare open-mouthed and wonder what to do with her.

ON THE MEND
Dumfries, Border Country, Scotland: Rupert Wythenshawe, Xenia

NOW AND AGAIN, increasingly often, Wythenshawe wakes up in his hospital room. Xenia is often there at the bedside. She mops at his brow, she tries to keep him calm. When he wakes with a start, he often imagines himself back at school.

"No, sir, it wasn't me," says Wythenshawe looking direct at Xenia with half-sedated, terror-filled eyes. "It was matron put me up to it, sir. It was her all along, you see. Not me."

"Yes, yes, darling," says Xenia. "Calm down dearest."

"And Svetlana's nothing to do with me either, sir. It was Rincke brought her up here. It was Rincke, sir."

"Yes, darling, yes. Don't worry about it now."

"I've told Svetlana to go, sir. I've told matron she's sick, she's diseased... I promise not to touch her any more."

"Yes, yes, dearest, of course, of course."

The consultants gather mournfully round the bedside, every other day, and all of them unite in saying Wythenshawe's on the mend.

"This sort of confused babbling," the consultant surgeon says, "is perfectly normal."

"As time goes by," opines the consultant neurologist, "the incidence of these delusional episodes will decrease."

"The patient will have longer and longer lucid spells."

"Occasionally, of course, patients reject the regular course of treatment."

"It wouldn't do to be rash..."

"More tests are advisable..."

Either way, Wythenshawe will soon be ready to return home, they tell Xenia.

DUE DESPATCH
Dulwich, London: Janice Primrose, Myles Lyall

WHEN JANICE PRIMROSE got back to London from Istanbul, she was desperate to talk about Shirin's disappearance, not herself quite believing it, nor wishing it attached to herself, so talking about it might make it real—yet detach it from herself.

That evening, after she'd pulled herself together, having sobbed alone for an age in the doorway, Janice made up her mind to go see her friend Myles. She'd already explained everything to him on the phone, but she needed to speak to someone face to face.

Myles was home alone babysitting that night. Fiona Lyall had gone out, so he was more than happy for Janice to come. He was looking forward to one of those sessions of intimate disclosure Janice so often regaled him with, when little in the way of physical detail was left untouched. But he also sensed the continuing tension in her voice on the telephone. Her tenseness came out amplified as she now spoke.

"Oh, shit, I don't know what else I can do. I feel so guilty about it. Did you speak to her boyfriend?"

"Azeem? No, he's on his travels. Macedonia, I think. I left him a message, though."

"Poor guy. So he doesn't even know..."

"I remember feeling sorry for him, that you were about to snatch his girl away from under his nose. That was the plan, wasn't it?"

"Yes, Myles."

"Something tells me my pity was well justified."

"No, stop it Myles. It's nothing to do with that, I'm sure something's happened to her."

Myles, tired, half-cut, did his best to comfort Janice, to relax her. He thought this was a lover's tiff perhaps, he didn't get it really. He did his best to make Janice let it all out. And so they spent the early evening drinking vodka getting tipsy, till Myles's wife Fiona's key could be heard in the latch.

... Soho, London: Azeem al Din, Myles Lyall

Next day, Azeem is back from Macedonia and meets Myles for a status report. Before they start, Myles says,

"Something funny cropped up, Azeem. I think I should tell you even if it may be nothing."

Azeem looks distracted.

"The traffic's murder," he says. I need to get back to Heathrow again by eleven."

"You'll want to hear this."

"Okay."

"It won't take long."

"Go on, then."

Myles takes a deep breath.

"A friend of mine called Janice Primrose knows your girlfriend. She knows Shirin."

Azeem nods and smiles a wintry smile.

He thinks this stinks.

A friend of mine knows Shirin.

It's too much to stomach.

She knows Shirin.

So fucking what? Everyone from Ghazan Khattak down to Myles Lyall seems to be getting involved in his relationship with Shirin. And Azeem thinks, why does everyone and his uncle feel justified poking his nose into our private lives? What makes them think it's any concern of theirs?

"I wouldn't normally mention it," continues Myles, utterly unabashed, "but something slightly strange seems to have happened. You know they went off to Istanbul together?"

Azeem, through gritted teeth: "Yeah. Girly weekend."

"Well, Janice now tells me they *lost* each other out there."

Myles looks apologetic.

"I know it's probably nothing," he proceeds, "but Janice was pretty upset about it... She told me last night."

Azeem flushes. His face feels cold. He instantly knows. Myles is avoiding his eye now.

"Janice seems to think Shirin may have been kidnapped."

Myles shrugs dismissively.

Azeem is energized with awareness—he knows what's happened.

"I've got to meet this Janice."

"Of course."

But Azeem is loud now, insistent. "Myles, I need to see this Janice as soon as possible. It's important!"

Myles is impressed by Azeem's urgency. He takes out his phone and dials Janice's number.

... Azeem al Din, Janice Primrose

Later, speaking directly with Janice, Azeem starts to sort his thoughts, such as they are.

Janice doesn't know much. She tells him about the men who passed themselves off as cops in the lobby. Maybe they were helping the kidnappers. She's not even sure a kidnapping's what really happened. All she knows is that Shirin was suddenly gone. Janice is vague, slightly out of it.

She tells him about Shirin's fear, the stuff she said about being followed.

"Followed? Who by?"

"A man in gray."

Janice pauses. How hopeless that sounds. She tries to explain more about Shirin's misgivings. Janice blames herself. She blames the police. She's confused.

She really doesn't have the foggiest what's happened, Azeem's thinking. *But I think I know. I think she went off to see Faisal. Faisal's the one she went to see. The man in gray was just a messenger.*

He'll have to follow it up himself.

... Azeem al Din, Ghazan Khattak

First, Azeem tries to reach Sheikh Faisal ibn Shabbir direct. But he only gets through to his Office. The flunkey on the phone is casually dismissive, vague. Azeem leaves a blistering message telling the sheikh to get back to him right away.

Even as he speaks, he knows his words will have no effect.

He's fiery with anger. It's clear enough what Shabby has done. Although part of him—a nagging whisper like an itch in the back of his skull—is beginning to think that maybe he can't really be quite so sure about any of that as he'd like.

How can any man truly know a woman?

He shouldn't be one hundred percent certain. It's *possible* Shirin has gone somewhere else. He well knows how frustrated she's been getting with him over the past few months.

But he *feels* one hundred percent certain he's right.

At any rate, when he calls again, Faisal's obstructive Office keeps putting him off, evading any direct questions, putting him on hold.

Azeem decides to call Ghazan Khattak. He also doesn't know for sure if Ghazan's involved. But he feels this inner certainty and calls him all the same.

"Shirin's gone," says Azeem when he gets through to Ghazan Khattak. Azeem's voice is sharp and cold as steel.

"What's that to me?" says Ghazan Khattak.

"That's what I'd like to know, Ghazan."

"I don't know what you're on about, mate."

"Sheikh fucking Shabby's got her in Istanbul."

"Don't talk crap."

"He's seduced her with his money. Seduced her. Taken her from me. Effectively kidnapped her."

"Make up your mind, man, he can't have seduced her *and* kidnapped her all at the same time."

"He's always been after her, the fucking creep."

"Well it's nowt to do with me, Azeem." Ghazan's uneasy. "Calm down, man."

"This is the worst possible thing he could have done, the fucking creep!"

"I keep telling you not to get distracted by this temporal side of life, these trivial temptations, man."

"Don't talk to me about temptations. This has got nothing to do with trivial temptations, Ghazan. This is *love* we're talking about here."

"Love is the worst temptation, man. The worst temptation of all."

Azeem sits silent in his grief, his anger robbed of words.

"Take it from me, mate," says Ghazan, "this will pass. I know it's rough right now, but these things happen. It's part of life. Lovers split, it happens to all of us, man."

Azeem sits still within himself.

"What will not pass," says Ghazan, "is our duty to fight for our faith. That is our fate, Azeem. To fight for our faith. That is our fulfilment. Not chasing after impossible shadows here on earth.

"Our fate is the eternal love of Allah," says Ghazan, "not earthly lust. You need to think of this some more. Remember our teachings. Jihad is ordained for you, man, even if you think you dislike aspects of it. Many people dislike things that are good for them. And many like the things which are bad for them. Almighty Allah *knows*, he knows everything, but they do not..

"Believe me, Azeem, you are no better than the mass of men. Allah knows, but you do not. The most Exalted said, in the Verse of the Sword: *So when the sacred months have passed away, then slay the idolaters wherever you find them, and take them captives and besiege them, and lie in wait for them in every ambush.*

"Believe me, it is time for us to *act*, to do great deeds for our faith. Everywhere our brothers are being oppressed. You feel this now, I know."

Ghazan's voice is a gentle incantation.

"You are being oppressed," he says, "but you think it is something else, even though much of it is because of your lust, and you try to wipe away that stain. It's all shadows, shadows in mirrors... shadows watching shadows...

"But oppression is real, and we can fight back, Azeem! We can fight back from the shadows of our torment! We don't have to take it lying down, like emasculated losers!

"Remember how it is written, *I only wish for reform to the degree that I am able*... What are you capable of, my brother? I feel it in my heart, you are capable of more, far more than you are doing! That is something we share, Azeem!

"We can rise above this stinking world! We do not have to live in this dark stinking hell, our minds infected with poisonous demons. We can rise out of it, we can rise above ourselves, find our inner nobility when we come out with our true fighting spirit. A holy martyrdom, Azeem, is a prize that will purify you. It will give you rewards in the afterlife so great that everything you thought was precious here on earth will seem petty and small, unworthy of you. Believe me, Azeem. Believe me, it's time for you to take the next step."

QUEEN OF THE CRUSADERS
Twinnington: Laetitia Wythenshawe, Frank Twynne, Sholto McClintlock

UP IN TWINNINGTON, things have been getting evermore hectic for Laetitia, a kind of miasma of mania hangs over all the things that happen to her now.

One night she is tossing half asleep in her bed. Through the open window she hears strange muffled sounds. She pulls open her drapes, sees shadows receding on the grass, and a strange glow of light which flickers and fades away in the shadows. She hears in the middle distance a roaring, as of fire.

She leans out of her window. She breathes the familiar air.

And now she sees a burning mass of flames. Three crucifixes are burning in the middle of the lawn. A naked female figure is nailed to the middle cross. The other crosses standing to either side have unidentifiable shapes hanging from them.

She grabs the telephone to call Twynne. He picks up at once, already awake and afoot.

"I've been tracking those keelie bastards the past few minutes," he says out of breath. "I'm heading up to the heath. There's three of them. Arsonists. Started a fire on the meadow. They look stocious, all shoogly, stumbling about like a bunch of barking loons! Andy and Rob are out there helping us. We'll take care of it."

Laetitia rushes downstairs. She unlocks the gun case. She runs outside loading her shotgun. Slowly she approaches the crucifixes. Their flames blind her in the darkness of the night.

The air is cool, the grass is moist underfoot. Laetitia looks up at the burning crosses, her eyes scrunched up against the blinding flickers of heat and the sparks that spit down specks of fiery spittle. The central figure, a naked woman wearing a crown of thorns, has half melted in the flames.

Attached to that cross is a sign, which reads, *Queen of the Crusaders*.

The figures on the other two crosses have partially detached themselves from their nails. One of them is flapping loosely in the wind.

King of the Jews.

It now tears free and starts ascending into the sky. Flames still emanate from it, as it coils and roils up in the wind.

It heads off toward the east, and it's slowly disintegrating, bits of burning plastic fall off and drop to the ground.

Sholto McClintlock, private detective, divorce consultant, sometime stringer for the *Border Gazette,* is putting a call through to his London contact, Danny Fleming at Boundless Television.

"I've got a story that may turn out mega," says Sholto.

Fleming, a cynical brute in his fifties, sounds skeptical.

"Yeah, right... big story, eh, Sholto? That's what you said about that lunatic kid and his deep-fried Mars bar eating record, remember."

"Aye, well, the Mars bars were just a piece of local color. This is something bigger, not just national but *international.*"

"Okay, Sholto. What's it all about then?"

"There's big trouble over at the Twinnington estate in Border country."

"The Twinnington Estate?"

As Sholto goes on, Fleming pictures a dismal underclass ghetto. A gray, treeless expanse of concrete, stewing in the juices of social deprivation. He imagines some picturesque, grimly Hibernian twists to add intrigue to its rainswept misery. A bare mountain side in the distance, a babbling brook, caber-tossing men in kilts, haggis-swilling crones, caterwauling bagpipes filling the glens with a hideous, tuneless din as the cold mist swirls in from the ocean. Bonnie Scotland. Then throw in the drug-addiction, racist graffiti, alcoholism, prostitution, knife-gangs—Fleming has to admit his interest is whetted.

"The Twinnington Estate, yes, Danny, it's a big old place not far south of Glasgow."

"An underclass sort of place?"

"It's beyond any conceptions of class, Danny... it's in its own league. Listen, there's so much I could tell you about oppression and squalor up here, man. You've got to remember, we Scots were the very first victims of English imperialism. Centuries under the English jackboot have left their mark, scarred our souls! It's in our blood, man! It's why we hate the fucking English."

"Riots, is it? How long's it been going on for?"

"My contact Dave just phoned me with it. I'm on my way there now."

"Who's behind it?"

"Islamist outrage. Crucifixions, burnings, the whole place is going up in flames."

Fleming's ears prick up.

"*Crucifixions* you say?"

"Yes, it's crucifixions, they've put up a huge burning cross with a sign saying *Queen of the Crusaders.*"

"Queen of the Crusaders? Is it some no-hope Scottish football supporters behind it?"

"Don't be daft. It's not Queen of the South. There's a *woman* on the crucifix, Danny."

"*What?* I thought crucifixes were for Christians?"

"What you talking about, man?" says Sholto, forgetting himself for a second. "They've crucified her *because* she's Christian, ye great bampot!"

"They've crucified a *woman* you say?"

Fleming is practically wetting himself in excitement.

"Yes, my contact says there's a naked female figure, nailed to the cross."

"The mind boggles," says Fleming now in the keenest state of newshound arousal.

Sholto presses home his advantage, eyes lighting up his ruined face. He's seized of a sudden with words.

"Some of the slime ye get up here is as black as the Earl of Hell's waistcoat!" he cries.

He knows this is laying it on rather thick. Better safe than sorry, though. He'll never see a better chance of getting on TV.

"Do you want me to shoot some exclusive live coverage and interviews or not? I can be there inside an hour, take my digicam, and I reckon you can have the first piece within two. Remember, Danny, no-one else knows about this yet."

They spend a few minutes coming to terms.

When they've finished, Sholto McClintlock knows he's on the brink of the big one, the one he's been waiting for all these years.

Laetitia stands on her lawn and surveys the crucifixes burning there.

Her factor Twynne now joins her, looking right dishevelled, his thinning hair wild and, like the collar of his Barbour, covered in burrs and bracken.

They watch as the *Queen of the Crusaders* blazes away into nothingness.

"They got away," says Twynne. "We last heard them heading up to the heath. Seemed to know their way about the place."

"It's quite an impressive sight."

Laetitia's voice is subdued, as if she's been struck half dumb by the sheer aesthetic quality of the outrage.

Twynne offers her his flask. She takes a long grateful swig of single malt.

For a moment or two they stand in companionable stupefaction watching the flames roar on.

All at once they hear a rustling behind them, and a fat, stumbling, ewe-necked apparition, wearing jeans and a filthy blue jersey, prowls into view, sprouting up between the bushes as if he's just jumped off a toadstool. He's carrying a digicam with which he is filming the scene of fiery mayhem.

"Hey, gaberlunzie-man, what are ye doing?" asks Twynne in a stern voice.

"Sholto McClintlock of BTV."

Sholto, a man with a face like a torn pocket, speaks authoritatively, not stopping his filming but casting his eye disdainfully over the two civilian bystanders as he continues his work.

"Oh God," says Laetitia.

"You the lady of the house then, hen? Would you be prepared to answer some questions for our viewers?"

... London: Dave Page

Dave Page is lain out on the sofa at home, a can of beer clutched to his chest. It's past midnight and he's been drinking with a group of mates. The last of them staggered out half an hour or so before. Dave is on his seventh can of Special Brew. A buzz of woozy, boozy benevolence is beginning to dull his wonted belligerence.

On the television an unflappable news-anchor appears. She has high-gloss, plastic features and hair that looks like a sprayed-on confection of honeyed flax, sprinkled with gold dust.

"We're heading up north, where we've been getting reports of large-scale unrest in Scotland. Our correspondent Sholto McKinnon is there now. Sholto, can you fill us in on the situation?"

The camera cuts to a still photo of a generic rundown dead-end council estate in the rain. *Twinnington Estate,* it says on the super.

Then Sholto McClintlock's reassuring, flinty voice comes on to say his piece:

"Well, Tessa, the situation's been getting out of hand here several hours now. Disaffected youths have been venting their many frustrations on the Twinnington Estate. These are youths from deprived areas, where a lot of irreparable damage has been caused to people's self-esteem by recent waves of unemployment figures. This despair's been building up a head of steam and it's boiled over in demonstrations, acts of vandalism on people's property. But the most dramatic scenes have only just happened. I was here on the scene in person, in a position of considerable personal danger. I was able to snatch exclusive footage of it, earlier tonight. I hope our viewers will excuse the quality, I was on the hop in the middle of a riot, as you can see."

Dave now sees the crosses, the crosses burning on a lawn. In the middle of the night, on the underlit film, the three crosses might be anywhere, there's no way of seeing where it is, from the footage Sholto has shot.

"The rage of the underprivileged spilled over in scenes which could only be described as the work of primitive creative impulses, or prankishness gone out of hand."

The camera pans in on the *Queen of the Crusaders*—the blowsy sex doll—as she slips the fetters which tied her to her cross, and she blows away into the sky.

Sholto's words drone nasally, flintily on.

"But the ability to escape deprivation—a rough deal in housing, a lack of employment prospects, crumbling social services—is a luxury only few are able to afford."

The camera lingers on the *Queen of the Crusaders*. The flaming love-doll flies out of sight, dipping down beyond the line of trees in the middle distance.

The scene now cuts back to the studio where concerned-looking Tessa sits composed behind her desk.

"Can you tell me what the mood is up there?" she asks, fiddling unflustered with something at her ear.

"It's terrible, Tessa, terrible," says Sholto in a doomed voice. "People are feeling betrayed. I managed to speak to some of the residents here.... they don't know which way to turn."

"Have the police or local government given any signals that they understand, that they're getting to grips with the source of the trouble, Sholto?"

"It's eerily quiet on the estate, now that the rioters themselves have slipped off, melted away into the darkness. There's no sign of any police presence at the moment. There is a very real atmosphere of menace here. People are very much being left to their own devices, they're being thrown in at the deep end of deprivation."

Dave is now utterly fazed by what comes on the screen. When he sees Laetitia appear and speak to the camera at first Dave thinks it must be the booze.

"I woke up about an hour ago," Laetitia says, looking very tired, very beautiful. "It was the noise. And then I looked out and saw the crosses."

"Can you tell us how you felt when you saw them?"

"I was quite taken aback actually. It's not the sort of thing you expect to see on your lawn."

"Do you feel let down by the authorities for letting it come to this?"

"No, not really. One supposes they probably don't even know what's happened yet."

"Will it be easy to get back to living your own lives, after an atrocity like this has ripped apart your world?"

"I'm sure I'll manage," Laetitia smiles.

"And we'll have to leave it there," Tessa now cuts in from the studio. "That was Sholto McKinnon from the Twinnington sink estate in Border country. Our apologies for the quality of that report. And now, it's time to get an update on the weather."

The weather-girl comes on chattering over her animated maps. Dave Page smiles to himself. Through his beer-goggle befuddlement, the realization sinks in that Laetitia has been well and truly violated by the lads.

He lies back, tries to savor the moment.

But he can't really enjoy it. Something about it makes him feel *had*, he feels vaguely insulted on Laetitia's behalf.

Before he can bring these feelings into focus, his consciousness dissipates in a fug of alcoholic fumes.

ENCAGED
Aegean Sea, Turkey: Shirin Shaarawi

JUST A FEW HUNDRED yards off the Aegean coast the *Jawhara* lies becalmed on the placid sea.

Shirin's encaged, locked up in a tiny stinking hole like a galley-slave below deck. The space has no windows, no lights, precious little air. Shirin has been stripped naked. Her arms and legs have been tied to the iron bunk. The crewmen are taking no more chances with her.

They're expecting their master aboard soon, Shirin can tell.

The only one who comes to tend to her is the toothy man who brought her food before. Now, he comes round every hour or so, during the day, to check up on her. He brings her a warm cup of water every once in a way, some scraps from the kitchen.

This man resents her doubly since her escape. He knows it was his *softness*, in letting her leave her porthole open, that allowed her to get away.

On the second morning after her escape he comes in smelling as always of mothballs. Framed in the doorway, he stares at her expressionlessly, as he always does. Today though, is different. For the first time, after he's looked her up and down, he closes the door behind him.

He locks it.

For a while there he's just standing leaning against it, letting his eyes get used to the light as he leers. Shirin lies back on her bunk.

He's playing with himself. She closes her eyes to avoid his leering look, eating her up.

Then she feels his hand between her legs. At first she's so surprised and shocked she lies stock still, tensing up. The man's breathing hard. He brings his hand higher up her thigh and with his other hand he squeezes the underside of her breast.

Now Shirin says, "Get that fucking hand off!"

The man takes no notice. His hands are roving across her body. He cannot curb his frenzied fingering, he's all over her, he's possessed by his hungry lechery.

As he rummages and fondles her, Shirin's mind is racing with horrible impressions, she's thinking how best to stop him—but a small part thinks *if I let him go on I might find a way to escape.*

But those thoughts pass from her brain in a second as revulsion overcomes her.

Now she screams.

"STOP IT!"

She screams out, and when he still doesn't stop she yells out wordless screaming fury. She's shouting out, she's thrashing at the ropes round her raw wrists and ankles—until at last there comes a sound of rushing feet, and then a moment's silence, and then an urgent banging at the door.

Now finally the man stops. He removes himself, reluctantly, from Shirin's moist, trembling body. He stands stock still, holding his breath.

The banging and shouting at the door go on, filling the room with sound. Finally the man rearranges himself into his clothing.

He opens the door. He gabbles out something Shirin can't understand. The harsh light from the corridor floods over Shirin lying spread-eagled on the bed. The shadow of her violator is cast over her before the others take him away.

She closes her eyes to the glare, and she tries to stop crying.

The door clicks shut again.

POETRY
Bloomsbury: Azeem al Din

AZEEM SAT ALONE in his dark space in London letting Ghazan's twisted words weave whorls of glumness his mind.

I should be doing something.

But he felt drugged, unable to act.

His mood blackened with each hour that passed. Brooding. Time had ceased to be, seconds and hours dissolved away, the idea of days and weeks too.

In his mind, an emptying was going on.

Shirin was a dream, gone. He felt trapped, static with nerves, with inactivity... full of new doubts about what had really happened with her. There was that rotten seed of a thought she could have gone off with Sheikh Faisal. Disappeared because she wanted to.

Why... why did she want to?

Maybe she wanted to punish him for his long absence from her? Maybe she wanted to be free of him forever.

Azeem sipped his mint tea, let his mind empty, uncoiling into the empty room, where it was dark all around him.

Even then, even there, in peace at home and all alone as if in hiding, Ghazan's presence, and his words, followed him like an unwanted incantation.

Ghazan's telephonic barrage—those hissing, immolatory injunctions to *sacrifice yourself*—battered at the fragile skein of Azeem's inner peace. But his hypersensitive, heavy mood wasn't caused by that alone. It wasn't just down to Ghazan's heated exhortations to martyr himself... but to Shirin's disappearance, and what lay behind it, his slowly chilling relationship with her.

Whatever else had happened, Shirin and he had lost so much. He drained the dregs of cold tea in his mug. His eyes passed over the framed picture on his desk. He didn't take it in, but remembered the two of them together, smiling and entwined, kissing—a party. Taken just last winter. Azeem remembered how the germ of his present despondence already lurked within him then, for all that outward glow of happiness.

These days, Shirin saw all he did through hostile eyes, eyes of enmity, eyes that could make him feel futile with a look. And that chimed in with developments at work. Now that Rania had pulled out of the *Voices* campaign, he felt the project was running into the sand.

He set down his mug on the desk. He sat back in his chair and listened to the passing night-time sounds of London outside his window. The air was cooler now, the fumes of the cars receding, the traffic sporadic in the square. Screech of a cat leaping at a bird—frantic swishing of feathers.

So much going on, so much passing me by.

In his workaholic daze, the more he carved out his strategies and images, the longer he labored to tell the world about his faith—the more Shirin mocked him at the very core of his purpose. The more bogged down Azeem got in his boundless, grubby networkings, from the energy they required to set up, to the dim dull diplomacies their upkeep demanded—the heavier that sense of futility clung to him, and seeped away his strength.

The only peace he found these days was in the Qur'an and in his poetry. He often lay down to read. Often he'd wake to find a volume flattened on his chest, its words still resonating in the rhythms of his brain. Sometimes he sat down to write. He'd lean over the blank paper, and out came words teeming in verses without end. They flowed from him in mad torrents of verbiage—like verbally regurgitating himself.

And always, when he'd done, he'd feel a sense of relief inside him.

So too tonight, he sat at his desk and wrote.

The telephone rang. Ghazan, he saw on the display. He let it ring. After a half dozen rings, it left off. The answering machine did its stuff in silence, punctuated by a few whirring clicks.

Azeem cast his eye over the final sheet of mad poetry he'd been working on.

Love like war
Can be a bloody thing —
                    If I'm at war
                    Then with myself —
My life-core
She who is not mine —
                    My warlike love,
                    My lovelike war —
                    For love is all I was.
The lovelight songs like torches' shine
In wartime sung by those who love —
                    All that is no more
For all that's sucked up in the whirlwind void of war.

                    If love long lost is all I'll ever be -
                    Ever was or once may have become,
Here in the now,
In my own self's vacuum
                    I am no more
                    And everything I felt is numb
It's nothing now — nothing rages —
I am at war no more,
No more lies of love to sing.
                    For love remains a bloody thing
                    When all that's fucked up, girl meets boy no more,
                              We live in different ages,
                              Each in a different war.

When Azeem's head's cleared, he comes to a realization, sharp and clear in his mind.

If Shirin really has gone to Sheikh Shabby, she's out of his life forever. There is really no more reason for him to keep hanging on to their love, as though it were his lifeline, the central fact of his life.

If Shirin really has left him, withdrawn into her new world, what's to stop him leaving this life behind?

What on earth is there to stop him putting an end to it all?

Why he is feeling so hazy, so apathetic? He doesn't even know what Shirin is thinking... He only knows she is gone. He's sure she is with Faisal.

She *is* with Faisal.

Anger rises in him. An anger which feels aimless, because it's aimed at himself.

My project's lost, my girlfriend's gone, and what do I do? Here I am, writing poetry, hiding behind words.

His anger irradiates his mind, throbs at the back of his eyeballs. His temples pulse, there's an itch in the palm of his hands. The moment breaks free from his brain, leaving nothing but that spark of certainty.

No more hiding.

He's done with hiding, done with his poetry, done with trying to keep the peace. He feels an urge to get moving.

It is time to spill some blood again.

FIGHTING MAN
Wembley: Azeem al Din, Muwaffaq, Hariz

EVEN THOUGH HE'S NEVER thought himself much of a fighting man, Azeem knows exactly how he can get his hands on a serviceable AK47. Months spent at the *madrasa* in Afghanistan, an experience which shaped him as radically as any other, have given him contacts he can still call on.

He had made his first choice of training camp with a great deal of care, paranoid about what he'd likely come across. People's ideas about them were very much of the brainwashing, school-for-terrorists kind.

He'd gone to see his mentor, Muwaffaq, about it.

They were in Muwaffaq's sitting room drinking sweet coffee. Muwaffaq was smoking his *nargila*. A tall man with gnarled brown teeth, he had the lean face, the thin legs and arms of a contemplative ascetic.

Azeem opened up, told him he'd been thinking about going to Afghanistan, his apprehension, everything.

Muwaffaq laughed, dismissively, bright-eyed, uneasily.

"Yes, I know what you mean, brother. Most religious training you hear about these days involves AK47s and suicide bombs, doesn't it?"

Muwaffaq, a man of great inner peace, didn't even try to sweeten the tang of bitterness dripping from his words, which were soft enough, but spoken in a calm species of seasoned ridicule. Barbed and prickly, he blew out his frustrations with his smoke.

"I know only too well what people think," he said, "what you, Azeem al Din, must fear, what you seek reassurance about. I know there is truth behind all that scandal. There is often a kernel of truth even in slander, even in lies... I cannot *change* how people think about us... and I cannot stop wrongheaded men from misusing our schools..."

It was something Muwaffaq didn't want directly to confront. He couldn't.

He put the mouthpiece of his nargila to his mouth and took a toke of *tobamel*, his eyes glittering.

"What can I say? I'm torn... broken in the bottom of my heart... these slanders on our *madrasas*—reputations spoiled by a few rotten apples."

Maybe it was because of his detachment that goodhearted Muwaffaq managed to convince Azeem he was bugging himself about inconsequentialities, that all those stories about *schools of terrorism* were rumor, wrenched out of proportion, beyond any relation to reality. Muwaffaq's rhetoric, wistful, and so all the more compelling in its fierceness, started to persuade Azeem against his better instincts.

Muwaffaq ended up recommending a *madrasa* he knew, a traditional, respectable establishment, where he guaranteed Azeem would receive heavyweight religious instruction.

Muwaffaq had been right about the instruction—but even so, he was more out of touch than he realized. There was no getting away from the whirling political undercurrents, the radical jihadi whirlwinds which stormed through that *madrasa*, no matter how pointedly most of the dignified, distinguished teachers might withdraw behind their disapproval.

They closed their eyes to much, knowing that unity was all.

And the time Azeem spent at the *madrasa* left him confused about a lot of things, but in no doubt that, should the time be ripe for armed action, he could play his part, and count on his contacts to set him down the right path.

At the time, nothing could have been more alien to Azeem's mind. He had never spoken about it to anyone. That wasn't the way they ran things there.

The less you know about us, and the less you know about each other, the less you can give away if things go wrong, if you are captured, and they torture you to make you talk.

But now, with all that had passed, Azeem had well and truly turned.

He accordingly arranged to visit Hariz, the jihadi point-man he'd met before, shortly after coming back from his first trip to Afghanistan. Hariz knew Ghazan Khattak, was connected to his network.

Hariz was conspicuously keen to speak with him. He made a fair speciality of deploying western converts in media-friendly jihadi roles.

Azeem—even if he was only half Western—must have struck him as ideally cut out to play such a part.

After some introductory spiel on the telephone, Hariz cut the pleasantries. He described his "activist" projects.

"We gotta talk," said Hariz in his sultry smoker's voice. "I'd like to tell you about them face to face."

They met next day. Hariz was a serious-looking fellow, scruffy, about forty. His office was in a rundown street in Wembley. He proceeded to give Azeem some plain speaking about jihad.

"Jihad isn't something you believe in or not."

He let out a demented sort of laugh—a laugh of that distressing kind whose mirth segues into retching.

"Violence is a fact," he cried, still smiling through his phlegmy coughs. "There's no way round it, these days. You've gotta act."

"I think that way, too."

"Of course."

Again the offputting laugh and that retching.

"You may be given an opportunity," said Hariz. "I need to check you out with people we trust."

Hariz took Azeem's number and told him he would call as soon as he could.

"I'll be waiting," said Azeem.

After a week, Hariz calls him. This time, they meet at another house, in another part of Wembley. From the outside, it looks much the same as the last place. But Azeem is ushered in by an attendant, and he sees at once it's much swisher and better kept-up than Hariz' previous place. That had just been a neutral sort of place, Azeem reckons, a place Hariz only uses to meet people he wasn't sure about. This is the real deal. He looks around at the opulent rugs and the smart modern furniture.

The times have been kind to Hariz and his trade.

Emerging from his study, in a glow of prosperity and success, Hariz' whole attention, as Azeem walks in, is on Azeem. He spreads out his arms, fawns over him like an obsequious servant.

"I spoke with Ghazan, he told me all about you, he said you were thinking about a project," says Hariz with gentle concern, letting him into the spacy white sitting room where refreshments await them. Another flunky hovers, discreetly murmuring, ready to pour.

"Ghazan tells me he's aimed the searchlights of doubt into your soul, Azeem. That can illuminate. That can highlight new sources of determination."

"A lot has come into focus," says Azeem.

"Much has changed," says Hariz unctuously, "but much has remained the same. What is important is what has changed in you."

"I wish to act," says Azeem fervently. "I want to act in accordance with my deepest principles. It is time. It is time for action."

"Without true faith, actions are barren."

"That is true. My faith is strong. It is time for me to heed my calling."

"I believe you, my brother. I believe you."

Something in Azeem makes his words vibrate with fervency.

"I can see that everywhere I look, my brothers are in mortal danger," Azeem says, his eyes ablaze with fervor. "Everywhere I see they are suffering oppression and the death of decadence."

Hariz nods blankly popping a *petit-four* into his mouth, swigging it down with a sip of soda water.

"We know that everyone shall taste death," says Hariz. "But Almighty Allah gives life to the earth, even after death. And so, if you are truthful, you should long for death, for you have nothing to fear, and only paradise to gain."

"I know."

"Even if you flee from death then it will surely find you. For death rides a fast camel."

"I do not wish to flee from my fate."

"That is good. I am glad to hear it. You must never let those who have no certainty of faith discourage you from conveying Allah's Message. That, my brother, is true death, much more so than the termination of the body."

"I was thinking of going to a country where our brothers are in especial danger from modern decadence. I really believe I've found my mission—to make a statement there—a statement not of words, no message, or mere poetry, not *tabligh*, but a statement in action *fi sabilillah*, in Allah's way. I will do something that will never be forgotten, it will blaze like a fresh blast of truth in the history of our faith."

Azeem's fervor still burns inside him, infusing his words with warmth. And enthusing with persuasive passion Azeem begins to tell Hariz about his plans.

Shortly before taking off for Istanbul Azeem rang up his agency contact there and fixed up a meeting.

"I want to update you on the *Islamic Reform* project," he said.

They fixed it up.

"There's something else, something you can help me with in the meantime," said Azeem. "I have to meet with my colleague, Sheikh Faisal ibn Shabbir. He's got his yacht, it's called the *Jawhara*? It's sailing along the Marmara or Aegean Coast. I need you to help me track down its exact location... If there's a problem, the police might help, he's the sort of a man they keep tracks on. If they can't, and you need professional help, a private eye or whatever, just bill me for the cost. The main thing is to find out where the *Jawhara*'s holed up. Let me know just as fast as you can."

Having put this in motion, Azeem boarded his plane. He was looking forward to meeting his *other* contact, the one Hariz had arranged for him.

SAFE HOUSE
Lewisham, London: Ghazan Khattak

GHAZAN KHATTAK was holed up in a safe house in Lewisham, alone. He'd gone to bed almost relaxed by his standards, his mind raw and wired, but ready to switch off for a few hours, to lie in the balm of sleep.

He was, as always, fully dressed in case something cropped up. He wasn't really anticipating anything. Things had been quiet of late.

He turned in for the night almost easy in his mind.

That morning, shortly after two, even before the first glow of dawn was spreading, his sleeping brain was shaken by an irruption of ringing — his cellphone. It was a call from a man he trusted.

The man was calm but abrupt. He warned Ghazan the police were hot on his trail, hot on a trail they seemed to know was fresh. The man told him he wasn't sure but it was possible they knew where he was now.

Ghazan threw himself out of bed. He was well prepared to leave the place at once. His few things were packed, waiting in a holdall.

He peered out the window through the net drapes. Two new cars were parked there. He could see blacked-up faceless figures moving about through the shadows.

His heartbeat picked up not in panic but in the awareness of the enemy closing in. The awareness filled his veins with pulses of energy.

Someone flicked a spotlight on. It was trained directly on the house and flooded it in light. It blinded Ghazan's sleepy night eyes.

A loudhailer voice boomed out.

"You are surrounded. I repeat, you are surrounded. You have no means of escape. Your only chance is surrender. You must surrender now. Your weapons are of no more use to you. Throw all your weapons out of the window. Then come out of the front door with your hands above your head. You are surrounded on all sides."

He got down on the floor. He crawled over to the bedside cupboard where he'd stashed his AK47. He pulled it out and sat with his back against the wall. Hands shaking, he mounted a 75 round Chinese drum magazine onto the gun. Kneeling, he clipped on the belt with his remaining ammunition.

He crawled out onto the landing, to the ladder up to the attic. This was his only route to a quick getaway, over the rooftops. He climbed as fast as he could.

Outside, the police had planted marksmen in trees and in neighboring houses either side of the house. The bulk of the police force was in front of the house, fully alert in that sleepy suburban street which had been silently evacuated.

They were sheltering behind their cars, training the searchlight onto Ghazan's safe house.

A contingent of twelve officers had already spread themselves out to the back of the house. That whole section of the street was cordoned off by now, the police working stealthily, putting everything into place at a cracking pace.

Up in the attic, Ghazan managed to get his head out of the window. He looked round. He spotted one of the sharpshooters in the trees and immediately fired off a single round. By a miracle, it hit the man.

Ghazan thought he heard him fall through the branches. But before the man hit the ground the bullets were splashing round Ghazan's head.

He drew himself inside as the ricochets tore into the roof tiles. A sharp edge, flying off, scratched his cheek. He smeared away a smudge of blood.

He bent down and launched himself back down the ladder.

Crawling across the landing he felt a sting where he cut his left hand on a shard of broken glass. He opened the bathroom window to the back of the house. He fired a rapid succession of rounds, sightless, into the black back garden. Returning fire shattered the window immediately.

He rushed to the window at the front, smashing it open with his elbow. The glass splinters showered at his feet. He threw himself back against the opposite wall.

Then he twisted round, let off another ten rounds or so at the cars, the dim figures he thought he saw there. His fire was returned fourfold.

He decided to go all the way downstairs. On his way down the bullets kept ricocheting all round him—ripping into the walls, they sent fragments of wood flying, clouds of plaster dust into his face.

The police, closing in, were throwing it all at him, emptying all their barrels in a furious onslaught. The air turned into screaming mayhem. For a minute Ghazan lay on the floor under the kitchen table. Bullets smashed into the walls and into the floorboards, everything came apart in howling splinters.

Ghazan lay there clenching his teeth. The taste of blood was on his tongue.

Abruptly, the firing stopped. Again the loudhailer boomed out calling on Ghazan to surrender and come out with his hands above his head.

He got up. His mind was closed. He gathered himself together. It was time. He took a deep breath, threw himself at the smashed kitchen window, those shards of smashed glass. He thought he might make it to the alleyway on the other side of the house.

But even as he was flying through the air the bullets hit him in waves, ripping through his flesh, and he tumbled down, holed and leaking blood.

He was dead before he hit the ground. His body fell smashed on its back on the tiles of the kitchen floor.

There his corpse lay bleeding alone, his clothes soaking in the liquid. His beard lay spread out over the bullet holes in his chest, red and sticky with gore. It was five minutes or so before the police had secured the building to their satisfaction.

Then they found him, drained, drenched and broken, his blank eyes staring at the ceiling, his AK47 cradled in his arms.

JEWELS
Near Babakale, Cannakale, Aegean Coast, Turkey: Ozgur Balikci

THREE THOUSAND MILES to the east.

He was very tired that day, could hardly focus his eyes. Another sleepless night of worry, waking nightmares about money. And now he was stumbling through the day, the sun glaring in his eyes.

At first, when he glimpsed it, in the corner of his eye, he was peering into the blue float he was holding up to the light, his attention caught by a movement gliding along the bottom corner of the glass. He thought he had spotted a blemish, a crack.

Something sparkled there, gleaming like a speckled jewel in the light. Then, when he held it further back and looked again, he thought it might be a bug, crawling on the pale turquoise glass of the float and reflecting the sun on its wings.

Then he saw that the movement was not on, but way beyond the float—it was way out there on the water. On the outer edge of the bay, he thought, maybe a dolphin had swum in splashing close to the shore—only a few inches free of the horizon, from his perspective, as if a dolphin were frolicking close to the beach at the far edge of the bay.

Only after three or four seconds did he see it wasn't a dolphin, it was a *yacht*, glittering in the sun like a gem, far off on the horizon, heading his way, entering the wide frothy bay in all its majesty and opulence.

Since then, Ozgur Balikci had been watching from the shore. A fifty-four year old fisherman, there wasn't enough work for him to do, just maintenance today, and so he'd been keeping an eye on everything through his binoculars.

It was a grand distraction. So many things going on aboard that yacht! Ozgur had never seen its like before, so sparkling, unearthly.

Jawhara, he read on its hull. An elegant vessel, pearly white, adorned with polished silver and teak, a vessel that could only belong to a man of the most exquisite wealth, the most expensive tastes.

Ozgur spread out his nets and his floats on the sand, half-heartedly doing his repairs.

Before dawn, very early, Ozgur is out on the beach again, gathering his equipment along the shore. The dark is melting away, and the dim morning light is like an invisible glow seeping up from the horizon. The gulls are out in force, screeching and yapping at him in the zesty, ion-filled breeze.

He glances out at the yacht. The surface of the water which spreads around it is very still, streaks of moonlight through the clouds. No sign of movement. Aside from the squalls of those pesky gulls, there isn't a sound to be heard in the bay. No lights are on, nothing living can be seen out there.

The boat bobs like a black shadow, quietly lurking in the bay's placid waters.

But then all at once, in a sudden shock of discordance, Ozgur makes out a figure, emerging with some difficulty from one of the cabin portholes, just there on the near starboard side of the *Jawhara*.

Ozgur takes up his binoculars and peers across the side of the yacht. To his astonishment he sees a naked, longhaired girl come crawling out of the porthole.

The girl crouching down creeps swiftly to the side of the boat. She raises herself up and looks down onto the water below her. She climbs onto the railings with urgent limbs. Ozgur watches her entranced, his heart beats faster, in sympathy with hers.

Then for a split second the girl stands outlined stark against the indigo horizon—the second before she launches herself headlong into the water.

A dull splash like a soft, far-off thud marks her entry into the cold sea.

Silence falls again, broken only by flurries of cries from the birds. The water reverts to surface placidity.

For what seems a very long time the girl stays invisible under the surface. Then, almost indetectable to his eye so far out from the shore, Ozgur sees a split second's spit of white surf. The water sprays up, maybe half a foot above sea level, before immediately falling back down.

Ozgur can only just see the white flashing breakers, where the waters ebb, he can only just hear the small echo of a splash when the girl comes up for air, can only guess at the pain that's bursting from her lungs.

But he sees what happens next through the clarifying blur of his own disbelief—which heightens its unreality in the same measure as its intensity. The net brought out in triumph from below deck by the burly running man has been gathered up and flung into the ocean before Ozgur's properly seen what they're all doing there on deck.

The net's pulled up dripping from the water, the girl knotted like a gasping mermaid in its meshes. Ozgur knows precisely how the cutting wire hurts when it bites into the skin. He has been cut so often. He can enter into her agony as she's hoisted up, as she swings through the air, twisting up, before being dumped down on the deck.

Ozgur, inflamed and sickened by what he sees, makes an instant decision of the heart. He decides—even before the men have dragged the girl writhing and bleeding back out of sight to her cabin—that he'll do something he's never before thought right...

Whenever he's witnessed murky acts committed under cover of darkness, contraband coming in, or altercations along the shore, he's always kept it to himself.

Not this time, not this morning. Not this disgusting persecution of a young woman trying to escape from people who are clearly not from here, not his sort.

He sees it's his duty, now—he'll inform the police... and not just the police, he'll tell his wife, all his friends, get them to spread the word.

Someone, somewhere, needs to know where this girl is... and I'll do all I can to make sure they do.

And in the meantime, he'll keep watching the *Jawhara*. He'll be watching and ready, if there's anything he can do to help the girl.

ESCOPETARRA
Istanbul, Turkey: Azeem al Din

AZEEM'S TAKEN A CAB to where he's been instructed to go, a deserted street in a town he's never heard of, an hour outside Istanbul. It's a smallish, dusty town. No-one's about. A long main street runs along close to the top of a bumpy, rocky ridge. Smaller streets and lanes lead off down the lower side into the valley.

Azeem's gotten out, the taxi pulled off.

Azeem paces the silent street uneasily for ten minutes or more. Then his cellphone rings. The voice tells him the way to walk.

Azeem waits on a corner four hundred yards away.

At length, another car appears, a battered, rusty red Toyota. He gets in. The driver speaks no English but smiles, offers a cigarette.

They drive on for twenty minutes before leaving the road. They go down a track entering a disused industrial estate, a sprawling factory complex surrounded by tumbledown sheds, anonymous huts, long, empty warehouses.

They pull up outside a dirty brown building. It has an old wooden door, blistered green paint peeling off its surface. The driver points that way.

Azeem gets out and pushes open the door. Inside, it takes a while to get used to the gloom. A man's short shape stands half obscured by the wall in the shadows. His arm reaches over to a switch on the wall and a light bulb hanging above the table flicks on.

Azeem, blinking, sees the man standing at a dusty table to one side of the room. The man looks middle-aged, Arabic, and is missing half his left arm.

A grubby white sheet lies folded on the table covering an unidentifiable mass of lumps. The man clasps it and unfolds the sheet, unfurling it with his good arm.

Inside, there's a mass of metal, bits and bobs of mechanical parts. The man gestures to Azeem to come over. Azeem joins him. They look down to where the gun lies in pieces on the table in front of them.

"Used one of these before?" asks the man.

Azeem nods and picks up the bolt and its carrier. "I'm no expert. Is it a Russian version?"

"It's a Yugoslav model."

"Even better."

Azeem picks up the barrel, he puts his eye to it to peer down it. He lifts it up, and looking through it at the light his eye fills up with a sudden blaze of blindness from that bright bare bulb.

Azeem sets down the barrel. He checks the bolt face, the gas tube and piston.

"It looks like it's been cleaned quite recently. Did you do that yourself?"

The man shakes his head. He's a short greasy-faced man wearing a cap. His expression is bulge-eyed, he looks like he's in a permanent huff. His bare right arm is thick and hairy. The stump of his left arm is three quarters covered by the sleeve of his T-shirt.

Azeem looks from the man to the parts on the table and seeing them lying there disassembled he smiles at an irrelevant thought, sparked off by the shape they've assumed, which creeps suddenly into his head.

"Have you heard about the *escopetarra*?" Azeem asks taking up the magazine in his left hand.

"Sounds like Spanish," mumbles the man. "Is it a South American weapon?"

He's got this strange twitchy expression of outrage in his eyes. Azeem stares at him, deadpan. The man's eyes look uneasy. Suspicion fidgets in them.

"That's right." Azeem now smiling broadly at the man to signal that an attempt at humor is being assayed. "The *escopetarra* is a South American invention. A guy called Cesar Lopez. He's a Colombian. He converts AK47s into guitars."

The man frowns at Azeem in consternation.

"Guitars!"

He splutters a globule of spittle onto the ground. He looks at Azeem as though he's taken leave of his senses.

Then, seeing Azeem still smiling, the man cracks a reluctant, uncomprehending grin. His eyes are still bulging, emitting suspicious little glints of disapproval.

"Guitars!"

"Guitars."

The man shakes his head. "What a waste of weapon!"

They laugh.

"Back in the *madrasa* I could assemble one of these in under a minute."

Azeem is serious again, tapping on the table.

"Blindfold. I'm pretty rusty now."

Azeem leans down and starts slotting the pieces together. He works calmly, without fuss. After just over a minute and a half of puzzling he snaps the magazine into place. He cradles the gun familiarly in his arms. He tests its balance, puts it to his shoulder.

The man's forgotten about the guitar-gun now, reassured. He smiles when Azeem finishes the reassembly, he can see Azeem isn't some kind of timewasting tenderfoot.

They start to talk about ammunition.

JAWHARA
Aegean Coast, Turkey: Shirin Shaarawi, Sheikh Faisal

A FEW DAYS LATER Sheikh Faisal landed on the *Jawhara*. That
caused quite some commotion on board. Everyone was on their
best behavior, looking to avoid the sheikh's cruel, unusual rage.
He seemed bland, so kingly and complacent, but beneath his
composure there lurked a coiled-up fury. His rage lay curled up
inside him, like a cobra preparing to strike, and everyone sensed
this, tried to stay out of its range.

Soon enough, one of his crewmen, taking him to one side,
whispered scandal into his ear, about how the balding,
mothballed guard had lost control of himself, and molested
Shirin.

Sheikh Faisal received the information in studied silence. He
sat and digested it for several moments. Then he looked up, gave
his orders quietly, calmly, with an ominously gentle tone, and a
punctilious concern for detail.

Immediately, the incontinent guard was dragged up from the
quarters where the others had confined him below. He was
thrown down at Sheikh Faisal's feet. He began to grovel basely
before his master.

Faisal now ordered him to be bound to the side netting, by
the railings, and to be stripped, in preparation for his
punishment.

While his orders were being obeyed, Sheikh Faisal went down to
Shirin's cabin. On his arrival she'd been put back into her
previous cabin, the one with the window and the Qur'an. The
crew had given her a simple abaya robe to wear.

He wanted to apologize to Shirin. He really wanted to make
it up to her. He walked in, but she didn't allow him to speak.

"What the *fuck* do you think you're doing, Shabby!?"

She was full of loud reproach, and contempt, to see him, and
to hear his pathetic, dolorous expressions of regret.

368

Faisal ordered his attendants to leave them alone.

Then he sat down and let her scream at him for several minutes, taking it as calmly and impassively as he could, whilst trying with his eyes to show her that he truly cared.

Finally, he persuaded her to at least listen to him.

"It has been brought to my attention that you were treated badly by one of my men," he said, picking up on what she was saying so much more graphically. "I apologize humbly that one of my servants could have done such a thing."

"He did with his cock... what you do with your money! Like master, like fucking slave."

Faisal remained coyly impassive. Shirin shouted and hissed at him, half crazed in her contemptuous rage.

Faisal saw that he had to show that he meant what he said.

He had to prove his love for her, show her what he was prepared to do for her honor.

"Now I should like you to come on deck with me, my darling. I think you should be there too, to witness the slave's punishment."

"He should be brought to the police!"

"He will taste humiliating agony," said Faisal with a complacent grin.

"He should be tried."

"My vengeance will be merciless on the guilty one."

He pondered his power. He laughed to himself. She saw that there was something wrong with him, something wrong in his eyes.

He isn't listening. Doesn't understand what he's done.

Doesn't know who he is, who I am...

"Have no fear, my treasure," said Faisal, ogling her with a happy eye. "He will be punished according to the will of his lord. So come, come, let me show you what happens to men who lay their hands on what belongs to Faisal ibn Shabbir!"

Shirin followed him up, her legs shaky, reluctant. She emerged into the sunlight blinking. The men on deck averted their eyes.

The falcons wheeled high above them in the gray-blue sky.

The man had been fed drugs to make him calm and apathetic as he awaited his punishment. Manacled to the netting he half lay, half stood on the deck. The sun beat down on him. His body was waxy having been locked away below deck the past few days. There was a sweaty pallor on his skin.

Faisal had instructed his crew to prepare the body with rancid oil. Rubbing then pummelling it into the pores with uninhibited hands, they softened him up till he was black and blue, in such a way as to make the birds above believe him to be a carcass—that he was soft carrion already, easy meaty pickings, putrefying.

From previous experiments Faisal knew full well just how hard it is to fool animals which are all but wild. Especially keen-eyed falcons, who retain their sharpness of eye even when they're maddened and ravening with hunger and thirst.

Shirin and Faisal emerged onto the deck. As they were settling into their seats, a falcon plummeted down. Like the strike of a missile, the bird hit the bald man in his bruised, naked flanks.

Talons gripped at his skin, tearing it into gashes, crimson ribbons. Then the bird's cruel beak ripped out a strip of the man's flesh, and began to gobble it down.

In a moment the falcon flew off again, bearing its dripping prize away.

The man, half-dazed and unaware of what exactly was going on, started up as if from a nightmare, half waking when the beak cut him. He howled in agony as the bird flew away with the meat in its beak.

His cries soon ceased. He fell back into his trance. The blood from his wound flowed freely and Faisal ordered one of the crew to staunch it.

At first, Shirin, despite herself, thrilled at the swift imperious swooping of the bird, its majestic grace, its greedy violence. She still felt vengeful, and was excited to see her tormentor made to suffer as brutally as he'd made her.

"When this is finished we shall have our lunch together, my darling. I've ordered some fresh squid."

A minute later, a second falcon struck. This time the man's right eye was ripped right out. Again, the man was unaware of what was happening, but he writhed up in agony as the bird flew away.

The sheikh marvelled with pride at the uncanny skill of his falcons. How tenaciously the birds ripped at the flesh with their talons, snipping off a piece in their beaks—the whole intricate operation over within moments, before the man had even had time to wake! His eyes shone with delight to see the success of his hard training.

The birds continued to plummet from the sky, one after the other, tearing out shreds of the man's flesh. But Shirin no longer thrilled to see the birds, the torture was too excruciating now.

She felt a cold sickness inside her, pity for the man, ashamed to be there to witness this sickness.

As the spectacle continued, a dark blue fisherman's boat approached the yacht, slowly chugging from the shore. A pair of fishermen stood at the rudder, wrapped up against the gusty wind, the choppy waves splashing their faces with spray.

Before them lay overflowing baskets—glinting as they caught the sun—their catch, moist fish and squid caught that morning.

Shirin turned away from the stomach-turning torture. The bloodied guard's screams increased in length and loudness, every time one of the falcons renewed the attack.

Shirin watched the boat approaching, and tried to drown out the horror.

The first fisherman climbed up the ladder, swung himself aboard, looked round him with an air of being openly impressed, overawed by the opulence of the yacht. He greeted the crew in Turkish.

Faisal, having instructed his falconer to keep the birds at bay, ambled over. He asked via a crewman who understood Turkish whether the fisherman had brought the precise squid he'd asked for. Yes, *hasmet*, he was told. And plenty of it? Yes, *hasmet*. And was it fresh? Faisal demanded. Just out of the sea, said the fisherman, it still needed to be cleaned.

Having got the replies he wanted, Faisal went back to join Shirin.

She looked over her shoulder to see where the fisherman leant down to his colleague, waiting in the boat below. This man now handed up a bulging sack from which protruded gleaming tentacles of squid. After a great deal of heaving—Sheikh Faisal's crew not lifting a finger to help—the two men managed to lug it on board.

"Just bring it down to the galley," said Faisal's interpreter with a dismissive wave of his hand.

The first fisherman started to haul the bag toward the stairs. It was a heavy load. With great difficulty, he managed to shift it just a few feet along the deck. As he struggled, the second fisherman appeared at the railings and followed him to help. One of the crewmen told him to stop. But the second fisherman ignored him, stepped past him.

"Stop!" shouted the crewman in Arabic.

The fisherman evaded him and carried on walking. Now two of the crewmen went after the fisherman. One of them took him by the shoulders.

The fisherman half turned, raising his hand.

As he did so, his scarf was dislodged.

Shirin recognized him first.

Something about the man's movements struck her as familiar, from the second he jumped from the railings onto the deck. And for a second her heart felt light, her head giddy. But she forced herself to put it out of her mind. The man walked off, following the first fisherman to the stairs below.

The noonday sun was beating down on the deck. Under her parasol, Shirin didn't move, seeing nothing.

When she looked again, it was because of the commotion the crewmen were causing. They had surrounded the fisherman. And they were poking and goading him, hitting his face with his fists.

His scarf came off.

She'd seen who it was at once. And she felt estranged, suddenly numb, woozy and weak.

But she kept still.

It was Faisal, peering across irritatedly, who broke the spell.

"Why it's Azeem al Din!" he said with a cordial smile. "Welcome aboard my humble yacht, Zimmie!"

Azeem is now hauled before Faisal.

"How kind of you to join us," says Faisal in his most polished tones. "We were about to pause for lunch. I must insist you stay for that."

He lifts a hand at the falconer and on cue a falcon fastens its talons on the unfortunate crewman chained to the railings. As the screaming rises, and the birds swoop down, Azeem says,

"I was watching the show on the way here, Shabby. Your... tastes... haven't changed much, have they?"

They watch another falcon ripping off another chunk of flesh.

"I have refined my tastes. I indulge tastes no other man can indulge."

"You're a sick man, Shabby."

"You're too fussy... too pussy... too *weak*," says Faisal, eyeing Azeem with a smile, his face lighting up every time a bird strikes, while Azeem flinches. "You always were."

"If you think it's weak to hate... this sickness of yours," says Azeem, "this sick sadism, this sick kind of murder... then I'd rather be weak."

"If you don't kill your enemies they'll kill you. I'd call that a weak way of dealing with reality. What would you call it?"

"That one doesn't look like he's about to kill anyone."

"He is a dead man already. Dead meat... since the minute he insulted me, insulted my darling princess! It was a mortal insult."

Azeem glances over at Shirin unable to meet her eyes.

"Your darling princess?" says Azeem.

Shirin makes a muffled moan.

"You mustn't imagine it gives me any pleasure to point out your gross failings," Faisal tells Azeem.

He murmurs something to his attendants. Two of them unholster their pistols and go over to Azeem. They stand beside him. Faisal gloats over Azeem, and he gloats as he looks from Azeem to Shirin, revelling to have Shirin here, in his power.

"Azeem, you've worked hard," says Faisal, "worked diligently, at my behest. But perhaps you haven't worked hard enough. Something was always wanting, I fear.

"You were sometimes impressive," Faisal concedes with a benevolent smile, "but you have a fatal, a *tragic* flaw. You lack the will to power."

He turns to Shirin.

"Don't you agree, my darling?"

He laughs, with so little amusement that the laugh seems designed solely to take the edge off fearsome internal stresses. She stays still, eyes bland and wide with fear. Pointing at the magnificent yacht and his crewmen standing fearsomely by, Faisal continues to laugh, feyly, keeping himself in check.

"How could you not agree, my princess?" he laughs. "Now you see us side by side. How could you fail to be silenced when, with your own eyes, you can see the evidence of my success? The final proof of my love!"

Faisal's eyes flash in scary triumph as he looks from Shirin to Azeem and back again, as if to satisfy himself that what he sees is truly there, not believing the scale of his own success. Then he looks stern again.

"Take him below," he says with a wave of the hand in Azeem's direction. "We'll work out how to deal with him later."

Azeem is taken below deck.

Faisal already has a perfectly serviceable plan up his sleeve for dealing with Azeem.

It is time for him to pay the final reckoning.

He will sail the yacht far out to sea that evening. Then, in the dog hours of the night, he will have Azeem injected with a sedative.

Azeem will then be dumped overboard.

Once Azeem's cadaver is leagues behind them, and the bright morning comes, he can tell Shirin that Azeem appears to have left his cabin, that it seems he's committed suicide.

And it isn't a lie. Azeem has chosen this.

He has truly chosen death.

Nobody will gainsay him, Faisal is quite sure of that, and he suspects Shirin herself is unlikely to sense anything amiss.

And even if she does, her mouth can be stopped...

Faisal, with this plan in the back of his mind, exults as they watch Azeem being taken below. He smiles at Shirin.

"When will you set him free?" she asks.

His eyes flash as he replies, "The only one who can set him free is himself. No-one can say when that will be, apart from him."

He chuckles mournfully.

"All in its own time, my darling, all in its own time. Allah knows all."

Azeem's pushed into a dank cabin in the hold where the fisherman, Ozgur Balikci, is also being held.

It's pitch black in there. Azeem is glad to hear his companion still has the sack with him. He scrabbles about in the dark in a frenzy of cold excitement.

As he works, he whispers to Ozgur, "You know that, as of now, we... we could be launched into paradise at any moment, Ozgur. You know that, don't you?"

Ozgur replies, "I know you don't really think that, Azeem... I don't think it myself."

Azeem continues to puzzle the pieces together. He assembles the AK47 within a minute. He sits back and breathes out a long, exhausted sigh of relief.

"Now we just need to wait," he says.

Azeem and Ozgur get to their feet and position themselves either side of the cabin door.

"It won't be long," says Azeem.

One of the crewmen comes to check on them. He's got a cudgel. For a split second after he's opened the door, he stands blinking blind in the darkness, his cudgel raised, at the ready.

Azeem jumps directly at him He smashes the gun into his face. The man sinks to his knees. His cudgel falls.

Azeem pushes him to the ground. Ozgur kicks him a few times about the head to keep him quiet.

The two men empty the remnants of fish in the sack on the recumbent crewman's head.

Ozgur gives him a final swipe to the chin with his fist.

Then they go up the stairs and climb up into the light and the deck.

Azeem reappears on deck, the AK47 at his shoulder. He shoots the first crewman rash enough to aim his pistol at him. The man falls with a choked cry clutching his bloody shoulder. His gun clatters across the deck.

The other crewmen are unprepared, aghast.

Another of them, from the shadows, raises his pistol. Azeem points his AK47 at him.

"Drop it!"

The man holds his gaze. A second crewman, to Azeem's left, makes an uncontrolled move with his rifle. Azeem fires, hits the first man in the forearm—the gun flies from his hand.

Azeem's already swung to the left, covering the second man.

His face is expressionless. He motions to the man to put down his rifle.

The man is staring back. He looks ready to risk it all—a man with no future, no fear. But he hesitates in the face of Azeem's calmness, his vacant eyes.

He bends down to put his gun on the deck. Ozgur ambles over to collect it. He throws it overboard.

Azeem orders the men to the side of the ship and they obey, slowly, with sullen, dragging steps.

"Throw your weapons overboard!"

Azeem walks over to where the manacled bald crewman lies bleeding by the railings. He orders him to be cut loose. The bloody man's body collapses on the deck.

He takes one look at Azeem and thanks him in broken words.

Then the man looks at Shirin piteously, whispers some incomprehensible phrases. His torn face is twisted with pain and remorse.

Azeem has been outwardly calm until now. But anger wells up inside him, unstoppable.

He flies into a fit of fury, spitting his curses at the crew. Before he knows what he's doing, he's forced them all to line up along the gunwale, their backs to him.

There they stand, trembling for their lives. They're balancing themselves with great difficulty as the boat tosses them back and forth.

They know this yelling berserker is capable of anything.

And suddenly, as he stands there, cradling his AK47, Azeem feels how easy it would be—just to let fly, shoot them all out of hand.

He knows, now, how sweet it would feel. But then, he also suspects how fleeting and momentary that sweetness would be, how quickly it would fade, how quickly he would feel shame.

He reckons that if he does it, he'll hate himself before sunset.

And yet... is it so bad to hate yourself when you hate the world? Is it so bad to do something you'll hate yourself for, if it brings you at least a passing semblance of relief?

He stands there looking at their backs—victims--and he fears himself, afraid of the way his hands are twitching as he looks at those trembling men, with their sweating, downturned necks, and he holds the gun in his arms.

"Jump overboard!"

A prod in the back, and the first man is propelled into the sea, his arms flailing as he falls. The second man needs no prodding—and then all in a heap the rest, relieved Azeem hasn't started shooting, follow him down into the welcoming waters.

Azeem watches them swim toward the shore, a mile or two away.

His anger has subsided again.

When Azeem has finished with the crew he turns back to the others—Shirin, Ozgur the fisherman, and Sheikh Faisal ibn Shabbir, all standing there watching him, all uncertain of him in their different ways.

The only one who seems remotely relaxed is Ozgur, Azeem notices. He gives Ozgur the crewman's discarded pistol and tells him to take command of the yacht.

He warns him to keep an eye on Sheikh Faisal at all times.

Azeem sits down at the table and takes out a piece of paper on which he begins to write. He asks Shirin to join him. They confer earnestly.

At length, Azeem finishes writing.

He calls Faisal over.

"Read this. Then sign it."

He hands him the document:

I, Sheikh Faisal al Hasan ibn Shabbir, B.A. (Cantab), am a member of Islamist terrorist mujahidin groups. I have supported and organized them. I am responsible for murders and violent attacks on innocent people, as well as planned conspiracies to undermine democratic governments.

Until his shooting by security forces, I was an associate of the proven murderer and terrorist Ghazan Khattak, late of Leeds. I helped him to plan, and supported him in numerous attacks on innocent people selected for their membership of racial or sexual groups—women, Jews and gays.

I have transferred monies for these purposes from bank accounts operated under company names under my control.

I personally ordered the kidnapping of Shirin Shaarawi, a woman with whom I am obsessed but who repeatedly rejected my advances. I imprisoned her in conditions of unbearable suffering and allowed my crew to mistreat her in unspeakable ways. I have personally ordered the torture and mutilation of a crewman on my yacht. This was carried out under my direct supervision.

I make these confessions and shall now surrender myself to stand trial for my contemptible murders, tortures, kidnaps and innumerable further crimes against Islam and humanity.

I have brought shame and infamy on Islam.

With effect today I herewith transfer the ownership of my yacht, the Jawhara, to Ozgur Balikci, a noble fisherman who has helped Azeem al Din expose and terminate my crimes.

(Dated and signed) Faisal ibn Shabbir.
(Witnessed) : Azeem al Din
*   : Shirin Shaarawi*
*   : Ozgur Balikci*

Faisal reads impassively. His eyes move steadily as he reads, his lips frozen in scorn.

He finishes reading and puts the paper down on the table.

Azeem hands him a pen.

"You have beaten me," says Faisal ibn Shabbir, after a long silence. "I acknowledge it."

He folds his arms.

"I will not sign this. You must kill me."

Azeem tightens his grip on his gun. He begins to raise it—

"No," he says. "That's not my way."

"You must do it."

"That isn't me."

"It *isn't you*, what do you mean by that? You think you have achieved a great victory in beating me, don't you? You may've beaten me—but there's a million others ready to take my place. So kill me. Kill me, I beg you! Enjoy your victory while you can. Kill me!"

"That's not the way, man. That's not the way things should be done." Azeem lowers the gun. "That's not me anymore anyway, man. And it's not Islam!"

Faisal's broken inside. As he begs Azeem to kill him, he tries desperately to think of himself as a martyr, worthy of paradise, dying for a higher cause.

But all Azeem will reply is, "That's not my way. It isn't the way of Allah!"

He says it again and again. He doesn't know why. He doesn't even know if he believes it himself.

What's the use? He's not listening…
He's very tempted to finish Faisal off.
Azeem looks at Shirin, he holds her gaze in his.

And now Azeem sees it is time to let his spirit fill the space above him, to rise above what he only knows. He looks at Shirin, sad, and scarred, and alone.

It is like seeing her anew again, the first time he realized he loved her. She looks just like she did that other night, that night on the steps of the Sacré Coeur in Paris. Her lips slightly parted, her eyes full of lively confusion, half excited, half afraid.

Azeem goes to her. Holds out his arms to her. She rises, and comes to him. They stare into each other's eyes for a long time, remembering who they are. They draw close, squeezing each other. They hold each other closely for some time.

And then they kiss.

Azeem kisses her. He is filled with love. His thoughts are overcome, overrun with passion. His fate is to love Shirin, to love Shirin forever. He looks into her eyes and sees something he thought he had forgotten.

Shirin, he sees, knows her fate, she knows her fate is his again.

Faisal saw their look. He knew what it meant he'd lost, something he knew, even then, he might never have had. He wondered whether he'd ever even come close, ever, to Shirin's love.

He also knew that, if he were not to feel debased and diminished for ever, he had to redeem himself in his own eyes. The only way he knew how to. His heart and mind were wrapped in this sudden realization of sadness and depression, a blackness of the soul engendered there.

And so, before anyone knew what he was doing, the sad sheikh took his deepest breath, and breathed it out again. He moved slowly to the railings. He stood there unseen, except by Ozgur, who was watching him, but unwilling to intervene. And then he climbed over, and he dropped himself over the side and into the sea.

And now underwater there was nothing more to see, he sank down, and the cold dissipated into his blood, his nose and ears filled with salt water; he tasted death, and span slowly round in the water, and only felt what is written: *The Day that We roll up the heavens like a scroll rolled up for books...*

Faisal's head did not reappear above the surface for a long time.

An hour or more later, his body had drifted a mile out to sea, seized by the currents, and already bloated, swollen. No one ever saw it again.

His beloved falcons, masterless, wheeled crawing in the sky.

NINE MONTHS LATER...

AT FIRST, FARAZ ZANDI thought he could adjust to his life in Pakistan. He tried his best to fit in with his new cousins, tried to work up some enthusiasm for his work as a mechanic's assistant, in a provincial town near the Afghan border.

But soon he realized how much he missed his family, his friends, the whole world he knew—and loved more than he knew—in Leeds. He misses the cool fresh air, proper cricket, the sleety rain, Yorkshire pudding, the banter of his friends, the TV, digestive cookies to dunk in his tea...

When he lies alone in his bed, Rania appears to him. Her face fills his mind as he tries to sleep. And often in his dreams he is haunted by her, by the knife, by her lying there as he backs away into the darkness.

More and more, these days, he thinks about going back home. He doesn't know how his parents would react. He's sure they will try to understand, try to see why he did it, why he was forced to do it... how the pressure on him to do it became unbearable, he was unable to resist, and now regrets it with all the power in his soul.

And even if they can't understand, he's sure they will try to soften their hearts toward him. Rania herself, he believes—he prays—might find forgiveness, to see how he was misled, seduced by the whispers, the impassioned exhortations and teachings of Ghazan, by the mutters he heard in the community, inspired by the spirit of *Iblis*, of *Shaytan.*

Every few hours, then, thoughts of returning home flit through his mind. He's even discussed them with one of his cousins, the only one he can speak English with.

Sometimes he dreams of England, of turning himself in.

And his sister, Rania Zandi?

She's recovered her voice. There's still a husky strain in it when she's tired, but not so you'd notice.

She's had a good year. The trip with Yass, when they went to Blackpool, was a laugh. She even got together with gorgeous Yahya the DJ, although he turned out to be a little more immature than she thought... not serious potential boyfriend material at any rate.

Her mom and dad, finally, are beginning to relax again. Rania thinks—no, she knows—they were far more stricken by this whole thing than she was. Slowly, though, they've stopped fussing around her so much, letting the past go. They're beginning to see that she's a responsible girl, they're beginning to let her be herself, with more of her own space, seeing as she's got her whole life in front of her.

Sometimes, though, she does think of the others, her fellow victims. The ones who weren't as lucky as she was, who *didn't* make it. Those other ones, killed for "honor", lie alone, she knows—for that is the custom—in unmarked graves. No tombstone marks their passing on this earth, their lives unacknowledged, except in the hearts of those who love them.

She tries not to dwell on what might have happened if Faraz had been less squeamish, had exerted a little more pressure on the knife that morning, in that cobbled alley off Kirkstall Road.

WAKE
Aegean Sea, Turkey: Shirin Shaarawi, Azeem al Din, Ozgur Balikci

OZGUR STEERS THE BOAT out into the open sea.

The *Jawhara* heads out toward the sun on the far horizon. Its wake spreads behind it like a peacock's trail, sparkling with rays of liquid sun.

Azeem and Shirin stand beside Ozgur. They watch the waves rise up and whip the prow in a lather, gutsy gusts of salty spray. The lovers, still entwined, are still oblivious within themselves.

Ozgur smiles over at the two of them, his companions. He smiles to see their happiness. He is happy himself, looking forward to coming home to his wife.

Then he looks away, in growing contentment, looking at his yacht, and at the sea, and at the birds wheeling high above their heads. As the yacht sails away, the birds follow them at first, but then they hang back, hugging the shore till their raucous yells fade in the distance, and the horizon swallows up the last cry.

THE END

Mad Bear Books hopes you enjoyed HONOUR and invites you to read a preview of Freddie Omm's stunning new thriller, **THE TRASHMAN**—the first instalment of his riveting series, **THE DARK GOSPEL**—out soon from Mad Bear Books.

PROLOGUE

ZOE MASTERS

CHAPTER ONE
Zoe Masters, Emerald Bay, Laguna Beach, California

I'M STANDING, naked and ashamed, on my balcony—the black night wrapped round me like a cloak, the seething ocean, dark and cold, sixty-five feet below, sending its waves crashing onto the cliffs, its spray onto my face, calling to me, calling on me to come...

I never dreamt a girl like me, an up and coming fashion designer with no cause for angst, would have a full-on existential crisis before I hit thirty.

And not just any old crisis. This one is designed to climax in my death.

These words will be my last... unless the unthinkable happens.

Of course, I never thought anything like this could happen to me.

But then no one like Daniel Farr ever came my way before.

Nor did anything as fatally tempting, as addictively pleasurable as *The Tabernacle of Gaia.*

Dan sucked me right into his life, his world, his whole dashing, debonair way of doing things. Forcing a rethink of all that made me me, he started fucking up my life the moment he knew he'd never fuck me...

It wasn't just his wealth, it wasn't just his fame... more the way he managed to wriggle himself right under my skin, searching out all my hot buttons and pressing them without mercy.

So here I am, alone on my balcony on Emerald Bay, talking into my headset like I'm reading a script, repeating the words I'm told I should say... The black sea swirling madly below, the drugs and booze beating crazily through my veins...

... and then there's that voice again, insistent in my left ear...

I'm holding a long knitting needle in my right hand, because he told me I had to.

Don't ask, he said (and I didn't).

But I know that knitting needle is meant to end up skewering my brain...

I know it, because that's what he does, that kind of sickness is like his signature.

Just like I know all this is being filmed.

Just like I can see the red laser sight, playing on my body, touching me in my secret places, like the eyes of that sick perverted mind, watching me through the night vision lens...

I can hear the rotor blades of the chopper sweeping in from over the sea. I can see the cockpit reflected in the pale moonlight.

And all the time the soft Californian breeze blows, mild on my bare feet...

This scene, so elaborately staged, so *ridiculous* in some ways—it'd be dead funny if it wasn't likelier to kill me than make me laugh.

I wish I could get free, just go inside, make some calls.

Frank—my almost-lost love Frank—would be over like a shot. He'd grab at the chance to wrap me up in his arms and protect me again. And once the nightmare was over, we could have one of our delicious nights in, crack open some bubbly... Give each other the comfort we need.

Not tonight though. Maybe no night ever again.

There have been just too many killings, murders which have terrified this city of stars and angels, made it a place no sane girl goes out alone at night—a place everyone feels watched, *scrutinized* by inscrutable, invisible eyes. A place where the stars are being snuffed out one by one, butchered, tortured in horrific ways—and disposed of, mixed up in the garbage by this arty, clever, creepily creative maniac..

My head is light and sick, and half of me hopes to be blown away, to sink, submerge myself among all those sickening images which will be part of me now, for as long as I shall think and breathe.

I remember Rita Valley, the reality TV star I found, cut to ribbons and put into the trash can—just the other side of town from here.

That was the first collection the Trashman made.

That was when it all began.

The sadism, the depravity, the sickness and the blood.

BOOK ONE

Rita Valley and Xavier Santos

CHAPTER 1
Rita Valley, Xavier Santos, Sammie the Dog, Malibu, California

SINCE COMING THIRD in the reality TV show *Heavy Losses*, Rita Valley had turned herself into a liked and successful celebrity. Snobs might sneer at her for being overnight-rich trailer-trash — but she really didn't give a rat's ass. Trading on charm and a figure which fluctuated from a trim ten to a buxom fourteen, she graced a succession of chat shows like *The Tyra Banks Show*, made a handful of special guest appearances on soap operas, on variety shows and comedies, and modelled in ad campaigns for Poundwatchers and the launch of the Nano car in California.

She was living the dream, a fat and waddling ugly duckling who'd turned herself into a swan by sheer exercise of will.

Rita Valley pulled into her driveway in her sleek black open top 6 Series BMW with the same feeling that always overcame her when she got home — the feeling of having *arrived*, having achieved all the stuff she wanted... things no one could ever take away from her. Her pleased, pouting pink lips matched the pink tortoiseshell sunglasses perched on her beehive wig.

She tippled out of the car in her sling-backs, a coiffed, neurotic pug nestling under her arm. The dog curled its lower lip and peered at the tarmac with canine superciliousness, but Rita indulged in a shiver of enjoyment, savoring her sense of possession to the full.

Of all her new possessions, she prized none more than her lover, Xavier, a toyboy she'd been playing with over a month. She smiled to herself, looking forward to the afternoon ahead. Just a half hour ago, she'd been in the depths of a stuffy dark studio, recording a radio commercial in her breathiest voice. Now the fresh blue sky, clear and smogless for a change this spring, was all that bounded her.

She was free. Free to enjoy her house, and her terrace with its view of the rugged canyon in the distance, and her Latin lover with his clean-cut smile, chiselled chest, well-defined limbs.

She pressed her little pug to her breast.

It's all so perfect, I wouldn't change a thing.

She turned the key in the keyhole. The heavy oak door swung open. She stepped in.

Inside, the dim hall was quiet.

"Lover?" she said into the silence. She walked toward the living room. "Lover?"

Not a sound. Before her, the cosy space with its big windows on three sides, a wide-screen TV along the wall, a long white leather sofa in front of it.

Maybe he's gone out to get us some more champagne.

She looked out the near window, her eyes gazing at the mountains and the sky. She put the pug down. Then she heard it—a dull scratching and banging sound coming from the bathroom. The dog raised a single paw, cocked an ear, and listened.

"What is it, Sammie?"

The dog pattered off toward the bathroom. Down the main corridor, then into the side passageway to the left.

Rita walked slowly behind it, the strange sounds still coming faintly. She was thinking maybe an animal had found a way in there, a raccoon or something. Her hand closed on the cold doorknob and twisted it.

The door wouldn't open at first. Something heavy was blocking it. She gave a push and it swung open halfway. She looked down.

Then she saw him where he lay. Naked on the cold white tiles. She screamed. He lay sprawled on his back, looking almost relaxed and comfortable, as if all that fresh blood had embalmed him, calmed him in his dying.

She knelt down beside him, shaking uncontrollably.

"What happened?"

He couldn't speak. Blood gurgled in his mouth.

"Oh lover, what'd you do?"

His eyeballs were bleeding, he couldn't see. His right arm was scrabbling hopelessly, scratching at the air as if he were trying to point at something to her left. He looked like he was drowning on dry land.

Then, in the corner of her eye, the door of the master bedroom pulled open.

CHAPTER 2
The Trashman, Malibu, California

THE TRASHMAN had been looking forward to making his first collection for so long he could hardly believe it was really happening now, today—the start of his new life.

Will I be able to see it through?

When he approached the house from the street his heart beat so crazily in his ribcage he could hardly focus on what was in front of his eyes.

Her lover, Xavier Santos, is waiting for her to return. He's in there alone.

He rang the bell at the trellised gate.

"LA Sanitation," he said into the intercom. "We've got an inspections appointment… to check the premises."

"We've got no problems here, man."

Xavier Santos had a rough, but *high* voice, it was almost shrill. It didn't fit to his physique, which the Trashman knew well, having cased the house and its occupants for several weeks. He'd seen Santos' body—an altar to ripped muscle, with all the abs, biceps, triceps, quads and pecs in place—he'd watched him doing everything a human body can do—sleeping, eating, shitting, fucking—everything except *dying*—and he'd formed the idea that Santos would sound like a gravel-voiced macho man. But Santos' voice rasped out of the speaker like the crawing of a startled fowl.

The Trashman smiled to himself.

He's ill at ease. He's right to be that… He's just a sleazeball. He doesn't belong in that house. He doesn't belong in that woman…

Then again… that woman doesn't really belong here either, if you think about it…

"Ms Valley made an appointment for us to check her sanitation, sir... this was like six, seven weeks ago?"

"She didn't tell me nothing about it."

"I can show you my documentation, sir. She must have thought there might be some waste issues coming up... blocked drains, pipes, the whole shebang... you name it, it's an ageing system, and it could start getting clogged up even as we speak."

Xavier Santos didn't reply. The intercom was silent except from a background crackle of interference. The Trashman stood tense and waiting beside the bougainvillea at the gate.

This is turning into a nightmare... is my début going to be a flop?

At length he said, "Is Ms Valley available, sir? I got a lot more appointments lined up today. This won't take long."

"Hold on," said Santos. "I'll let you in."

The intercom buzzed, releasing the latch.

Lights! Camera! Action!

The Trashman was on the property.

The curtain's rising on the greatest show on earth!

MAD BEAR BOOKS

Mad Bear Books is an independent publishing imprint — owner-run, free from big-business corporate pressures. We publish books too edgy, controversial and non-compartmentalized for old-guard publishers to touch.

Other recommended titles:

The Sky is Not Blue by Sandie Zand: *A dark tale of oppressive friendship and the fallibility of memory.*

www.madbearbooks.com

www.ingramcontent.com/pod-product-compliance
Lightning Source LLC
Chambersburg PA
CBHW060811030726
47503CB00002B/439